D0343346

More Praise for Bruce Wagner's *Still Holding*

"In blazing, high-speed prose, he tears into his subject with a taboo-breaking savage rage disguised as wild comedy."
—Salman Rushdie

"A millennial heir to Nathanael West, he captures the stone-cold nihilism lurking just beneath the city's glossy, cellulite-free surface and the deceptions and self-delusions that fuel so much of the deal making in town. . . . Mr. Wagner serves up [his] themes with his customary black humor and unforgiving eye, proving to fans of *Force Majeure* and *I'm Losing You* that his knack for satire is as cutting as ever."
—Michiko Kakutani, *The New York Times*

"With *Still Holding*, Wagner surpasses everything he's done before . . . this is the crowning achievement of his Cellular Trilogy. While reading it you'll find yourself thinking: This is the great Hollywood novel."
—Bret Easton Ellis

"Imagine Dickens without London, Dostoevsky without St. Petersburg. It's like that for Bruce Wagner and Hollywood. He owns this fetid, steaming lump of a town."
—*Los Angeles Times Book Review*

"It's a gorgeous freak show, and part of the pleasure is that Wagner seems to be having so much fun. . . . The return of the novelist most often compared to Nathanael West. (But guess what: He's better.)"
—*New York*

"Exquisite satire."
—*Details*

"*Still Holding* is Bruce Wagner's greatest novel. It is as if Louis-Ferdinand Céline were retelling the Arabian Nights. . . . It is an uncompromising, hilarious, achingly sad, flat-out brilliant book."
—Jonathan Carroll

"Bruce Wagner—Tinseltown's answer to Emile Zola—offers up *Still Holding*, another scathing, keenly observed tragicomedy of manners (and lack thereof) among Hollywood's wannabes, already-ares and couldn't-get-arresteds."
—W

"*Still Holding* finds the Nabokov of New Age Angeleno life in the best form of his career—which is saying something. . . . [Wagner] has simply made [Hollywood] his own territory, with as much genius and ferocity as Faulkner applied to laying bare the gloriously unsavory humanity of Yoknapatawpha County."

—*Elle*

"A fable of the restless, millennial American self . . . the novel's characters are so tightly and persuasively conceived against the sprawling absurdity of their setting that *Still Holding* never feels forced or didactic. . . . Great satire has always been deadly serious business, and *Still Holding* is very good satire indeed."

—*The Washington Post Book World*

"Wagner has the odd but marvelous ability to be resolutely kind and unsparingly cutting at the same time, a contradiction played out in the third [of] the Hollywood-set trilogy."

—*Entertainment Weekly*

"Another razor-sharp exploration of the depths of Tinseltown's black heart, with clueless young actors, surreal interior monologues, faux Buddhism, and creepy celebrity look-alikes."

—*The Hollywood Reporter*

"At root, Wagner is a moralist. He captures a world far more horrifying than any of us suspected. No Hollywood novel is quite as upsetting as *Still Holding*. Even Wagner's earlier stories pale in comparison. Wagner's Hollywood is a world truly beyond redemption, one that deserves not adulation but profound moral outrage. It's to Wagner's credit that it mesmerizes—even as it horrifies."

—*Rocky Mountain News*

"A brutal phantasmagoria on the pleasure and perils of the dream factory."

—*Kirkus Reviews*

"At its best his prose reads like some unholy combination of Rick Moody, Anthony Lane, and the Page Six gossip columnist Richard Johnson. . . . the hippest, funniest, and most angrily humane novel written about Hollywood in the last twenty years."

—*The New York Times Book Review*

Also by Bruce Wagner

I'll Let You Go

I'm Losing You

Force Majeure

Still

Simon & Schuster Paperbacks

Holding

Bruce Wagner

NEW YORK LONDON TORONTO SYDNEY

SIMON & SCHUSTER PAPERBACKS
Rockefeller Center
1230 Avenue of the Americas
New York, NY 10020

This book is a work of fiction. The characters, conversations, and events in the novel are the product of my imagination, and no resemblance to any actual conduct of real-life persons, or to actual events, is intended. Although, for the sake of verisimilitude, certain public figures do make incidental appearances or are briefly referred to in the novel, their interactions with the characters invented are wholly my creation and are not intended to be understood as descriptions of real or actual events, or to reflect in any way upon the actual conduct or character of these public figures.

Copyright © 2003 by Bruce Wagner
All rights reserved,
including the right of reproduction
in whole or in part in any form.
First Simon & Schuster paperback edition 2004

SIMON & SCHUSTER PAPERBACKS and colophon are registered trademarks
of Simon & Schuster, Inc.

The author gratefully acknowledges permission to reprint the following material:
"Hot Property; Her Extra Territory" by Ruth Ryon, © 2002 Los Angeles Times. "The Logical Song" words and music by Rick Davies and Roger Hodgson © 1979 Almo Music Corp. and Delicate Music. All Rights Controlled and Administered by Almo Music Corp. All Rights Reserved. Used by Permission. Excerpt from *Bardo Guidebook*, Chökyi Nyima Rinpoche. Rangjung Yeshe Publications. © 1991 Chökyi Nyima Rinpoche & Rangjung Yeshe Publications.

For information about special discounts for bulk purchases,
please contact Simon & Schuster Special Sales at
1-800-456-6798 or business@simonandschuster.com.

Designed by Paul Dippolito

Manufactured in the United States of America

1   3   5   7   9   10   8   6   4   2

The Library of Congress has cataloged the hardcover edition as follows:
Wagner, Bruce.
Still holding / Bruce Wagner.
p.   cm.
1. Hollywood (Los Angeles, Calif.)—Fiction.   2. Motion picture industry—Fiction.
I. Title.
PS3573.A369S75   2003
813'.54—dc21   2003057256

ISBN 0-7432-4337-4
0-7432-4338-2 (Pbk)

This is for Seven McDonald

Contents

Pray for those that eat,
The things that are eaten,
And the act of eating itself.

—BUDDHIST MEALTIME PRAYER

The Three Jewels

Her Drewness

AS A GIRL, Becca hadn't resembled Drew Barrymore at all. But now, at twenty-five, especially after gaining a few pounds, she had grown used to comments from bartenders and store clerks, and the half-startled looks from passersby.

That was funny because her mom had always gotten the Sissy Spacek tag, even if Becca thought that was mostly because of a bad nose job. Still, Sissy and Drew were worlds apart, physically. It was a subjective thing; sometimes people could see the Sissy, sometimes they couldn't. But no one ever seemed to have trouble with Becca's "Drewness." Her boyfriend Sadge, who on a good day looked like a piss-poor Jack Black, got his kicks from playing it up—like the time he booked a table at Crustacean under Drew's name. He made sure to get there first and had Becca come forty minutes later in huge sunglasses, head swathed in a knockoff Hermès scarf. They were high, and the maître d' wasn't thrilled. (He must have been on to them from the beginning because Sadge had been ushered to the "civilian" zone.) A few diners turned their heads when Becca arrived, but she didn't have as much fun as she might have because Jordana Brewster was in the house, just on the other side of the glass partition, with a trim bald man Becca assumed to be her manager. Whenever Sadge laughed raucously or cued Becca to ham it up, the aspiring actress felt foolish, as she was certain Drew and Jordana knew each other. Jordana didn't look over once, and the whole thing kind of threw water on it for her. Suddenly Becca felt cheap, like a character in her friend Annie's favorite movie, *Star 80*.

That was the week she saw Drew on a Jay Leno repeat. Her divorce from Tom Green had just been announced, but there she sat, surrealistically giddy about the marriage. She gushed that her husband had sent a dozen roses and a note saying good luck on the show, and the audience sighed. Jay volunteered that it was actually a statistic that comedians stayed married longer. Drew said how great was that. It was so horrible and depressing that Becca actually got nauseated then angry that someone in programming would have been so careless as to rerun that particular show. She thought it might have been deliberately perpetrated, like when those malicious video store clerks splice porn into animated classics. Jay Leno struck her as a good and decent man, and she told Sadge—who'd laughed throughout the segment until Becca hit him—it was the kind of thing that if it was brought to NBC's attention by Drew's management (she hoped), the talk-show host would definitely apologize to her personally. Becca actually considered being the "whistle-blower," but then her own career concerns overtook her.

•   •   •

"THAT WAS GREAT," said Sharon. "I think you've got the potential to be quite a *comedienne.*"

She gave the word a Frenchified emphasis, and Becca was lost. Did she mean stand-up? She was too intimidated to ask for clarification. Maybe she meant Becca should be doing gigs at the Laugh Factory instead of wasting time trying to get movie and TV roles.

She decided she didn't care what the woman meant. She would simply persevere, perseverance being the one quality all successful actors had in common. She'd just gotten her SAG card and had finally found a commercial agent but didn't yet have the all-important "theatrical." Still, she thought of herself as a winner because only a month or so after a general meeting with Sharon Belzmerz, one of the big casting directors on the Warners lot, she had been invited back to do a taped audition for a WB pilot. Sharon's friend, Becca's acting coach, made the initial contact. What you always heard was true—it was all about personal connections.

"That was really fun!" said Becca. "Thank you *so* much for seeing me." She glanced at the video camera on the tripod opposite her. "Can I get a copy?"

Sharon smiled at her naïveté.

"Well, the director has to see it first—then we usually recycle."

"Oh! That's OK," said Becca, hiding her embarrassment.

"You're really very good. Don't worry, you'll have tape or film soon. You'll have a whole reel."

On the Boardwalk

WHEN HER FATHER had a stroke, Lisanne took the day off.

She worked for Reggie Marck in the penthouse offices of Marck, Fitch, Saginow, Rippert, Childers, and Beiard, at Sunset near Doheny. She was thirty-seven and had been Reggie's crackerjack executive secretary for thirteen years, beginning with his stint at Kohlhorn, Kohan, Rattner, Hawkins, and Risk. When he heard the bad news, he encouraged her to get on a plane and go home. That wasn't so easy. Lisanne had a profound fear of flying (a condition long predating 9/11). After a round of phone calls to her aunt, she went to the Venice Boardwalk to clear her head.

The shoreline was windswept and absurdly pristine. Since the bike path's renovation and the rebuilding of a few burned-out boardwalk apartment houses—not to mention the arrival of Shutters and Casa del Mar—the beach had lost some of its funky grandeur. There wasn't much to be nostalgic about anymore. The shops, vendors, and performers were forced to clean up their acts, and the city hadn't sanctioned Fourth of July fireworks on the pier in years because of the gangs.

Lisanne bit the bullet and took possession of her wistful stroll; she had some serious mulling to do. There was the dilemma of her father's grave condition, plus imminent jet travel. . . . Still, it was diverting to take in the scene. Because it was a weekday, there weren't many people out. Interspersed with the homeless was an upscale cadre of citizens busily exercising their right to play hooky at watery world's end. They spun or sprinted past doing "cardio" or simply sat and stared at the passive ruthlessness of the sea whence one day they would return, if they were so lucky. Heads tilted, faux-contemplative, to regard the occasional chandelier of gulls.

Lisanne waited for a woman in her late forties to jog by before crossing the path. A tribe of drunks sat on the grass. One of them yelled, "You go, girl! You c'n do it! You c'n *do* it, girlie!" The runner pretended to ignore him, but Lisanne could tell the bum had found her prideful nerve. Later, she saw a different drunk approach a gorgeous twentysomething couple. The boy's pants slung stylishly low, and the drunk said, "Hey, your fuckin pants are fallin down your ass!" The boy, smiling and trying to be cool, decided to say, "I know," to defuse the harassment. His girlfriend was being cool too, but the drunk wouldn't have it. "Then pull 'em *up*! Pull 'em *up*!" It was like the commedias dell'arte that Lisanne had studied in school. The bums and winos were there to keep it real, to deflate the ego and remind that all was vanity.

Lisanne slunk away to avoid being heckled. She was forty pounds overweight—a perfect target.

She tried to imagine herself climbing onto a plane. As a girl, she didn't mind flying so much, though she remembered only a few trips. The 747s were so big and she was so small that somehow it was OK. But now it was different. Reggie would have to hook her up with his doctor for the big gun sleeping pills, and if she timed it right, she'd wake up as they touched down at Newark. That was the best of scenarios. Aside from the obvious fantasies of wind-shear-induced nose-dives, messy hijackings, human-debris-scattered cornfield fireballs, and charismatic pilots greeting her with gin-laced coffee breath as she boarded, Lisanne considered some of her lesser concerns to be laugh-out-loud comical. What if the pills put her out so deep that her snoring became shamefully stertorous or she drooled on the passenger beside her? What if her throat closed up or she had a reaction to the pills and vomited in her sleep? No—try as she may, Lisanne couldn't see herself getting into some fucked-up cylinder and hurtling through space. She wasn't ready to play that kind of Russian roulette. In heaven or hell, the biggest bunch of losers had to be the ones who crashed while flying to be at the side of a stroked-out parent.

She would take the train.

Does a Dog Have
Buddha Nature?

KIT LIGHTFOOT WAS in his trailer, meditating.

He was thirty-four and had meditated at least an hour a day for nearly a dozen years without fail. Out of carefully enforced humility, he had never shared that statistic with anyone, though the urge to do so frequently came upon him. Whenever he felt the pride of a Zen valedictorian, he smiled and soldiered on, letting the feeling wash over him. Years of *zazen* had taught him that all manner of thoughts, feelings, and physical sensations would arise and clamor for his attention before falling away.

His career as an actor had barely been launched when a friend turned him on to Buddhism. He took up meditating and, a short while after, visited a monastery on Mount Baldy. It was freezing cold, but there was wordless beauty and a stunning quietude that pierced him to the core. That was the week, he used to say, where he got a taste of stillness. Monks and dedicated laypersons came and went like solemn, dignified cadets amidst the ritualized cadence of drums, chanting, and silence—his unthinkable siren and dangerous new friend, for silence too had a cadence. (*The hard poetry of silence,* his teacher once said.) He watched a man being ordained and later found out he had once been a powerful Hollywood agent. Kit grooved to that kind of convert. He loved having blundered into this magisterially abstract Shangri-la of the spirit, a flawless diamond-pointed world that might liberate him from the bonds of narcissism, the bonds of self.

He got deeper into his practice. Between theater and film gigs he traveled to far-flung countries attending monthlong *sesshins,* awakening at four in the morning to sit on a cushion eleven hours a day when not immersed in the meditation of food preparation, tea ceremonies, groundskeeping. He was glad to be young and strong while learning the art of sitting in stillness. Older initiates had a hard time with *zazen*'s physical demands.

It became well-known within the show business community, and outside it too, that Kit was a serious practitioner. He rarely discussed his thoughts or beliefs with interviewers unless the venue was a magazine like *Tricycle* or *Shambhala Sun*. He didn't want to trivialize something so personal or, worse, get puffed up in the process. There were enough celebrities talking about yoga and Buddhism anyway. He gave generously to the Tibetan cause and funded clinics and ashrams through an anonymous trust. That satisfied him more than any public discourse ever could.

In those twelve years of practice, Kit Lightfoot, the celebrity, was often the People's Choice. He'd finally been snagged by James Lipton (Hoffman and Nicholson were among the remaining holdouts) and photographed in *Vanity Fair*'s Hollywood issue with the simple caption "The Man." He even won Best Supporting for a remarkable, artfully thrown away performance in a fluky, borderline indie lark filmed just before the death of his Buddhist teacher, Gil Weiskopf Roshi. After the fact, it seemed so perfect. It was Gil who had said: *Throw it all away.*

.   .   .

IT WAS THANKSGIVING time, and a whore was at his Benedict Canyon home. That used to be his thing, but he hadn't been with a whore since the early nineties. And he'd never cheated on Viv.

They were coked up in the living room, and he laughed as she held the dog's head between her legs. It kept trying to break free, and that made the whore laugh too. "Jus' like his master," she said. "Real *picky*." She laughed again and released him, then stood to pee. When the whore came back, she knelt by the Buddha at the fireplace and lit a cigarette. There were flowers and incense and tiny photos of enlightened men. She asked about the altar, and Kit said reflectively that it was a gift from Stevie Nicks. Then he gave her a little flash-card intro—Zen 101. Stillness. Sitting. The Power of Now.

"You meditate every day?" she said.

"Every day. For fifteen years."

A Star Is Born

BECCA WAS PART of Metropolis, a modest theater company that leased space on Delongpre. The roof was undergoing repair, having been damaged in the rains, so the class was temporarily on Hillhurst at the home of one of its founders. Becca thought Cyrus was a wonderful teacher and a good director too. He was for sure an amazing promoter. Aside from agent and exec heavies, he always managed to get people like Meg Ryan and Tim Robbins to show up at openings.

For two weeks, she'd been working with Annie on a scene from a Strindberg play. She had never even heard of Strindberg until she met Cyrus but had to admit she loved Tennessee Williams more. She loved Tennessee's letters and poems and short stories—everything he wrote was so sad and beautiful yet filled with such tenderness. His women were at once tough and unbearably fragile, just as Becca imagined herself. She'd seen all the films made from his plays and liked *This Property Is Condemned* best. In real life, Natalie Wood was sad and beautiful too and just as tragic as anything. August Strindberg was brilliant and ruthlessly true to human nature, but sometimes he scared her, leaving her cold. She preferred Ibsen and Chekhov.

After rehearsal, they went to a coffee shop on Vermont.

"Did I suck?"

"No!" said Annie. "You were *great*. Why? Did *you* think you sucked?"

"I always think I suck."

"You *so don't*. You're always *amazing*. Cyrus *loves* what you do."

"You think?"

"Totally. He so totally does."

"You mean he loves the one line per play he sees fit for me to declaim."

"You'll get there," said Annie. "Anyway, do you see me majorly treading the boards? Do you, Miss Declaimerhead?"

Becca laughed. "I'm just so freaked out—about *everything*. Ohmygod, did I tell you Sadge might be going to Tasmania for this reality show?"

"No! What is it?"

"I don't even know."

"Where's Tasmania? Is that, like, near Transylvania?"

"Maybe Czechoslovakia?"

"I *so* want to go to Prague. You should go, Becca! You should go with him and use his hotel as a base. You could do absinthe. Like Marilyn Manson! It would be so rad."

"I don't think so, Annie."

"But won't it be good, though? I mean, weren't you saying you needed space?"

"Yeah. But it'll be weird suddenly being alone."

"Can't you not have a boyfriend for *one minute*?"

"It's pilot season, and I haven't gone up for anything."

"That's why you're freaked out," Annie said knowingly.

"I guess."

"But you saw that casting woman."

"It doesn't matter."

"What did she say?"

"That I could be a 'comedienne.' "

Annie scrunched her nose the way Becca loved. "What does *that* mean?"

"I have no idea."

"You should do open-mike night at the Improv," said Annie. "You could be the next Margaret Cho."

"I could waitress at the Cheesecake Factory and after work do open-mike at the Laugh Factory."

Annie laughed then said, "I think that rocks."

• • •

ONE OF THE Metropolis ensemble players who guested on *Six Feet Under* got sick with the flu and gave Annie his tickets to the show's season premiere at the El Capitan. Becca splurged on a dress from Agnès B.

They lingered in the lobby, getting free drinks and popcorn before going in. Stars like Ed Begley Jr. and Brooke Shields were milling around. The air was electric with showbiz bonhomie.

When they entered the theater, the girls were led to a special roped-off area to sit among the luminaries. They were just an arm's length from Jeff Goldblum, Kathy Bates, and Pee-Wee Herman. The head of the network got up and said they had all made history and that the cast was the greatest ever assembled. He said the creator of the show was a dark, special kind of genius who had written a drama that was ostensibly about death but actually turned out to be profoundly about *life*. Then the creator, the ubiquitous Alan, a handsomely nerdy, sweet-faced man, took the stage to a tumult of applause. He comically prostrated himself, saying "Thank God for HBO!" and this time there was a thunder of laughter along with the applause. Becca had never been to the premiere of a television show and was confused when he began to speechify like it was the Academy Awards. He acknowledged this person and that, occasionally interjecting "Thank God for HBO!" and everyone laughed, hooted, and clapped their hands. The audience seemed so happy, healthy, and rich, and ebullient men were kissing each other on the cheeks and mouth. She felt like part of them, like part of the HBO family— she was among the roped off after all, and the same men smiled back at her whenever Becca caught their eyes, as if it were a given that she was one of their own. They were kind and open and not cliquish even though they had every right to be.

The "after-party" was across the street in the building where they held the Oscars. It was fun walking the short distance because there were lots of photographers and police, and pedestrians straining their eyes to watch the privileged make their crosswalk pilgrimage. They passed the Chinese Theater, and for little micromoments Becca pretended she was famous. It gave her goose bumps.

While Annie was in the rest room, a woman approached and asked if she was an actress. She was casting for a show and gave Becca her card.

When Annie came back, Becca giddily marched her friend to a corner before uncrumpling it from her sweaty hand to examine:

THE LOOK-ALIKE SHOPPE PRODUCTIONS
ELAINE JORDACHE, FOUNDER/CREATOR
HOLLYWOOD, CA

The Great Plains

LISANNE TREATED HERSELF to a deluxe bedroom on the Amtrak. It was such an intense relief not to be getting on a plane that she found herself almost sensuously relaxed as they left Union Station. She would keep in touch with her father's caretakers by cell phone and with the office as well, fielding any questions the temp might have. Getting to Chicago took two days. Lisanne would change trains there, arriving in Albany within twenty-four hours.

She kept to her room, hunkering down with a paperback filled with transcribed tapes from the recovered black boxes of crashed airplanes. She laughed a little at her own morbidity—it was so Addams Family-bedtime-story of her—yet each time she dipped into the book, her decision to take the rails was sustained anew. Oh God, thought Lisanne. My fears are completely justified.

One of the transcripts was particularly harrowing. An Alaska Airlines jet on its way from Puerto Vallarta to San Francisco had plunged into the Pacific. It was clear from the dialogue that the captain knew they weren't going to make it. But what haunted Lisanne was his intercom announcement to the passengers. He said Los Angeles was off to the right and that he didn't anticipate any problems once he got "a couple of subsystems on the line"—this, after the plane had shakily recovered from a nosedive. Anticipated arrival to LAX, he said, was under half an hour. Lisanne presumed that, by the time of his speech, the doomed passengers, many no doubt injured from the free fall, would have been in a state of shock. For months, she read the account over and over, thinking of Flight 261 as a kind of ghost ship, its wayward souls' eighty-eight sets of eyes (the book's favored term, each airborne drama typically ending with "all souls aboard were lost") forever fixated on Los Angeles, condemned to circle a destination at which they'd never arrive. The moment the captain directed their attention toward L.A.—"off to the right there"—Lisanne imagined the last thoughts and wishes of the passengers focused upon the sprawling city with an incomprehensible, laserlike force, a desperate longing that may ultimately have outlived their physical bodies. (Maybe that was just her father talking. It was the kind of impassioned, fanciful theory he would have advanced over the dinner table, spookily transcendent, darkly romantic; the sort of argument that intimidated her mother and made her feel small.) *Our intention,* said the pilot to the control tower, *is to land at Los Angeles.*

On trains, one ate communally, but Lisanne didn't have the energy for small talk or passing personal histories so she took meals in her cabin. Once in a while, to break the monotony, she had coffee in the observation car. The tracks were dicey, and the cars shimmied and shook. Her body shook too, but Lisanne didn't feel self-conscious because so many people on the train were fat—L.A. wasn't the way Americans looked, *this* was how Americans looked. Cushy and invisible, safe from wind shear, she clicked into cozy "observer" mode. . . . A family threaded its way through the shifting aisle. The studious-looking little girl said to the others, "Now, if you hold on as you go, you'll be just fine." Such a darling, so distinctly American: the budding caretaker. She reminded Lisanne of herself. A young man with a shaved head passed by, wearing a T-shirt that read PAIN IS WEAKNESS LEAVING THE BODY. She saw a hermit-looking fellow staring out the window, with a heavy slab resting in his lap. She thought it was a food tray before getting a closer look—he'd been whittling a finely detailed memorial to the police and firemen of September 11. "How beautiful," she said. She really did think it an extraordinary example of folk art. The hermit thanked her indifferently, never averting his eyes from the mysterious panorama of the Kansan plains. So American too, this eccentric! Americans all.

One thing Lisanne thought strange: They had traveled hundreds of miles through small and midsize towns, but she rarely saw a human being. The locomotive whooshed, clattered, or lumbered past clapboard houses, some abandoned, others half built, many clearly lived in, yet Lisanne never saw anyone in the yards or driveways—no scavengers or children, idlers or train watchers, no one working in the yard, or even seen through windows, baking, yelling, reading or restive, writing or resigned. She searched her mind, but there was no way to account for it. She thought of Alaska Airlines again—of ghost ships and ghost trains, ghost moms and dads on a ghostly plain. What was that movie she saw on pay-per-view and liked so much? *Ghost World.* That just about said it all.

The porter, a slow black girl, brought dinner. Lisanne fastidiously arranged the food on the metal tray that dropped down from the cold window of her private compartment. It was pleasurable to eat in solitude with the sun dipping and the scenic world moving by. Had she flown, she would have arrived long since.

Just before sleep, Lisanne thought of the family she'd read about in *The New York Times* who had perished in France, in a fire aboard a high-speed train. Only those in the deluxe sleeper car had died. The same thing happened in the States some years ago, but she couldn't get it up to care. Phobias were like that—either you had one or you didn't. Bed down, tucked beneath the requisition threadbare pink blankets, Lisanne felt safe and secure, certain she'd survive any old little fire or derailment that came her way.

⋅ ⋅ ⋅

JUST BEFORE ARRIVING in Chicago, Lisanne showered in the closet-size bathroom. The water was nice and warm, and she smiled at the comic absurdity of hosing herself down in the upright plastic coffin of a train toilet. Looking at the big white folds of skin, she felt like an animal at the county fair. She laughed when imagining herself stuck in the stall, the dull-witted porter having to pry her out.

She had four hours to kill and went to Marshall Field's for lunch. The grandiose dining room was shopworn and depressing, so she ate lunch in an ill-lit, pretentious chain-boutique hotel with giant, ludicrously stylized chairs and lamps. After the meal, she strolled to the Sears Tower. It was windy, and her mind imbecilically repeated: *The Windy City, the Windy City, the Windy City.* She tried calling her aunt but couldn't get through.

It was good to get back on the train. She saw herself traveling like this forever, city to city, station to station, coast to coast, working for Amtrak incognito as a secret inspector in quality control, a plus-size spinster who kept to herself and legendarily took meals in sequestration. She thought seriously about changing her return ticket so that instead of coming through Chicago again she could take the southern route to Jacksonville then over to New Orleans.

By the time she got to Albany, her father was dead.

The Benefit

HE FLIPPED THROUGH the paper. Viv was still getting ready. The driver waited outside to take them to the benefit.

Kit was always looking through articles in the *Times* for movie ideas. Maybe there would be something to develop that he could direct. Shit, his friend Clooney had done it. Nic Cage and Sean, Denzel and Kevin—name the film and the chances were that some actor had "helmed." There was an item about a woman accused of feeding her young daughter sleeping pills and shaving her head in an effort to convince the community she had leukemia and was worthy of multiple fund-raisers. She even put the kid in counseling, to prepare her for death. Another told of two Wichita brothers who broke into a town house and forced a bunch of twentysomething friends to have sex with each other before staging executions on a snowy soccer field. At the bottom of the page was the story of a pole vaulter who had freakishly crashed to the ground and died during his run. The last thing he said before jogging to his death was, "This is my day, Dad."

"What's this thing we're going to?" Kit asked as Viv strode in, cocky and perfect-looking. He could smell the hair on her arms.

"A benefit for Char Riordan," she said. "She's a casting agent—*so* great. I *love* her."

"Television?"

She nodded.

Viv Wembley was as famous as her boyfriend but in a different way. She was one of the stars of *Together,* the long-running, high-rated sitcom.

"She cast me in my first play and my first TV movie. I was bridesmaid at her wedding on the Vineyard."

"So what's wrong with her?"

"Scleroderma."

"Gesundheit."

"Very funny."

"Sclero*what?*"

"*Scleroderma.*"

"What *is* that?"

"I don't even know! It's in the tissues or something. She looks kind of like a monster—like she's rotting away."

"Always attractive."

"If I ever get anything like that, promise to shoot me."

"After I fuck you. Or maybe during."

She swatted at him as they got into the Town Car. When it pulled up to the hotel, the photographers shouted their names in a frenzy. Alf Lanier, a younger movie star in his own right and a friend of both, nudged his way over, doing jester shtick as the trio posed in a seizure of strobes.

"What the fuck are *you* doing here?" asked Kit, playfully sotto.

"Isn't this the Michael J. Fox thing?" said Alf.

"You are *such* an asshole," said Viv, with a scampish smile.

"You stupid cunt," said Kit to Alf, whispering in his ear to be heard above the vulturazzi. "Didn't you know this was the Lymphoma Costume Ball?"

"You guys better shut up!" said Viv, enjoying their banter.

Alf looked outraged and shot back to Kit: "This is the cystic fibrosis–autism thing, you insensitive prick."

"Oh shit," said the superstar, contritely. "I fucked up. But are you *sure* this isn't the bipolar Lou Gehrig tit cancer monkeypox telethon?"

They went on like that as Viv dragged them into the ballroom.

Fisticuffs

THE OFFICE OF the Look-Alike Shoppe Productions was on Willoughby, not far from where Metropolis had its theater. It was Saturday when Becca came in. Before taking the stairs, she noticed the dented Lexus with the customized plate:

Elaine Jordache, a hard fifty with jet-black, dandruffy hair, had predatory eyes that somehow still welcomed. She sucked from a Coffee Bean & Tea Leaf cup festooned with lipstick. Glossies of actors covered every available wall space; Xeroxes and boilerplate contracts littered floor and desk in a parody of industry. She rid a chair of papers and bade Becca sit amid the shitstorm. If the phone rang, Elaine said she would have to take it—her assistant was out sick, and she was expecting an important call from Denmark. As it happened, she said, the Look-Alike Shoppe did a ton of business with Denmark.

"What did you think of the show?" she asked.

Becca was flustered until she realized Elaine was talking about the *Six Feet Under* premiere.

"It was *amazing*. Ohmygod, did you cast it?"

"A close friend of mine," she said, shaking her head. "A protégée. She handles the extras. She'll be doing principals soon, wait and see— they all just won Emmys. The girls who cast the show. They do a *great* job too. But you burn out doing a series. It's an assembly line. That's a fuck-load of faces, each and every week. They'll be wanting to move on." She took a long cigarette from an antiquey silver case, then shuffled beneath the contracts, hunting for matches. "Fun when you're younger, though. They really work you. Everyone wants a lot of bang for their buck. I've been with all the biggies—Altman, Ashby, Nic Roeg. Do you even know who Nic Roeg is?" Becca shook her head. "Well, why should you? My God, I worked with Nic when I was a *baby*—your age. Married to Theresa Russell. Were *they* the couple: hot, hot, hot! I've got a *fabulous* Theresa Russell, but I can't use her. Saw her on the street—not even *she* knows she looks like Theresa. Who's heard of Theresa Russell anymore?"

Elaine found a matchbook and lit up. She dipped into a steel file drawer and passed an eight-by-ten Becca's way—a pretty girl with wavy blond hair dangling from beneath a fedora, like a starlet from long ago. "There she is," said Elaine. Becca noticed some acne on the chin that should have been airbrushed. "That's my Theresa, for all the good it'll do me. I don't even know where she is. Phone disconnected. She was working at either Target or Hooters, can't remember which. Maybe Costco. I get all my kids confused."

"What is it that you do here?" asked Becca ingenuously.

Elaine literally threw back her head and laughed. " 'Do'? I do *look-alikes*! Ground control to Becca! I mean, that's what it says on the card, right? Look-alikes. I cast look-alikes." Becca still seemed per-plexed. "For trade shows and special events, OK? Meet-'n'-greets. Con-ventions. Comedy sketches. Ever done comedy?"

"I've done improv. I'm in Metropolis—the theater group."

Elaine wasn't impressed.

"Last week, Rusty was on the Leno show—my Russell Crowe. You know how Jay sometimes does movie takeoffs? Like Johnny used to. God, I used to book Johnny like crazy. He's got emphysema now, poor man. But he's richer than Croesus so I ain't gonna feel too bad. I flew Rusty to Japan just last month, they're *crazy* about Russell Crowe in Japan—and Drew too," she said, with a wink. "They did a nine-eleven memorial thing over there. I had my Russell, my Clooney, my Bette. She did 'Boogie Woogie Bugle Boy.' Does she have a voice on her! I'm *desperate* for a Nicole—lost mine to pilot season, what can you do? I'd kill. I actually *do* have a couple of Ewans, believe it or not. Thought they'd be harder to come by. Audiences eat the duets *up*. But the Nicole really has to be able to sing. *Moulin Rouge* has become a cash cow for us. *And,"* she said dramatically, "I've got a Cammie Diaz and a Lucy Liu . . . *but no Drew."* She inhaled deeply. "That's where *you* come in."

．　．　．

THAT NIGHT, BECCA made Annie go with her to a nightclub in Playa del Rey that Elaine recommended. Some of her people would be performing.

The show was a cavalcade of look-alikes. Most of them were tacky, but a few had natural talent as impersonators. Annie was stoned and couldn't stop laughing, but Becca was moved in a way she couldn't explain. A bad Kit Lightfoot did his thing, then a Russell Crowe came onstage in a cheap gladiator outfit and Becca thought him awful. He was muscle-bound and inelegant, his accent was absurd, and you had to squint even to imagine a resemblance. Her opinion of Elaine Jordache's judgment soured right there.

Toward the end, after a few peculiar acts—a lurid Celine Dion, and a ranting John McEnroe being interviewed by a long-haired Larry King—a second Russell Crowe took the stage. Becca thought this one to be nearly charismatic as the real thing. He did the hand-to-forehead tic of the character from *A Beautiful Mind* and spoke in "schizophrenic" tongues, a creative stream-of-consciousness monologue that Becca found funny and poetic, with pointedly scathing asides directed at his earlier, idiotic incarnation. *This* Russell was someone who didn't relish sharing the stage.

Afterward, the two girls went out for a smoke. Annie got woozy from the wine and the weed and they decided to go home. On the way to the car, Becca saw the second Mr. Crowe and called out, "You were amazing!"

"Thanks," he mumbled, head down, as if still in character.

She walked a little closer. "I'm a friend of Elaine's," she stammered. "Elaine Jordache. She told me you were in Japan—that you went to Japan."

He eyed her warily. "Oh yeah? That was no thanks to her. She's a cunt—worse—a Jewish cunt. And she's trying to fucking rob me."

His ears pricked like an animal's and he bolted, sprinting down the block. Annie gasped then broke into laughter, while Becca's mouth remained open in astonishment. They ran for the car and tussled awhile, Becca trying to wrest away the keys. Annie insisted on driving and made a screeching turnabout, stopping at the light in time to see the Russell chase down his inferior. He threw his shadow to the ground and pummeled him. Like puppet and despotic puppeteer, the weaker Russell squeaked and moaned, squirming under the rain of blows.

"*Ohmygod!*" muttered Annie, and floored it.

Sleepless in Albany

HE HAD BEEN dead just forty-five minutes when Lisanne arrived. The nurses stayed out of the room while the aunt and one of her father's neighbors sat vigil. All of the medical equipment had been disconnected.

His skin was like tallow. The aunt spread baby powder on the hairless, purple-bruised arms, draping a small towel over the genitals, then gave Lisanne the powder and gestured for her to do the legs. She wasn't sure why they were doing it, but it was somehow a comfort. His shins reminded her of slick wood handrails. The cologne of the talc commingling with death smells faintly sickened. His mouth twisted to one side, like that of a whispering conspirator in a medieval religious painting.

• • •

AFTER HE HAD been cremated, Lisanne kept dreaming that she was a victim of one of those undertaker scams and that what she thought were the dusty remains of her father were actually those of animals or indigent men. Finally, to break the cycle, she went downstairs.

Her aunt sat in Dad's favorite chair half asleep, the cool, ash-filled vase poised on a thin shellacked table beside her. It took four hours—four whole hours to burn a body then grind its bones to dust. Lisanne picked up the urn, revolved it, then quietly set it down. She traced a half circle around it, then tapped the tabletop's veneer.

Just the kind of piece people bring to *Antiques Roadshow,* she thought randomly.

Lisanne heated up milk in a saucepan. While her aunt slept, she padded to the library to browse the bookshelves so she might further distance herself from the soot of nightmare. Her father had been a professor, a learned man. She drew a forefinger over the spines: *Poverty—A History*; Wedekind's *Diary of an Erotic Life; The Norton Dictionary of Modern Thought; The Hundred Thousand Songs of Milarepa; The Book Lover's Guide to the Internet*; a cool green, five-volume set called *Mexico—A Traves de los Siglos*; Hardy's *Selected Poems*. She never really knew him, nor would she now by his obscure and bloodless books. They would crumble soon enough, like the body of their collector, whose exit she'd been too late to observe.

"Why didn't you fly?"

The aunt appeared in the door like a dark oracle.

"Because it terrifies me."

Lisanne paused, wondering if she should go on. Why should she have to explain herself to this crone?

"And because I would have had to drug myself into a coma, which always makes me uncomfortable."

The old woman winced at her niece's low comedy but said nothing. She left the room.

Lisanne climbed the stairs and returned to the same bed she'd slept in as a girl—the same bed her mother chose to die in, ten years back. She had missed that death too.

She took half an Ativan and settled under the covers, imagining herself on a 747, first class, selecting wines and cheeses offered by the handsome steward . . . joshing with a flirty fellow passenger after a spate of turbulence . . . the uneventful landing . . . the connecting plane and swift arrival to hospital . . . Dad's deep-water eyes rising just once more to surface sea brightness at the unexpected sight of her, and the aunt's tearful relief as she entered the room . . . a convocation of hands prayerfully entwined as he shanty-sighed his last respirations, sinking back to the briny depths.

As the first wavy softness of the drug entered her bloodstream, Lisanne's thoughts drifted to her high school boyfriend. The aunt said Robbie had moved back to town six months ago. It was at least ten years since they'd spoken and she decided to see him before the train left for Chicago on Sunday night.

Command Performance

"WHAT THE FUCK are we doing here?" asked Kit.

They were at a club on the Strip frequented by young television stars.

"My roots, baby," said Alf. "Television made me what I *fucking am.* Jus' *loves* comin back to look after the little ones." He scanned the room with a vulpine smile. "You're so mega, Kitchener. Your very fucking *presence* makes 'em *nutsoid.* Look at 'em! Look! Trying to be all cool and not make eye contact—sad but *so sweet.*"

Kit looked around in exaggerated disgust. "I meet enough TV dickheads through Viv."

"Think you're gonna marry her?"

"Man, I don't know. It's hard. It's fucking hard. Sometimes I think that'd be . . . kinda great? You know, I love her—I really do."

"I know. I know. Great gal."

"Sometimes I think: OK. Let's *do* it. The whole yadda-baby thing. Because she's *hot,* she's in my blood, man. Other times, I just stare at the fucking ceiling. And it's like . . . whoa! *Can't give up the whores.*"

Alf got quiet.

They erupted in laughter, tilting back shots.

"Still into the Buddhist thing?"

"Still into it," said Kit, by rote. He was used to the tepid inquiries. "I'm a lapsed Buddhist," he added with a smirk.

"Fallen monk."

"That's me, honey. After the fall."

"I read this interview with Oliver Stone? He said he was attracted to Buddhism because it wasn't on some morality trip like most religions."

"That's bullshit," said Kit. "Buddhism's all *about* morality. Right thought, Right action."

"I think I'm really gonna try it," said Alf.

"Uh huh."

"I'm *serious*—at least the meditation thing. Friend of mine has this machine, this mask and headset that put out these crazy lights and sounds. Very sixties, bubba. Supposed to put you in an alpha state without having to sit for ten hours a day. Kinda jump-starts you. He drops the shrooms, then straps it on. Cause I don't know if I could do that—the whole sit thing that you do. I mean, I got discipline but . . ."

"You're disciplined at getting blow jobs."

"From your daddy. And he's good, too. Guess you gave him a lot of practice. I was listening to these Joseph Campbell tapes on the way to Vegas. The ones with Bill Moyers? Downey's totally into them. We were on our way to see the Stones. Did you ever listen to that Campbell shit? He's a trip."

"Get thee to a monastery. I'll hook you up."

Kit flinched at his own words. He hated his behavior of late, the way he acted, spoke, thought. His only comfort was in telling himself that he was in the at-least-conscious throes of some sort of perversely pathetic karmic regression. For years he had been meticulous, impeccable, mindful—now he was frivolous and inane, wasteful, asinine. A flabby bullshitter: every gesture and every breath was false, vulgar, wrong. He was a poisoned well. It was becoming intolerable to be in his own skin. He'd long since betrayed the precepts and spirit of his practice. When he thought of Gil Weiskopf Roshi, his root guru, monitoring his lifestyle from the afterworld, Kit shuddered with embarrassment before noting that even his shame and remorse were bogus and hypocritical. This sort of masochistic digression formed the backdrop of his days.

Alf saw a friend come toward them from the bar. "Heads up for my man Lucas. Good little actor—got a Golden Globe."

Lucas was upon them. He said hello to his old friend, then turned to Kit, awestruck. "I just wanted to tell you what a big fan I am of your work."

"Thanks."

"And Viv's great, too. I just did an arc on *Together*. She's good people. *Very* cool."

Alf stood up. "Be right back. I see someone I think I want to fuck."

"Boy or girl?" said Kit.

"Girly-man," said Alf. He leaned over to Lucas and stage-whispered, "Try not to drool on my bro, OK?"

Kit wasn't thrilled to be left holding the bag with Golden boy.

"You're into Buddhism, aren't you?"

"Right."

Oh God here we go. Suddenly he felt how drunk he was.

"My sister's *deep* into it. She spent nine months at an ashram in the Bahamas. What's it called, the meditation?"

"There's different kinds."

"It starts with a *v*—"

"Vipassana?"

"Yeah! That's it—vipassana. That stuff is *serious.* She's way into yoga too. She's really close to Mariel Hemingway, who's *completely addicted.* She wrote this memoir?—Mariel, not my sister—with the chapter headings all named for yoga poses? Did you read that?"

"No."

He kept his ego in check. What was the point in dissing this nervous kid?

"So, how long you been knowing Alf?" asked Kit.

"We did this series, a summer replacement. Kinda were roomies—lived down the hill from Hustler's. On Sunset? Before that, we both tended bar at the Viper. Went on auditions together, slept with each other's girlfriends. You know the drill. Alfie's gone a little farther careerwise than I have. Can't complain."

"You won the Globe! That's pretty major. What was that for?"

"*Savage Song.*"

"Right! The software guy with Tourette's? Man, I *saw* that. Viv thought you were amazing. Kept buggin on me to check it out."

"Thank you. I can't believe you actually watched that! Thank you. Yeah, that was difficult, cause there were, like, *so many Tourette's* flicks. It's hard to stand out."

"Ever think you'd fuck it up? I mean, you go out on a major limb when you do the disability thing. I don't think I have the chops."

"I researched it pretty well."

Alf came back to the table accompanied by a redhead with a tiny dragon tattoo on her neck. They ditzed around while Kit and Lucas hunched over, talking between themselves like new best friends.

"I kind of got to know a lot of those people. My accountant's actually got Tourette's."

"You *have* to do it," said Alf, having overheard. "You gotta reprise your Golden Globe–winning performance!"

"You mean, *now*?" said Lucas, a twinkle in his eye. Alf knew his buddy would do anything in front of The Idol, for a laugh.

"Kit, you gotta see this!"

"What?" said Kit, with a half smile. He swallowed another shot.

"OK, I'll show you," said Lucas. He spoke directly to the superstar, as if it were Kit, not Alf, who'd been egging him on. "But only if you put me in your next film."

"Done," said Kit, along for the ride.

Alf rubbed his hands together and said, *"Let's roll."*

Lucas stood and instantly adopted his small-screen persona, barking, spitting and spewing obscenities with startling spasmodic accuracy as the clubbers reacted first with stunned silence then shrieks, laughter, and war whoops.

Chagrined, Kit found himself laughing louder than anyone—to the starstruck onlookers it almost seemed like he was part of the show. He'd been feeling so miserable and so derelict, and now all his self-loathing tumbled forth with unstoppable fury.

Asses into Seats

BECCA GOT TO the L.A. Convention Center early. She went to the Subaru exhibit, but no one was there.

As she left the hall to find a coffee, Elaine arrived with a gaggle of look-alikes in tow. She was glad to see "Drew"—she insisted on calling her brood by their celebrity names—and quickly introduced her to Cameron, Louie (Anderson), Cher, and Whoopi. Shoving Cameron at her, she bemoaned that Lucy (Liu) had car trouble and wasn't going to make it. Today, the Auto Show would have to get by with just two Angels.

A few aloof staffers appeared and faintly sniggered while Elaine gathered the ducklings round for an impromptu seminar. Subaru had a Hooray for Hollywood! theme going, and the idea was for the look-alikes to encourage spectators to sit in the cars, kick the tires, and whatnot. Before Elaine even finished, Whoopi dived right in, spritzing a Japanese couple with *Hollywood Squares*–type zingers. The Louie was heartened and impulsively uprooted a prepubescent girl, forcibly settling her into one of the car's open trunks so that she stood in it upright. The dad took pictures of his bemused, giggly daughter.

The Cameron was awkward at first but in between entertaining consumers spoke excitedly to Becca of Elaine Jordache's *Angels* Master Plan. She was tall and had no ass. Becca thought the most Cameron-like thing about her was definitely her smile, which shone grotesquely without requiring cue. She wore clear braces (she said she was "currently under construction"), with a view toward making wideness and whiteness closer to Cameron's; the lips were chapped with grape-colored gloss ill-applied. Becca couldn't understand why the girl couldn't at least have given the mouth—her prime asset—a little more prep time.

Some kids came over and hassled them. "Are you supposed to be Drew Barrymore?"

"That's right," said Becca, extending an arm to one of the cars. She thought she may as well use them for practice. "Now be an *angel* and take a seat in the new Impreza—it never fails to impress!"

"Take a seat on my *face*," muttered his friend. They cracked themselves up until a mean-looking staffer sent them scurrying. Out of harm's way, one of the boys shouted: "Hey, everybody! Drew Barrymore! Over there! It's Drew Barrymore and Cameron Diaz of *Charlie's Angels*!" His buddy added, "Free blow jobs, free blow jobs! They're giving out free blow jobs!"

They disappeared into the crowd.

Becca introduced herself as Drew (per Elaine's instructions), showing browsers to their cars. All in all, people were kind, and flattering about her resemblance. She had read that a lot of Hollywood power-types came to the Auto Show—you never knew who you'd make an impression on. Her Southern charm and sunny spirit lightened everybody's load. She even won the staffers over.

After an hour or so, she took a break. She saw Elaine over by a customized SUV, having an argument with the handsome man who had impersonated Russell Crowe in Playa del Rey. Becca hid herself behind a display and eavesdropped.

"I told you to bring the armor!" she hissed.

"I *said* that I couldn't find it. I didn't want to be late."

He was docile—a far cry from his brutish behavior of the other night.

"Well, *next* time I say bring it, *bring it*. Or there won't *be* a next time. They specifically asked for the *armor*, and now I don't even know if they're going to *pay* for you, understand? If you ask for Mickey Mouse, you damn well expect the *ears*." She tapped her foot with irritation. "*Start paying attention or there won't be a London and there won't be a European tour*. Understood?"

"You're a little over the top, don't you think?"

"There won't be a European tour, Rusty! Am I making myself understood?"

He stared at the ground in the diffident way that had charmed Becca when they first met. "Understood."

Elaine stormed off.

Rusty—she wondered what his real name was but liked Rusty just fine—approached the Subaru space, defeated. She was reminded of the scene where Joaquin Phoenix stabs Maximus, mortally wounding him before their Colosseum showdown. Becca discreetly circled around so that they both approached the exhibit at the same time. When he saw her, he seemed to reach out and retreat all at once. She said hello, and he nodded in a way that broke her heart. Becca saw him deflate as he stood there in his shabby *Beautiful Mind* suit, watching the Louie cavort with people's kids. He listened to the other look-alikes introduce themselves by their celebrity names, and seemed to steel himself; then, in a remarkable rally, he approached a young black couple and vigorously said, "G'day, mates—I'm Russell Crowe. Come have a seat in the Subaru Baja! I assure you its south of the border qualities won't disappoint. As a real *Insider*, let me tell you *this* little vehicle's no croc—*or* 'Crocodile' Dundee! So c'mon over, put a shrimp on the Barbie doll and let me give you something strictly *L.A. Confidential:* I got half *A Beautiful Mind* to give *this Gladiator*"—arm sweeping toward polished passenger door—"an Academy Award—for Best Car of the Year!"

The Fireman's Fund

THE COLD, MOLDY, red-shingled string of cottages was called The
Albany. A voice inside her—the snotty L.A. voice, the wry deadpan
voice of her boss, Reggie Marck—said, *Hey: it doesn't get much more
imaginative than that.*

Robbie wouldn't take her home, and she knew that meant he was
involved. Though maybe not. Lisanne wouldn't ask. Maybe he had a
roommate he was embarrassed to parade her in front of, the kind
who would tease him about porking a porker. She understood. She'd
never made love at this weigh-in. He seemed excited enough, and
besides, she didn't care. She only wanted communion. She had
almost forgotten what that was like.

He was an athlete in high school. It was torrid between them, but
when Lisanne got accepted to Berkeley they broke up. Robbie stayed
behind and drove an ambulance, with the idea of eventually enrolling
in med school. When the company went bankrupt, he took the EMT
course for paramedics in training and began working for the city. His
story was that he injured his back lifting a gurney and wound up
addicted to painkillers. He moved back in with his mom, inheriting a
small amount of money when she died. Lisanne didn't want to know
too many details.

The sex was still good. She got vocal and cried out to God. That
surprised her. He went down on her, and that was rough; she instinctively covered the fatness of a thigh with one hand while drawing up
folds of belly with the other. While he worked down there, she
thought about enrolling in an obesity program at UCLA. You ate
seven hundred calories a day for months and lost three or four
pounds a week, the only drawback being that your breath stank as
your body began to devour its stores of fat. There was a moment of
embarrassment when he spoke up and said it looked like she had

some discharge. She switched on a lamp, but it was only a small wad of toilet paper. He went back to his labors—nothing seemed to turn him off.

Robbie lit an après-sex joint and proceeded to get all happy. She smoked and choked. He asked if she wanted to come see his house (the one he had bought and was slowly fixing up) and glowed like a cheap guru when she assented. Her cohabitation theories might have been wrong after all.

The ride was freezing and quiet. The truck smelled of desuetude and cigarettes, old mud, junk mail, torn vinyl promises. She hadn't been this loaded in a long time. She became focused on the long, trembling metal stick that ruled the roost, the crystal of its eight ball cupped in Robbie's hand like an animal's heart. She watched the arcane, manly, unfathomable patterns of his upshifts and downshifts with the attention of an adept. The engine provided heat; there wasn't even a radio. Her ex seemed to lose impetus as they drove, but Lisanne thought maybe that was because there wasn't any more weed. Robbie clearly had a tolerance.

A light flurry of snow blew down as they pulled into the drive. It felt like high school, playing hooky to do something dirty.

"How long you been here?" she asked as they stepped out.

"About a year," he said. "My grandma stays with me."

"I thought Grannie was dead!"

"That's *Mom's* mom—remember Elsa?"

"Sure do," she said.

"Well, Elsa died about a year after Mom."

"That's terrible."

"Yeah, well, it was time for her to go."

"So this is your dad's mom?"

"Uh huh."

"I don't think I ever met her."

"She lived in Rochester. She's kind of a hermit."

When they entered, the house was filled with shadows. A cloud of perfume pressed on Lisanne like a rag of chloroform. A petite, hawk-like figure watched them from the other side of the kitchen counter.

"Maxine?"

"Yes?"

Lisanne was suddenly self-conscious that she hadn't showered. Robbie's eyes were bloodshot. She felt dodgy and illicit.

"This my friend Lisanne, from L.A.—her dad died. I told you about her," he added. "We went to high school together."

"Hello," said Lisanne, brightening like a loser.

Perky whore.

The pot was still kaleidiscopically working on her.

"Hiya," said the woman.

Her features grew more distinct as Lisanne's eyes adjusted to the light. She looked around seventy, of slender frame and predatory countenance. She was meticulously groomed, and Lisanne pegged her wardrobe as vintage—Chanel or YSL.

"I was just getting ice cream," said Maxine. "Y'all like some?"

Robbie turned solicitously to Lisanne, who shook her head. In the full fluorescence of her stonedness, her man looked wild and bereft, startled to have put them in this wrong, weird predicament.

"Actually," said Maxine, "it's soy. They call it Soy Dream and it's raspberry. I am *absolutely* hooked and don't care who knows. Do I, Robert?"

"No ma'am!"

"Aren't I absolutely hooked?"

"Yes ma'am!"

"Hook, line, and stinker. Bell, book, and candle."

"May I use the bathroom?" said Lisanne.

She could feel her smile becoming fixed and ghoulish; Robbie pointed the way.

Lisanne listened to the voices engaged in low argument as she douched.

The Greenroom and Beyond

"HE'S BEEN VOTED *People* magazine's 'Sexiest Man Alive' more times than anyone on the planet—and he can type too. Ladies and gentlemen, please welcome . . . Kit Lightfoot!"

The supernova took the stage with his patented self-effacing panther walk. The band raucously played the well-known theme from an early megahit. There was a large contingent of fans and screamers toward the front.

They embraced. After the applause died down, Jay did his jokey debonair thing. "Those screams—if our viewers at home are wondering—are partially for me. Something in the aftershave."

Laughter. More swoons, hoots, and hollers.

"All right," Jay chastised. "That's enough now!"

He turned to his handsome guest. "So how the hell are ya?"

Hair-trigger whoops came before he could answer. Kit raised an eyebrow at the audience and chuckled. A few isolated screams.

"I'm great. I'm great, Jay."

First words greeted by more electric commotion (everyone was having fun, and fun was what it was all about) which gradually though never completely faded away.

"I saw you at a benefit last week," said Jay.

"For scleroderma," said Kit, nodding.

"Yes. For a lovely lady who Mavis, my wife, has actually known for years—Char Riordan. They're doing wonderful research."

"Yes."

"Making great strides. Do you go to a lot of those things? I would imagine you get asked to lend your name to causes."

"This business is so frivolous, Jay, and so many of us have been absurdly blessed. I mean, let's face it, I put on makeup for a living—"

"You could always work on Santa Monica Boulevard . . ."

"Don't quit my day job, exactly! But I think we get compensated on such a ridiculous scale, that we're . . . *compelled* . . . to do what we can. Otherwise, you're just a kid in a sandbox. I try to do my share."

Applause kicked in, soberly encouraged by Jay. "So you went last week—"

"I had a personal connection. Viv and Char—the woman being honored—are very, very close."

"That's of course Viv Wembley," said Jay, pausing to acknowledge the audience as they whooped and applauded. *"In case the folks out there didn't know,"* he added with a wink. "The very lovely, and by the way very *funny* star of *Together*. And I want to get to some other things—it's well known you have an interest, a long-standing interest, in Buddhism, and you've agreed to talk with us a little about that tonight in connection with an upcoming event—which is something you rarely do and I'm thrilled you're going to enlighten us, so to speak. But first, I'm dying to ask you a question."

"Shoot."

"Someone told me you and Viv have nicknames for each other."

The audience hooted while Kit squirmed appealingly. "Who told you that?"

"*Vee haff ways.* Now come on, Kit, tell us what she calls you."

He hemmed and hawed. The crowd cajoled.

"She calls me Bumpkin."

The audience let out a happy groan. Warm laughter. Wolf whistles.

"Now come on!" said Jay, admonishing the mob. "I think it's *very sweet.*" He turned back to Kit. "She calls you Bumpkin."

"That's right, Jay."

"And . . . what's your nickname for Viv?"

"I don't think we should go there."

The audience protested, then began to plead.

"This is a family show," Kit added.

Laughter. More pleading. Isolated begging whoops.

"Now, you were supposed to do a cameo on *Together*—"

"Jay! I thought we were moving on!"

"We are, but this is *important.* I heard Viv was *mad* because that cameo hasn't yet happened."

Kit looked at the host with keen-eyed admiration. "Oh, you are *good.* You are *really good.*"

Audience laughter.

"Bumpkin's been a very bad boy," said Jay.

"Yeah, she's not too happy. But I'm busy! I'm in the middle of shooting a picture! I'm in a little bit of hot water here, Jay, help me out!"

"I'm trying to be sympathetic. But to most of us, being in hot water with Viv Wembley probably isn't the worst thing in the world."

"Think you're man enough to handle it?"

The audience laughed. Jay cracked up, blushing.

"When we come back, I want to talk about the Dalai Lama—he's a friend of yours, right?—and the important work you've been doing building clinics over there."

"Helping to," Kit added, with a modest smile.

"Where are they, India?"

"Yes," Kit said matter-of-factly. "India."

"For the refugees."

"For whoever needs them."

Jay looked straight into the camera and said, "Kit Lightfoot. Right here. Right now. Wearing makeup. So don't touch that dial."

How Verde Was My Valle

RUSTY INVITED BECCA to his apartment. They met instead at the Rose Café, a few blocks from where he lived. She wasn't ready to be alone with him just yet. There was something so tender about him but something dangerous too, like the actor he portrayed.

When she asked his real name, he said Rusty, without a trace of irony. He said he was from Sarasota. His father was a wealthy entrepreneur who, among other ventures, had been involved in business dealings with Burt Reynolds, a pal from college. About himself, Rusty used the term jack-of-all-trades. He had worked as a racetrack stable hand, a private nurse to the wealthy ("like the guy who killed that billionaire in Monaco," he said with a laugh), and a thief whose expertise was delivering the items on grocery lists of antiquarian books for reclusive bibliophiles. He was so disarmingly forthright that Becca didn't know which fanciful story to believe.

She immediately regretted asking if he had an agent. She should have known that Elaine Jordache was his lifeline to the business, such as it was. When Becca mentioned her work with Metropolis, Rusty said he did theater too, when he could, preferring it to the game of auditioning for film or television, which disgusted him. He asked if she was single, and Becca felt foolish because she told him about Sadge and how everything was between them—just blurted it out. He put his hand on hers and she laughed nervously then got teary-eyed, the two of them like an image from the cover of an old Pocket Books romance. He asked again if she felt like coming to his home. Becca shook her head. He smiled, pleased by her reticence.

"Then let's go to Magic Mountain."

She left her car in the lot.

.   .   .

THEY WERE ON the freeway, heading north. She wanted to be cool around him and not make any missteps. She was glad when he turned up the radio because it calmed her not to have to make conversation. He knew all the words to "Baby, I'm Yours," and even though half-goofing, his voice was sensuous and beautifully modulated. He kept looking over, winking devilishly. She felt like she was high.

Rusty took an off-ramp and after a few miles, they pulled onto the grounds of a sprawling hospital. When Becca realized that Magic Mountain had been a joke or a ruse, she got nervous. They parked and began to walk. To allay her fears, he began a little travelogue. He said that, fifty years ago, Valle Verde had been featured in a Brando movie about paraplegics in rehab. He had lots of Hollywood trivia like that in his head.

Rusty confidently threaded his way through a maze of polished linoleum corridors, with the occasional nod to a passing nurse. He was an old hand. No one stopped them or asked who they were visiting. Young, heavily tattooed men loitered in wheelchairs, alone or in quiet groups. Most of their heads were shaved. One bore the legend CLOSE COVER BEFORE STRIKING on his skull. Rusty said they were gang bangers whose luck had run out.

He led her into a patient's room. A brawny, shirtless man stood by the bed with an attendant. He looked at Rusty with cold hostility before breaking into a grin, as if for a moment he hadn't recognized him.

"Hey now," said the man.

"Hey now," said Rusty.

(Old *Larry Sanders* freaks.)

Becca hung back while the men embraced.

"Jesus, it stinks," said Rusty. "What'd you, just take a dump?"

"Nature's finest."

"This is my friend Becca—Becca, this is Grady."

"Hello, Becca."

"Hi."

"Grady Dunsmore, at your service."

His hand felt damp when she shook it.

"Need servicing? Give Grady a call."

"Hey now," said Rusty, chastising. "Heel, boy. Stay at your curb."

"Hey now."

Grady wobbled on his good leg while bracing himself against the slim Filipino man who was helping him dress.

"Wish I knew you were coming, motherfucker. Always so *sly*. Slip and slide. Stealth-Man."

"Into the night, baby."

"See, cause now I gotta go do my thing. My get-better thing."

"They gonna work you?"

"You better believe it."

"Put you through some major pain?"

"I already prepared." He voodoo-rattled a bottle of pills. "Gots to take the vikes before Ernesto puts me through my paces."

"How long you gonna be?"

"I don't know—forty-five? Maybe an hour. Can you hang?"

"Absolutely. I'll try on a prosthetic or two."

"Knock yourself out, Mad Max."

"Hey now."

"Eat me." Then, to Becca as he left: "Pardon my Spanish. And watch him closely. See that he doesn't steal any of my shit."

Benefits

IT TOOK LISANNE a few days to shrug off the torpor of the trip back across America. There was so little to do on a train that one's cycle shifted—Lisanne's did, anyway—she slept practically from sundown till dawn.

Reggie kept her workload to a minimum. At the end of the week, he asked for a favor. A longtime client and somewhat eccentric old friend, Tiff Loewenstein, copresident of Fox, was being honored at Casa del Mar. Reggie and his wife were unable to attend. He knew how fond Tiff was of Lisanne (through the years, she'd become so much more than the firm's amanuensis) and asked her to do some hand-holding. He said Tiff was a wreck. He'd been drinking and had thrown up in the living room, like a dog. His wife kicked him out.

When Lisanne got to the penthouse suite, Tiff answered the door, sobbing and half-dressed.

"Hi, baby," he said with a scary smile. "Thank you for coming! Can I get you anything?"

She trailed after as he cried his way to the bathroom.

She had come to his rescue at her boss's behest before, when Tiff was depressed and holed up in the Colony. (Once he even tried to kiss her. He was drunk and begged forgiveness the next day.) They had an easy intimacy. In the summers, the Loewensteins asked her to Malibu on weekends, and she grew to be a kind of auntie to their kids.

She was a commodious, safe harbor, someone he could pour his heart out to. He appreciated her wit—and they had more than a few phobias in common. Lisanne had never become acquainted with the man who was a feared Hollywood player; she knew only the vulnerable, courtly, rollicksome bear, and thought the world of him.

"Roslynn threw me down the stairs, did Reggie tell you?"

A butterfly bandage graced his temple.

"Are you all right?"

"I had Armani send a tux over . . . this one's from Dolce, think it's too long? They say that's the style, but I think it's for a younger man. Roslynn wouldn't even let me back in the house! I don't know if I can squeeze into this." His hand rose to a second bandage when he caught her looking. "No, no, that's from the cancer. Can you believe? They did a little scrape. You know, I was one of those kids who didn't even like to swim in a pool. *Never* swam in the ocean. Never been a sun freak—that's Roslynn. Thank God it isn't melanoma." He sighed, wiping away fresh tears. "Thank you for coming, Lisanne! So that fucker your boss couldn't make it, huh? Well fuck *him*. I'm kidding. Reggie's one of the good guys." He sat and sipped his drink. "Everything OK? Everything OK with Reg and Janie and the kids?"

"Everyone's great."

"Christ, what a year. I got hit with prostate, did Reg tell you that?"

"No. He didn't."

"They irradiated, which was fine—until two weeks later. That's when you wake up in the middle of the night screaming. Top of your lungs. I'm not kidding, Lisanne. You try calling the doctor and you get one of those messages saying which buttons to press but you *can't* because you're *screaming*. I told him I wanted liquid morphine. He said, 'I can't do that.' Didn't want to give it to me. I said, *Then I'll kill myself* because I can't live with that kind of pain. *No* one can. And I know myself. I told him I would kill myself and take him down with me, and make sure everyone in this *city* knew his name before I went. So he gave it to me—two drops under the tongue. And I've hardly used it, Lisanne, but I just had to know it was there on the nightstand. Makes me feel better. Because you don't want to live, Lisanne. You *can't* live—not with pain like that. Michael Milken's been a godsend. And Dominick. Talked me through a lot of it. I even talked to Giuliani." He started crying again. "You've *got* to take care of yourself, Lisanne! You're a beautiful girl but you've *got* to take care of yourself. Lose some of the weight. Will you please? Cause you're open to the heart stuff and the diabetes. You look beautiful, by the way—you're a gorgeous lady. Do you know I've completely changed the way I eat?" He hoisted his glass in the air. "This is a recent thing—the wine—I *never* drank the way I'm drinking now. And it's gonna stop tomorrow.

The cigarettes too." He took a deep drag then lifted his shirt like a tease, to show the nicotine patch. "Know what it's all about? Changing the environment of your body. Cancer likes acid, acidic foods. *Loves* acid. And sugar. That's where it likes to grow. You've got to go alkaloid, acid versus alkaloid. Raw veggies—alkaloid. Broccoli. I have wheatgrass every day, Lisanne, like a fucking goat. Colonics three times a week to flush out the toxins. They did some tests (all I do are tests) and found I had high levels of mercury. Having all the old fillings taken out. Ever had a colonic? I don't have a choice. You can do it over in Culver City, there's a marvelous place, I'll make the call. Seema—she's the girl to ask for. You've *got* to take care, Lisanne, while you're young. My daughter in Michigan—Kittie—you've never met Kittie—from my first marriage—had a double mastectomy. They took the tits, the implants, the whole shebang. Shitty implants to begin with. She's got a South African doctor, a real Christiaan Barnard type. He cut everything off. She's got tattooed nipples now. He put a hose in there—she comes to the office and he pumps 'em up with saline, right under the muscle. She calls 'em Magic Tits. Know what Kittie said when they were wheeling her down to surgery? 'Dead tits walking!' The *schvug* orderlies turned white. Then she wasn't healing so they put her in a hyperbaric chamber. She's been through major *tsuris*. Remember Michael Jackson and the chimp and the hyperbaric chamber? We're Ashkenazy, so Kittie's getting herself tested for genetic markers—if they're positive, he's gonna rip her ovaries just to be safe. She was taking this nausea pill during chemo. I went to pick the prescription up and the pharmacist says, Boy, she's got great insurance. It was fifty bucks for thirty pills. I say, So how much would it be without insurance? He goes to the computer. Thirteen hundred dollars! For thirty pills, Lisanne! The country's a nightmare. They *stick* it to you cause you've got cancer and can't do without. Who wants to be nauseous? So they *rob* you. What are we gonna do when the smallpox comes if we can't even deal with fucking nausea?"

"Tiff," she said, taking away his drink. "Why don't I call room service and get you some coffee?"

He sniffled, patting her hand. "Thank you, dear. Thank you. So glad you're here. You're a real mensch. What do they call a girl-mensch? A womensch? A wench? Listen, sweetheart: any time you want to leave that slick bastard and come work for me, you've got a job. Pay you *twice* what he gives you. But you've got to take care of yourself, Lisanne." He went and stood before the mirror. "Know what my friend Feibleman said? Do you know Peter Feibleman? I love him— brilliant writer. You should eat his fuckin paella. One day he'll make us all dinner. Sylvia Plath was a huge fan. Not his cooking—his novels. He just went through the prostrate thing too. Said the radiation took away the 'punctuation' of sex. And that's true. All the commas and semicolons are gone. There's no catharsis. You're chemically fucking castrated. That moment where life used to hang in the balance— that 'little death'— gone. You come, or *think* you do, and then you say, *Was that it?* Feibleman says, 'I don't have that *seizure* anymore, that *paroxysm*. I go right to wanting the cheeseburger.' Don't you love that? The cheeseburger! But I'll tell you something, Lisanne: I *always* wanted the *fuhcocktuh* cheeseburger. I wanted it *before* the shtup. Know what I'm addicted to? Know what sex is for me now? Tributes. The cancer took away food and sex and left me with tributes. I'm worse than Quincy—Jesus! They can't stop giving and he can't stop getting. Did you know he got a Grammy for Spoken Word? For reading his autobiography out loud! Is that not genius? King Coon goes to Cancún," he said nonsensically. "A sweet sweet man. Beautiful spirit. We're supposed to go to Africa in September with Bono. Next month we've got Sting and the Poitiers and Medavoys at the Kofi Annan dinner. I got the Ark Trust Genesis in two weeks at the Hilton. (In my honor.) Then the 'Starlight Dream' gala-thing at the Kodak—for me *and* Quincy. Then Roslynn and I have the cervical thing—what's it called?—whatever, at the Peninsula. Would you go with me, Lisanne? Unless some miracle happens with Roslynn by then, which appears doubtful. Kittie's flying out for that, you'll love her. A funny funny lady. And that's all in one weekend!" He laid upon the bed and sighed. "You wade through crap all day and then you put on a tux and feel less like a putz. Hey, that rhymes. And you know what? The applause ain't so bad either. But I wanna tell ya, I'm seriously addicted. Does that make me a terrible man, Lisanne?" he asked tearfully. "Does it? Does that make me terrible?"

A Beachside Reunion

KIT WAS IN the trailer with Xanthe, his assistant. He was at the beach opposite Temescal Canyon, shooting a film with Jennifer Lopez and Anthony Hopkins. Alf and Cameron Diaz, sometime flames, dropped by the set.

"Thought you might like a little orgy to start your day," said Alf.

"Hope you like to watch," said Kit to Alf, then belched.

"Ready-teddy," said Cameron. "That's what I'm here for. To be fucked like a righteous animal."

"Careful what you say around the Man, Cam," said Alf. "There have been some fairly ugly rumors about Mr. Raffles."

Kit gave Alf the evil eye.

"Oh yeah? Who's Mr. Raffles?" she asked.

"His dog. Mr. Raffles seems to have that certain je ne sais ménage à trois quoi."

Cameron laughed, and Kit got off the subject by asking if next week they wanted to go to Harrison's ranch in Jackson Hole with Callista, Ben, and Jennifer. Cameron couldn't because she had to be in Monaco for an AIDS costume ball.

Xanthe answered a knock at the door. She took Kit aside and said his father was there to see him.

. . .

BURKE LIGHTFOOT SAT at the end of a catering table. He stood when he saw his son approach. The waves crashed weakly a few hundred yards off, lending the reunion a petty dramatic touch.

"Hey there, Kitchener!" said Burke, with an oily smile. (As any Kit-watcher knew, the star had been whimsically named after the first Earl Kitchener of Khartoum.) He extended a hand, and Kit reluctantly shook it, squinting in the sun so as not to fully take the man in.

"Hey."

"I was on my way to Santa Barbara," Burke said unconvincingly. "Saw all the trucks and asked about the commotion. Cop said it was a Kit Lightfoot movie. 'Now wait a minute, that's my son!' "

"Yeah, right," said Kit, sucking in snot and tapping a cigarette against the bottom of his boot. "I'll have that guy fired."

Burke laughed it off. Kit wasn't sure why the man bothered to lie anymore.

"Saw you on Leno," he said.

"Uh huh."

"I didn't know you did all that fund-raising."

"Yeah, well, I don't."

His father shone with good health and good cheer. He was a handsome, lanky New Englander; Kit's mom was an American beauty with a touch of Cree. It was a right-on gene pool.

"Anyhow, thanks for seeing me," said Burke. "I know it was unannounced."

"That's your thing, right? 'Unannounced.' "

"Your mother was rather spontaneous herself," he said folksily.

"Don't drag her into it."

"All right." Burke knew when to acquiesce.

"Look," said Kit, cynically. "I don't know what you think we got goin. Or what you think we're gonna *get* goin—"

"I don't have an agenda, Kitchener, other than seeing my son. Fathers tend to want to do that."

"Oh really? Well, *this* father"—he jabbed a finger toward Burke—"didn't tend to want to. Didn't tend to want to do shit until I started making bread."

"That isn't true," said Burke, stung.

"Why don't you tell me what husbands tend to want to do? Now that I know all about dads."

"I was there for your mother—"

"Right!" Kit exclaimed, with a nearly out-of-control donkey laugh.

"—as much as she wanted me to be. And you know that. But she had *you*. R. J. didn't want to see me when she was sick. She had you and that was enough."

They listened to the waves. Crackle of a walkie.

"Look, son . . . I won't take any more of your time. But while I'm here, I wanted to tell you I came across some of her things, from when we were in college. Love letters—beautiful. Thought you could drop by the house and see 'em this weekend. If you'd like."

Kit blew a ring of smoke. "Call Xanthe," he said. "She'll give you a FedEx number and an address."

"I'd rather not send that precious material through the mail," said Burke, shrewdly playing out his hand. "I'll wait till you're in the neighborhood."

"You might have to wait a long time," said Kit, standing. "And it's probably not a good idea to drop by without calling. In fact, it's probably not a good idea to drop by at all."

"You're the boss." His father gathered up an old leather satchel. "One more thing—may I trouble you? Grant School's having a benefit. Remember Grant? They had some pretty severe water damage to the auditorium. That's where you did *The Music Man*. 'Trouble in River City! With a capital *T* and that rhymes with *P* and that stands for *pool!*'" He pulled a stack of headshots out—Kit at the beginning of his career. He drew a fancy Waterman from his coat. "I told them I'd help. If you can sign some eight-by-tens, they'll be the hit of the auction."

Pool Party

THE REALITY SHOW relocated from Tasmania to the Canary Islands. Sadge kept Becca on a tight leash until he left. He wouldn't even let her answer the phone. A guy kept calling at all hours, asking for her. It gave Sadge the creeps. Whenever he picked up, the voice would say, "Is this fat Jack Black and the Heart Attacks? Is this Tenacious D?" Becca had given Rusty her cell phone but didn't know how he got the home number. She didn't think Elaine would have given it to him. He denied making the calls.

. . .

SHE ASKED WHY he called himself Rusty and he said because that was his name. Then he said it was Elaine's idea. Anyway, he liked using his counterpart's "appellation." There was a purity in it, he said. Like the servants in that movie *Gosford Park* who took the names of their masters.

. . .

SADGE WAS IN the bathroom when Becca's phone vibrated—it said UNKNOWN in the little luminous window. It was Rusty. He asked if she wanted to go to a party Grady Dunsmore and his wife were having. He was out of the hospital and celebrating in his new house. Rusty said he'd pick her up at Ürth Caffé at nine. She impulsively called Annie and asked her to come. Becca told Sadge that Annie was having monster period cramps and she was going to bring her Vicodin and stay for *Six Feet Under.*

Rusty wasn't thrilled that Becca had invited her friend along. When he called her the chaperone, Annie got feisty with him, which he seemed to like. Becca was quiet as he drove, subdued, entranced, in her mind already his girlfriend. Annie hassled him about beating on that guy in Playa del Rey. Rusty enjoyed the razzing. Becca could tell that Annie thought he had his redeeming qualities.

They drove up Laurel Canyon to Mulholland. Annie asked about his friend's house. Rusty said it had been in escrow for six months and finally closed, and that Nicholson and Brando apparently lived right across the street. Annie asked about Grady's injury. Rusty said he'd been shot by the police a few years back. The girls left it at that.

A valet took their car. Decorated golf carts ferried guests to the house, but the trio chose to walk through the gate and descend the long, steep drive. The fractured tiara of a mansion lay below. There were crowds of people, and Becca gradually made out a South Seas theme. Fiery tiki torches surrounded the pool. Women in grass skirts served drinks and canapés.

They saw Grady beaming at them beyond the sliding window of the living room. Music boomed from inside and liquor sloshed from his glass as he limped out to give his old bud a modified bear hug.

"You did it," said Rusty. "It's a fucking palace."

"Yes, we did it, we fucking did! Absolutely. But all this?" He put an arm around Rusty's shoulder then took in the pool, the revelers, and the evening air itself before glancing Becca and Annie's way. "Everything you see? A tribute to Questra. Wish she could be here to see it."

"She *is* here. She's *here*." Rusty thumped Grady's chest at the heart. "Here, there, and everywhere."

His maudlin friend let it sink in. "Thank you. Thank you for being here and thank you for fucking saying the beautiful shit that only *you* can say." Grady turned to Becca. "An *awesome* cat. He's crazy—and fuckin *awesome*. But you probably already know that."

"You remember Becca," said Rusty.

"Hey now," said Grady. "I'm not gonna forget Becca. Ain't nobody gonna forget *Becca*. Welcome. Welcome to my righteous home."

"This is my friend Annie," she said.

"Hi," said Annie.

"Hey, Annie Fannie." Suddenly energized, Grady looked all around him again. "Place is a trip, ain't it? We got Hefner beat."

"It's incredible," said Annie, in earnest. Grady's hoarseness and cock-eyed brio reminded her of a younger Nick Nolte.

"Three acres! That's one more than Marlon. But the house is a pile—it's a teardown. Used to belong to Russ Meyer. Know who Russ Meyer was? Ol' Russ was *seriously* into the female anatomy, with special emphasis on the breast. The *large* breast. Man was my hero. Did you see the pool yet? Check it out. There's an observation room down below. Super sixties! Ol' Russ used to like to sit and watch *titties* float by. I don't even think they had implants back then—no silicone, anyway. No Viagra either. Fuckin Stone Age."

Grady got pulled away. He waved at Rusty and the girls as he was sucked into the house.

"What does Grady do?" asked Becca as they headed toward the pool.

"Personal trainer. He was Kevin Costner's stunt double—before he fucked up his leg. They still work out together whenever Kevin does a movie. He's K.C.'s camera double too."

Annie said, "I don't understand how he has this place."

"A settlement from the city."

"The shooting?" asked Annie.

"Nah, that's a whole different deal. Their little girl drowned in a municipal pool. A light in the tile shorted out or some such shit—the kid he had with Cassandra. Questra. Electrocuted her. Took five years, but they got eight million. You'll meet Cass. She's around somewhere. Trippy lady. Hard-core."

They passed the tiki bar, where drinks were being dispensed from an enormous ice sculpture. Blue-tinted gin flowed over the massive crystalline chunk into high-stemmed glasses. Just before the stairway that led beneath the pool came a makeshift shrine. The framed photo of a shiny-smiled toddler was surrounded by leis and votive candles.

They went down the storm cellar opening to a small booth with a glass wall allowing a view of the swimmers. Their shoes puddled. It was dank and smelled of mold. A girl smoked a joint, nodding her head in stoned, silent assention at what she saw through the aquariumlike window: a disembodied woman, about six months pregnant, sat on the steps of the pool getting head from a fat old Hell's Angel type. Everything was below the water from the breasts down. The bearded biker wore only Levi's. Every twenty or thirty seconds, he surfaced for air before going down again.

"That's Cass. Grady's old lady." Then, with a smile: "I told you she was hard-core."

Impermanence

LISANNE THOUGHT ABOUT letting Robbie know that she was expecting. She would have e-mailed, had he been an e-mail person. Anyhow, she was glad he wasn't.

It would have been so easy to have the doctor flush it away. She wasn't showing and was hefty enough to think she never would, even if she carried to term. For the moment, Lisanne had the perverse luxury of putting the whole thing out of her head. She went to yoga a lot that week over on Montana. There was a kind of remedial class for fatties, newbies, and old folks.

To her shock, one morning Kit Lightfoot and Renée Zellweger slipped in, just as class was beginning. (She wasn't sure if they came together.) The ninety-minute session was difficult though not nearly as crowded as the advanced levels—a hip choice, thought Lisanne, for a celeb. She could deal with Renée, but having Kit there made it tough to concentrate. She'd always had a crush on him: now there he was, barely ten feet away, sweating his tight, insanely famous butt off. The teacher kept telling everyone to "stay present," and Lisanne thought she must have picked up on her delirium.

After the group *Namastes*, Lisanne lay in the corpse pose, trying to time her departure from the sweat- and sage-scented room with Kit's. When he left, she waited a beat, then got up to stash her mat in the anteroom. She retrieved her things from the shelves and laced up her shoes in slow motion. Her mind wandered. The next thing she knew, Kit brushed past. He looked in her eyes and smiled and Lisanne's heart actually fluttered. With a surrealistic pang, she thought of her pregnancy. Renée emerged from the large room. The two stars said quietly enthusiastic hellos. They left, and Lisanne discreetly followed.

Her car was conveniently parked a length away from Renée's. Lisanne opened the hatchback so she could fuss around while eavesdropping.

"Gonna go see the monks?" Kit asked.

Renée grinned inquisitively.

"The Gyuto monks," said Kit. "They're making a sand mandala at the Hammer."

"Oh! I *heard* about that," said the actress excitedly.

"It's *very* cool. You should really try to get over there."

"Those are the guys who do that weird throat-chanting thingie?" She imitated the gargling sounds, and Kit laughed.

"Tantric monks," he said, nodding. "They had a school in Tibet for like five hundred years. They were forced to go to India in 'fifty-nine—like everybody else. They've been making a mandala all week."

"At the Hammer?"

"Uh huh."

"That's so cool."

"It's really a kind of meditation. You sit, don't you?"

"Yes. But not as much as I'd like."

"No one ever sits as much as they'd like. So you know a little about what they're doing, then."

"A *very* little."

Lisanne got the feeling Renée was vamping.

"When they're finished designing the mandala, they destroy it."

"*Destroying the mandala,*" she said, with a respectful laugh. "That really sounds amazing."

"It's not about making art. That *is* a component—because the mandala and the meditation itself are both art. It's really more a way of showing dedication and compassion to all living things."

"Sentient beings."

"Right. It's about impermanence."

"And they're doing that today? They're still doing that today?"

He nodded and lit a cigarette. "The deconsecration ritual isn't open to the public, but I could definitely arrange for you to go in. If you want to see it. I'm kind of a patron of the San Jose Center."

"Kit, that would be so great! I would *love* that."

.   .   .

LISANNE PLANNED to take off early from work and finagle her way into the mandala ceremony, but everything conspired against her. A string of tiny crises kept her longer at the office; when she finally got in her car, traffic was gridlocked. Her repertoire of residential street detours failed abysmally.

When she got to the museum, the guard signaled that the exhibition was closed. She stood there downcast.

Moments later a monk in orange robes appeared, on his way in. He was short and radiated a cliché, childlike bliss. Unexpectedly, he took Lisanne's arm, gently ushering her into the large hall. She felt like Richard Dreyfuss at the end of *Close Encounters.*

While her eyes adjusted, she looked around for Renée, but the actress wasn't there. Neither was Kit. One of the masters had already begun sweeping away the colored sand. The Yamantaka deity, an emanation of the Bodhisattva Manjusri, was disappearing. The eight heads and thirty-four arms, two horns—"the two truths"—and six-teen legs (sixteen kinds of emptiness), the nakedness that symbolized abandonment of the mind, the self, and its worldly concerns were all being swept into a container. The monks would offer the commingled grains to an undisclosed local body of water. Water, which reflects both the world and infinity at once.

Now Lisanne had no doubts.

She would keep her baby.

Reunions

KIT GUNNED the Indian down the 60, toward Riverside—the famil-iar, unfamiliar route. The faux-stucco skin of the old house was thick with cement spray-on coatings, ordered throughout the years by Burke in varying fits of mania. Seasonal cosmetic makeovers were his thing.

The sun-bleached DeVille was in the drive, and a junk car too. It was less than a beater—no wheels and up on blocks. Urchins ogled the chopper.

Kit sat in a ratty chaise, feet propped on a tire swing, sipping beer while scanning love letters and ghostly Polaroids of Rita Julienne. Burke came from the house bearing gifts: coleslaw, corn, and KFC. "If I knew you were coming, I'd have provided something a little more sumptuous," he said, delighted his son had shown up.

"That's cool," said Kit benevolently, softened by the words and images of his beloved mother.

"See? You're like your old man after all. You arrive unannounced."

He let the remark slide. "I see the neighborhood hasn't changed. Still shitty and depressing."

"That's Riverside!" said Burke.

He talked about a methamphetamine lab that had been busted up a few blocks from there. A chemical odor hung in the air for weeks—no one could figure out where it was coming from until someone's lawn caught fire.

"I'm telling you, it was straight out of David Lynch." He looked over Kit's shoulder at a snapshot. "Catalina. You were conceived on that trip. Did we ever take you to Catalina?"

"No."

"We had a wonderful time there. Years later we went back and had a not so wonderful time." He sighed. "Such is life."

"Look," said Kit, neatening the documents. "I think I'm gonna head back."

"But you didn't eat," said Burke, waxing paternal. "Have a bite before you go."

"Some other time," said Kit, lighting a cigarette. He lifted his feet off the tire.

"Don't you want to see your old room? It's exactly as you left it."

"Got to keep it authentic for the tour groups, huh, Burke."

"I thought we could go by the school and have a look at the future Kitchener Lightfoot Auditorium."

"They're not going to do that, are they? Name it after me?"

"I know they want to. I'm told ten thousand will make it happen. It'd be nice press," said Burke, smiling like Cardinal Mahony. "I'm always looking out for you."

Kit got the notion to fuck with him.

"Do you need ten thousand, Dad?"

The man chuckled like a bad actor.

"I don't *need* it. I could *use* it but I don't *need* it. Not personally. The alma *mater* needs it: Ulysses S. Grant."

"I'll send a check over, OK?"

"That would be a beautiful thing."

"Now who should I make that out to? You, Dad? Or the school? If I made it out to the *school,* that'd probably be better. For *me.* I mean, tax-wise."

"Either way," said Burke, staring off with stagy indifference. "Either way'll do. To the school would be fine." A pause, then, "It's just . . . I'm not one hundred percent sure if Grant School is the right entity. I'm not sure they have their funding entity together yet. They could be calling that project something else. So if you write the check to *me,* that's fine too, I'll hold it in escrow then funnel it to the correct entity. No problems. Make it out to me, son—or leave the pay to line blank—not the amount—and I'll turn it over. Save your business manager the hassle of a reissue."

Cela appeared at the front fence and made a dash to Kit's arms. Pleased at the fortuitous arrival, Burke said, "Kit Lightfoot, this is your life!" He went inside so the high school sweethearts could be alone. Kit was certain his father had alerted her, because she was dolled up more than a Saturday afternoon would call for.

"What a *surprise.*"

"How you doin, Cela?" She was still gorgeous to him, but drugs had taken their toll. She was old around the edges.

"Slummin today?"

"Just a little," he said.

Some preteen girls pressed up against the driveway gate and giggled.

"You look great," said Kit. "You been all right?"

"Not too bad. Burke and I have a pretty good thing going—we do the Sunday Rose Bowl swap, in Pasadena? Find all kinds of stuff then sell it on eBay. I know *you're* doin OK."

"Can't complain."

"Oh and hey, thank you for the eight-by-tens. That was a bonanza. People at the swaps go *nuts* for anything of yours that's signed. Especially when Burke says he's your dad—which, to his credit, he doesn't a lot of the time."

The Afterworld

IT WAS COLD but fun laying on the slab.

Thanks to Elaine Jordache and her connected friend, Becca had been hired to play a cadaver on *Six Feet Under.* She was a little embarrassed to tell Annie, even though the casting people said it was the most coveted "extra" gig in town. Evidently, the producers were superfinicky about who they hired. Becca's mom was thrilled. She immediately ordered HBO.

All the actors were really nice. They felt bad for the extras because they had to spend so much time on their backs, sometimes wearing uncomfortable prosthetics.

"You look *so* much like Drew Barrymore," said a regular.

"I think she might be a little bit heavier than I am right now," said Becca. She didn't mean to sound catty.

"She's a big fan of the show. Her agent supposedly even talked to Alan about coming on, but I don't know if that's going to happen."

There were actually two Alans. Everyone was always mentioning one or the other without using last names. (If you were "family," you knew who they meant.) Becca had met the executive producer-sometime director Alan, but not the executive producer-director-writer-creator Alan.

"The show doesn't really work that way," the regular went on. "They don't usually cycle in movie stars. It's not like *The Sopranos.* Thank God."

The actor went away, and a few minutes later another actor who Becca thought was gay sort of hit on her. He asked if she'd read about the mortician who had been caught posing bodies so a friend could take arty photographs.

"It was so Witkin," he said. She didn't know what that meant. "We actually did a story line kind of like that—life imitates art. Did you see *L.A. Confidential?"*

"Uh huh."

"Remember the whole thing with Kim Basinger? The call girls who looked like celebrities?"

"Uh huh."

"Wasn't she supposed to be, like, Veronica Lake? You could seriously do that—I mean, as Drew Barrymore!"

Becca smiled politely from her cold metal tray. Even though she knew he was just being friendly, she didn't like the suggestion that she could capitalize on her looks by being some kind of whore. But she was a captive audience and not in any position to take offense. All the cadavers spent their time praying that Alan—*any* Alan— would bestow upon them lines for, say, an impromptu dream sequence or that in some future episode they'd at least be allowed to cross over to the living for a speaking role. A speaking role was the Valhalla.

The first A.D. called camera rehearsal.

She lay there quietly amid the tumult, pondering her life. The relationship with Sadge was coming to an end; a strange and powerful new man had entered the scene. The strange and powerful new man frightened her, but Annie said that wasn't necessarily a bad thing. It wasn't a great thing, but it wasn't necessarily a bad thing. It could even be a good thing.

Becca played a game with herself between takes, seeing how long it took to get wet while thinking of him.

School Days

"SCHOOLS NEVER LOSE that smell, do they?" asked Kit.

"That smells-like-teen-spirit smell?"

He cocked an eye.

"Did we ever fuck anywhere on campus?"

"Hey, mister," she said. "I held out a *long* time. Don't go mixin me up with somebody else."

They sat on a plastic picnic table outside the auditorium. Padlocked vending machines, scratched with graffiti, hibernated against the stained cinder block wall.

"I wish I could have seen your mama before she died," she said. "I miss her, I truly do." She shook her head. "That was a rough time for me—'Cela Byrd: The Rehab Years.' It's all about me, isn't it?" she said, sardonically.

"You doing OK now?"

"Still peeing in a bottle. Hey, my birthday's coming up! AA—six months. Wanna give me a cake?"

"Love to."

"So . . . you gonna marry Viv Wembley?" She smiled as Kit simulated a blush. "Well you *should*. She's pretty! And I *love* that show, it's hilarious. She's from L.A., right?"

"Orange County."

"Michelle Pfeiffer's from OC too. I read that somewhere."

A faraway girl approached on a bike. The sight of her summoned a memory.

"Remember when we got loaded at that Christmas party?"

"Yeah," said Kit.

He fished a roach from his wallet.

"And we went into that room where everybody left their coats and purses and shit? And you, like, *stole all the money—*"

"I wasn't the only one! You had some magic fingers."

"I did, didn't I?" she said, sex creeping into her voice.

"You surely did."

"Please don't call me Shirley. Remember that from *Airplane!* I *loved* that movie." She put her hand on his leg. "We had something special, huh. First loves . . ." She unbuckled his belt. He lit the roach. "You don't know how *fucked up* it's been, Kit. Sitting in rehab, watching you in a movie. Reading about you in *People*. Or wherever. At the *premieres*. Always with someone else. There I am thinking: That girl should have been *me*. I used to tell people we went out, but I stopped. I was in jail once, all like, 'He was my boyfriend! You don't understand! He took me to the prom!' That was a low point. As worsts go, that was a personal best."

She kissed him lightly once or twice to see how amenable he was, then drifted down and put him in her mouth.

The faraway girl was closer now and stood on her bike, watching.

A Gathering at the Rose

BECCA DROVE SADGE to LAX. He would be away about three months. It was understood that when he returned, he'd find his own place. He would for sure have the money by then, anyway.

On instinct, Becca drove to the Rose and parked in the lot. She decided to go for a stroll and check out Rusty's building. Why not? He had described it to her. It was right on the boardwalk, a few doors up from the Figtree.

Suddenly, Elaine Jordache emerged from the café. She dawdled, then Rusty came out holding a coffee and talking animatedly to a blondish young man of slight build. He wore an incongruous dress shirt and tie along with a warm and wolfish, slightly bemused grin. Becca slid down in the car seat to watch.

A boy barely out of his teens was the last to join them. He held a binder and hung behind the blondish man with subtle, efficient obsequiousness. The trio strolled toward a vintage convertible with the boy lagging behind. The blondish man enthusiastically shook hands, first with Rusty then with Elaine. The boy-assistant got into the convertible and started the car. Becca couldn't quite hear the words but thought Rusty was complimenting the blondish man on his car as the latter climbed into the passenger seat. There were a few more good-byes as boy-assistant and blondish boss pulled away.

Becca slunk lower as Rusty walked Elaine to her car. They stood talking awhile in earnest. The mood got lighter, and Becca's heart sickly speeded as she wondered if he was going to kiss Elaine on the mouth. He bussed her cheek. Becca, vindicated, swore eternal allegiance. Elaine drove off. Rusty strolled from the lot toward the beach.

She considered going inside for a fruit plate then embarking on her mission, as planned. She could linger at the pier or have a cappuccino at Shutters before dropping in at Rusty's on the way back. Take him by surprise.

Then she thought better of it, having had enough excitement for the day.

A Brief History of
Tantric Buddhism

IN HER BED, Lisanne McCadden dreamed of Kit Lightfoot.

They were by the ocean, making a movie. Filming was delayed because an animal got caught in a generator and the crew was trying to free it with long, lacquered sticks. Kit lay on his side on a peaceful promontory overlooking the water. He was sketching in the sand, and something about the way he concentrated reminded Lisanne of the monks she'd seen at the Hammer Museum. A talking baby was there, like in one of those old *Ally McBeal*s. When Lisanne woke up, she couldn't remember anything the baby had said.

She thought the dream was psychic because a few minutes after she arrived at work, Reggie gave her a pair of tickets to see the monks perform that very evening at UCLA. She thought of who she might ask but no one seemed handy. She decided to go alone.

.   .   .

THERE WERE ABOUT a dozen of them onstage, but this time they wore elaborate costumes and headdresses. A small photo of H.H. the Fourteenth Dalai Lama rested on an altar, with an architectural model of a many-layered temple beside it. Microphone headsets were the monks' only bow to modernity. The characteristic amplified *yoy-oy-yoy-oy-yoy* throat chants accompanied drums and weird metal instruments, creating a haunting cacophony of sounds. At varying times, the holy men looked as if they were making signs and signals with their hands like ballplayers, but Lisanne hadn't rented binoculars so couldn't be sure. The man beside her was snoring and no one seemed to mind. A row ahead, a bored little boy fidgeted. Lisanne thought it sweet that his father had brought him to the ceremonies.

Slowly and fantastically, it dawned upon her that just one aisle over and four rows down, sat none other than Kitchener Lightfoot, flanked by Viv Wembley and the comedian Paul Reiser. Kit's eyes were closed. He looked as if he was mediating.

After a few minutes of obsessing, Lisanne looked down at her program to distract herself. It said that tantric meditation was considered the "quick" way to enlightenment. Books of the tantra described not just one Buddha but thousands. A tantric meditator was supposed to visualize that he or she was actually one of those Buddhas, and she wondered if that's what Kit was doing that very moment.

Her mouth moved as she silently read that

Vajrabhairava's name means "Diamond Terrifier." His bull-like face indicates that he has overcome Yama, the bull-headed Lord of Death. From the top of his head emerges the small peaceful

face of Manjushri, who embodies all of the wisdom of all the
Buddhas; Vajrabhairava symbolizes that wisdom transcends death.

Maybe Kit was just going over lines in his head, for tomorrow's
shoot . . . or maybe he was thinking: Who is that girl across the aisle,
four rows back, the Rubenesque milkmaid who charmingly does not
even notice how totally into her I am? Who is that amazing, secretly
pregnant, sweet-faced executive assistant who could have no possible
way of knowing that I am only sexually excited by similarly propor-
tioned women who also happen to be phobic about flying? I need to
have her in my life!

She gave herself the chuckles amidst all the sacred rituals. But try
as she might, she couldn't imagine what was going on in the head of
Viv Wembley or Paul Reiser.

A Colony of Angels

ELAINE LEFT a message for her to call back as soon as possible. It
was urgent.

Cameron Diaz—the true Cameron—was throwing a birthday
party for Drew and got a brainstorm to have the "Angels" there, along
with half a dozen other look-alikes. Elaine had already managed to
get hold of the Cameron and the Lucy Liu, Cher, David Letterman,
Donald Rumsfeld, Jim Carrey, and the Pope. When Becca asked if
Rusty would be there, Elaine said no. Becca was relieved.

• • •

SHE HAD NEVER been inside the Colony. The guard waved her
through, and she felt a curious, unexpected sense of belonging. When
she saw the true Kid Rock climbing into a pickup, her nerves got all
jangled and she wondered if she'd be able to pull this off.

A stern coordinator was waiting—the party wasn't yet under way—
and Becca was ushered into a kind of bull pen set up in the garage.
Costume and makeup people descended on her with pins, Pan-Cake,

and cigarette breath. The Cameron was sitting in a chair having her zits covered, Lucy's hair was being straightened, and a bug-eyed, too-old Tobey Maguire was in the middle of a close shave. The Cher, who Becca thought to be a really good Cher, wandered in smoking. She said she didn't think this was the true Cameron's house; a makeup person concurred, but no one seemed to know who the house belonged to. Sting supposedly lived down the street but was never in residence, and the coordinator said Elaine told her that he rented the house out during the summer for ninety thousand dollars a month. Becca had a hard time believing that anyone would rent a house for that kind of money.

The true Cameron poked her head in and shrieked when she saw Elaine's Angels.

"Oh my God! It's fantastic!" she said, clapping her hands together. "You guys are *incredible*."

The Lucy said, "Flip the goddamn hair!" and that went over big— the true Cameron split a gut. The true Selma Blair wandered in, and Becca was beside herself. She couldn't wait to tell her mom. And the party hadn't even started!

The Angels were brought in for maximum effect, when the birthday was in full swing. Ben Stiller was there with his wife and baby, as were the true Demi Moore with the true Ashton, and the true Tobey. When Cher showed up, she clucked her tongue at her double—Becca figured the singer had seen her share of impersonators and wasn't as psyched as the younger stars about having a look-alike. The true Rose McGowan arrived with Pink and Pamela Anderson, the latter sans Kid Rock. Rose went and talked to the Cher, who evidently she'd once hired for Marilyn Manson's birthday. Tom Hanks mingled with the look-alikes and seemed to get the biggest kick out of the hammily decrepit, hunched-over Pope, whose "day job" turned out to be that of a somewhat wealthy Valley restaurateur. Becca and the Cameron were hoping against hope that Sting would drop by. No such luck.

There were so many famous people that she became numb. (She spaced out after seeing Jackie Chan with Owen Wilson. It all became a blur.) But the celebs weren't very engaging; except for Tom and Rita, they preferred talking amongst themselves. Becca liked schmoozing with faces she *didn't* recognize—that was much more intriguing. She figured that anyone who had been invited in the first place was by definition "a player," a behind-the-scenes heavyweight. Those were the people who might actually be helpful in the long run. One turned out to be the writer of her all-time favorite movie, *Forrest Gump*. He lived a few doors down. His mom had just died, and he was so sweet and open about it that soon there were tears in his eyes and in Becca's too. They were joined by a cordial, unassuming fellow named George and his exuberantly pregnant girlfriend, Maria; he turned out to be a bigshot *Simpsons* writer. They talked about all kinds of interesting things, and then the *Forest Gump* man introduced her (first as Drew Barrymore then as Becca Mondrain) to Tom Hanks just as Tom was leaving. Rita was saying her good-byes but soon came over. Tom was funny in a pretend-dark kind of way and started chatting with Becca like she was the true Drew. Then he did a kind of triple take, as if he'd been tricked, screwing up his eyes to have another look. "Drew better watch her back," he said menacingly, as he sidled out. He did this cute thing where he kept looking over his shoulder at her with hooded, accusing eyes before smiling warmly then tipping an imaginary hat in good-bye. Rita looked like she wanted to stay a little longer, but her husband gently led her by the wrist. Becca was sure to make eye contact with her, though, mindful of the fact that it was Rita who discovered *My Big Fat Greek Wedding* as a stage show, and Rita who convinced Tom and everyone else to take a chance on putting up the money for a film version. Maybe she would see Becca onstage one day and extend her the same opportunity. Hollywood was full of those kinds of stories.

Drew Barrymore approached with two gays in tow. It was Becca's moment of reckoning.

"You are *so scary*. Do you think I could call you on the phone? Like when I'm having a shitty moment in a relationship? Which is pretty much *all the time*." She turned to the gays, who laughed in chorus. "Or how about when I just really don't want to deal with my family—or lawyer or agent or whatever? Couldn't you just, like, come over and kind of *live through stuff* that I'd rather not?"

"Drew," said Becca, gasping from the thin air. "I'd come and *wash dishes* if you asked."

She knew she sounded like a rube, and the queerfolk winced, but Drew laughed, laying a hand on Becca's arm to put her at ease. Becca nearly burst into tears.

"Oh my God!" said Drew exultantly, a lightbulb going off. "You could have a baby for me!"

The gays laughed some more and one said, "She could fuck for you."

"Thank you, no," said Drew. "I'd rather do that myself. *For now.*"

More laughs from the gays. The beautiful black girl from *Saturday Night Live* came over with the true Cameron, who saucily threw an arm over Becca's shoulder. "Well," she said. "If it isn't Dylan Sanders . . ."

Becca sucked it up and said, "Flip your goddamn hair!"

Everyone laughed and she felt redeemed.

At 20ᵗʰ Century-Fox

LISANNE CALLED Tiff Loewenstein. She'd been meaning to do that as a friendly follow-up to their gala at the Casa del Mar, but she had a hidden agenda as well. Tiff got on the phone right away. His lunch had canceled and he asked her to join him at the commissary.

It had been a while since she'd been on the lot. Lisanne loved the bustle of a studio. The hallways of the executive building were cool, creamy, and hushed, for that wonderful retro mausoleum effect. Everything was perfectly production designed, with a forties ambience. Deeper into the honeycomb and closer to the offices of power, posters of blockbuster films gave way to gauzy Hurrells of bygone stars: Davis, Cagney, Crawford, Hepburn.

She was met in the anteroom by one of three secretaries, then led back to his plush Art Deco domain. Tiff rushed over from his desk, kissing both her cheeks. He immediately informed her of two upcoming events for which he "sorely" needed companionship on the weekend. Friday, he was to receive the KCET Visionary Award (Biltmore ballroom); the following night, he would be honored at a benefit for the Children's Burn Foundation (Beverly Hilton). "What, may I ask, is your availability?" he said, somewhat wryly.

It didn't seem like the right time to ask how things were going on the home front, or if they were going at all. Since he was dateless for his tributes, she assumed the worst.

"You're in luck. As it turns out, I've been relieved of my duties as Karl Lagerfeld's muse. I'm completely at your disposal."

He laughed, took her arm, and swept her out.

.   .   .

"HOW'S THE KIT Lightfoot movie going?" she asked, after ordering.

Tiff occasionally waved to well-wishers—only rarely was he approached in full greeting. As a rule, it was understood the mogul was not to be disturbed.

"Phenomenal. I think it's gonna be a big hit."

"He's really good."

"Number one. Very down-to-earth—an old-fashion movie star. And he gets the biggest compliment I have. Know what it is?"

She shook her head.

Tiff said, "He's not a prick."

"Do you know him? I mean, very well?"

"What, you have a crush?" His antennae were up.

"I meant, do you ever *socialize*—"

"Because he's very much a twosome, you know," he chided.

"So I heard," she said, rolling her eyes.

"I'd be very jealous if you wound up on his arm at a benefit."

"I would never be unfaithful," she said, patting his hand. "Unless, of course, I was the honoree—then I just might drag him along. Naturally, he would have to consent."

"Fair enough. All's fair among love and consenting honorees."

"Are they still shooting?"

"For two more weeks."

She got very brave and casually said, "I'd love to visit the set." Better just to come out with it.

Two men interrupted to say hellos, then the food arrived. She would have to find a way to circle around again.

Since they'd been seated, Lisanne had noticed heads consistently turning toward one of the booths in the back.

"Is that Russell Crowe?" she asked, narrowing her eyes.

Tiff glanced over and laughed.

"See the blond kid? *Adam Spiegel*—Spike Jonze. He did *Adaptation* and *Being John Malkovich.*"

"I know who he is. I love his movies."

"He's sitting with Charlie Kaufman."

"*That's* Charlie Kaufman? God, he looks like J. D. Souther."

"Who's J. D. Souther?"

"He wrote songs for the Eagles."

"Well, that's *him*—Garbo himself. Two Jews from Verona. Spike's a rich kid. The Spiegel catalog. *Der Spiegel* says that's a myth, but he's full of shit. You know who he's married to, right?"

"I love her. Are they doing a project with Russell Crowe?"

"I wish. They've got a *meshuga* project that Charlie's writing, about look-alikes. That's who that guy at the table is—a Russell Crowe look-alike."

"What is that."

"Bottom feeders who come to Hollywood and get jobs impersonating movie stars."

"Sounds kind of interesting."

"Maybe too interesting. When someone wants to spend forty million of the studio's money, I need more than 'interesting.' Now, if we could get the *real* Russell Crowe to be in their movie and pay him 'look-alike' prices, that *would* be interesting. Who knows. Could happen. You still didn't give me an answer—which benefit would you favor, Ms. McCadden? The Friday or the Saturday?"

"That's a tough one."

"Tell you what. Go to both and I'll make you a deal."

"Shoot."

"You can bring something to your friend for me."

"My friend?"

"Mr. Lightfoot. See, I have a gift for him. Come to both benefits and you can be the messenger. I'll so anoint you. Because I'm a very anointing person."

The Varieties of
Religious Experience

KIT SAT ON A cushion in his private zendo, facing the Benedict Canyon hillock that rose up like a ziggurat. A landscape architect had trucked in tons of dirt for the effect.

He stared at an abstract, shifting patch of sun on the teak floor a foot or so beyond his knees.

His next film, an Anthony Minghella, had fallen through. He was scheduled to do a Ridley Scott but not for at least ten months.

He thought of going to India for the Kalachakra Tantra, the annual Wheel of Time rite in which thousands of initiates experience rebirth en masse, coming through childhood to visualize themselves as buddhas. Seeing the Gyuto monks had triggered the notion of pilgrimage. The Dalai Lama, his teacher's teacher, was scheduled to preside over a gathering of some quarter million devotees. Kit had attended such a ceremony before with His Holiness in Madison, Wisconsin, albeit on a far smaller scale.

There, in that unlikely place, the actor had spoken words of promise, before infinity: "O all Buddhas and Bodhisattvas, please take heed of me. I, Kit Lightfoot, from this time henceforth until arriving in the essence of enlightenments will generate the excellent unsurpassed mind of intention to become enlightened in just the way the Protectors of the three times become definite toward enlightenment." A sand mandala representing a palace was created, and the pilgrims were mentally guided through it. After a number of days, the rituals and blessings ended when the Dalai Lama himself swept up the colored sand with a broom, in readiness for dedication to the waters.

It seemed like a lifetime since he'd been to India. He had journeyed there with his teacher, Gil Weiskopf Roshi. They had visited Lumbini, birthplace of Prince Siddhartha Gautama; Bodh Gaya, where Siddhartha was realized beneath the Bodhi Tree; the Deer Park at Sarnath, where he gave sermons on the Four Noble Truths; Sravasti's great park that hosted the Buddha's meditation retreats, and where he converted a notorious murderer; and a saal forest in Kushinagar, the final, unglamorous place in which he left the world. The trip saturated him, and he craved India's sounds, smells, and heart. He craved his teacher too, who had died a year after his mother passed on, to the day—craved the Dharma anew. A few months ago, he'd made vague plans to travel with Meg Ryan at Christmastime to see Ramesh, a disciple of the great sage Nisargadatta Maharaj. But now he was thinking he should make the trip alone, confining his visit to Bodh Gaya, where this year's Kalachakra would be held.

He readjusted himself on the cushion and focused his breath, suppressing a smile as the mischievous, deconsecrated image of his old friend Alf bobbed before him. Alf wanted to go to a Golden Globe party at the Medavoys', but Kit had bailed because he didn't have a film out and was envious of those who did, jealous of the actors— some unknown, others long forgotten and now rediscovered—whose fates had contrived to cast them in one of those overrated, dark horse indies that infect hearts and minds each awards season like a designer virus. He felt defunct, used up, ashamed of his body of work. In the middle of his meditations

he returned to his breath, pushing through. He focused on another trapezoidal tile of sun. Insect buzz. His attention flitted from the face of his root guru, Gil, to a page of Rita Julienne Lightfoot's love letters to the smell of her hospital room to the taste of Viv's mouth to the little girl who watched as he came in Cela's mouth on the edge of the playground of Ulysses S. Grant School.

Alf loomed again, the irrepressible jester, trickster. Shapeshifter. He got his kicks by tweaking his more famous friend and knew what buttons to push. Yesterday, he'd made a point of telling him Spike Jonze was up to something big—Spike was about to do a really wild film, "more genius than Adaptation," about celebrity look-alikes. Alf said he didn't know much more than that, but did know Spike was supposedly out there looking for a "Kit Lightfoot type." When he heard that, Kit had laughed out loud, playing it cool. (He'd secretly resolved to phone the director at home and get the friendly lowdown. If there was something for him, he'd most likely have

heard. Spike would have called or his people would have approached.) Kit
wanted to do challenging work; it haunted him that he hadn't yet made his
bid. He was desperate—so he told himself—to do something magnificent, to
work with an art house hotshot, any hotshot, young or old, step right up. He
completely understood Tom's need to have done the Kubrick thing. Respected
it. Admired it. Then the Master went and died, as if in homage to Tom's
great taste and timing, Tom's great luck. Kit kept telling himself that he
wanted to do a film to challenge him in his core the way his practice once
had, back in the day. But even if he found the right project, there were obsta-
cles to surmount—he knew that he needed to be empty enough to exceed real
or imagined boundaries. Maybe he just didn't have it in him; never did and
never would. Maybe he was just a pretty boy with swagger, gutless and not
that bright, the King of People's Choice. And that was that.

He shivered, straightening his spine.

The zendo had been built by master carpenters from five-hundred-year-old Japanese cedars without benefit of nails or glue. Each morning, the *toryos* had made offerings of sake and rice to their tools before setting to work. *Architectural Digest* wanted to put it on their cover, but Kit turned them down in his nobility. He flashed on the whore and the extemporaneous *teisho* before the shrine of the Buddha: the pornography of hubris. How had the path led him to this? He felt in danger of dying.

Like a warlock, he summoned a Kalachakra invocation to clear the air—"I will achieve complete enlightenment through the four doors of thorough liberation . . . emptiness, sinlessness, wishlessness, and non-activity!" These words he had said in Wisconsin, before his mentor and friend, the Dalai Lama. These words he had said before Prince Siddhartha, before timeless Shakyamuni, before Nothingness. He whispered *Om shunyata-jnana-vajra-svabhavatmako ham* and bowed deeply to the void, the hum of his words merging with the drone of a faraway leaf blower.

Stagecoach

RUSTY PICKED BECCA up around seven. Even though Sadge's things were still in the apartment, she felt single. It was a turn-on. He came in and sniffed around like a cartoon dog. He sniffed his way to the bedroom, and she laughingly had to keep hauling him out.

They drove to Beverly Hills and parked near the big church where Bo Derek got married in Becca's mom's favorite movie, *10*. Suddenly she got the crazy notion Rusty was going to take her to Crustacean. She started worrying about the sullen maître d' but figured he probably wouldn't recognize her—tonight, hair and makeup were in anti-Drew mode.

Rusty walked them toward Wells Fargo, saying he needed cash. He went past the ATMs and into the building's lobby. It was already after seven.

"The bank's staying open late," he said, with a smile. "Just for me."

For a fleeting moment Becca thought he was going to commit armed robbery, but then she saw a gala group on the other side of the tall windows. A guard was at the entrance. Rusty said, "We're with Grady and Cassandra Dunsmore," and he let them in without a hassle.

A peculiar, festive scene greeted them within. Gang bangers and their relations, some in wheelchairs (she was reminded of Valle Verde), upended slim-necked Coronas and sipped champagne from plastic glasses beside jovial white men in suits and loosened ties. A table had been set up with Costco deli platters, some as yet unwrapped; people seemed more thirsty than hungry. Motown played on a boom box. The high-spirited wives wore satiny dresses and as many tattoos as their spouses. Toddlers ran manic circles around their grandparents. Some of the gray-haired folks also had tatts.

"Hey now!" shouted Grady, on seeing Rusty come toward him.

"Hey now."

They did their bear-hug thing.

"The gravy train has finally pulled into the station!"

"You mean the *Grady* train," said Cassandra, waddling over, napkin filled with canapés and little sugar-dusted donuts. Her belly had grown since Becca last saw it underwater.

"You got *that* right," said Grady.

"You're both wrong," said Rusty. "It ain't the Grady *or* the gravy—it's the 'bullet' train."

"The bullet train!" exulted Grady. "That's right! That's dead-on! It's the motherhumpin bullet-in-the-leg train!"

They had a laugh, then Rusty said, "You remember Becca."

"I ain't fuckin senile." Grady turned to his wife. "Tha's Rusty's lady."

Cassandra nodded, in Barbara Stanwyck–*The Big Valley* mode—all steely, matriarchal approval. They'd actually met at the party but Cassandra didn't recollect.

"Honey," she said, taking Becca's elbow with mock intimacy, "would you make one thing clear to your boyfriend for me?" She paused for dramatic effect before saying, "*He ain't gettin any*! Not a *dime*, OK? He ain't gettin even the *caboose* of the bullet train! Not a red Indian cent!"

Cassandra choked as she laughed, fizzing up tiny sprays of Diet Pepsi that cooled an exhalation of cigarette smoke.

"Now, hey, Cass," rebuked Grady. "Don't *be* like that. When *we* party, *everybody* parties!"

A bank bureaucrat spoke up, and the lawyers motioned their clients to gather round—time to get serious. The families of the men hung back respectfully.

"What's going on?" whispered Becca.

"Payback," said Rusty in like tones. "I told you: Grady got shot by Rampart. LAPD planted dope on him. Did nineteen months. Got out three years ago, when Perez talked. Took this long for the settlement."

"Settlement?"

"One point eight."

"One point—"

"Mill."

"But who are the others?" she asked, not really comprehending.

"All plaintiffs. Grady said some are detainees—guys held in jail longer than they were supposed to. That's a no-no. Class action, big time." Becca couldn't keep up. "The county had to fork over twenty-seven million. See the chick standing next to him? To Grady? She got busted on some domestic violence thing. They held her an extra day and strip-searched her. *Ugly* bi-atch. Screws must've been hard up! Well, she's rich now. For that kind of money, I'd do twenty-four hours standing on my head—or sittin on a dick. That's what's called a detainee. Most everybody here has the same attorneys." He nodded toward a charismatic, black-stockinged woman in a pantsuit. "Ludmilla Vesper-Weintraub. She's got a thousand clients, I shit you not. And every one of 'em is gonna be motherfuckin rich."

"But the money they got for their little girl . . ."

"That don't have nothing to *do* with this. Can you believe it? They won the lotto twice! Can you fucking believe the karma of these people? *Wheel of Fortune*, man. *Blazing Sevens.*"

Grady bounded over. "The moment has come! The time is upon us!"

"What's happening?" asked Rusty.

"They're gonna dole it out, soul man. Then we are going to get our asses over to Gardena! We are going to get in that limo and cruise on down to Hustler Casino! Gonna play me some *twenty-one.*"

Cassandra kissed her husband, deliberately regurgitating a stream of soda into his unsuspecting mouth. Grady belched it back at her, and they both laughed gutturally.

"See that jail-face?" said Grady to his friends. He pointed surreptitiously to a short, muscle-bound skinhead standing in a corner with his wife and kid. "He got two million for doing less time than *I* did. Fucker already spent half his life in the penitentiary. I asked him what his thing was, and you know what he said? 'Raping niggers.' "

Deities

LISANNE FINALLY CALLED to say she was pregnant. Robbie didn't have much of a response. At the end of the brief conversation he told her to take care of herself, as if she'd said she was down with a cold or the flu.

· · ·

TIFF'S OFFICE LET Sotheby's know that Lisanne would be picking up the item. When she got there, they were friendly enough but made her show ID.

She'd thought about bringing Kit something personal—a flower, maybe, to grace the gift—but discarded the notion as amateurish. No coy upstaging allowed. Something like that might get back to Tiff. No, she would just have to be as charming and low-key as she could, in spite of her schoolgirl jitters. Besides, Tiff was the one who deserved the flowers. It really was awfully grand of him to have engineered the meet.

When she arrived at the beach location, a cop directed her to a parking space beside the famous Indian motorcycle. That's when her heart began to pound. A baby-faced A.D. appeared and led her to Kit's trailer. She cracked herself up with wild, nervous thoughts along the way. She imagined the star, a legendary on-set practical joker, coming to the door nude with a big veiny hard-on. They knocked at the trailer's door, and there was no answer. Just as they turned away, Lisanne said, "Wait! Something's wrong. I can *feel* it." Before the A.D. could restrain her, she burst in to discover Kit on the floor, facedown. She began resuscitation efforts as her escort ran for help. The star, in diabetic semicoma, dumbly began to explore her mouth with twitchy, treacly tongue as she breathed warm life into his grateful bronchi—

A slender brunette in a headset answered the door. She smiled in a way that made the already paranoid Lisanne certain that Mr. Loewenstein had tipped them off about the "messenger" and her minor crush. The gorgeous, multitasking assistant motioned her in.

"What's happening with Aronofsky?" The unmistakable voice came from deeper inside. "Are we supposed to meet?"

"Darren's on his way back from Boston. We're trying to set a place and a time."

"He can come to the house—wherever. And, Xan? I want to call Spike. At home."

Without warning, Kit emerged, barefoot in blue jeans. At first, he didn't see Lisanne. He wore a tight cotton T, and actually stretched in front of her. A tattooed spiritual symbol floated above a hipbone.

"I want to find out if my homeboy Alfalfa is full of shit," he said, winking at Lisanne. "But that's not really accurate. I *know* he's full of shit. I just want to find out how much." He turned his full attention to the visitor and said, "Hi."

"Hi."

She waited to see if he recognized her from that time at yoga (she hoped he didn't) but there wasn't a flicker. Lisanne introduced herself, announcing that she was an emissary from the "offices" of Tiff Loewenstein. She said it drolly, as if speaking of a cardinal. She wanted to come off just a little bit sophisticated, and it seemed like he appreciated that and got where she was coming from. She reiterated that Mr. Loewenstein was adamant in his desire the package be delivered personally, and that she was performing her duties as his "special envoy."

He took the box and opened it as he parodied the studio chieftain railing about his "tribute addiction." Aside from the occasional impulse to prostate herself at his feet, the besotted go-between was relatively at ease.

"Wow," he said, pulling the figure from a beautiful velvet sack. Xanthe came over to gawk.

It was a golden Buddha, mounted on dark wood, without question the most beautiful thing Lisanne had ever seen. Kit read from a creamy insert card that fixed its provenance to the thirteenth-century. His finger delicately transcribed the air above its head.

"The crown symbolizes reaching enlightenment," he said, with casual authority. "Usually they're five-pointed."

The transcendent sculpture sat in lotus position. With deft elegance, one of its hands reached over a leg to touch the ground.

"Touching the earth," said Kit. "To touch the earth spirit means that he's conquered Mara, the world of illusion."

"It's so beautiful," said Lisanne.

That was all she came up with, but she was glad to have said anything.

"What's it made of?" asked Xanthe.

He traced a hand over its belly. "Copper." Kit leaned over, crinkling his eyes in scrutiny. "See the gems in the crown? Whoa. What is that, lapis? And the tiny symbols on the sash? See the little symbols?"

He bade them draw closer. Lisanne could smell him. She felt her leg touch his.

Xanthe called his attention to an envelope tucked within the box. He opened it, reading the note from Tiff aloud. "But I should have got you *this.*" Kit removed the paper clip and looked at the photograph beneath that had been ripped from the auction house catalog. The mogul had underscored the accompanying text.

AJNA-VINIVARTA GANAPATI
COPPER ALLOY
TIBET CIRCA 15TH CENTURY

The exotic form of Ganapati is supported by a <u>monkey goddess engaged in fellatio</u>, sitting on an amrita vase flowing with <u>jewels and menses</u>. He is depicted with three heads: the elephant-headed Ganesha (primary) with a rat head to its right and a monkey head to its left. The role of the deity is to appease the suffering of insatiable beings.

$10,000 – $15,000

Kit laughed, then became almost somber.

"Get Loewenstein on the phone, OK, Xan?" He shook his head. "That's a serious gift. That's a *very* serious gift."

Xanthe immediately got through. She handed him the cell.

"Mr. Loewenstein! Mr. Loewenstein! *Head,* from a *monkey*! Yes! Yes! The gift that keeps on giving!"

Then he expressed awed appreciation and began his sober thanks, disappearing into the bedroom as he spoke.

There was nothing for Lisanne to do but go.

Hustlers

HUSTLER'S WAS ONLY forty minutes away. It was a shock to Becca that casinos existed in places other than Vegas, Reno, and Atlantic City. Rusty said that gaming was all over the place—even Palm Springs. Cassandra said the American Indians owned more casinos than Donald Trump. You could even gamble on-line.

It was their third consecutive night. (And their last, according to Cassandra. "Cause our money's gettin royally flushed.") Rusty's guesstimate to Becca was that the couple had dropped at least two hundred thou. They were given the royal treatment. They had their own private blackjack table if they wanted, and everywhere they went security guards politely followed, even standing outside when the girls used the powder room. Cassandra sometimes needed help walking, and the guards were there for that too. Now in her eighth month, she claimed to have stopped drinking but still took painkillers. She said that was OK because she knew a doctor who prescribed certain pills that wouldn't hurt the fetus. Grady was sloshed and kept wanting to hire the affable men away (he kept slipping them hundies) to be personal bodyguards. Cassandra put the kibosh on it, in a friendly way. "I don't want no *cop* knowing where I live," she said to Becca under her breath.

Each night, Larry Flynt was supposed to be tooling around the premises in his gold-plated wheelchair, but whenever they asked, a pit boss would say he wasn't in town. Larry's brother was there, though. *Well, whoop-dee-doo.* The Dunsmores weren't too eager to meet frère Flynt. But the casino manager said the Dunsmores and their friends should come to Bel-Air and join Larry for cocktails when he got home from wherever. The funky invitation only rankled them more.

"Shit," said Grady, "Larry can come to *me*. Wheel his diapered ass on up to Mulholland!"

Cassandra made a point of laughing louder than she might have.

"Got a bigger house than him any*how*," said Grady. He thought about that and said, "Well, maybe not." The Dunsmores had a real conniption over that one. No one was feeling any pain.

Becca was returning from the rest room when she saw Rusty and the decorous blue-haired lady. She was in her seventies and clutched his arm with arthritic hands.

"Now young man, I *know* who you are and I *respect* your privacy, your right to privacy as a human *being*. But *you*, young man, belong to the *world*. And *you* are in a public place—not a very *wonderful* public place, I may add—so you cannot mind if I call you to task. I know that you are Russell Crowe. And I cannot remember if you are an Australian or a New Zealander, but I am of a certain age that allows me to say what's on my mind. I am an *elder*, and while we do not honor elders in this country as we should and as they do in others, I *know* that you will not object—and I don't care if you do!—if I tell you, young man, that you are simply *marvelous*. A *marvelous* actor. And a wonderful *lit'ry man*. You are *authorial*. I have never *heard* such marvelous acceptance speeches in my life! So marvelously composed and thought out, with such theatricality! I wish, young man, that you would write a *book*—not one of those damn tell-alls but a *real* book, a book of *poetry*, the poetry that's *within* you. A *memoir* or a marvelous *novel*. *Dylan Thomas* is there, *inside*. Now I know when to shut up, I've lived long enough to know *that*, and I will leave you be, young man." She clenched him hard and fast. "Don't let them be your master!" she said, cautioning like a feral gypsy. "You are the *artist*. You have the *power*."

She winked, then hobbled away on a tripod cane.

Becca slipped her arm in Rusty's. They ambled to the sushi bar.

"California roll, Ms. Barrymore?" he said.

"No thanks." She was happy to see him in such good humor—and that he hadn't taken offense at the old woman's eccentric ambush. "Been gambling?"

"A bit."

"Does Grady give you money?"

Wrong question. She saw his face cloud over, then reappear.

"I assure you that when he *does*, it won't be for gambling. Not this kind."

She softly tickled his knuckles as if to undo her crassness.

"I think they're just about ready to leave," said Rusty. "Want to go over to the Four Seasons? Or do you want to go home?"

"What's at the Four Seasons?"

"I think they're going to get a room. We can hang awhile then split."

Next Day Delivery

VIV WORKED LATE. They judiciously kept separate homes, but she stayed over most of the time. She didn't always tell Kit when she was coming, and this time the house was dark. He might be out. She was on her way to draw a bath when Viv saw his shadow in the living room.

"Oh my God, you scared me! Bumpkin, are you OK?"

She turned on a lamp. He was on the floor beside the couch, drunk. He looked as if he'd been crying.

"Bumpkin?" She kneeled beside him, like a nun to a homeless person. Softly, she said, "Honey, what's going on?"

"*This*," he said, proffering a script. "*This* is what's going on."

Viv opened it—there was no title page.

"*Special Needs*. That's what it's called. Though Darren said that may change."

"Darren?"

"Aronofsky."

"He wrote it?"

"I don't know, Cherry Girl. I think so."

"And you love it?" she said, with a broadening smile.

"God wrote it," he said. "Bin Laden wrote it. Jeffrey Katzenberg wrote it. Cherry Girl wrote it. My dead mother wrote it . . ."

"Kitchener—do you think you're going to *do* it?"

She knew how unhappy he'd been, how much he wanted to work on something amazing. She had never seen him like this before. Shattered and ecstatic.

"If I don't do *it, it's* gonna do *me.*" He reached for the shot glass, downing its contents with melodramatic finesse. "A script comes from nowhere—and it's like *whoa,* 'beginner's mind.' You don't bring anything to it, it just is. You can *see* it—the way you *used* to see shit. Before the shoe dropped or the whatever and you became a product. A corporation. Brand-new again. *Beginner's mind.*"

Viv grabbed him and gave his neck a hundred little kisses while he squirmed and smiled, pouring and swallowing another shot.

"Bumpkin, do you know how lucky we are? How fucking *lucky* we are? That you can just *stand* there—for however long—and whisper in the wind: *I want something crazy and brilliant, something I can finally be* passionate *about.* And when you're ready—when you're ready to *receive*—God just *returns* that, returns all that *energy,* he fuckin *FedExes* it to you cause you're so *pure* and you've worked *so* fuckin hard, Kit— not just on *yourself* but you have helped *so many people*—God just sends it right back to you on the whirlwind!"

"Hey, Cherry Girl, you know what? I think I wanna marry you."

At Sarbonne Road

LISANNE WENT to her favorite Level 1 at Yoga Circle. There were only five people in attendance—a guy fatter than she was; a sixty-something socialite type with a wrist splint and a ton of face work; an even older, hollow-cheeked Nefertiti type in a turban, with weirdly elongated muscles; a grumpy, inflexible fellow in his fifties who looked as if he'd been forced by a probation officer to attend; and Marisa Tomei.

Afterward, she overheard the actress talking to the hippie girl at the front desk about a meditation class that night. Lisanne boldly asked if anyone could come. Marisa was sweet as could be and actually wrote down the address for her.

THE CLASS TOOK place at a private home in the Bel-Air hills.

The Yoga House sat on the edge of a vast property belonging to the producer Peter Guber and his wife, Tara. After Marisa left, the hippie said that Tara used to be Lynda, before taking a spiritual name. She said that Tara was one of the Buddhas who took female form, specifically to help women. Tara was born of tears shed over the suffering of sentient beings. Lisanne thought that if you had to give yourself a new name, that was a pretty good choice.

The night was windy and spectacular. The zendo sat on Sarbonne Road, high on a hill. Lisanne was surprised at how quiet it was, the kind of sepulchral stillness that, in the midst of an enormous city, only the very rich could afford. She parked on the slope and descended the driveway on foot.

A small group (Marisa was nowhere in sight) milled about or sat on cushions in preparation for what a flyer on the desk called *satsang*. Lisanne slipped off her shoes and signed the guestbook. She wrote out a check for the suggested "dana": $15. She retrieved a Mexican blanket from the corner of the studio and on her way back to the sitting area studied the black-and-white wall photos. Some were of a woman doing yoga while pregnant; others of the same woman, older now, in symmetrical yogic poses with a man. Lisanne assumed the woman was Tara Guber.

A handsome, fortyish guy came in—the one in the photographs with Tara—and quietly bantered with a few of the sitters before stepping onto the platform. He assumed the lotus position, facing out. He was lithe and unpretentious, smiling at the group.

"We're going to begin in silence," he said. "The Upanishads said the only thing of real value is silence. That's where the answers are. Tonight, we'll begin with silence—and end with silence."

He said he wasn't going to guide them and they should just close their eyes. He told everyone to slowly find their breath (an instruction that puzzled Lisanne). After ten minutes or so, he said, "Open your eyes." They were now free to ask questions.

Lisanne couldn't quite grasp the evening's format—because of what Marisa Tomei had said, she thought she would be attending a meditation class. But her back was already hurting so she was glad to have respite. The man beside her kept doing the kind of desultory leg stretches that dancers do, even though tonight clearly wasn't about movement. Another woman took her watch off, positioning it so she could constantly read the time. Lisanne related to that. She had always, to her chagrin, been a clock-watcher.

Someone asked about "chakras." How does energy move up to the head then out the crown? The teacher gave a thoughtful, seemingly roundabout answer, in which he invoked a tantric prayer called "The Power of Regret." He said that during certain meditations, one visualized the Buddha dropping light and nectar down like a purifying stream through the crown of the head so that it filled one's totality with bliss. Another woman asked if it was all right to meditate between one and four in the morning. The teacher said *his* teacher told him that a yogi should be asleep during the day and awake at night. By that he meant "awake while sleeping. As with Christ: 'I am in the world, not of it.' " As a rule, he cautioned them against baroque, late-night gestures. He said that if you were awake at that hour, it probably meant that you were "over-amped." There was, he added, a tantric practice where one meditated in the middle of the night, in water up to one's belly, during a full moon. Meditated on the moon in the water. Even though the teacher seemed learned, Lisanne found herself judgy and cynical. He just seemed too handsome to be taken seriously. Too California, too Malibu surfer. Too something-something.

After the Q & A, he led the class in breathing: stomach-tucked rapid breaths, and "bumblebees"—in through one nostril and out the other. (It suddenly occurred to her that it was probably time to have a doctor check the fetus.) This part was hard, but she liked it when, at the end, he had everyone breathe "into your hearts," then out to infinity.

He asked them to settle into lotuses for closing meditation. Lisanne kept adjusting her legs, occasionally opening her eyes in slits to observe the serene, sandy-haired Aryan *guru erectus*. He made no perceptible movement; she couldn't even see his respirations. Her stomach growled and gurgled as she listened to the electronic rush of hedges just outside the window, buffeted by the Santa Anas. The hypnotic sound of the leaves and her own breath led her back to that magical visit to Kit Lightfoot's trailer and how he had patiently explained, like a kind, scholarly Adonis, the recondite attributes of the golden Buddha. At last, her mind alighted on the soot that was the residuum of her father.

A few minutes before the hour, the teacher chanted a mantra that began and ended with *AUM*, and they all joined in. Lisanne liked that part even though the man next to her—the irritating stretcher, who, instead of even attempting a lotus was the only person to have deployed one of those portable back-support chairs that were stacked along the wall (Lisanne had thought of using one when she first came in but couldn't figure out exactly how they worked)—began to consciously harmonize, annoying her to no end.

Riding in Cars with Boys

THE BAR AT the Four Seasons was mobbed. Big-bellied Cassandra sat on her stool and got dirty looks for nursing a snifter of Petron. Becca wasn't sure when she had begun drinking again.

Mrs. Dunsmore grunted because there weren't any celebrities. "I guess Thursday's bridge and tunnel night." Becca never understood that phrase.

Grady waved his arms from the lounge—their suite was ready. Rusty helped Cassandra up, and Becca followed. A familiar-looking woman touched her arm.

"Becca? It's Sharon—Belzmerz. You came in to read for me."

"Oh, hi!" she said, gushing. "How *are* you!"

"The director *really* liked your tape," said Sharon.

Becca was so flummoxed to be "recognized" by a professional that she didn't know what the lady was talking about.

"He finally looked at it—he's a little slow."

"Oh! That's . . . great!" stuttered Becca, feeling like a fool.

"Are you still at the same numbers?"

Sharon was tipsy. It was loud and she pushed in so close that Becca could see down her throat.

"Yes! And you have my cell—"

She made a move to her purse for a pen, but the casting agent stayed her hand. "I'm sure we have it. Anyway, I can always reach you through Cyrus." She asked if Becca still studied with him. Then she changed her mind, and they exchanged phone numbers and e-mails. Becca couldn't believe Sharon Belzmerz was actually giving out her home phone.

"That is *so* great," said Becca, referring back to the director. "I thought they had *totally* decided to go with somebody else."

It was Sharon's turn to be puzzled. A light went on: "Oh! That director did! He *did* go with someone else. *I'm* sorry." She tapped her glass. "Too much wine. *Another* director saw your tape, and he's *very* interested. Spike Jonze."

She dropped the name with the brio of a homespun pimp.

"Spike Jonze?"

"He *really* likes you. But now I have to get back to my friends. Call you Monday!"

"Nice running into you!"

As Becca moved through the crowded bar, her skin was flush with the excitement of the encounter. She felt that all was preordained and that she'd just been moved by an invisible hand (in the form of Sharon Belzmerz) upon the great magnetized Ouija board of show business destiny.

For the first time since she came to L.A., she felt like a celebrity.

•　•　•

THE SUITE WAS HUGE. Grady lit a joint, and Cassandra said, "Hey, didn't they tell you this was a nonsmoking wing?" Room service brought pizza, caviar, ice cream, and booze, and everyone broke apart, then came back together again, disappearing into the bedroom for lines of coke. When Rusty told her the cognac cost eight hundred dollars, Becca said, "Sorry, but I cannot compute." Cassandra said she was drinking only tequila now. She said it was the purest and actually benefited the baby homeopathically.

At one in the morning, she began to cry over her drowned daughter. "I'm sorry, sweetheart!" she shouted, through pugnacious tears. Whenever Grady went to her side, she shoved him away like a diva.

"Baby-girl Questra, I am *so sorry* I didn't protect you! Forgive me! Forgive your mama!"

Repelled at the sight of the stoned, egregiously mawkish woman, Becca became sickened by her own response—who was she to judge? She, who didn't know the first thing about the blood, sweat, and tears of birthing a child, the agony and the ecstasy, the *responsibility,* and maybe never would. . . . What gave *her* the right to sit on high? How could she dare resent someone who'd been through what Cassandra had? Becca shuddered with the realization: It was their *money* she resented them for. Disgusting! As if they didn't deserve every dollar! The police had cold-bloodedly shot Grady down, then planted the dope—and if that wasn't enough, they'd watched their little baby girl die through the negligence of a city maintenance crew. *Becca Mondrain, you ought to be ashamed.*

Rusty took her to the bedroom. They did more coke, and he kissed her on the bed awhile. When he got overly sexual she became uncomfortable (he hadn't shut the door), but he kept on. She could hear Cassandra petitioning her unborn son as she roved the living room like a wounded animal.

"I'll protect you," she blubbered. "God help me, I *will.* I *won't* let them take you away from me!"

"Come on, Cassie girl," said Grady, helpless to assuage. "Ain't nobody gonna take our baby away."

"They will, they will, they will!"

"Why'd they want to do that, Cass?" His gently logical tone was that of a hostage negotiator.

"The motherfuckers—"

"Why'd they wanna try and take our baby away? Huh, Cass? Why—"

"And *if* they do," she said, inconsolably, "someone's going to righteously *pay,* understand me, Grady? Someone's going to fucking pay! Because *no one* takes my babies! No one takes Cassandra Dunsmore's babies, I showed 'em that *already.* I *made them pay.*" Chin lowered, she addressed the womb. "And they're not going to *touch* you, OK? Mama Bear ain't going to let them fucking *touch* you!"

Becca was dizzy and drunk. Rusty was eating her out when the couple came in, Grady holding his wife's hand like she was a child just retrieved from Lost and Found. Becca tried to get up, but Rusty was too heavy on her. Grady went to the bed while the half-dressed Cassandra wailed through her soliloquy, incognizant of anything but faceless oppression and grief. Her gut protruded like a cruddy seed-pod. Grady stripped off his clothes. He showed Becca his cock—HARD TIMES was inked on it—then let it dangle down. He fastened his mouth to Becca's freckled tit.

"They killed you!" shouted Cassandra. "But *you're not dead*, Questra—you're not dead! I *know* you're not dead. You're *right here with me*. Such an old, beautiful soul . . . how *could* you be dead? You *can't*. You're *not*. And we're *rich* now and so are *you*. And when your little bro's born? We're gonna go to *Disney World* and *Hawaii* and *Ground fucking Zero*—we're gonna do *all* the things families do, OK? *Together*. And if something happens to little bro at Disney World, if he gets fucked up on Space Mountain, we are gonna take care of business! We gon' take on Eisner, the King Jew! Better *believe* it. Cause the jury is our *friend*, Questra Girl, the jury know how to take *care* of the Dunsmores. Oh, my baby! My precious baby, baby, baby! You're gon' have *everything* your mama never did, that's right. That's right! Cause your mama loves you *so much*. OK? Loves you *so much*. Loves you *so much*. Loves you *so much*. Loves you *so much*. Loves you . . ."

Storming the Temple

KIT MET DARREN Aronofsky in the courtyard of the Chateau. They talked around the project awhile. Matthew McConaughey came through with his dog and said hello.

The director said he wrote *Special Needs* in just two weeks' time. His friend Paul Schrader (who loved the script) thought that was a good omen—Paul said the screenplays that exploded out of you always proved to be the most enduring. The germ of the idea had occurred to him while he was watching an old Cliff Robertson movie called *Charly*; as it turned out, *Special Needs* was *Charly* in reverse. What would happen, he wondered, if a famous actor set out to do a film—say, a character study of a retarded man—and before shooting began, sustained injuries in an auto accident that left him "neurologically impaired"? As the story wrote itself out, Darren said that his conceit, which seemed at first a kind of knee-jerk satirical response to a genre that had become a perennial audience pleaser and vainglorious actors' showcase staple, revealed itself to be more layered and poignant than he could have imagined.

Whatever its origins, Kit thought the script was incredibly complex and controversial. The role would allow him to walk several high wires at once. It was risky (there was always the danger of falling; he recalled his conversation with "Mr. Tourette's"), but he knew he had no choice. He would face his shame and his fear. Each morning when he awoke, Kit felt like a dud, a popinjay, a cosmic fraud—the biggest travesty of all being that he dared call himself a Buddhist. He was diseased, and further from the Essential Truths than ever. Now, in desperation, he at least owned that terrible, shiny thing his teacher had warned him of:

Hope.

He knew the battle was not in Bodh Gaya—it was in Hollywood, the place where he practiced his craft, the place he had seduced and been seduced by, that had brought him godhood then brought him to his knees. This was his crucible. He remembered Gil Weiskopf Roshi telling him of an enlightened master who refused to allow soldiers into his temple. With joyful indifference, the monk set the room ablaze. "To meditate, seek not the mountain stream—to a still mind, fire itself is cool and refreshing." The conflagration would be here, not there. And it had already come.

Darren asked what the rest of his day was like. Kit said he was free, and the director suggested a field trip.

·   ·   ·

THEY WERE MET in the waiting room by a thin black queen of indeterminate age. He wore hospital whites, a hairnet, and aviator glasses with smoky green lenses.

"Mr. Aronofsky!" He shook the director's hand, then looked at Kit and smoldered, as if wanting to take a bite. "And *you* must be *Mr. Lightfoot*. Been *expecting* y'all—though your girl didn't say when. Don't get me started, you can drop in any time you like! I know y'all'd like to get straight to business, but I have to do my official meet-and-greet thing. Won't take but a minute. My name is Tyrone Lamott, and I am Valle Verde Liaison for Television and Motion Pictures. I am media liaison, that's right. And Mr. Lightfoot, Tyrone is a *very* large fan and thought he would just get that out of the way so he don't *salivate* over y'all while y'all are here. No no no, that just wouldn't do. Now just so's y'all don't think we are *pikers,* I must inform that we've had 'em *all* come through, the full gambit—Mr. DiCaprio for *Gilbert Grape* and Mr. Hoffman for *Rain Man,* Mr. Ford for *Regarding Henry*—we have seen quite a few. Because we are the best. But, Mr. Lightfoot . . . Tyrone will say *for the very last time* that you are the one among *all* the others who thrill him most!"

As they toured, the staffers gawked. Tyrone sternly, comically shooed them away. "G'on, now! G'on about your business!" After walking what must have been three city blocks, they approached one of the stations.

"Roy getting bath," said a Cambodian nurse, with a curious eye to the guests. "Be done in few minute." She broke a toothy smile as her giggling cohorts gathered round. "Is Kit Lightfoot?"

"Yes, Connie. Is Kit Lightfoot." He turned to the men. "That's Connie *Chung.* I give all my girls names. Freshens 'em up. Now go check on Roy, girl!" he said, with outrageous dispatch. "These are busy, busy men! Go tell Roy he gonna meet hisself a movie star!"

"Tyrone," said Darren humbly. "What happened to Roy?"

"Glioblastoma multiforme. Now I don't know if that's what y'all are looking for—"

"Is that a tumor?" asked Kit.

"Uh huh," said Tyrone. "But he's doin real well."

Nurse Connie emerged from the room and said they could go in.

A pale, beleaguered man stood at the bed, poorly draped by a shabby robe. He was around forty and attended by an orderly, who wasn't thrilled to be part of any dog-and-pony show.

"Roy, you got y'self some visitors! This is *Dar-ren.*"

"Hi, Roy."

"He's a *very famous* director. And *this* is *Kit Lightfoot.*"

"How are you?" the actor softly inquired.

Roy took them in, blank-faced.

"Do you recognize him from the movies?" said Tyrone. "Huh, Roy? I'll bet you do. I'll bet you recognize him from the motion picture big screen."

Kit was mildly uncomfortable with the approach but let it go.

The man spoke up, in a garbled drone. With Tyrone's coaxing, the words became apparent:

"I . . . fuck. I fuck. I—I fuck."

Connie Chung held a hand over her mouth, embarrassed.

"Roy Rogers fucks a *lot*," said Tyrone, rolling his eyes. "Least he *say* he do. If you believe Roy, he get more pussy than Julio Iglesias."

"I fuck! I fuck! I fuck! Fuck! Fuck!" barked Roy, smiling gleefully as he got up to speed.

"He gettin excited—cause *you* here, Mr. L."

Other nurses gathered in the doorway. More hands to giggling mouths. Nurse Connie and the orderly lowered the patient back on to the bed.

"Roy Rogers had his own business. Didn't you have your own business, Roy?"

"Fuck!" He laughed, messy and unnerving, full of spittle. He stood up again. Tyrone put a comforting hand on the man's shoulder and said indulgently, "Naw, it wasn't the 'fuck' business. I think he had a McDonald's."

Kit noticed a horseshoe-shaped scar over his temple.

"Those Golden Arches made lots of money for you, too, didn't they, Roy. Roy got some grown-up kids," said Tyrone, turning to Nurse Connie. "I guess it ain't been no Happy Trails."

"They no come," she said.

Tyrone took a framed photo from the bedstand and handed it to Kit and Darren—Roy and his family, in happier days.

Kit went over and steadied the man with his hands, murmuring softly while helping him to sit. The orderly dropped his sullen demeanor and pitched in, supporting Roy's other side. The patient's obscene perorations faded. There was something so touching and fearless about Kit's tender mercies, and Darren knew for certain that he had found his man.

Field Trips

LISANNE SET OFF for Riverside. It was Sunday. Apart from her main plan, she wanted to scope out the famous brunch at the Mission Inn that her boss was always raving about. It turned out to be a tad Waspy for her taste. She had a general rule never to eat where women of a certain age congregated in colored hats.

She went to Denny's instead. Lisanne thought she felt the baby kick, but maybe it was too soon for that. *Maybe it kicked when one of those big fat pancakes I promised myself I wouldn't order thunked it on the head.*

It was easy to find the house. There were a thousand Kit Lightfoot links and Web sites that listed the address of the local landmark, many containing interviews with Lightfoot Senior. He spoke freely, almost defiantly, of his son's early years, glibly advertising himself as a good parent, a tough but caring dad, an all-too-human family man who had done the best he could under great hardship, insurmountable medical bills, beloved wife dying of cancer (he fudged time lines and history), a sorrowful patriarch benevolently bewildered by his boy's estrangement. "He'll come around," said Mr. Lightfoot. "He knows I'm there for him anytime he needs me." In a more current posting, Burke Lightfoot bragged that Kit had indeed come around, and not too long ago at that, to visit the old homestead. ("I still live in the same house my son was born in. I have nothing to hide.") In fact, it was noted, that with his father's recent urgings, the star had made a generous donation toward the rebuilding of his grade school's auditorium—see? Reparations were well under way, all across the board.

Lisanne took the leisurely route over to Galway Court. The Lightfoot residence was on a cul-de-sac, making it harder to do a simple drive-by. She parked a few blocks away and hid behind the classifieds, as if looking for rentals. After a few minutes she glanced around, absorbing the sights and sounds of the neighborhood. Maybe she'd take a stroll. Then she thought that wasn't such a great idea (the street probably had its share of lookie-lous) and decided to leave. Her mood plummeted. She felt common, aimless, unveiled, one more fat, lonely fan in a vast, uncelebrated throng. In a few short moments, she had lost her special connection.

She was embarrassed at having come at all.

.　　.　　.

THAT AFTERNOON, SHE accompanied Tiff and his wife to a luncheon at a house in San Marino. The Loewensteins were being honored as the most generous of the American Friends of the Salzburg Festival. She'd been invited by Tiff before the couple had reconciled but they insisted she come. Roslynn had always been kind to her and was grateful for the neutered companionship she provided during Mr. Loewenstein's sundry postmidlife freak-outs. As a reward, she invited along "a catch" to be Lisanne's date.

Phil Muskingham was the anemic thirty-nine-year-old heir of a San Francisco telecom clan. He had a minor facial tic and a bad haircut. He wasn't witty, but he wasn't unfunny either and seemed to genuinely like her, in spite of her weight, which definitely made him more appealing. (Lisanne had been steadily gaining and thought that Roslynn must have broached the issue to the "catch" beforehand to make sure it was OK.) He was flirting with her, and she wasn't used to that. He could have been one of those people who got turned on by fatties—hell that'd be OK too. *Bring 'em on.*

The awards part of the luncheon was to begin soon. As coffee was served, Phil asked Lisanne if she wanted to walk the grounds. They set off.

"I know where I've seen you before," he said. She couldn't imagine. "Were you at a gathering a few months ago, in Bel-Air? Kind of a yoga thing?"

"Oh my God, yes!" she exclaimed in disbelief. "But—what were *you* doing there?"

"The Gubers are old friends of the family. Lynda—*Tara*—is always after me to start meditating."

"*The Yoga House.*"

"I call it Yoda House. House o' Yoda."

"I remember *you*. You were *next to me*. You were *fidgeting.*"

"Back problems. I can't sit like that."

"That is *so funny*. You were *harmonizing.*"

"Gettin spiritual," he said, with a goofy smile.

She thought he was cute.

"I can't believe that was you!" she said. Maybe it was a sign from matchmaker heaven.

"Hey, didja hear about the swami at Pink's? They asked how he wanted his hot dog, and he said, 'Make me *one with everything.*' "

"I've *heard* that," Lisanne said, sweetly groaning.

"So . . . you wanna go somewhere sometime?"

"What do you mean?"

"I don't know. We could go out. We could go to Pink's and be one with everything."

"Sure," she said, insouciant. "Why not?"

She was actually being asked on a date. *We could go to a movie. Or to the delivery room together.*

"Well," he said, drolly. "I guess that's better than just 'Why?' "

They laughed. A downsized version of the Vienna Philharmonic began to tune itself, and they headed back so as not to miss the encomiums about to be sung for the studio mogul and his wife.

Dashed Hopes

BECCA DIDN'T TELL Annie about the orgy at the Four Seasons. She avoided Rusty the following week. She had a yeast infection anyway.

When she thought about it, her stomach turned. She knew everyone was really stoned, and that made the reality at least a little less harsh in her head. She didn't think Grady had been inside her but wasn't really sure. It made her paranoid that she might catch something. Becca flashed on fooling around with Cass, smelling her smells and licking her pussy, reaching up to rub the taut, protuberant belly while Cassandra sucked the men. She was obsessing so much about the evening and feeling so guilty that she got a flu. At her worst moment, Becca was dialing home to Virginia to confess. But then the fever broke, so to speak, and she decided on a new tack: she would pretend it hadn't happened. When they were together again, if anyone made some smarmy reference or even hinted at a replay, she would tell them they could all go fuck themselves.

• • •

WHEN THE CASTING director called to say that Spike Jonze wanted to meet, Becca nearly fainted. Sharon suggested they go to the Coffee Bean on Sunset, to "strategize."

She said that Spike was making a film about "the nature of celebrity and what this town does to people." The script was by the genius Charlie Kaufman, and they were already signing up big actors (Russell Crowe, Raquel Welch, Cameron Diaz, Benicio Del Toro, John Cusack), but the *real* stars—the heart and soul of the piece—were look-alikes. Supposedly, Spike didn't want to do any special effects like he did with Nic Cage and his "brother" in *Adaptation*; that it was important the actors *resembled* the stars instead of being exact duplicates. They were throwing out a wide net for look-alikes who could act, and of course Becca qualified because, as far as Sharon was concerned, she was an exceptionally talented actress who just happened to moonlight as a Drew Barrymore impersonator. Becca asked if Elaine Jordache was involved in the production. Sharon hadn't heard the name.

In the parking lot, they clasped hands and Sharon said that she had a really good feeling about her meeting with Spike. She kept gently pinching the pressure point between Becca's thumb and forefinger. It hurt a little but felt good too. Becca closed her eyes and asked how she knew about that kind of thing and Sharon said she'd actually trained in shiatsu and deep tissue massage; that was what she did in her college years to get by. She told Becca she would do bodywork on her if she wanted. Then she gave a quick, firm rub to the back of Becca's neck, saying she had "a few rocks back there." She kissed Becca goodbye on the lips but with mouth closed.

· · ·

HEART IN THROAT, Becca immediately called Rusty. She was eager to share the news with him. Also, it was a feel-good way to close the book on the whole creepy sexcapade.

"What are you saying?"

"I'm saying," she said enthusiastically, "that I'm supposed to go see him tomorrow morning—some place on Gower. Rusty, I am so totally terrified!"

"Supposed to go *where*," he said testily. Obtuse.

"This address on—no, Ivar. To see Spike Jonze! Oh my God, I have to rent *Adaptation* . . . I mean, I already saw it but not for a while. And I never saw *Human Nature*—but that's by a different director, not Spike [she was already on a first-name basis]. Still, it's by Charles Kaufman— I mean, he wrote it—so I probably *should* see it. . . . And Annie says there's some other movies—the one George Clooney directed, that Drew's in—I should— *Ohmygod*, Rusty, I looked on IMDb and Spike's from Maryland, where *Annie's* from! Did you know he was an actor? He was in that movie *The Game* and that movie *Three Kings*? But I don't think I'm going to rent those. Not until he gives me a part!"

"*Would you please shut the fuck up?*"

"What?"

The air went out of her.

"So you called Elaine?" he said accusingly. "Or did she call *you*— did Elaine call you, Becca?"

"No! Rusty, what is *wrong*? Elaine had nothing to *do* with this. Sharon never even *heard* of her. Sharon said—"

"Sharon?"

"Sharon Belzmerz—"

"Sharon *who*?" he asked sarcastically.

"Sharon *Belzmerz*. She's a *casting director*, at *Warner Brothers*. I *told* you about her—I met her through Cyrus. She put me on tape."

"Oh. Sharon Bullshitz put you on tape. Oh! Oh. Right."

"I ran into her that night we were at the Four Seasons"—here she did start to cry, with the forced, fractured memory of in-suite high jinks. *Don't go there.* "Sharon said that someone saw my tape, some-one— But *why*—why are you so—"

"I *met* with Spike Jonze, OK? OK, Becca? I already fucking *met* with him. Do you hear what I'm saying? I know *all about* the 'look-alike' project. And they're not trying to find any 'Drews,' OK? I read the script, which not even the fucking *studio* has read, OK? He *gave* me the script. And they're *not* looking for *Drews.*"

"OK. All right." Her voice grew thin as she capitulated. "He just said he wanted to meet me." Hating herself for whining. For backing down. Hating him. Fighting for breath. "He saw my tape."

"Well," he said, voice dripping acid, "maybe *Sofia,* who's probably your *new best friend,* maybe *Sofia* is having a surprise party for old *Spike.* Remember the one you did for Cameron? In the Colony? The Colony's your hood! Well, maybe they need a *Drew* to hand out hors d'oeuvres and blow jobs."

"*Why* are you being so *mean?*"

"I don't like people doing snaky things around my back."

"But I *didn't*—"

"I'll take it up with Elaine."

"I *told* you, she didn't have anything to *do* with it."

"There isn't any reason for you to go see Mr. Jonze tomorrow, OK? Unless you want to be humiliated. But maybe you do. I forgot who I was talking to. Maybe that's your thing."

One-Man Show

KIT WAS ALONE onstage.

He had sublet the Delongpre Avenue space from the Metropolis troupe for a private, weeklong intensive with Jorgia Wilding. When he first landed in Hollywood, he'd attended the acting coach's legendary class. She was in her seventies now but hadn't lost her acumen—or her bite.

He slouched à la Monty Clift, slurring and stammering his words as he flailed about in bravura Method mode.

"No!" she yelled, cutting him off from her middle-row seat. "No no no no *no!*" She stood and shuffled toward him. Her head poked through an immense wide-knit purple poncho, like some crusty cartoon character caught in a fisherman's net. "You're gonna win an Oscar for this, all right—*an Oscar Mayer*. Cause that's what you're doing. You're *hot*dogging."

She climbed to the stage. Kit hung his head and waited, as a prisoner might to receive his blows.

"What are you doing? *What are you doing?* You doin brain injury? Or you doin retard? *I'm asking you:* Is this traumatic brain injury or is this mental retardation?"

"It's, uh, it's both," he said lamely.

"Both," she said, slack-jawed. As if that were the dumbest thing yet uttered by actor or man. No one could've said anything dumber.

"I guess I'm not sure," said Kit. "I'm finding my way."

"Well, you sure as hell are. We finally agree! And by the way, 'brain injury' for 'retarded' is like Cockney for Bostonian. They're *completely different languages*, OK? With their *own aphasical rhythms and syntax*." She took a deep, disappointed breath. "Kitchener, we've known each other a lot of years."

"Yes ma'am."

"Unless you dig deeper you're gonna be laughed off the screen. Folks are gonna think you're in a Farrelly Brothers movie. Sling Blade you're not; Sling Blade you don't want to be. But this isn't some TV movie, am I right? This gonna be a TV movie?"

"No ma'am."

"This is *Aronofsky*. He's very demanding. I know— I worked with Ellen for *Requiem*. *Very* smart and *very* demanding. And he won't let you get away with it, honey. So guess what: you've got homework. We need to unlearn you some bad habits. Bad movie star habits."

"If you say so, ma'am," said Kit.

He laughed, breaking the tension.

"Yeah, well I say so," said Jorgia, softening. "You want to be on Jimmy Lipton's show, doncha?" she said facetiously. "Have you done *Actors Studio* yet?"

"In fact I have, ma'am."

"You did?" She seemed genuinely surprised.

"Yes ma'am."

"I missed that one."

"That's probably a good thing."

"Well, you want to be asked back, don't you?"

"No ma'am, not really."

They both were laughing now. It was the end of their day and he was exhausted. She was indomitable.

"All right then, let's stop wasting time. I want you to sit on that cushion and center yourself!"

He assumed the pose of the Buddha, spine erect, eyes half-closed. Jorgia, an old yoga hand herself, sat opposite. She began to speak, trancelike: "All those years of meditating. All those years of clearing the mind. The discipline. The energy. Call on it. Call on emptiness. *Dérèglement*. Derange the senses. *Breathe*. Pull, from your root. Everything flows through you. Empty the mind. *Astonish* me. Astonish your*self*. Be still, in the core of you. Untangle. Undo. Erase Kit Lightfoot. Kit Lightfoot is overpaid for what he does. Kit Lightfoot doesn't *know* what he does. Kit Lightfoot doesn't have a clue. Kit Lightfoot doesn't know what he's capable of, the heights and depths he can reach. Kit Lightfoot is retarded, brain-damaged! Kit Lightfoot is the enemy. Erase Kit Lightfoot. Breathe. Go to that yoga place. *Yoga* means 'union.' Erase the self. Breathe. Forget the self. Breathe . . ."

Entities

REGGIE MARCK HAD a three o'clock meeting with a married couple. They had been referred by Rodrigo Muñoz, a well-known attorney who specialized in civil rights violations stemming from police misconduct. He was seeing them as a favor to Rodrigo, who'd sought Reggie's services after being too closely portrayed in a *Law & Order* episode a few seasons back. He felt maligned. Reggie had gotten a small but reasonable settlement and they'd become friends.

Rodrigo had told him some colorful stories about "the Munsters," and Reggie thought Lisanne might get a kick out of meeting them.

Lately, she'd been so dispirited. It seemed like she was gaining weight by the week. His wife thought he worried too much, but for Reggie, Lisanne was family. He asked her to sit in and take notes.

"Rodrigo said you were the Man," said Cassandra.

"I hope I can be helpful," said Reggie. "How's the big guy doing?"

"El jefe?" said Grady. "Still causin trouble. Stirrin it up."

"He keeps it real, though, that's for damn sure," said Cassandra.

"Sounds like Rod," said Reggie. "He's sharp."

"I call him the Brown Man of Renown."

"That's better than the Brown Turd!" said Grady.

They bantered like that until Mr. Dunsmore finally got to the point. "See—the thing is," he said, "that we want to make movies."

"But we don't know too much about it," said Cassandra. "Ain't our world. I mean, we're *learning*, don't get me wrong. Learnin *quick*. And we know a *shitload* of people—"

"A shitload."

"—in the business, but the bottom line is, if they're *successful*, they ain't really in too much of a hurry to say hello. Not to no *virgins*. And I can understand that. Shit, I'd be the same way. Show business is a *motherfucker*, it ain't a charity. Took 'em this long to get to where they're at and here comes some asshole wanting to know the secret of their success. *Hey, how'd ya do it! I wanna be rich too*! Know what I'm saying?"

"Absolutely," said Reggie, nodding.

"There are only so many pieces of the pie," said Grady.

"That's what *they* think," said Cassandra. "That's the fallacy in a nutshell, see, cause that is one hundred percent, gold-plated *bullshit*. There's *plenty* of apple pie to go around—cherry and blueberry too! Motherfuckers just *greedy*."

"*Greedy*," echoed Grady, like a pilgrim at a tent meeting. "Damn straight."

"And I ain't even sayin it's the Jews. Cause hell, they're the ones we need to be learning from."

Lisanne kept her head down and scribbled furiously, trying not to laugh.

"Rodrigo said we got to form a production company."

"That would seem a logical way to go," Reggie said.

"Goodie!" said Cassandra, clapping her hands. "Can you do that for us?"

"Not a problem."

"Does that cost a lot?"

"A few thousand dollars."

"We want to get into music publishing too—we want to own catalogs. Rodrigo said that's where the *real* money is."

"If the soundtrack of one of our movies takes off," said Grady, eyes on the prize, "we want to be *ready.*"

"We know *lots* of movie people," said Cassandra. "Actors and directors—agents and managers too. Hey, they come to *us*. Jimmy Caan calls us Playboy Mansion East."

"We live up on Mulholland, right across from Jack."

"We started renting the house out for movie locations—the Strokes are doing a video tomorrow, and Drew Barrymore might be there cause she's going out with someone in the band—but not cause we need the money. It's a cool way to make connections. It's all about networking."

"We're right across from Jack Nicholson."

"You already told him that, fool!"

"And Brando. We keep asking him to come over, and one day he will. He don't answer the phone. He's famous for that. We heard you gotta leave a message on the machine for his pet rat or somethin. That's the only way he'll pick up."

"We tried that. But he ain't called back."

"Oh he will. I know he will," said Grady, winking at Reggie like a crazed hillbilly. "Cause he's stone nuts. And he knows we're crazy enough for him to want to get to know us. We're his people!"

"Mr. Marck," said Cassandra. "If you can help us with the *legal* then we can have more of a foundation. Cause we're already lookin at scripts. Gonna put up a whole Web site like Kevin Spacey did so unknowns can submit screenplays."

"Tha's right."

"Gonna be *all over* Sundance. Want to do us a Project Greenlight too. But right now we couldn't get nothin goin if we *wanted* to. Rodrigo said we need an 'entity.' "

"Like a poltergeist!" said Grady.

"*Can* it, goon," she said, kicking at him.

"What you've got to do," said Reggie, "is come up with a name for the corporation. Lisanne will send the papers to Sacramento, and they'll do a search, for clearance. If the name isn't being used, you're good to go."

"Can we put you on retainer for company business?"

"You know, unfortunately, much as I'd like to, I wouldn't be able to take you on—that's not really my thing. But I'll happily refer you to someone who has that kind of day-to-day architecture already in place."

"Cool," said Cassandra. "We like architecture!"

"Ain't it cool?" said Grady, doing his Travolta.

"We already come up with a name," said his wife, proudly. "For the entity."

She rested a hand atop her gigantic stomach and smiled. Grady reached over to pat her swollen fingers.

"QuestraWorld," he said, beaming.

"QuestraWorld Film and Television Productions," Cassandra added. "Incorporated."

The Life of a Working Actress

SHE LAY ON a towel, on a *Six Feet Under* gurney.

They'd brought her in for another show. This time, the casting lady said that her face would probably be featured. Becca wondered if one of the actors who'd hit on her had arranged it. That seemed a little far-fetched.

She was bewildered that Rusty had been so harsh when she tried to tell him her good news. It came as a shock that he could be so insecure. But then she felt bereft and asinine, because she really knew nothing about this man. The first time she saw him, he was beating up some pathetic look-alike! She wondered if she should be afraid. With a shiver, she flashed on Grady trying to shoehorn his dick inside her. An upside-down Rusty looked into her eyes while reaching over to put his hands on her legs, spreading them for his friend. Thank God Grady was too loaded to do anything. Rusty was panting, and she could tell how much it excited him to be pimping her. (She still hadn't told Annie.) That's the kind of person she was dealing with. The man she'd fallen in love with.

Her back was killing her. When they were done shooting, she decided to treat herself to a massage. She was calling Burke Williams on her cell when Annie rang through. She said Becca should drive over to the theater on Delongpre *right now*—Kit Lightfoot was inside, rehearsing with Jorgia Wilding.

. . .

THEY SAT IN Annie's car smoking and waiting.

"What are they rehearsing for?"

"I don't know. I think a movie. Cyrus didn't say. I don't think he knows."

"Are you sleeping with him?"

"With Kit Lightfoot?"

"Heh heh."

"Oh! You mean with Cyrus."

"No, I meant with Jorgia."

"Hey, if it would make me a better actress . . ." They laughed, then Annie reconsidered the question. "Cyrus and I? We're *kind* of sleeping together."

"I love that. 'Kind of.' "

"Kinda sorta. Are you sleeping with *your* friend?"

Becca nodded reluctantly.

"Well *that's* not very enthusiastic," said Annie.

"Oh, it's pretty enthusiastic all right."

"*Really,*" said Annie, intrigued.

"Be careful," said Becca, putting it back on Annie. "I mean, he's the *director.*"

"I know. It's that old saying, 'Don't shit where you act.' "

"It's much harder to find a good acting company than it is someone to fuck."

There was movement at the front door of the theater. A worker-type came out—false alarm.

"I'm gonna split," said Becca. "Are you staying?"

"Guess I'll go. And don't *tell* anyone about this."

"About what?"

"Kit Lightfoot! It's supposed to be a *total secret.*"

"You should come get a massage with me."

"Where?"

"Burke Williams."

"I'm going to Koreatown for a sauna. It's cheaper."

*   *   *

WHILE BECCA GOT rubbed, her thoughts drifted lazily to the Colony. She fantasized that the look-alike movie was a big hit. Charlie Kaufman had written a part especially for her, and Rusty was OK with that because now Rusty was famous too. He and Becca were known in the magazines as having one of those reliably unreliable on-again, off-again relationships like Ben and Gwyneth, pre-J. Lo. But they would always be great friends. She was in Malibu, at a party at Spike and Sofia's. George Clooney and Nicole Kidman were there, and Pink and Drew and Leo and Kirsten and Tobey. Sofia's cousin Nic Cage was grilling Becca a hamburger while they talked to Charlie K about something funny that had happened during the making of *Adaptation.* She was walking on the beach with the wise and amazing Shirley MacLaine (always one of her faves, and her mom's too) and Francis Coppola, and Becca told the director how much she loved *Rumble Fish* and how she'd always thought of herself as the girl floating above the classroom. Then Becca was on Leno telling the already famous story of once being hired by Cameron Diaz as a Drew Barrymore look-alike for a surprise birthday party for Drew and how funny and ironic that was because of course now she and Cameron and Drew were *thisclose,* with Becca having subsequently been cast in *A Confederacy of Dunces.* Critics said she'd stolen all her scenes.

The masseuse dug too deep, interrupting Becca's pleasant jag. She was the type who never really listened when you said you wanted it light; you could tell them a hundred times and they'd just keep digging. For the rest of the rub, Becca tensed beneath the onslaught.

The Omen

ON HIS WAY to the production office, Kit zipped into the Coffee Bean, on Sunset. By now they were used to seeing him. Even though most of the customers and employees were actors, they kept their cool. They were careful not to get too ruffled.

"Next guest in line, please!"

The server was mildly retarded. He spoke loudly, with a perceptible slur—straight out of *I Am Sam*.

"A large latte please," said Kit. "With no foam."

The server called to the nose-ringed barrista at the machine. "One no-foam latte *large* for guest, please!" he exclaimed, turning back to Kit. "We are *living large*!" He used a gloved hand to point. "Your drink will be *there*, sir, in ohnee one minute!"

The barrista seized the quirky moment to exchange warm, sidewise looks with the superstar. Kit could see her tongue stud.

·   ·   ·

HE DROVE TO the Valley and hung with Darren. They were shooting in ten weeks, but the kind of barely suppressed anarchy that typically characterizes preproduction hadn't yet kicked in. Today, everything seemed under control.

A P.A. came in to say that Marisa had arrived.

Kit had met the actress before socially, with Viv. They small-talked before reading through the scene. Then Darren made a few suggestions and they started over, with a different approach. The director liked the way they worked off each other.

At the end of the afternoon, on the way to his car, Kit saw a man scurry toward him with a cockeyed, swivel-hipped gait. It was the retarded server from the Coffee Bean.

"Hi!"

He was nonplussed. Was the kid delivering cappuccinos on the lot?

"Hey," said Kit tentatively.

"Sorry to bother you but—I just wanted to say that I think the project with Aronofsky is *killer.*" The tilt and slur had miraculously evaporated.

"Who *are* you?" asked Kit.

"Larry Levine!" said the man, sunnily. "I'm an actor. Goin up as one of your rehab buds. *Kit Lightfoot* and *Darren Aronofsky*—I am *so stoked.* It was a total omen running into you this morning! I've only been there a week but it took me *months* to get that job. They don't even know I'm doin my 'research' thing. It's a whole different world out there when people think you're 'challenged'—"

"Hey, *fuck off.*"

Larry Levine stood there, perplexed and bleary-eyed.

"Don't draw me into your bullshit *process,* man. You want to perpetrate that nonsense on people, fine—"

"But Darren said—"

"I don't *give* a shit. Why would *I* want to fucking hear about it?"

"I'm sorry, man," said the dismayed actor. "I'm really sor—"

"Just stay away from me, OK?"

"I *totally respect* you. I—"

Kit got in his G-wagen and gunned it.

• • •

THAT NIGHT KIT and Alf were at the Standard, drunk on scorpions and laughing their asses off.

"You didn't get spammed, you got *Samed*! He fucking *Samed* you!" cried Alf, showering spittle onto his friend. "He *I Am Samed* you!"

"One *large* no-foam latte for guest!" said Kit, in spot-on imitation.

"That is *so fuckin genius.* Tell you one thing, man. You better make sure they don't *hire* this guy—it's Eve Harrington time!"

"We are *living large!*"

"Café latte?" said Alf, in his best Sean Penn improv. "Excellent choice, excellent choice!"

"Mr. Tourette's" stumbled over to join the dysfunctional fray.

"Shit motherfucker!" ticced Lucas, dusting off the clinical signs of what Alf called Golden Globe syndrome. "Shitpissfuckcunt. Tampaxdick down Grannie's throat! Fuck Mommy's hairynaziniggerass!"

Kit convulsed.

"I love my li'l guhl!" whimpered Alf, in emotional paroxysm. "Why you no think I c'n love her? You cannot take my li'l guhl! She the only-est thing I have!"

"Fuckpissnigger! West Nile smallpox shitstained babycunt JonBenet Elizabeth Smart sucksbeanerdick! Arf! Arf! Arf! AIDS! SARS! Sickle Cell! Arf! Arf!"

"Stop!" cried Kit, clutching his gut. "You have to stop!"

"Excellent choice! Excellent choice!"

"No more! No more! No more!"

Beginner's Mind

SHE WENT TO the Bodhi Tree on Melrose. A child was forming within her, already the size of a toenail. She was lost.

There was too much to learn. She stared awhile at the statues of saints and bodhisattvas inside the glass case. Of course, none compared with Kit's. There were crystals, beaded necklaces, and all manner of fetishes with centipedal arms. She wandered past meditation pillows, through aisles of Vedic texts and theosophy, to the only section that made any real sense: fiction. She scanned the volumes, her fingers settling upon *Siddhartha*. She dimly remembered reading it in high school. The pretty black-and-white cover hadn't changed.

Poetry followed, and she saw the fat book from her father's library—*The Hundred Thousand Songs of Milarepa*.

Loitering in Eastern Religions, she quick-study gleaned a Buddhist 101 introductory: the Three Jewels (*the Buddha, the Dharma, the Sangha*) and the Four Noble Truths—(1) suffering (*duhkha*), (2) origin of suffering (*trishna*), (3) cessation of suffering (*nirvana*), and (4) the Eightfold Path (*marga*). She flipped through the primer's pages but couldn't focus. Instead, she selected a book called *Spiritual Tourist.* That was what she felt like.

She grabbed the Upanishads, recognizing the title from the blond Bel-Air guru's mention. She picked up some incense, a poster of the Wheel of Becoming, and a few yoga magazines before returning to the shelf for *The Complete Idiot's Guide to Understanding Buddhism.* (Just thinking about which Eightfold Path to take first seemed exhausting.) She was going to buy a statue—a Tara or a Kali—but they were sort of pricey so she got some beautiful laminated cards instead. One was of the "Shakyamuni Buddha."

Tad Yatha Om Muni Muni Maha Muni
Shakyamuni Ye Soha

Seated on a lion throne, Shakyamuni Buddha holds his right hand in the earth-touching mudra. With this gesture he called upon the earth to witness his lifetimes dedicated to attaining enlightenment for the benefit of all beings and triumphed over Mara, Lord of Illusion.

Lisanne stood at the cash register while they ran her credit card. She was somehow ashamed—ashamed of her life—and was looking over her shoulder with random paranoia when Phil Muskingham materialized.

"Well, hello!"

"What are you doing here?"

She looked stricken, as if caught shoplifting.

"My therapist told me to pick up a lingam stone." He held the egg-shaped thing in an open hand for her to see.

"What is it?"

"It's supposed to balance energy—or something like that. What, are you a complete idiot?"

Lisanne was taken aback until she noticed him nodding toward the Day-Glo orange tome as the clerk bagged it.

"Yup, that's me," she said. "A total spiritual moron."

"I was going to call you," he said. "Are you free? I mean, do you have some time?"

"Sure."

"I mean now. Because you know what I was going to do? I was thinking of going over to the Self-Realization Center. Ever been?"

"I haven't. But you're so funny!"

"Why?" he said, with a smile that charmed her.

"I have trouble seeing you as the mystical type."

"Don't judge a book by its cover," he said, nodding again at the hidden Idiot's Guide. Finally, she laughed.

.   .   .

FOR SOME REASON, Lisanne had never been to the Sunset Boulevard Self-Realization temple or church or whatever it was. She'd passed the white-domed tower a thousand times and every once in a while read about the organization in the *L.A. Times* or heard from a friend how beautiful the grounds were. Phil said it was founded by the man who wrote *Autobiography of a Yogi*.

The adjoining well-kept park was peaceful in that cliché kind of way, and politically correct in its respectful inclusion of all major religions. A trail circled the lake (an entry sign warned not to feed the fish, who only "pretended to be hungry"). People sat on benches reading or meditating. Unobtrusive shrines to Gandhi and the Buddha garnished the walkways, along with plaques engraved with quotes from Bible and Bhagavad Gita alike. Phil couldn't help but remark what a valuable piece of real estate the parcel would be should the Fellowship ever decide to divest.

They sat on a small viewing platform by the water. He broke the requisitely contemplative moment by offering sympathies on the death of Lisanne's father—evidently, the Loewensteins had filled him in. He spoke of his own loss. His parents, in their late forties when he was conceived, had died within a year of each other not too long ago. Until then, Phil said he had deliberately shunned the trappings and responsibilities of the family fortune. A wry proviso of his dad's will (he didn't elaborate) forced him to leave the cocoon to help his sister run the charitable foundation that bore their name.

"You'd love Mattie," he said. "In fact, you'll love her on Saturday. Because that's when the three of us are going to have lunch."

Catharsis

RUSTY TOOK BECCA to Les Deux.

On the way in, they wandered over to the restaurant-owned gallery on the far side of the courtyard. There was an exhibition of bright, poster-size photographs, self-portraits of a fortysomething woman frankly displaying her genitalia. The lady behind the desk said that the subject of "the suite" was Randy Quaid's wife, a film director. Becca couldn't really make any sense of it. Was it porno? She tried to summon an image of what Randy Quaid looked like but kept seeing Dennis Quaid instead.

"I'm sorry," said Rusty, a few minutes after the waiter took their order. "I didn't mean to go off on you the other day."

"It really hurt me."

"I know. Sorry I'm such a dick."

"I didn't even know anything *about* it, Rusty," she said, quickly becoming emotional. She felt like a child. "I never even *talked* to Elaine."

"I know." He delicatedly put his hand on hers. "I know. Look— there's going to be a read-through of the piece."

"What piece?"

"The script. The Spike Jonze thing, on Saturday. I think you should come."

"But I already called Sharon and told her I *couldn't*. That I couldn't even *meet*—" She whined and fidgeted in her seat.

"It's perfect that way—almost better. That it doesn't come through 'official' channels."

"I just think it would be weird."

"No, it's fine. It's better that you were 'reluctant.' "

"How can I just *show up*, Rusty?" she asked, with a touch of anger.

"Cause you'll be with *me*."

"So you're doing the read-through." She stared indifferently into space, resigned to the web he had woven. "I think I saw you with him, at the Rose Café."

"You show up, looking totally Drew. Everyone'll say: 'That's the Drew girl! The one we were supposed to meet.'"

"Why can't I just call Sharon?"

"Go ahead. Call her," he said. She couldn't tell if he was getting nasty again. "But at this point, I think it'd be a mistake."

"She's *mad* at me."

"Then don't call her," he said, laughing amiably.

"She got really mad when I told her I didn't want to do it," she said, tearing up again. "After you yelled at me, I called and said I didn't want to go up for a 'look-alike'—this whole long thing about how I was just doing that kind of work to pay the bills and if I was going to make it, I wanted to make it as *myself*. And Sharon said I was being really stupid and that she was the one who discovered the guy who won the Golden Globe for playing James Dean *and* the girl who played Judy Garland on that TV movie and how *those* actors were doing really, really *well*. She said that if you have *talent*—and I did, she said that I did!—then that talent comes shining through and that if you really want to make it you just have to take whatever opportunity comes your way. She said it was a really incredible opportunity to have a meeting with a famous director and that I'd come out a winner either way no matter what because even if they didn't think I was right, I would stay in their minds for future projects. She said that actors would *kill* to have a meeting with Spike Jonze—and I felt really bad, Rusty!" She began to cry, full-blown. "I came off as such a jerk! Because I was loyal to you and didn't understand! I was loyal and I didn't understand why you wouldn't want nice things to happen for me! I just couldn't understand!"

A Gathering at the Gubers'

KIT AND VIV went to a gathering at the Gubers' for a visiting holy
man. H.H. Penor Rinpoche was the head of a monastery in Mysore
whose lineage was associated with Kit's teacher, Gil Weiskopf Roshi.

It was an odd assortment of people. Matthew Perry, Ray Manzarek,
and Paula Poundstone listened in rapt attention alongside a contingent of poets, meditators, and a dozen or so saffron-robed monks. But
the person whose presence interested Kit most was Ram Dass.

They'd met a number of years ago at a benefit in San Francisco,
long before Ram Dass had suffered a debilitating stroke. The onetime
Harvard professor and cohort of Timothy Leary had always been
charismatic. Now, paralyzed on one side, he radiated "fierce grace."
His dancing eyes still burned with celestial fire; the famous white hair
ensorcelled his head like candescent wisps of cloud. After the talk, Kit,
Viv, and Matthew went over to say hello.

Ram Dass spoke slowly but without the slur-and-drag Kit had
expected. He remembered seeing Kit at Tassajara in the early nineties
and knew Gil Weiskopf Roshi quite well. He spoke fondly of his own
guru and said that when Maharaj-ji was alive, he wished they could be
together more often. But now that his guru was dead, "I'm with him
all the time!" Kit asked about the experience of having a stroke, and
Ram Dass showed his sense of humor to be fully intact. He mentioned a book he once wrote called *How Can I Help?* The moment had
come, he said, to write the sequel: *Who's Going to Help Me?*

 .   .   .

"I FELT KIND OF mercenary," said Kit, as they drove down the hill.
"When I saw Ram Dass, the whole actor thing kicked in. I couldn't
wait to go say hello, then listen to how he talked. I wanted to try it out
on Jorgia."

"You are *so bad*," said Viv, smiling. "But that's why you're so good."

"I thought he'd be much more Kirk Douglas." He shrugged sardonically. "I was extremely disappointed."

"You know who Ram Dass kind of reminded me of? Larry Hagman. But I *loved* the man who spoke. What was his name?"

"Penor Rinpoche. He's the real deal."

"You met him before?"

"In Mysore."

"I've seen pictures of that place. A real eyesore."

"Haw haw."

"Heh heh. Now *who* is he again? Penor—"

"A Nyingma master. A *tulku.*"

"What is that?"

"A reincarnation of one of the lamas of his tradition."

"Are you going to help them?"

"They do very well without me, thank you very much. I'm going to give them money for a clinic, in honor of Gil. That's who first took me there."

They fell silent. He stared out the window as the dark, luxurious world whooshed past.

"I was reading," said Kit, "about this tantric practice where you learn to use your cock like a straw."

"What do you mean!"

"You, like, put it down and suck stuff up."

"*No way.*"

"Hoover time. First you practice with water, then milk—then some kind of oil. At the end, when you're a certified master, you're supposed to be able to do it with mercury. *Suck it up.*"

"That is so weird."

"It's about drawing your semen and the woman's come up to the soma chakra."

"Oh! I'm all about that! Kids, don't try that at home. Penor Rinpowhatever doesn't do that, does he?"

"He hasn't shown me, personally."

"Tara Guber should have a workshop."

"Peter would be all over it! Hey, are you hungry?"

"Kind of. Want to go to the Polo Lounge?"

"Or we could just go to the Bel-Air."

"Nah—too tired. Let's go home."

"We've grown elderly, huh."

They passed through the gate, onto Sunset.

"Getting psyched about your movie?" she asked.

"Yeah. Yeah, I am. *Super*psyched."

"That's so great, Kit. It's not scaring you?"

"Why should it?"

"People are gonna think you're making fun of retards."

"People are going to think whatever."

"Do you want an Academy Award?"

"Do I want an Academy Award?"

"I asked you first," she said, impishly.

"You know what I want? You know what I *really* want? I want to be *excited* about what I do while passing my time on this fucked-up, dying planet. *That's* what I want. And you know what? This little movie has me juiced about acting again. This little movie has me juiced about my fucking *practice*. At the end of the day, I just want to be able to live with myself, Viv. Which lately, hasn't been so easy."

She paused before serenely repeating: "But do you want an Academy Award?" Her tongue licked her lips. "Just answer the question."

"Don't fuck with me," he said, mad-dogging her.

They laughed.

The Getty

KIT MOANED then screamed.

Viv bolted upright.

"Baby, you OK?"

"Yeah. I'm OK."

"What was it?"

"Whoa! Fuckin *strange*."

He shook himself like a beach dog after a wave.

Viv passed a bottle of water.

"I was hugging him or some shit."

"Who?"

"The Getty kid."

"What Getty kid?"

"The one with the cut-off ear. But there was something *really fuckin creepy* . . ."

"What."

"I met John Paul—man, a *long* time ago. I don't even think I was into my practice yet. I was hanging with Gianna Portola. She was fuckin *wild* before she got sober." He laughed. Viv was glad he was out of the panic zone. "She brought me over to meet him. They used to be lovers. Somehow I kind of remember that she was still balling him, after it happened."

"After he was kidnapped?"

"After the stroke."

"It was a drug thing, right? A coma thing?"

He shivered again and pulled from the Aquafina. "I was curious, so she took me to see him at his house in Laurel Canyon. He got around in this supervan, *Ironside* style. Shit, maybe he still lives up there. It was like a very cool house with an elevator to the master bedroom. We rode it up and Gianna introduced me. Kinda ghoulish but kinda cool. He and Gianna started talking. It was a trip! The guy was talking like this, Viv, I swear to God: *argabuggagoogagoolalalalmamamaooga-googuhgooguhgoo.* I couldn't understand shit! But Gianna was just *gabbing* away. Back and forth, back and forth. And John Paul seemed to be having a really good time. He was excited that I was there—like having anyone new around was a fun thing for him. I think that's why she brought me."

"So what did you dream?"

His face darkened. "It was *sad*. Sad, sad, sad. And he—in the dream—he, like, gave me a weird hug. Weird. Like *prolonged*. I don't know. Can't remember now."

She softly rubbed his head. "Poor Bumpkin!"

L.A. Confidential

HE AWOKE TO the jingle-jangle light of morning. He heard voices and stood, swaddling himself in the duvet. He lit a cigarette and stepped over Mr. Raffles.

Her voice grew louder as he neared the guest bath.

Viv sat on the toilet. Her assistant stood a few feet away with pad and pen. The bath was running. The room was steamy and rank.

"I am *so* backed up from the codeine," she said when she saw Kit, before directing her words to Gingher. "I need you to get me a laxative from Wild Oats. I think it's called Quiet Moment."

She farted loudly then laughed.

"They should call it Unquiet Moment," said Kit. "Jesus, Viv, why don't you let Gingher take five?"

"Because I *can't*, Bumpkin, I'm on a *schedule*. I need to get gifts for the *crew*." To Gingher: "Or Metamucil, but it has to be sugar-free." To Kit: "What do you think about those Prada cell phone holders?"

"What do I think? I think you should concentrate on moving your bowels."

"We *have* to get one of those Japanese toilets, Kit. They douche and dry you. You never need to use toilet paper again."

"You wouldn't be able to wipe in front of people. Won't that be a deprivation?"

"I'm getting everyone a Mini Cooper."

"The crew?"

"The *cast*, silly. Cell phone holders for the crew. And I'm going to New York in about forty-five minutes. You knew that, didn't you?"

"No. Why?"

"I already *told* you, Bumpkin. I'm doing Letterman."

"You told me two weeks ago. When you comin back?"

"Sunday. So give me a smooch."

He edged past Gingher and knelt at the altar of the bowl, hands on Viv's downy thighs, fingertips reaching the matching ॐ at the fold of her crotch. The assistant shyly averted her eyes while the actress closed her own to receive the courtly kiss. As their lips touched, she oopsed and the water plashed. Kit stood, shaking his head in mock disgust. Viv guffawed, involuntarily farting.

"*Sorry*, Gingher," said Kit. The efficient, overweight girl had comically stepped back, with a forced smile. "Jesus," said Kit to Viv. "Who have you become, Anna Nicole Smith? Who have *we* become?"

"Liza Minelli and David Gest."

"Right," said Kit. "I'm Liza, you're David."

"Don't worry, honey," said Viv, regaining composure as she wiped herself. "Gingher signed a confidentiality clause. It's ironclad."

Viv farted again. This time, everyone laughed.

"I'm outta here," said Kit. He turned to Gingher and said, "Can you see why it took me so long to pop the question?"

"Maybe you should have *pooped* the question," said Viv.

He had something to say about that, but she was laughing so hard she couldn't hear. He took his wraparound floor-length comforter and shuffled out, shaking his head.

"Bumpkin!" shouted Viv. "Buy me something nice while I'm in New York! There could be a terrorist attack! You might never see me again!"

Supreme Bliss-Wheel Integration

LISANNE WAS ENTERING the second trimester. All the mommy magazines said that any day now she was supposed to start feeling better. Less fatigued, sexy even. She felt worse than ever.

A cashier at Erewhon vibed her pregnancy and told her about yoga with Gurmukh at Golden Bridge. Lisanne got the time wrong and arrived at the end of a class. She stood outside the musty, lily-scented room while rich, distended women danced to drum and sitar. When they began to chant, Lisanne fled.

. . .

MATTIE MUSKINGHAM, Phil's older sister, was petite and unneurotic. Lisanne liked her right away because she was one of those no-nonsense gals who called a spade a spade. Lisanne still couldn't believe her luck—she had the feeling this sort of luncheon was arranged whenever Phil met someone who was potential relationship material. But she felt so fat. Her self-esteem was at its lowest ebb, and on top of it all, she was living a serious lie.

Rita Wilson was at a patio table with a girlfriend, and Mattie went to say hello. The Hankses were on the board of the Muskingham Family Foundation.

When the bill came, Mattie asked Phil if he'd forgotten about "the meeting," and he rolled his eyes. He pretended to cop an attitude and said he would go only if they brought Lisanne. Mattie (who it seemed to Lisanne was also playacting) told her brother that he knew it was "strictly against the rules to bring in outsiders." Her delivery was a bit arch. "We'll just say she's family," retorted Phil. When Lisanne asked if they were talking about AA, the two laughed out loud. "I wish," said Phil, cryptically.

As they left the Ivy at the Shore, the sibs were as giddy as children initiating a new friend into a favorite game. They told her not to ask anything more about where they were going; it would be their little surprise. Phil made Lisanne promise that, if pressed, which was unlikely, she would inform "the group" she was their half sister. No, said Mattie, not half sister—first cousin.

They swept through the lobby of Shutters, taking the stairwell to a lower floor. Lisanne was steered toward a series of conference rooms at ocean level. A few nondescript types congregated outside one of the smaller suites. The Muskinghams called some of them by first name, casually introducing their "poor relation" before going in.

A caterer put the final touches on a buffet. The arrival of Dr. Janowicz, an affable, fiftyish man in horn-rims, made for cohesion. In rumpled tweeds, he was a parody of the congenial, humanist professor, with a touch of *New Yorker* cartoon psychotherapist thrown in. In short order, everyone gathered fruit, bagels, and coffee, finding seats at a round table in the room's center.

Desultory chatter was broken by the unexpected, somewhat jarring words of the ringleader. "I want to die in my sleep, in peace, like my father," Dr. Janowicz said somberly, initiating a hush from the group. With the timing of a pro, he added, "Not like the *other people* who were in the car!"

When the punch line sunk in, they all busted a gut. Decorum restored, Dr. J, as they called him, said he wanted "to just throw a theme out there" and see how people reacted. He interlaced his fingers and hung his head a moment, as if summoning a word from the depths. He looked up, grinning, and said, "Envy."

Group groan.

"Oh God," said a thin-faced woman in ivory bangles. "Do we *have* to go there?"

The roundelay began, unruly and hilarious, anecdotes in which the covetousness of friends and strangers was given subtle shade or boldly drawn. Avarice segued neatly to rage; rage to impotence; and finally, to envious feelings of their own—envy toward those with simpler lives and the imagined serenity that went along. Eating disorders, insomnia, and depression were blithely noted (and their Rx handmaidens too), along with yo-yoing self-worth, psychosomatic illness, free-floating anxiety, and general feelings of impoverishment amidst plenty. Toward the end, Dr. J asked each person what nice thing they were planning to do for themselves in the coming week. When he got to Lisanne, she surprised herself by saying she was going to buy a mandala that she'd seen in the glass case of a bookstore but had thought too expensive. The group thought it a glorious idea. The puzzling session ended with everyone standing and holding hands in silent prayer.

•   •   •

"LONELYHEARTS," said Phil as they drove her home.

"I thought some of them were really nice," said Lisanne.

"Kibbitzers," said Phil. "Whiners. How many meetings do we have left to go to, Matt?"

"I think maybe four?" his sister said. "It is by far the single most perverse thing Dad ever engineered."

"And that's saying a lot."

"I don't understand," said Lisanne.

"We *have* to go to the meetings," said Phil.

"Or we're disinherited," chimed in Mattie.

"Attendance being mandated by a closely monitored stipulation of our eccentric father's last will and testament."

"But what *is* it—exactly? I mean, who *are*—"

"A support group for rich people," said Phil. "No one in that room has less than fifty million."

"The meetings were hatched during the dot-com boom and kept on. For what they call sudden wealth syndrome. Funny thing is, I don't think anyone in the industry has that kind of money anymore."

"Oh bullshit," said Phil. "Tell it to Larry Ellison's grandkids. Them that got, still got."

"Not for much longer," said Mattie, ominously. "Don't you read *The Guardian*? America isn't long to be. The great experiment is nearly done! As the Romans', our population shall be leveled and its cities rendered unto farmland. Hopefully, Bechtel will do the rebuild—we still have shares."

"That joke he told about his father dying," said Phil, "may have been the funniest joke I have ever heard in my life."

.   .   .

LISANNE LEFT FOR the Coffee Bean & Tea Leaf on Larchmont. She had just scooped up her blue-wrapped Sunday *New York Times* and was walking to the car when a man came toward her with a package.

"Are you Lisanne McCadden?" he said.

"Yes."

"I have a delivery."

She signed and went back in the house, thinking What kind of messenger delivers things on a Sunday? She opened the rich wooden box, gingerly removing the gold-flecked tissue that surrounded the dark, dense core. She gasped. The object in repose was an exquisite lotus bud, its metallic petals sensuously opened to expose what a typed enclosure identified as the tantric deity at its center: Paramasukha-Chakrasamvara—otherwise known as Supreme Bliss-Wheel Integration Buddha.

" . . . to save you the trip to the Bodhi Tree," read the handwritten note. "Anyhow, *my* mandala can beat up *your* mandala. Ha ha ha. Ever yours, Phil."

Top of the World

HE SAID THEY were there for the Spike Jonze table-read, but the valet in the Chateau garage told Rusty that he had to park in a lot down the street.

Becca, in full Drew mode, turned heads when they entered the penthouse. She wasn't an official invite and was paranoid that someone was going to eighty-six her, but the crowd (and crowd of look-alikes) was large and the mood, casual and festive. She blended in.

Rusty went straight over to Spike and introduced Becca as "my girl-friend Drew." The diffident director grinned and said he was glad they could make it. He was quite the gentleman. The whole "Sharon controversy" about her canceling or not canceling never even came up, and suddenly she was grateful to Rusty for his thoughtful insistence that she join him. She liked the "my girlfriend" part too, though she *was* a little disappointed when Spike said the true Drew wasn't able to make it. Becca started tripping, wondering if that meant maybe *she'd* be reading Drew's lines, but then she snapped to the fact that she was clueless—Rusty hadn't told her a thing about Charlie Kaufman's screenplay, so she had no way of knowing what kind of lines the true Drew had or if she had any at all. (Maybe the Drew look-alike had some, or maybe the part was silent.) She decided the best thing was to just keep her mouth shut and have no expectations. Don't worry, be happy—happy to be there at all and *super*happy to have been chatting with Spike Jonze, the amazing auteur.

They got some diet Cokes and wandered to the terrace.

The city view was awesome. A cluster of look-alikes huddled in a group: the Cameron that she already knew, a Kit Lightfoot, a Benicio, a Billy Bob, and a guy named Joe Sperandeo, who had been featured in *Los Angeles* magazine because of his resemblance to Brad Pitt. Some girl who got fixated on the true Brad and broke into his house to take a nap ended up getting fixated on Joe too. Becca heard the laugh of the true Cameron, who came clopping onto the terrace with Sofia in tow. She laid eyes on Becca and yelped with pleasure, throwing her arms around her like a long-lost friend. Becca almost peed her pants.

"Isn't she *amazing*?" said Cameron to Sofia. "She was at Drew's birthday—you were in Japan. Drew was *so freaked out*. I mean, it was *really disturbing* for her, but in a *good* way."

Becca did her "flip your goddamn hair" shtick and Cameron tittered. Then Sofia, who seemed even nicer than her husband if that could be possible, told Becca how incredible she looked and Becca was bashfully glad. She somehow mustered the poise to say how much she loved *The Virgin Suicides* before Rusty reclaimed her, rakishly introducing himself while the other look-alikes excitedly hovered close by. Cameron giggled over Rusty's resemblance to his temperamental counterpart (there had been a buzz that the true Russell, already cast, was expected for the reading) and howled when she saw her own doppelganger eavesdropping at the edge of the impromptu clique. The Cameron look-alike's teeth looked like giant, lipstick-stained Chiclets.

As Becca and Rusty wandered back to the living room, John Cusack arrived. He was much taller than she had pictured. Benicio Del Toro came in close behind him, and his eyes were so hooded that she thought she would die; he was the only man in the room who could compete with her Rusty. Someone pointed out Charlie Kaufman, who was there with a girl named Kelly Lynch, not the actress but the personal assistant to the songwriter Leonard Cohen. Along with working actors and Sofia's friend Zoë, other Silverlake denizens arrived—Donovan Leitch and his sister Ione Skye, Moon Zappa, Amy Fleetwood, and a daughter of Robert Wagner and Natalie Wood (Becca didn't catch the name). They grabbed scripts from a box and took seats.

Annie was always telling Becca about hip industry table-reads, and now she was finally participating in one herself. (She wasn't actually at the table; she was on a folding chair just behind Rusty, and that suited her fine.) She was so proud to be with her peers, and her dashing man. Her looks had got her in the door, and of that she wasn't going to be ashamed. She was determined to be assessed by her merits as an actress alone. The others—the cheap Cameron and the Kit, the sleazo Billy Bob and off-the-rack Benicio—were lame and starstruck. They looked sad and out of place, like the losers left standing in musical chairs. She hoped the people who mattered would see through her Drewness to the Becca Mondrain within. If anyone in the world had the genius and sheer aplomb to look and *really* see, to make the most of who she was underneath it all, well then surely that person was Spike Jonze.

Coup de Grâce

KIT PLAYFULLY POSED with a family of German tourists outside Fred Joaillier, on Rodeo. A small crowd began to gather. More tourists with cameras ran over from the other side of the street.

It didn't take long to pick out the engagement ring—a pear-shaped sixteen carats. He flirted with the older saleswoman throughout the transaction. A guard had the valet bring the car to the alley. Kit ducked out, to avoid the mob.

. . .

THAT NIGHT HE and Alf had a late supper at Bar Marmont.

"Where's Viv?"

"Letterman—I already told you that."

"Well excuuuse me."

"Goin senile?"

"Nope. Goin retard," said Alf.

"Retread."

"Tardo. Tardatious."

"So what's happening with you and Cameron?"

"Why?"

"You still having a thing?"

"Uh . . . it's not really going on."

"What the dillio?"

"I think she was playin me."

"Oh. I see. You got your heart broken."

"No—"

"Oh man, you *did*."

"*No*—" said Alf, suppressing a smile.

"Oh shit! Oh no! She blew you off!"

"Don't bust my balls."

"Threw you away like a fuckin tampon! Took your heart-cherry and *stawmped* on it!"

"You are *outta control*."

"*These boots are made for walkin'! And that's just what they'll do!*"

A square in a sport jacket walked over.

"You're Kit Lightfoot." He looked at Alf and said, "I know you too."

"You won the lotto," said Alf, in freeze-out mode.

"You guys are really great actors. Can I bring my girlfriend over? She *said* it was you, but I didn't believe her. She's a big fan. Maybe you could sign her hand—or her tit!—or something."

"You know what?" said Kit. "We're off tonight."

The square didn't understand.

"We're not workin. We're just hangin," said Alf, grinning professionally.

"That's cool," said the square. He was embarrassed but sucked it up. "How bout if you don't sign anything. Just come and say hi when you leave. That'd mean a whole lot to her."

"I don't think so," said Alf. Can you believe this?

"Sorry," said Kit.

"We're not doing the Universal Tour thing tonight," said Alf. "We're off the tram."

"Some other time," said Kit.

"OK—right on. Catch you later."

After he left, Alf said, "Are they letting anyone into this fuckin place now?"

A security guy came and apologized. When Kit was in the club, they liked to keep a closer watch.

"We're off the tram," said Kit, with a laugh. "What the fuck does *that* mean?"

. . .

THE VALET HAD the G-wagen in front. Alf got in while Kit bolted to the liquor store for cigs. He was at the counter paying and didn't see the square, who swiftly approached and brained him with a bottle. The girlfriend screamed. Kit collapsed. They ran out. The clerk gave chase. The actor's foamy rictus looked like a sardonic smile.

"And fuck you too, superstar!" yelled the square from the street.

Late Bloomers

HE SHIFTED IN her belly as she tried to sleep. (She'd finally gone to the OB-GYN and learned it was a boy.) The movement stopped. She drifted off.

Yesterday, Robbie had called to inquire listlessly about the baby. She didn't feel at all connected to her high school lover. It didn't even seem like he could be the father, but no other possibility existed. She had a fleeting born-of-the-ether thought.

Midnight. She stirred awake and padded to the living room. The petals of the mandala were closed. (She liked closing them at night and opening them in the morning, but now that she had awakened, Lisanne wanted to commune. She wanted the deity to share her bumblebee breaths—she'd become official celebrant and caretaker of the numinous, night-blooming mandala.) Leaning over to delicately midwife the Buddha's coppery dilation, Lisanne had a wicked thought: I could sleep with Phil then tell him the baby is his.

She lay on the couch and drew the blanket up. A cold lunar light shone down upon the spirit-machine. She remembered the handsome guru talking of the moon-in-the-water meditation and wondered why she hadn't gone back for the weekly dharma talks. She wanted—needed—to know more about the nectar that dripped from

the crown of the head, saturating one with bliss. She wanted—
needed—to be in the world, not of it.

And more than anything, she wished to learn the prayer called
"The Power of Regret."

Absent Without Leave

"YOU CAN GO ahead and see him now," said the nurse.

Alf was in a special waiting area, away from the civilian hordes.
Two cops were finishing paperwork in the corridor. The tallest
approached with pad and pen; Alf instinctively knew what he was
after.

"Mind if I get your John Hancock? My wife would never forgive me."

"I'll give you my Herbie Hancock too," he said, taking the pen.

"Her name's Roxanne."

He signed: "To Roxanne (put on the red light!), All my love, Alf
Lanier."

• • •

THEY LED HIM to a curtained ER stall. Kit was sitting up. An
unused, blood-speckled emesis basin rested in his lap. His hair was
matted at the wound. His face looked pale and drained. The right eye
was puffy, but he smiled reassuringly.

"How ya doin, Dog?" asked Alf, in the grimly serious tones of an
intimate.

"I'm OK," said Kit.

"Man, you scared the *shit* out of me." Alf was relieved and excited
at once. "The liquor store guy ran out screaming your name— I was
like, *What?* I went and saw you lying there . . . it was very Bobby-
Kennedy-at-the-Ambassador! I was, like, *Where's Sirhan Sirhan?*"

"What time is it?"

"Almost three."

"This bullshit's gonna be in the papers," said Kit. "I better give Viv
a shout or she'll freak. Can I have your cell?"

"That mother*fucker*—it was the asshole who wanted us to sign his girlfriend's tits."

"They catch him?"

"I don't know. The cops had me signing fuckin autographs, I was too busy to ask. They *will*. The liquor guy supposedly totally got his plates. He's my hero, Dog."

Alf handed him his phone. Kit swung a bare leg out from under the blanket. "It's six o'clock in New York. Fuck it, I'll call from home. Let's go."

"Whoa whoa whoa! What?"

"I'm outta here. I don't like hospitals."

"Did they say it was cool?"

"Frankly, Scarlett, I don't give a shit."

"*Whoa.* Dog, you have to *seriously chill.* I mean, you start shooting in, like, a week, right? You should stay over so they can observe you."

"Observe *this.*"

"Just overnight, Dog—"

"You know what? This is the place where my mom died, OK? And you know what? Just *do this* with me, Alfalfa. I'll be cool. Everything's everything, Dog. Come stay at the house. Have a sleepover. You can observe me all you want."

"Did you tell them you were splitting?"

"Yeah, because I have a splitting fucking headache."

"Hey man, I'm *serious.* That guy didn't just give you a little tap. Did they give you something for pain?"

"They don't do that with a head injury."

"They should give *me* something."

"Viv's got all kinds of shit. Beaucoup Vicodin from her root canal." A pause, then: "So, you gonna stay over? Cause if you can't, that's cool too. I'll be fine by myself."

"Of course I'm gonna stay over. I just don't think it's one of the brightest ideas you've ever had. But whatever."

"Thanks, Dog. Just don't make a move on me while I'm sleeping."

A Letter Home

BECCA WROTE a long letter to her mom.

She told how she met Spike Jonze because Sharon, a wonderful casting agent, had given him her audition tape and he'd been duly impressed. She enclosed a printout of his bio and credits from the Internet, in case Dixie didn't know who he was (highlighting the part that said he was married to Sofia Coppola). She had planned to be on the conservative side and not reveal much more, but couldn't help herself and wrote that Spike was in preparation for a film and that the writer Charles Kaufman, Mr. Jonze's frequent collaborator (who of course had written *Being John Malkovich,* starring John Cusack and Cameron Diaz and *Adaptation,* starring Nicolas Cage and the venerable Meryl Streep), was quite possibly, if everything turned out right, going to create a small role tailored for yours truly. She was careful not to say anything about the new project actually being about look-alikes or bearing a look-alike "theme" because Dixie already knew about her daughter's occasional private party and convention gigs where she was employed to be a Drew, and Becca didn't want to give her the wrong idea or confuse her. She didn't want her erroneously thinking that she was being considered for a part in any capacity less than that of a legit, featured player.

At first, she didn't include anything about the new man in her life either. She *did* mention that Sadge was on the other side of the world editing a reality show and how that was probably not such a bad thing, "because between you, me, and the bedpost" they hadn't been getting along all that well. But then she couldn't help herself and, after inquiring as to the general health of her dad and brother, hinted that she was "kind of interested in someone" who also happened to be under simultaneous consideration for a role in the upcoming "Spike Jonze Untitled." She added that "this person" was incredibly handsome and people thought he looked like Russell Crowe, whom she knew to be one of her mom's faves.

She wrote these things down instead of saying them on the phone because it was easier that way to sort her thoughts. Whenever Becca called home, she thought she sounded like a flake. Dixie always wound up asking when was she coming back to Waynesboro—like her stint as a Hollywood failure was, in her mom's use of the phrase, a "fate accomp." Anyway, Becca was superstitious that the more contact she had with family, the less chance she would have at success, by her own lights. It was better, she surmised, to keep a healthy distance between oneself and one's roots (not just geographical)—that, in order to grow, a person needed to allow a great big space for the mystery which was their birthright to shine through. Besides, by writing everything down she got a kind of overview of her life; it untangled her mind and gave her ballast. (She'd kept a journal as a girl, so it was second nature.) Putting pen to paper, she even got a funny sense of entitlement as an actress, though there was nothing really yet to show for her little boasts and efforts. At the end of the letter, she thought of mentioning the Dunsmores, because after all they *were* potential Hollywood players with whom she might find herself in production, but decided not to, feeling still somewhat tainted from the drug-fueled encounter at the Four Seasons. It mortified her to imagine her mother ever knowing such a thing had happened.

There would be plenty of time to call Dixie, down the line—and who knew? Maybe by then she'd have married a big wig or won a Golden Globe newcomer's award or won a million dollars on a reality show (that, preferably, Sadge had nothing to do with). Maybe, God forbid, she'd get a weird settlement like the Dunsmores. Stranger things had happened . . . Maybe she and Rusty were on their way to being famous and she could go on the Leno show the way Brittany Murphy did, talking all sweet and humble, if that were possible, but Brittany pulled it off, about how before they broke up she and Ashton rented their first private jet so they could go back to Cedar Rapids, where Ashton is from, for Christmas, and then on to New Jersey to spend the rest of the holidays with Brittany's family. (She wasn't sure if the thing with Demi was trading up or trading down. But she knew it wouldn't last.) Still, Becca made sure to say to herself that if she never did the Spike film, if it wasn't in the cards, that would be OK too. She could always go back to Sharon. After the debacle, she sent the casting agent flowers and everything had been patched up (with promises of a "shiatsu date"): Sharon would get her auditions and meetings whether she scored the Spike gig or not. And if she didn't, Becca theorized that, at the very worst, which really wasn't that bad, it would be OK to be known as "the Drew girl" who almost worked with Spike Jonze. Sometimes that kind of reverse buzz was just what it took to launch a star heavenward. Elaine Jordache told her that for a long time Kevin Costner was known around town as the guy who got cut from a movie called *The Big Chill.* For a few years, the more he was edited out of projects, the more his stock kept rising. Those kinds of stories were legion.

Morning Tide

KIT WAS PROPPED in bed while Alf, who had already swallowed a Klonopin and a few extrastrength vikes, ate cold pasta and watched a *Jackass* DVD on the plasma. He kept an eye on his friend and gently shook him whenever he nodded off.

"They said you shouldn't sleep."

"That's only for the first few hours."

"How's your head?"

"It's better. Much better. So chill."

        •   •   •

8:00 A.M. AND ALF awakens to a Vicodin hangover.

He lays on the living room couch. Outside, preanarchy of bird chirps. For a half second, looks around in where-am-I? mode.

Hungry. Stink breath. Bladder three-quarters full.

Should have closed curtains—intolerably bright.

Mr. Raffles is on the patio, splayed indifferently upon flagstone, wide, soft belly slowly rising, falling under cold spotlight of sun.

Hears a frightful noise: garbled, prolonged scream. *What what*

what—is it even a scream? Leaps to feet. Enters bath, shocked at what he sees:

Kit vomiting—a broken, blasted hydrant—onto walls and mirrors. Both eyes monster swollen. Stops. Retches. Convulses while still standing. Hunches. Straightens. Vomits again as if overtaken by spirits. Alf tackles him—what else to do?—slaughterhouse wrestling ring, infernal tag team. Tries holding him down—holds him—what else to do?—meaninglessly, irrelevantly, crazily—to stop time in throes of gale-force throw up while Mr. Raffles canters in, slip-sliding, paws in muck, yelp-yawn groaning. Kit bellows to sky, inciting Alf to yell himself—pure *Dumb & Dumber* shtick—cradles him, helplessly, hopeless, Kit blind, desperately clutching hem of Alf's wifebeater in grand mal pietà, the Great Dane twitchy, and basso barking. Now Kit impossibly manages to look—*really look*—straight into Alf's eyes, in the panic room: locked gazes, primordial silence, close fetid stink, drowned shouts in flooded engine rooms, paws and kneecaps slipping, ducking, and feinting, dog near to retching itself, forgotten grotto's dank, drippy bacterial stench, Kit gone finally limp, Alf's continuous scream solo now while he lurches with brotherly burden, crablike to phone, any phone, deadweight of fallen People's Choice tucked hard to rib cage bosom as would sibling sailor's washed-up warrior body be, figures in a majestic tempera, ruined ship loitering offshore, charred and luminous—sudden skeletal descent, descant, plainsong to ocean floor, grateful aquamarine entombment silent everlasting.

The Three Poisons

The Morning After

"I CANNOT *BELIEVE* they discharged him," said the lawyer.

Counsel, agent, managers, and publicist converged on Cedars (Alf too—he hadn't left since the early A.M. return) while friend and client underwent emergency surgery to relieve pressure in his skull.

The surrealistic events had left the whole team powerless, breathless, and aghast.

Marooned.

"He signed a release?" asked the agent.

"Yeah," said Alf, boyishly vacant. The handsome, uncombed head hung low. Semidirty fingernails scratched reflexively at grizzled jaw. "He was pretty adamant about it. There was no *way* he was going to check himself in. He seemed OK—while they had him here. And he was OK at home. I mean, last night."

"He was *not* OK!" shouted the lawyer.

"Whatever," said Alf, shocky and depressed. Not up for chastisement. The agent shot the lawyer dead eyes, on the kid's behalf. "All I'm saying is, he was totally lucid. He was worried about Viv finding out before he got a chance to call." He huffed and snorted, congested by mucus and inchoate tears. "I tried to tell him that going home was a shitty idea—that he should just stay overnight and be observed." He cleared his throat. "He said that his mom died here—"

"That's true," said the agent, grateful to be able to glom on to some other tragic factoid, one at least that had resolution. "That's absolutely right." She began a series of short, nervously rhythmical nods, telegraphing historical longevity and the pedigree of her special relationship with the concussed superstar, a tenured, privileged intimacy with his life that naturally included an acquaintance with R.J., and charnel knowledge of that awful, protracted womb cancer. "That is completely correct. It was horrible for him. Horrible for him. Horrible."

"—that's why he wanted to go home. Hey," said Alf, resigned. "I can't go up against Kit. Never could. He's like a big brother."

"I don't give a *shit* what he signed," said the attorney, mostly to himself. Alf should have called someone right when it happened, but he was a dumbo—an *actor*. Not the target. Counsel's wrath became focused: rustle of lawsuits, hubbub of press conferences, briefs to be filed. "It is *completely* negligent, *completely* irresponsible. This is a major fucking personage here! Would they have let Spielberg discharge himself against medical judgment? Just stroll on out with a buddy? What on God's earth were they thinking?"

"It's just so insane," said one of the traumatized managers, staring into space. "It's just . . . so *wrong*. Everything is *wrong*."

"I'll tell you one thing," said the lawyer, in high dudgeon. "When I am through, Kit Lightfoot is going to own this fucking hospital and the ground it sits on."

"Did someone finally call Viv?" asked the other manager.

Alf nodded, snapping gum long bled of flavor. "A few hours ago, after we got here. She's on her way back."

"That couldn't have been an easy call to make," said the agent. She touched Alf's arm as a mother would.

"I hope you didn't tell her right before she went on Letterman," said the publicist.

"He said *a few hours ago*," said a manager, testily. "Jesus!"

"After," said Alf, by rote.

"My poor attempt at black humor," said the publicist, contritely.

"She's flying back with Sherry on the Paramount jet," said Alf.

"What are we doing about crowd control?" said the lawyer to the publicist. "It's *Day of the Locust* out there."

Just then, Darren Aronofsky was led in by a hospital guard.

"What's happening?" he asked.

"He's still in surgery," said the agent.

"Jesus." He turned to Alf. "Was it a fight?"

"No. This guy just . . . blindsided him. He was hassling us before at the bar. He was pissed because Kit wouldn't sign his girlfriend's left tit or whatever."

"Jesus. Jesus." Darren shook his head, sucking in air. "Are you OK?"

"Under the circumstances," nodded Alf. "Yeah. I'm cool."

"Where's Viv?" said Darren, turning to the others.

"On her way back from New York," said the publicist.

"Have they said anything?" asked Darren. "I mean, the doctors?"

The agent began to cry. A manager put his arm around her.

"Oh my God," she said. "What if he's really, really hurt and can't get better? This is so horrible! The world is *such* a horrible place!"

"There's a lot of people who love him, Kiki," said the other manager, forlornly. "A lot of people who care."

The comanager said hollowly, "We'll see him through."

"He's a stubborn motherfucker," said Alf, cocking his head—smiling, as they say, through the tears.

"That's for damn sure," said Darren. "He's a survivor."

"Plus it'd *kill* him not to do your movie," said Alf, wryly.

"Oh, he'll do the movie," said Darren, with that unsinkable old-fashioned brio only a film director can muster. The agent found his remarks vastly comforting.

"I have never seen him more passionate about a project," she said. "I mean, it's *amazing.*"

"And he'll be amazing *in* it," said Darren. "We'll push the start date, that's all."

"It's a wonderful thing," said a manager, "for him to know—even if he doesn't know *today*—that the project's waiting for him."

An uncomfortable pause in the wake of those absurd, well-meaning sentiments; the agent began to cry again.

"It's just so . . . *weird.* Darren!—your film—I mean, *that's what it's about*—in a sense. No? *Special Needs?* I mean, has anyone even *thought* about how *weird* that is? That the story line mirrors—"

"That's where the press is going to go," said the publicist. "Just a heads-up: that's *straight* where they're going to go. You know, 'Life imitates art.'"

"All we can focus on now," said Darren, keeping it real, "is Kit getting on his feet, ASAP."

"I know. I know. I know," said the agent, centering up. Regrouping. Steeling herself. Blotting her eyes.

"He'll kick ass," said Alf, rallying the troops.

"Oh, absolutely," said a manager.

"It's going to be a battle," said the attorney re the epic, looming lit-igations. "But let me tell you something. There *will* be serious casual-ties on the other side."

"Jesus," said a manager, with sudden emotion. "Has anything like this even ever *happened* before? Has a major film star ever been *attacked*?"

"Sharon Tate," said the publicist.

"I'm *sorry*, but Sharon Tate was *not* a major star!"

Vigil

LISANNE WAS AT the Coffee Bean when she heard. The washroom was occupied, so she dashed to the parking lot and threw up. She got in her car and went to the hospital.

Barricades held a crowd of fans and bystanders at bay. Media vans sprouted tall white antennae. Nasty policemen banished drive-through traffic. She valet-parked at Jerry's Deli and crossed the street.

She scanned the upper floors of the building, wondering if he was out of surgery. Her eyes wandered back to Beverly Boulevard, in vague lookout for Tiff Loewenstein's Bentley. Too soon, she thought. A visit from Tiff would come later in the week, if at all.

She felt like she might faint. She called the office to say she had the flu. She was talking to one of the girls when Reggie jumped on. He asked if she'd heard what happened, and Lisanne pretended that she was too sick to talk.

On impulse, she drove to the Loewensteins'.

.   .   .

WITH GREAT KINDNESS, the housekeeper led the ravaged woman in. She knew why Lisanne was crying.

Tiff was talking loudly on the phone, in a faraway room. Roslynn appeared on the stairs in her robe, looking so frail and everyday that suddenly Lisanne thought she'd made a grievous error by coming and burst into tears.

"Roslynn, I'm so sorry!" she said, face distorted. "I went to the hospital—I thought you might be there . . ."

They embraced and Roslynn asked the housekeeper to please bring them some tea. She led Lisanne to the living room and sat her on the divan.

"Darling, you look awful!"

"It's just so *terrible*—"

"I know." She put her arms around her, gently rocking as Lisanne wept. "We've been watching CNN all morning. We know a muck-a-muck at Cedars, Mo Biring. Mo says Kit's still being operated on—could be hours. Our spies are working on it. We know *lots* of people at Cedars."

Tea was served. Tiff came in, completely dressed, and regarded Lisanne oddly—again, she felt a trespasser's twinge. When he tenderly touched her head, Lisanne sobbed anew, throwing herself on the mercy of the cruel cosmos.

"He's out," said Tiff. Lisanne didn't know what he meant. "Of surgery."

"Is that what Mo said?" asked Roslynn.

"I just talked to him."

"Is he all right?"

"They don't know—*won't* know—not for a while. They think there may be some damage." He hesitated to say it but thought he'd better. "Brain damage."

Lisanne seized up and stopped her crying as if doused with cold water.

"My God!" said Roslynn, hand rushing to mouth. "My God."

"They *still* can't find the sonofabitch who clobbered him," said Tiff. This time, it was his wife's head he caressed. He nodded at Lisanne and said, "Got the fantods, huh." He said to Roslynn of their guest, "This one's got the fantods."

"He was just so *wonderful* when I brought him your gift," said Lisanne, from the heart. "So smart and so *sweet*."

"I had her bring him the Sotheby's Buddha," Tiff explained. "To the set."

"He's so *young* and so *talented* and it's—*just*—so—unfair and so *terrible*!" The Loewensteins drooped their heads in sorrowful affirmation. "So *kind,* so *unaffected.*" She fought for breath. Roslynn touched her arm. "I just had the feeling—I mean it was *so obvious*—that he was such a *warm and generous person.*"

"That he was," said Tiff absentmindedly, as if in eulogy.

"For someone to just *do* that to him—"

Annoyed with himself, Tiff quickly amended: "That he *is.*" Thinking aloud, the executive said, "We've already wrapped, but that's a ninety-million-dollar summer movie. We'll need someone to loop his voice—that's done a helluva lot more often than people imagine." He scratched his ear and stared through the Cézanne, cogitating arcane postproduction stratagems. "You two should play hooky today," he said, trying to lighten the mood. "Go see a movie at the Grove. Go to the beach house. Hey, we heard you had a few dates with Phil Muskingham."

"He's sweet."

"He's really smitten with you," said Roslynn.

"You could do worse than marry *that* one. I'll be working for *you* one day."

"Are you going to see Kit?" asked Lisanne.

"No," he said adamantly. "No point in sitting vigil. It's gonna be a circus over there. I'll wait till he wakes up."

"Do you think we should bring him the Buddha?"

"What?" said Tiff, nonplussed.

"Maybe it would be something he . . . his assistant could bring it from the house. He's a Buddhist and maybe—"

"Let me ask you something, Lisanne. Where was the Buddha when he got whacked on the head? The Buddha didn't help *then,* and I sure as hell don't think it's gonna to help *now.*" Roslynn gave him a look. "Roll your eyes, Roz, but that's why I'm agnostic. Besides," he added. "Too expensive to have laying around a hospital room. It'd be gone within the hour."

"What about the Courage Awards?" Roslynn called after, as her husband turned to leave.

"Sunday," said Tiff. "What about 'em?"

"Are we still going?"

"I'm not understanding you," he said combatively. "Of course we're still going. Why wouldn't we be still going?" She regretted her remark. "You mean, because of the bad thing that happened to Kit Lightfoot? Who are they going to give the award to if I'm not there, Roslynn?"

"I don't know, Tiff," she said, turning inward.

"To one of the waiters? To Suzanne Pleshette? Or how 'bout 'Frasier'? *I'm* getting the Courage Award, right? There's a shitload of people who worked their asses off organizing that—months and months of hard work. They're gonna raise three million dollars. That's their goal. And you know how? From the people who are in business with me who buy the fucking tables and spend money at the fucking silent auction. So I don't understand you, Roslynn. You think they're gonna *not* raise three million dollars because of what happened to Kit Lightfoot? It's a terrible thing, kids, but it ain't the Twin Towers."

"Enough, Tiff," she said.

Lisanne instinctively moved closer and held the older woman's hand. Roslynn was gratified to have a witness to her husband's noxiousness.

"Burt Bacharach's presenting. Did I tell you?"

"No."

"I guess you didn't know. I thought I told you. I thought I told you four times. Burt may do a thing with Elvis Costello, and I think he asked Paul McCartney, as a surprise. If Paul's in town, which I think he is. And I just happened to have given money to his one-legged cunt of a wife for the land mines. So voilà: the stars are all in alignment. So what, dear Roslynn, are you saying? That you don't want to go?"

"*Nothing,*" said Roslynn, con brio. "I'm saying *nothing.*"

"Of *course* we're going," said Tiff. He turned back to Lisanne as he left the room. "And you and Phil should come too."

Hot Property

THE *L.A. TIMES* real estate section showcased homes that were bought, sold, and leased by celebrities, and sometimes Becca clipped and mailed the features to her mom. Annie said that a lot of the brokers were former actresses, and Becca could understand why. She admired them—it took guts for a girl to look in the mirror at twenty-eight or twenty-nine and say, "It's over. I'll never be famous." But it took real smarts for that same girl to take the bull by the horns and go into a field that one day, if she were creative and industrious enough, might allow her the trappings of celebdom that would otherwise have been beyond her reach: say, a hillside manse. Because that's what a Realtor could have for herself if she put in enough blood, sweat, and tears. Realtors learned all the tricky ins and outs of buying and selling, and Annie said they were in a great position to join that exclusive club of people whose passion is to buy homes and do makeovers, then sell them at tidy profits (Courteney Cox and Diane Keaton were masters of the art). Becca thought the best thing about being a Realtor was that you got to dress up for work, sometimes to the nines, and you drove around all day in one of those cute little Mercedes with the saucy butt-trunk. (Though when she occasionally saw middle-aged brokers, thick in face and gut, carting for sale signs around on sky blue Sundays, it scared her in terms of thinking, Ohmygod, could that happen to me?) Becoming a Realtor was the kind of thing her mom might do; she was pragmatic that way. In fact, the next time Dixie started leaning on her to come home, Becca thought a viable thing would be to say that she was considering becoming a real estate agent and that she needed to stay and study for the test. Call the dogs off for a while.

Her heart raced as she folded the paper back to the front page and read the banner.

HOT PROPERTY
HER EXTRA TERRITORY

BY RUTH RYON, TIMES STAFF WRITER
Actress Drew Barrymore has purchased a Hollywood Hills home on nearly 1.5 acres for about $4.5 million.

Barrymore had been leasing since her former Beverly Hills–area home sustained fire damage in February 2001. She subsequently sold that property.

Described as a "two-story mid-century ranch with a long private drive," the compound she bought includes a four-bedroom main house with a two-story living room, a guesthouse, and a guardhouse that is staffed full-time. The estate, estimated to have about 9,000 square feet of living space, also has a gym, five fireplaces, and a billiard room with a bar. The grounds, behind gates, have a motor court, views from downtown L.A. to the ocean, a pool, and a yard with pathways and gardens.

Barrymore, 28, who starred opposite Ben Stiller in *Duplex,* also has a leading role in *Look-Alike,* to be written and directed by Spike Jonze and released in 2004.

She costarred with Cameron Diaz and Lucy Liu in the movie versions of the 1970s TV series *Charlie's Angels,* which she also produced. Barrymore also appeared at age seven in *E.T. the Extra-Terrestrial,* rereleased in 2002.

Brett Lawyer and Ed Fitz of Nourmand & Associates, Beverly Hills, represented Barrymore in buying, according to sources not involved with the deal.

She hadn't thought about the fire in a while, but now she remembered news footage of the bantering couple climbing into their BMW in the middle of the night to good-humoredly flee the flames—there was something about them that was a little too manic and Becca knew their marriage was already in trouble. Just thinking about that homely idiot Tom Green pissed her off. He is *so* majorly fucked up! Drew gave him *everything:* her house, her heart, her invaluable connections . . . stood by him for his lame-o ball cancer (Annie wondered if it was a stunt but even Becca thought that was going too far because she knew the comedian had truly suffered), and *never wavered*! Tom Green could have learned *so much* from Drew the producer, Drew the businesswoman, Drew the icon and showbiz vet. But in the end, all Tom Green wanted was to be in shitty, shitty movies, party with whorey-looking supermodel rejects, and host a fifth-rate Conan loserfest. In the end, all Tom Green wanted was to whine about how you should be careful never to marry someone who had a team of publicists. Oh! How galling! Tom Green should be so lucky! And like it's Drew's *fault* to be the legend she is! It's Drew's *fault* that Steven Spielberg is her godfather and that she was in *E.T.* when she was a baby and that for a *hundred years* her family was theatrical and cinematic royalty! But the worst of it was, they were *married*—they exchanged *sacred vows*—and now that it was over, Tom Green didn't even have the decency or common sense to keep his chinless cancer mouth shut. People were like that. People were ungrateful, fickle, boring, greedy, vindictive, and morally bankrupt. All anyone ever did was cover their own ass and Tom Green was covering *his*, busily rewriting history. Not *Drew*—Drew let everything hang for the world to see. She had her weaknesses, but you could *never* say she wasn't a stand-up person, that was Drew to the max, and when Green got that final (spread-to-the-brain) tumor Becca was certain Ms. Barrymore would be there for him 1000 percent. She wasn't one to hold a grudge at death's door.

Becca sipped at her latte and savored the description: "two-story mid-century ranch with a long private drive." It was like the beginning of a novel! Four bedrooms seemed cozy—just right. A guesthouse was always nice for friends or relatives (that was the kind of arrangement she dreamed of for Dixie), but if she so desired, on nights when Drew had the compound to herself, it also gave her the luxury of crashing elsewhere on the property, like a gamboling gypsy, for the fun of it— the wherewithal to mix it up, if she felt moody or devil-may-care. "A guardhouse, staffed full-time . . ." probably a necessity, because of stalkers—still, Becca couldn't imagine what *that* would be like. You could wake up at three in the morning freaked out from a bad dream and wouldn't even have to call 911—all you'd have to do was shout for your private live-in police! Annie would die when she told her. Becca reread "gym, five fireplaces," and suddenly the house didn't sound so snug anymore, though she was pretty sure it would *feel* snug because Drew probably did it up in the Topanga–Beverly Glen–Laurel Canyon hippie style, all dark wood and stone, dog-friendly Shabby Chic couches and worn, deceptively expensive Native American rugs. "A yard with pathways and gardens . . . ," pathways leading God knew where. I would give anything, Becca thought, to pitch a tent at the end of one of those trails, if only as an in-residence Pilates teacher or masseuse.

But this was the part that stirred her most:

> Barrymore, 28, who starred opposite Ben Stiller in *Duplex*, also has a leading role in *Look-Alike*, to be written and directed by Spike Jonze and released in 2004.

Becca's movie! Just that morning, Sharon phoned to say that Spike Jonze had been charmed at the table-read and wanted to put her on tape. She told Becca *not* to say anything to Rusty yet, and Becca read between the lines that Sharon didn't want to get burned again. But it came to mind there was the possibility—Rusty seemingly so close to Spike, having coffees at the Rose and whatnot—that maybe he already *did* know and would be punishing if Becca failed to mention. No need to get paranoid; she decided to think happy thoughts. She still had the fantasy of both of them getting cast and becoming stars. The whole fame scenario flitted through her head again, this time with the capper that she became the proud new owner of the "two-story mid-century ranch" when Ms. Barrymore got the urge to relocate. One thing Becca knew she *wouldn't* need was a private mod squad. Though it'd be fun to put a mannequin in there—a mannequin and a big dusty bunch of artificial flowers in the guardhouse might be memorable.

A young man interrupted her thoughts, asking if he could share the table. She blinked.

"I'm sorry," she said. "But you look really familiar."

They made a few guesses as to where they might have met before. He said, "Do you ever go to the Coffee Bean, up on Sunset?"

"Sure."

"I used to work there." She squinted at him. "I looked a little different. My hair was shorter. And I"—he smiled sheepishly—"I was 'impaired.'"

He slurred his words, refreshing her memory.

"Ohmygod, yes! But—I don't understand."

"Research—for a film role. The Kit Lightfoot movie. I was going to play a retard. If I may be so politically incorrect."

He reached out a hand, and Becca shook it, though she wasn't sure how to respond. Something about him was so refined yet flamboyant that she couldn't stop smiling.

"I'm Larry Levine. And if you're not Drew Barrymore, you've got some serious explaining to do."

Postsurgical

VIV WEMBLEY STEPS *from a Suburban, deep inside the hospital garage. She wears large Fendi shades and scuffed Dries boots—straight from the airport in Van Nuys, with minimal freshening up on the plane as it landed. Sherry offered to go with her, but Viv graciously, gratefully declined. She smells her own breath as she walks, fetid and stagnant. Grief-breath.*

She is ushered through the bowels, as they say, to a white room where doctors prepare her for what she will see.

A friend who is also her yoga teacher has come. The logistics of that rendezvous were a security hassle, and there's some delay—Viv will not go in to see Kit without her—finally the two meet and embrace.

They go in a room by themselves, and the teacher engages Viv in deep yoga breaths.

They ride the elevator up.

Outside the guarded room: Prana, prana, prana.

Viv enters, the way first-timers jump from planes.

The private nurse nods, smiles, and leaves. The yoga friend stays in the room, just inside the door, now closed behind them. Respectful. Moved. There for her friend. There for Kit too.

Viv stands beside him, holding his hand. Her awkwardness melts away at the humanity of it. The reduction of love, horror, and agony. The sheer bizarre unlikelihood . . .

Head shaved, face twice its normal size.

"Honey?" she says, choking up. She casts a look to her friend, who quickly looks away from Kit then to Viv's eyes, but Viv has already turned her gaze back to her fiancé so that her friend and yoga teacher missed the exchange.

"Bumpkin?"

He does not see: eyes swollen shut.

Two incisions in skull.

Tubes in nose, throat, cock.

"Baby, I'm here. It's Viv. It's Cherry Girl. She's here."

Stifles tears, certain that if she breaks down he will know. Will hear. Her yoga friend said, "Remember, he is aware." She doesn't want to put out any kind of fucked-up energy. No fear energy. Her yoga friend said how important it was to be calm, still, centered, comforting.

.   .   .

CORRESPONDENTS, IN FRONT of hospital, talk to cameras. Local news and foreign too—England, Germany, Italy, Spain, Japan. A distraught fan is interviewed.

.   .   .

A FOX NEWS lightweight talks to camera in front of the Bar Marmont. Ambitious, cadenced, sexed up by celeb tragedy. A run in her stocking the audience will never see. Camera follows as she walks to liquor store, reenacting Kit Lightfoot's ill-fated path. Interviews clerk who ID'd plate.

.   .   .

SPECIAL EDITION electronic newsmagazines on the topics of Celebrity Stalking, Celebrity Worship, Celebrity Murder.

Also, special subedition electronic minimagazines on Nightclub Security, Celebrity Bodyguards, Violence Prediction.

Also, on Head Injuries, Stroke Rehab.

Also, on film insurance and bonding, and what happens when a star dies in the middle of a shoot—Natalie Wood, Brainstorm, Oliver Reed, Gladiator—even though the movie Kit Lightfoot shot has already wrapped and he is not dead.

.   .   .

SHE CRIES AND cries and cries. She doesn't leave her bedroom for three days. A clot of yoginis come and go. Friends and professionals and gentle folk she doesn't know all that well (from Kit's sangha) stop by to cook and be of service. Her agents come. Her publicists come. Her manager and even her accountant. Finally—finally—she laughs. Then she cries like a thunderstorm and everyone cries along. There is some hilarity too, that very special kind of hilarity in extremis, and she drinks her favorite margaritas and mixes them with Vicodin and some Co-Proxamol she got in London. She takes big messy bubble baths with girlfriends. Everyone gets massages. It's Massage Central. Sheryl Crow, Darren Aronofsky, Joely Fisher, Renée Zellweger, Helen Fielding, Paula Abdul, and naturally, Alf Lanier drop by—at overlapping times—and of course all of the Together costars. Then a parade of industry demigods until she says, Enough. (She joked that Dr. Phil would walk in next.) She has Gingher shut it down except for the inner circle. Her crew. She dances alone in her room to the Stones and Freddy Mercury, Nirvana and White Stripes. She pulls her friends in one by one, then slams the door, and they dance with her, one by one, as a goof, a poignant goof. Everybody's sweating and crying and singing Dusty Springfield songs. She sobers up. Everybody does yoga together. Sometimes she cries in the middle of a pose. Sometimes when that happens she laughs, and then everyone laughs and then everyone cries too. When the teacher inadvertently says "corpse pose," Viv loses it. Everyone eats pizza and Häagen-Dazs and sushi and takeout from Trader Vic's, and they watch nothing but AMC—Bette Davis and Maureen O'Hara and Montgomery Clift and Jeff Chandler and Jennifer Jones. Then they smoke weed and watch a Britney concert and a Bangles concert and a Cher concert on DVD and then some PPV porno. What a hoot. Periodic solo retreats to the darkened bedroom, where she tries and fails at masturbation. Dares to watch CNN, awaiting taboo redundant reports of her fiancé's relentless nonprogress. Perversely cadges on-air quasi-eulogies and career summing-ups. Alf goes to Kit's house and finds the ring that he bought at Fred Joaillier. He brings it over. Horror.

•   •   •

ALF, PUFFY-EYED and disconsolate, at Kit's bedside.

An RN empties a catheter bag.

He smirks, then hangs his head low. Aggressively mutters, "Fuck this shit," and bolts.

Darkness. He is met by a frenzy of paparazzi shouting his name. Across the street, behind barricades, fifty die-hard fans—bundled up in the cold dead of night—gather with signs, candles, flowers. Calling, "Alf! Alf! How is he? How's Kit? Is he talking? Have you talked to him?"

Alf smiles tight-lipped. Gives a thumbs-up. Some applaud.

The lesser outcry, jokey, not really meant to be heard, of a prankster cuts through: "Hey, Alfie, did Cameron dump you?"

Paparazzo with an old grudge.

The others shout the insensitive shutterbug down, officially registering their distaste.

Alf ducks into the waiting Town Car.

. . .

A SPECIAL CREW obliterates all traces of biological debris from Kit's bathroom. (A CSI producer had referred them to Kit's agent, Kiki, who insisted on handling that sort of detail.) She told Alf that, supposedly, the company was profiled on the Discovery Channel. The LAPD hires them for crime scene scrubs—they restore rooms to their original pristine state. Kiki said they use chemicals that eat "smell" molecules.

. . .

HE EMERGES FROM coma, pulling the feed tube from his throat. Gagging. One eye won't open—the muscle controlling the lid is damaged. A rakish pirate patch is provided, but he keeps tearing it off.

Viv and Alf rejoice in his feistiness.

Lightfoot Senior revels in his boy's stubborn, genetic heroism. Headstrong.

There is some cause for celebration among Kit's management posse, though Kiki still can't see the light. She thinks people are grasping at straws.

Doctors are cautiously optimistic. In a press conference, they guardedly announce that the actor is no longer comatose. Condition upgraded to serious. They refuse to talk details of status or prognosis.

Kit makes sounds—gibberish. Sings in his sleep. Jerks awake, as if he was falling. Gains weight. Likes to spit. As long as he holds on to something, he can stand by himself and try to whistle or make barking noises. His face still looks like a Francis Bacon. He cries. He laughs. He is diapered.

. . .

HE STANDS AT bedside, dazed. Combative.

Flails at his caretakers and finally connects, punching an older female nurse, who reels and falls, abrading herself. Burke holds him tight to his chest, to restore calm—he scuffs at the floor and tries to break free. Finally submits to his father's ministrations.

Burke is the only one who can soothe him.

*   *   *

VIV SITS IN a chair, facing him (Kit in a chair too, but seat-belted in).

She takes his hand and traces it over her cheek. Flashes on Anne Ban-croft and Patty Duke in The Miracle Worker. *Sometimes he looks at her and seems to smile. She calls a nurse when she smells feces.*

*   *   *

VIV AND ALF, in a dark back booth at Chianti.

They commune in relative silence and eat their comfort food: red wine, bread, and bouillabaisse.

Occasionally, Alf says something to cheer her—crazy gossip about some actor they know or the beggar he saw on the median with a cardboard sign that said, I LEFT HOME WITHOUT IT. *She says she saw one on San Vicente with a sign that said,* START AGAIN.

She takes his hand and traces on her cheek to show how things went with Kit.

Nothing sexual about it.

Just sorrow and fatigue.

As always, she begins to cry. He is helpless to comfort her.

*   *   *

KIT RAISES UP as the RN removes the bedpan.

An LVN enters and hands a little camera to the RN, who tells him to shut the door.

They wiggle him into a shirt before posing with the superstar.

They take turns.

The poses are wholesome, not scurrilous.

Mother and Child Reunion

LISANNE WAS BESIDE herself, thinking that any moment she would learn that Kit was dead. She couldn't rely on the media for updates, and whatever leaked from Tiff Loewenstein was invariably grim. It was like a bad dream. She couldn't sleep anymore and watched *Lord of the Rings* DVDs nonstop. She was afraid to take pills because of the baby.

She went back to the Bodhi Tree in desperation and bought the *Bardo Guidebook*, which delineated the Buddhist experience of dying and being dead. Much of it frightened and overwhelmed. The *bardo* was described as a kind of twilight zone or in-between state. (When Lisanne looked the word up on the Internet, she got cross-referenced to Robert Bardo, the stalker who murdered the television actress Rebecca Schaeffer. That creeped her out further.) There were actually five or six different bardos, but the easiest one to understand was called the "natural bardo of this life." Apparently a human life span was merely an "in-between" to the states that came before and after. The guidebook said that what followed life was "the painful bardo of dying." (Whoopee.) It said how, at the time of death, the white essence of the father descended from the head like a moon sinking in the sky, while at the same time the red essence of the mother ascended from below the navel like a rising sun. The essences merged in the middle of the heart.

What really interested Lisanne was the book's assertion that, after death, those who had meditated a lot in life—people like Kit—still had a window of opportunity to be "realized" or liberated. The guidebook said that when consciousness left the body, a person became confused and disoriented. "Karmic winds" blew around and made a person wonder where his body was. At the coming of the winds, it was especially important to keep your wits and realize that whatever you saw or heard (say, the blinding of 100,000 suns or the clapping of 100,000 thunderclouds), no matter how wrathful, peaceful, or seductive, was the demons that befell you, it was essential to realize that all those things were just a manifestation of your ego. They represented the part of you still clinging to something called *samsara*. If you could just see that those visions, those hideous or beautiful sounds, feelings, and experiences were only projections of the self, then you could escape the cycle of rebirth, or the Wheel of Becoming. You would then be totally realized. That was the state they called enlightenment or nirvana.

If you got stuck on the wheel, the next bardo lasted forty-nine days and seemingly offered a little more time to achieve buddhahood. But even if you panicked and failed to "recognize the essence of your own mind," you still had the chance to steer yourself toward a human rebirth, which the Buddhists said was a rare and privileged thing; that was why it was important not to squander one's limited term in the so-called natural bardo of the living. Meditation and devotion to the path resulted in liberation. Animals couldn't meditate—they were trapped in the animal bardo and could be liberated only by those who had escaped the Wheel of Becoming.

It was fascinating to her and a welcome distraction from the self-imposed deathwatch. Lisanne read pages of the guidebook aloud when she couldn't sleep. She was amazed by something called *phowa*, an ancient technique in which a person literally shot his consciousness into space at the time of death, like an arrow. Mind mingled with *prana* ("life-wind"), ejecting itself through the central channel and out the top of one's skull into infinity. Lisanne thought that was intriguing because supposedly an experienced *phowa* practitioner could actually liberate someone *else's* consciousness upon that person's death—meaning that if you weren't the world's greatest meditator (she'd bought some instructional tapes but wasn't really into it), then fortunately a qualified guru or high lama or whatever could come along and give you that final shove.

There was something called the ground luminosity and the path luminosity. At death they merged—in Buddhism, there was lots of merging and lots of death—"like a child jumping onto his mother's lap." She thought it achingly beautiful, and her respect for Kit and his years of dedication "to the cause" grew. How admirable it was that in the midst of Hollywood shallowness he would have been drawn to such a world! But she wondered . . . Was the Buddhism of the guidebook the particular form that he practiced? So much of the teachings seemed morbid and impossibly esoteric. It was one thing to have a book lay everything out in concise, no-nonsense terms. But if a person meditated, did he, at least over time, become privy to all of the rules? Did he get rewired? Was the educational material sort of magically downloaded as a consequence of incredible discipline? Lisanne wondered if the experience would be like living among a foreign people then one day waking up to speak the language, or at least realize one was dreaming in it. How many years did that take—two, five, twenty, fifty? And if a person finally *did* understand, by some kind of osmosis, was his knowledge something he was allowed to share with others if he was even able? Lisanne was possessed by the thought that Kit was *nearly* liberated but hadn't, say, fully mastered a way of ejecting his consciousness, and was terrified that he would be trapped in some miserable bardo. Did he apprise Viv Wembley of his progress or lack of, before he got hurt? If Lisanne could learn something from the actress that was pertinent, it might give her comfort. Though it could be that Buddhism was like Scientology and you weren't allowed to tell anyone about anything. Or did that apply only to outsiders? (Which maybe Viv technically was, not being, as far as Lisanne knew, a practicing Buddhist.) Not that she knew anything about Scientology, but you *never* heard Tom Cruise or Jenna Elfman or Lisa Marie Presley sharing their personal experiences. Lisanne thought that if she wanted to find out anything about Kit's proficiency in terms of his struggle to be liberated, she would probably have to approach other Buddhists who knew him well. But why should they tell *her* anything?

The guidebook said that near the end of the forty-nine days, if you were destined to take a human rebirth, you began looking around for couples who were engaged in intercourse. The rule of thumb was that swarms of lost souls were always hovering around the entrance of a woman's womb as she made love, "like flies on a piece of meat." The book was scandalous! Maybe Buddhism was just an elaborately kinky sham.

There were so many questions. Did the fact that doctors had drilled into the skull to relieve pressure, bored into and broken bone in the crown chakra, from where consciousness waited to launch— did the surgical holes make "ejection" easier or, instead, somehow traumatically seal his fate and his doom? Anyway, the classical texts declared that a person had to be dead in order for *phowa* to occur. What if Kit didn't die but remained imprisoned in his body, conscious but unable to move or speak? He could stay like that for years. What then?

There were evidently three different ways of dying (there always seemed to be three ways of doing this and three ways of doing that)— like a child, like a beggar, or like a lion. To die like a child meant to have no concept of dying or not-dying. Dying like a beggar meant not to care about the circumstances of one's death. Dying like a lion meant to die in solitude. It was lovely, but what did any of it mean? She imagined that Kit would prefer to die like a lion, but with all those doctors and nurses injecting, monitoring, and restraining, how could he possibly have the chance?

She lay prone on the couch and closed her eyes. Phil's gift, the Amazing Technicolor Supreme Bliss-Wheel Integration Buddha, was close at hand. An ashtray overflowed. Lisanne shifted onto her side, drifting. Her nose pressed against the cushion, and she smelled the musty imprint of her heavy body. In conscious imitation of the Bliss-Wheel's counterpart—the Sotheby's gift—she let her left hand lay atop the gravid belly while the right dangled down to touch the carpeted floor. In her mind, the cautionary words from the guidebook regarding the afterlife struggle absurdly merged with sorcerers' voices from *The Lord of the Rings*.

> Like the confusion in the dreams of one's sleep last night,
> later on it will be difficult to practice in the bardo.

If he could not die as a lion, she mused, it would be better to leave the world as a child than as a beggar.

Ladies Who Lunch

BECCA, ANNIE, LARRY, and Gingher had lunch at Swingers in Santa Monica.

Becca and Larry had met a few times for coffee since first sharing a table at Peet's. Whenever they were together, she felt like the ingenue of a novel about the early days of a group of starving actors and artists, some destined for fame, others for tragic obscurity. When she finally made a date to introduce him to Annie, Larry brought along his chubby friend.

"Tell them how she shits in front of you," said Larry.

Gingher laughed, jiggling all over.

"Oh no!" said Annie. "I *really* like her show—*please* don't tell me she's one of those people who get off on that."

"Let us just say," said Gingher affectedly, "that the lady tends to be rather unself-conscious in the washroom."

"What do you *mean*?" asked Becca, wide-eyed.

Larry was smitten. "Girl, you are *so Southern—très naïve et gentille.* Or should I say gentile. You are so *Virginia*."

"That when she goes to the bathroom, she . . ."

"We have meetings every morning," said Gingher, "where she like gives me the list of stuff to do for the day?"

"You meet in the *toilet*?" said Becca.

"You betcha," said Larry. "That's when she's apt to pinch off a large one."

"Oh my God!" said Annie, laughing. "That is *so gross.*"

"The mirrors steam up like a jungle. *Jungle fever.* No: jungle feces!"

"Larry, you are crazy!" said Becca.

"Would I shit you, honeybear?" asked Larry. "Does a Viv shit in the woods? Who's shittin who? Horton shits a Who. Tell it, girl."

"I think it's like some kind of power trip," said Gingher. "But, you *guys*, you *cannot* tell anyone. She'd fucking *sue* me."

"You'd never shit in this town again," said Larry gleefully. "You'd be blacklisted—you'd be shitlisted!"

"I don't even care. I'm walking. She is such a cunt."

"You will never leave that job."

"Watch me."

"How did you even start working for her?" asked Annie.

"Doing craft service on her show. Actually my *friend* was doing craft service and I was helping him out. And Viv was really, really nice to me—this was before they were making like a million dollars an episode. Viv had this really horrible relationship with her mother, so she does this maternal thing where she likes to take in sick puppies. I was puppy-of-the-week. But she really *did* do all these nice things for me."

"You ungrateful whore."

"She paid for me to have my tattoos removed at UCLA. They were really gnarly. She has this whole side of her that's really sweet and nonjudgmental. She just started asking me to do stuff for her. Errands and shit. She liked having me around, I guess. Like while she was getting ready for big auditions or premieres. She'd like ask my opinion on her clothes or her makeup. Even though most of the time she totally had stylists and makeup people come in and do her. I never even really said anything except that she looked really good but I guess I calmed her nerves."

"She *is* really beautiful," said Annie.

"And when this other person she had working for her quit? *Honeychile,* I moved *right in.* That girl was *so* fucked up. Chartrain."

"*Chartrain?*" said Larry.

"Chartrain, Soul Train, whatever. Viv helped get me a car, and she was cool. But then I, like, saw this *whole other side* to her."

"How's she dealing with what happened?" asked Becca, in hushed tones. "Weren't they engaged?"

"That's actually really sad," said Gingher. "Because Kit is *very* cool. Very sweet and down-to-earth. We always got along. I've, like, *almost* gone to see him at the hospital a bunch of times. But I heard the security was so intense."

"Does she visit him?" asked Annie.

Gingher nodded. "She did at first, but now it's like a lot less. A *lot* less. She never asked me to go with. But he's really doing better from what I understand. I mean, they don't know what's going to happen—with his mind—but he's supposedly doing a *lot* better."

"A mind is a terrible thing to baste," intoned Larry.

The girls ignored him. "I don't know why they hooked up," said Gingher. "Well, I guess I know why she hooked up with *him*. She's got that TV-inferiority thing. Kit gave her street cred."

"A mind is a terrible thing to taste, said Hannibal Lecter."

"He wouldn't *even* say that! Would you shut up? God, you are so annoying!" She turned back to Becca and Annie. "I guess it's just a stone sex trip. Or *was.*I know they're kind of out there."

"Our Lady of the Perpetual Potty certainly is."

"But he's like—intellectually and just as a person—Kit's like, her *total opposite.*"

"Really?" said Larry. "When I met him he acted like a total prick."

"You bring it out!" said Gingher.

"You met him through Gingher?" asked Annie.

"I *told* you," said Becca, reminding her. "They met while Larry was working at the Coffee Bean."

"I was going to do that movie," he said, filling Annie in. He loved telling the story. "The Aronofsky thing—*Special Needs.* But I got fucked by Mr. Brain Dead."

"That's not nice," said Becca.

"Sorry, Virginia."

"You don't *know* that you didn't get the part because of Kit," said Gingher. "He's not vindictive like that. Maybe Aronofsky thought you couldn't act."

"Well fuck Mr. *Requiem for an Avant-Garde Blow Job* too, honey-child, cause my audition was *kick-ass.* I was on my second callback when Mr. Lightfoot and I had our little run-in, and I got axed the next day."

"I will always love you for working at the Coffee Bean as a retard!" said Gingher.

"He went off on me, and I just looked at him and said, 'I'm *sorry.* I mean, you're only like making *twenty-five million a picture*, or what*ever*, and I'm out there doing what I have to do so I can pay my fucking *phone bill—*"

"You *didn't* say that," said Gingher, agog.

"Under my breath."

Gingher guffawed.

"And how do *you* guys know each other?" asked Annie.

"We met at the Grove," said Larry.

"We were by ourselves," said Gingher. "We'd just broken up with our boyfriends."

"We were *crying.*"

"It was so pathetic! We were sitting an aisle away from each other at *E.T.*"

"The rerelease."

"*E.T.* is the *perfect movie,*" said Annie.

"Gertie!" exulted Gingher. "How *cute* is Gertie?" She addressed the last to Becca, whom she deemed to be ambassador to the land of Drew.

"What was that, like four years ago?" said Larry. "I'd never even seen it."

"Can you believe that?" said Annie to the others, outraged.

"I saw *Close Encounters,*" he said, "but I never saw *E.T.*"

"You know how the Grove—I love the Grove!—has those armrests you can lift up?"

"Lovebird seats," said Annie.

"So Larry and I see each other crying. And we like started whispering to each other, *really loud.* Then Larry changes seats—"

"I thought you were Julia Sweeney."

"—and we sobbed through the whole movie!"

"People were telling us to shut up."

"Larry told this one person that he was really sorry he was crying but he just found out he had tuberculosis *and* AIDS. After the movie, we went to the Farmers Market and ran our stories."

"About the mutual breakups."

"Who were you going out with?" asked Becca.

"Some pimply-faced Puerto Rican trash," said Larry. "I think he was, like, twelve."

"Research for yet another amazing movie role," said Gingher, with a wink. "And speaking of *E.T.*, ohmygod, you *do* look *so* much like Drew!"

"Thank you," said Becca, as if in rehearsal for when she would finally come into her own.

"Larry said you might be doing that Spike Jonze movie."

"I hope so," said Becca. "Because the look-alike stuff doesn't pay the rent. Not this month anyway."

Larry was saying how he read somewhere that look-alikes were always being flown to Japan for private parties, when Gingher gaped at a pregnant woman passing by their table. She took one look and blurted out, "*Ohmygod*, I can't even believe I, like, *forgot—Viv miscarried.*" She clapped an embarrassed hand over her mouth, in exaggerated fear that the woman had overheard.

"No!" said Annie.

"When?" asked Larry, eyes agleam.

"You guys so *totally* have to swear you won't tell anyone."

"I didn't even know she was pregnant," said Becca.

"*No one* did," said Gingher. "I mean, probably not even *Kit*."

"Wouldn't it have been weird," said Larry, "if they had a kid and it turned out to be retarded?"

"That's *so sad*," said Becca. "I mean, she probably lost the baby because of what happened. The stress."

"Ohmygod, that is *so sad*," echoed Annie.

"But you guys have to *swear* you won't talk about it until, like, after it's in the tabloids. I signed a confidentiality agreement and could *really* get in trouble. Will you so totally swear?"

Transmigration of Souls

LISANNE'S WATER BROKE in the Century Plaza ballroom, at Tiff's Heart Giver Courage tribute.

When she stood from her seat, she felt a pang and told Phil she was having a "bladder problem." By the time they got to the dance floor, everything was soaked. She collapsed in a chair at a table of old people who went on picking at their veal. She was shaking and crying. When the Loewensteins rushed over, Lisanne said she was pregnant and that her water must have broken. Tiff kind of took over. There were five top OB-GYN guys in the house, and all of them kept wanting her to agree that maybe she'd only peed her pants. Just when Lisanne thought it had ebbed, she got flooded anew. They plunked her in a wheelchair and laid her out in the stretch limo. Phil was white as a sheet. One of the OB-GYNs went ahead to Saint John's.

The nurse told her she was having contractions every five minutes, but she couldn't feel them. They gave her something to stop the labor, though the discharge was continuous. Phil was so shell-shocked that Tiff, who had already received his crystal figurine and was exhausted as well, announced he would escort the scion home. Roslynn stayed on. She was a great comfort, kind and discreet. She left around midnight without ever broaching the issue of paternity.

.   .   .

LISANNE LAY THERE and assessed. She thought of calling Robbie— but why? Her boss would be shocked when he learned, though in a way, she was relieved. Her secret was out, or nearly so. Earlier in the day she had taken the deepest, most restful nap of her life, awakening at peace. Her concern for Kit was still there, but the agonized worries over his health and well-being had evaporated. She knew he would be OK. The water had broken and a rainbow now shone.

At 3:30 A.M. the nurse said the tests showed the baby's lungs to be "mature." The doctor wanted to deliver right away. The C-section took forever, and at delivery, the bloody boy screamed with elemental force—healthy, at thirty weeks.

They fed him through his nose because the suckle reflex hadn't yet developed. Lisanne used a breast pump for milk, but it was hard to be productive. She was still able to make small quantities of what the RNs called "liquid gold," which they added to the feeding tube. The hotel sent a basket of fruit and cookies. No one ever had her water break in the ballroom before.

.   .   .

THE SOUND WAS off while she watched Larry King.

"Do you know she here?" said a Mexican nurse who came in for the dinner tray.

"Who?"

"Viv Wembley. The girl from the show who go with Kit Lightfoot. The show *Together*."

"What do you mean?"

"She miscarry."

"She—"

"She miscarry. Ectopic—very dangerous. She right here! Same floor."

"In the hospital?" The woman was confusing her.

"Right now! But I no tell you—is secret. Is terrible what happened to her fiancé. Handsome! Now no big fat Greek wedding. No baby. Is terrible. Is terrible."

.   .   .

THAT EVENING, Lisanne saw her.

She went for a walk and saw Cameron Diaz and a woman with a turban on her head leave one of the rooms. Against their tender protests, Viv shakily emerged to escort them to the elevator. That was when the weakened actress looked at Lisanne and smiled. (She remembered the time Kit made eye contact after yoga.) She thought how pretty Viv was without makeup, how vulnerable looking. Lisanne looped back toward her own room so they wouldn't have the same trajectory.

The moment they exchanged glances, she knew.

She felt the same peace she'd experienced after her amazing nap. They looked into each other's eyes and Lisanne knew, was certain.

The Bardo of Becoming

BUT HOW IS HE?

He farts, grunts, giggles, howls.

Words remain in throat, stillborn. Incipient thoughts—autochthonous ideation—aborted.

He is in love with his body, its pain, pleasure, and rapturous stink. Becomes fixated on arbitrary landscapes of skin—hair, follicle, pigment. Flake and fingernail.

A stage actor warming up, he spends hours fogging a hand mirror, watching himself gesticulate, crease, pucker, twitch, startle, suspirate, belch, yawn, coo, whisper. Therapists stretch muscle and rub ointment; he submits like a dog, belly up, with unannounced pleasure. He takes businesslike joy in their grooming and bodywork, as if thespian instinct has informed that the vessel is preeminent and must be maintained at all costs.

Sometimes his head is stabby and migrainous. He presses, imploring the scarified points of incision, feeling the heat beneath sutures, vents to a still-active furnace, mistakenly—catastrophically—soldered shut.

Boosters and cheerleaders are certain he's more "present" than he appears to be, the gray matter busily rerouting and reknitting "as we speak." But he has trouble standing, and, once standing, has trouble standing still. Trouble walking too, the gait ticcy and belabored.

Sometimes he awakens bellowing. High-priced nurses, privately hired, burly, stalwart, do their best to soothe without injections. Sometimes he surfaces from REM sleep cackling, knee-slapping, with attendant nefarious dysphonic outbursts. Sometimes he weeps, soft and plaintive like a child—or ragged, seizured, ugly.

Always heartbreaking.

He seems to know Alf but doesn't recognize his bride to be—or at least won't let on. Boosters and cheerleaders (led by Kiki) fantasize his indifference to be a shuck, a heroic way of letting the actress off the hook, nobly

allowing her to break the engagement. No fault, no contest, nolo con-
tendere, gentleman to the end, even in debilitation. Dad agrees, up to a
point. The dad says Kit knows damn well who she is but "just doesn't want
to go there."

Viv fears his eventual acknowledgment of her, no matter how gradual,
will cause great suffering. Stops visiting. Wants her man to focus his ener-
gies on recovery. She martyrs herself, shamefully hating her secret involun-
tary mantra: "I can't do this. I can't do this. I can't do this."

Alf disappears. He's doing a film that, mercifully, is on location, out of
the country. He was going to stop coming, anyway. In a fit of tiredness that
he regretted, he told Burke it was just too depressing. Mr. Lightfoot said, as
a lawyer would to a prospective juror whom he was about to dismiss, "Thank
you for your candor." Go recharge, Burke added expansively. Stop guilt-
tripping. You'll reconnect down the line. (You piece of Hollywood shit.)

Kiki still comes. A tough broad, said Burke. He tells the Buddhists she's
one hell of an agent.

· · ·

HE WISELY LIMITS access for those who would see his son. But the Bud-
dhists are allowed to come and go as they please—all Kit's friends and prac-
titioners from the sangha. *Burke calls them the* sanghanistas *and knows*
they want nothing from Kit. They're not morbidly curious. Their religion
demands they act in the most ethical, dignified, compassionate, "mindful"
of ways. They are patient and generous with their time. Burke respects them
and is comforted by their inconspicuous, warmly obeisant spirituality.

He feels his son to be comforted too.

· · ·

OLD FRIENDS ARE pleased the father kept open this vital aspect of his son's
life. They're happy not to be banished and glad he didn't trash Kit's beliefs
because they know it is the foundation that will heal him. They had heard
stories of the tyranny of this man—some from Kit himself—but in this terri-
ble time Burke Lightfoot had, for whatever reason, opened the door, and for
that, they are profoundly grateful. So they honor him. They see the Buddha
in his gesture and honor Burke Lightfoot's heart.

The sangha visit at all hours, even meditating at bedside while Kit
sleeps. They serve him while he is awake. They bring cooked food and read

scriptures and sutras out loud. They massage him with emollients and encourage him to stretch. They do baby yoga. They even teach the nurses—child's pose, downward dog, easy twisting warrior, spinal twist, neck release. They are courteous and helpful to staff, dependable, soon indispensable. Many have worked in hospices, and the nurses let them do funky, menial things. Bedpan and hygiene. Stripping the sheets and making the bed.

Burke watches the Meditators come and go, fingering their beads, reading texts aloud, intoning lengthy prayers, sometimes in English, sometimes in Japanese or Tibetan or Whatever. They wear civilian clothes and close-cropped hair, but now and then smiling monks, bald men or women in saffron robes, come to sit. They do not speak.

Tara Guber even brought Penor Rinpoche, the lama from Mysore.

· · ·

NOW IT IS TIME for him to leave.

The hospital is happy to see him go—he is just too big a celebrity, and difficult to accommodate. An unruly tabloidal pall had wrapped the complex in gauze. So much to contend with: the twenty-four-hour media presence, the police and additional security, the concrete barriers and parking disruptions, the predatory paparazzi eyes invading other patients' and their families' privacy. Donors and in-house benefactors were becoming restive.

At four in the morning, he emerges from the elevator and is rolled into the garage by wheelchair, flanked by doctors, nurses, and a half dozen private guards. (One has the sense the doctors are there so they can eventually boast that yes, they were present for that strange and historic release.) Burke engaged Gavin de Becker, the man who oversaw the details of George Harrison's last days, to facilitate his son's relocation. An armored van with blacked-out windows awaits, plus two dark Buick sedans with three men apiece.

Suddenly Kit becomes agitated.

His father, already inside the van, emerges to calm him. It takes but a few minutes. The dad gives a thumbs-up to the others and says, "Good to go." Whatever feelings anyone has about Burke Lightfoot and his questionable motives, it is clear the man has worked hard to establish an effective, easy kinship with his volatile, traumatized son. Things would have gone a lot rougher without him.

With media none the wiser, the convoy makes the forty-minute trip to Valencia.

The facility awaits. An entire wing has been cleared.

•   •   •

MR. DE BECKER HAS PROVIDED *round-the-clock guards on-site. Rehab employees have been screened and Tyrone Lamott, among others, duly briefed. Those immediately under him were seriously cautioned—warned— by Mr. Lamott himself that any breach of the celebrity client's confidentiality would be harshly dealt with.*

(Tabloid stories and their sources will be tracked. Photographs taken and sold will be tracked.)

Tyrone's heart sinks when he sees Kit lifted from the truck and set in the wheelchair. He puts on that pixillated smile.

"Well hello, Mr. Lightfoot. We meet again!"

Kit says nothing. A promising laugh—then sudden Stygian hollowness of features.

"Hello, Tyrone," says Burke, generating a kilowatt smile and a firm handshake, even in the chill of near-dawn. They've already met. The search for the right rehab was undertaken with the secrecy and precision of an Olympics hunt; once selected, there were many details to personally attend to.

"Hey, Mr. B—well, you made it."

"We made it. We sure did. He made it. He's the hero."

"He sure is. And we're sure happy to have you with us, Kit. There gonna be lots of people around you, twenty-four/seven, making sure you git better. Your daddy's got hisself a room right next door to y'all so y'all won't have time to be lonesome! We gonna have ourselves a party. Gonna have ourselves a get-well party."

Burke nods, and one of the men pushes the wheelchair toward the building. The interior lights blaze.

"Well, well," says Tyrone to Kit, clucking. "I thought you might at least bring Mr. Aronofsky with you."

He's a faggot negro that gets on Burke's nerves—a pain-in-the-ass queen whom he nevertheless cuts some slack, knowing Tyrone is ultimately a very important player, and that their dramatic arrival has made him overwrought.

"That's OK," continues their sardonic host, as he rushes to keep ahead of the men. *"Mr. Aronofsky isn't here and we jus' gonna have to* deal with it. We gonna deal with everything. *And we gonna have us a good time doin it, too."*

They reach the front door and Tyrone winks at Burke as they all go in.

An Actor Prepares

BECCA GOT A SMALL part in what *Daily Variety* called *Spike Jonze/ Charlie Kaufman Untitled A.K.A. Look-Alikes.* Rusty got a *big* part, which had been kind of expected, and that was OK too, because Becca didn't even want to think about the amount of shit she would have taken if given a commensurate role. Rusty seemed nicer now all around.

The look-alikes were scheduled for two weeks of rehearsal with Jorgia Wilding. (Rusty got privates.) The old woman was dismissive, demanding, and formidably gruff, but it was an incredible privilege to work with the legendary coach of so many greats—Al Pacino and Jessica Lange, Dustin Hoffman and Sally Field, Shelley Winters and Robert Duvall. Annie said that she'd even worked with Sofia on *Godfather III.*

For reasons of secrecy, scripts were mostly withheld; everyone got "sides" instead. (The pages were printed with invisible ink so they couldn't be Xeroxed.) Decoy scripts had been circulated because the producers knew that sooner or later someone would type scenes straight onto the Internet. The look-alikes had to sign waivers stating they wouldn't talk about the movie to friends, family, and especially the press. They'd be fired and fined if they did.

From what she had gleaned, *Look-Alikes* was one of those movies about the making of a movie. Becca played Drew's camera double (which she actually would be, during the shoot. Spike came up with that idea, and Becca thought it was great because, aside from helping her get into character, she'd be paid extra too.) Her role was kind of mysterious—Charles hadn't written her that many lines—but there was a dream sequence where she and Drew were supposed to kiss. Larry Levine said it sounded like "a postmodern *Cruel Intentions* thingie," but Becca just couldn't believe it. Her first film role and she was making out with Drew Barrymore!

She already knew some of her on-screen cohorts but got particularly friendly with the Barbra Streisand, who had a little cameo. When Becca asked if she had ever met the true Barbra, she said she'd only met Barbra's mother, Diana Kind, on the celebrity mom segment of a defunct TV show called *Photoplay*. Diana had invited her home for lunch.

"So here I am in Barbra Streisand's mother's *house*. Now you can't imagine what that was like because all my life people are telling me that I look exactly like her. And I'm gazing at the memorabilia, the framed photos and all, and it's like I'm surrounded by my *life* because every image has a history—for *me*—you know: everyone said I looked like *this* one when I was twelve . . . and *this* one when I was eighteen . . . and *this* one when I was thirty. And it's *very*, very strange. And I can never forget what Diana said. We were having our tea and chatting and whatnot and after a while she said that her daughter was so busy, 'I'll have to cart *you* around with me.' Can you *believe*? I saw her a *lot* after that—we went shopping at Robinsons-May for Barbra's brother's wedding present. We talked on the phone. She'd tell me how to make chicken, how you have to *clean* it and be careful of the *germs*, how you have to let it *soak*, then wash your *hands*. And the fact she was Barbra's mom gradually kind of disappeared—she was just a person. You know, I had a feeling that she liked the idea that people thought I was her daughter. To a point, I guess. I was a missing link. It *was* pretty strange. People occasionally said things . . . like once I was waiting in the car for her and some girls walked by and said, 'It's Barbra Streisand!' And Diana could hear them and I know that part of her liked that but part of her didn't. Maybe she was thinking, But this *isn't* my daughter. Where is my daughter? This is an impersonator! Then one day I got a call from her saying she'd won an award from the Jewish National Fund. She asked me to go along, and I took my fiancé. I thought Barbra might be there, but she was in Europe at the time. It was a luncheon. There weren't a million people. I got stared at in the elevator. I wasn't really introduced; she never said who I was. My fiancé and I didn't sit at the family table, but people were *looking*, I think, and wondering, Who is she? Barbra's sister was there, and we took a picture—me, Barbra's sister, and Barbra's mom! I called to thank her and she said, 'People didn't know if you were *Barbra*, if you were a *relative* . . . ' My feeling is that it got to the point where it was uncomfortable for her—though not for me. And when I heard she died, I just broke down. Because I always thought of getting in touch to see how she was but I never did."

. . .

TALKING WITH THE Barbra made her want to call her own mother in the worst way. She had a sudden, overwhelming need for Dixie to come to L.A.—it was primal, and Becca felt that if she didn't make contact, *now,* she would surely die.

She had actually thought of phoning all week because she was short on rent. She hadn't gotten a paycheck yet, even though SAG rules said that everyone was supposed to be compensated for rehearsal time. She wasn't complaining. But here she was with a Spike Jonze gig and not only was she broke but she *still* couldn't get theatrical representation. (Her so-called hip-pocketed commercial agent had done diddly-squat.) She told Elaine she was available for bookings, but ironically, the *real* look-alike work had pretty much dried up. She thought she should probably call Sharon but didn't feel like submitting herself to the seduction thing either.

Mom wasn't home. She hung up and played back messages.

"Becca? It's Gingher Wyatt. Larry Levine's friend? *Remember me?* Larry gave me your number. Listen, I'm moving back East—which means I'm quitting my lovely job! Which means I need to find someone to *replace* me and thought maybe *you* would be interested. She doesn't pay much because Viv Wembley's a cheap cunt—ha!—and of course you would have to interview, which is always fun depending on what mood the lovely and talented Ms. Wembley is in—but I have a feeling she would *really like* you. Anyway, I already talked you up with her and she thought the look-alike thing was a crack-up. (I hope it's OK I said that's what you sometimes do.) She was laughin it up, which means she was probably completely loaded. Hey, were you at a birthday party at the Colony once? Cause Viv said something about a Drew look-alike being there a while back or whenever. I think it really got her nipples hard. I'm *kidding*. Anyway, I don't want to use up your *entire machine* for this message, so if you're interested in gainful employment call my cell, 892-3311. Three-ten. The *good* part is, if she likes you she'll just *hire* you cause she's *weird* that way. But *really good*—I mean, the part of her that's *trusting* is good. Oh my God, it is *so* like the best part! Call me! Ciao for now!"

Out of Hospital

SHE NAMED THE boy Siddhama Kitchener McCadden. He was in the neonatal ICU for a month. Once he was able to breast-feed, Lisanne gave him her teat every two and a half hours. She did that for ten weeks.

Reggie said she could come back whenever she felt strong and that it'd be fun having a newborn around the office (he had one of his own). The man was a saint. She was even visited by Wendy, Reggie's wife. Mrs. Marck was on the board of a home for unwed moms, and suddenly, after all these years, she reached out. They sent flowers and sweet-tooth care packages and messenger-delivered all kinds of handy sundries. Wendy even sent her reflexologist to give Lisanne a foot massage.

The Loewensteins became unofficial godparents. Roslynn arranged for a cleaning lady and a nanny too so that Lisanne wouldn't be entirely housebound. They got her an amazing stroller and a $2,500 gift certificate at Fred Segal Baby. The studio sent over a ton of crazy reality shows and DVDs, and Tiff wrote Lisanne notes urging her to heal quickly so that he could exploit her natural-born talent as an award-show "walker." "So many tributes," he wrote, in surprisingly elegant cursive, "so little time."

She finally got the gumption to invite Philip to her apartment (that's what she called him once the baby was born, as if to formalize and atone). Lisanne was generally mortified at having concealed her condition: in retrospect, she felt duplicitous even though the word wasn't accurate. If the pregnancy had been unreal to her, how could she have made it real enough to have shared with Philip? She fruitlessly wondered if she might somehow have been forced to tell him the truth if only she had started to show. Maybe she'd have told him it was a fibroid tumor or just cut him off and fled. All she knew was that by hiding it from him, she had caused Philip tremendous pain. If she'd simply been honest (Lisanne used the word *simply* in her head and had to laugh), it probably wouldn't have been that big a deal. She had become pregnant as the result of a fling with an old boyfriend—in the wake of her father's death, no less, which actually, among excuses, was pretty much close to perfection—and couldn't imagine Philip not being understanding. And if he *wasn't*, so be it. Lisanne was frankly surprised that he still wanted her in his life at all. (He did, according to Roslynn.) She genuinely liked him, even if the physical attraction wasn't there, though a selfish concupiscence lay in Lisanne's suspicions that he got off on her obesity. She really did like the part of him that seemed damaged, the part that forced him to remain a goofy bachelor, the murky part he kept hidden— not so much that he was afraid to reveal himself but that he didn't possess the language. She also enjoyed the part that was kind and inquisitive and gentlemanly, too.

"I should have told you a long time ago," she said.

"It really doesn't matter."

He hadn't been able to look in her eyes. He watched Sidd nurse instead. Philip's glance furtively darted from suckling teat to Supreme Bliss-Wheel Integration Wheel and back; from suckling teat to plastic hangie thing above the crib; from suckling teat to the proximity of Lisanne's pale, implacable brow.

"But it does. It does matter. And I'm sorry for that."

"You don't have to say anything."

"I do. I guess that I was, just, really *confused*." Pause. "I've been confused about a *lot* of things lately. When I got pregnant, every-thing, just, kicked into overdrive. It's probably a cliché to blame it on hormones, but I think maybe it's true. Or partially. Maybe totally! I kind of 'unhinged.' I'm glad I'm not one of those women who drown their kids in the tub! I *could* be, but—anyway, I'm not, and I'm just, I'm just *really sorry*, Philip—that I didn't talk to you. I mean, about it. And I think another issue is that I really kind of really *like* you. *Being* with you. Maybe more than like. Which is unusual for me, I hope this doesn't make you uncomfortable because I know it's *crazy* what I did. Not talking about it with anyone, especially you. (But it wasn't just you.) And I'm not trying to justify it. I think part of me was in shock. Disbelief. At the timing. You know? And it's weird because I think I knew that I would never carry it to term. Which I ultimately didn't. And maybe part of me thought that if I told you, you would have just *run*. I know that sounds like bullshit because *I'm* the one who was running. And I probably would have too if I were you. But you didn't—or you haven't. Yet. And that shocks me! Scares me but in a good way. *I think*. I mean, I'm just really kind of *impressed*. By that. Is any of this making sense?"

"Are you still involved with the father?"

"No," she said, emphatically. "I never was! That's what's so ludicrous. He doesn't even *know*. I haven't *told* him—"

"You haven't told him?"

"I called a few months ago to say I was pregnant. When I knew I was going to keep it." She got tearful. "Philip . . . I'm going to be thirty-eight. I think that was *definitely* part of why I decided to go ahead and have it, knowing there wouldn't be a dad. Because Robbie Sarsgaard is *not* dad material. Then you came along—"

She wondered if she had spoken too much. Lisanne wasn't sure why she'd said half of what she did (she realized she'd been talking like someone in a melodrama) but was pretty sure she meant most all of it.

"Well, listen," said Philip. She sighed deeply, ready for the Dear Jane. "I've been thinking—and I know this sounds, *whatever* it sounds. Here's—well, this is just what's been going on in my head. I have a house in Rustic Canyon. I have this house. There's a bunch of rooms, mostly empty, except for the little part I live in. But you—if you wanted—could come stay. You'd have a full-time nanny and whatever you and the baby needed. You wouldn't be alone, Lisanne. And that would make me more at ease."

She broke into sobs. He lurched forward, kissing her neck. It felt bruising, and the skin there got sweaty and hot. Then it happened, like a dream, head sinking down to breast while the infant worked beside him, Philip's face beet red as they sucked and panted in tandem. He chewed hard on the already tender nipple, and Lisanne cried out as he quickly turned away, mouth open in a creamy, spastic glower as he came, lips fixed in a hellish hobbyist's grin, shamed and sated. His entire body quickly shrank in retreat, as if dissolving into an aerosol of corpuscles soon to finely speckle the walls before passing, microbe-like, through board and stucco to emerge on the other side, evaporating in the noonday sun.

A Successful Interview

"IS YOUR CAR INSURED?"

"Uh huh."

"You're gonna need to send a photocopy of proof of insurance to my business manager. Cause if you hit someone, I'm responsible. People *love* to sue a celebrity."

She sat in the living room of her new boss's Beachwood Canyon home. The *Together* star had moved in just a few years ago, and Becca made a mental note to go on-line and see if the transaction was ever listed in "Hot Property." She was curious how much Viv had paid and which celebs if any had lived there prior. She enjoyed researching pedigree and provenance. The high-roofed concrete house sat on five acres; Becca felt like she was in Griffith Park. It was awesome, if a bit modern for her taste—not really in keeping with the surrounding environment. Architecturally, the place definitely had a "Kit" vibe and she bet he had influenced the purchase.

She wondered if the actress had been planning to move in with him once they got married. Now that things were up in the air, she'd probably stay put. But you never knew—sometimes celebrities changed properties just because they could. The great thing about having so much money was, you could ditch everything at a moment's notice and check into any five-star hotel you liked. You could lease at the Colony or buy a ranch in Ojai or Idaho or Wyotana or wherever. Celebrities were always moving, sometimes upsizing, sometimes downsizing, but mostly they upsized. Still, Becca prided herself on being able to read between the lines of "Hot Property" blurbs to intuit when celebs were unloading because they needed cash—a sure sign being when a home was described as having been sold because so-and-so (faded rocker/older comedian/onetime game-show host) "found he wasn't spending that much time in Los Angeles" or so-and-so (forties film star/fiftysomething model with fledgling cosmetics line/Broadway icon) exchanged her house for a Century City condo because "her children were now in college." Anything going for under a million was another sign of trouble, though sometimes the charming "first home purchase" (usually Studio City or Silverlake) was inserted by the wily publicist of a young and up-and-coming USA or WB series star. Becca noticed that if a house was sold at more or less the same amount it was bought for, that was another sign of a celeb on the skids. All that being a far cry from the rarefied strata of perennially housenivorous dinosaurs like Stallone or Willis or Schwarzenegger, who still bought multiple lots (and even whole towns) with impunity, tearing down mansions so as to surround themselves with the luxury of undeveloped land. "Hot Property" said that Schwarzenegger and his wife had been looking for a place to stay while their home was being redone but couldn't find "a suitable lease"—and wound up buying a place for $12 million instead, which they planned to sell upon completion of the makeover. Becca's mom couldn't believe it.

"My business manager will have a confidentiality thing for you to sign. And they'll probably run a background check. Ever been to jail?" Viv said, with a laugh.

"Not that I know of!"

"They'll need a urine sample, for drug testing." She saw that Becca was taking her seriously and laughed again. "I'm kidding! We'll have fun. It won't be so bad, contrary to whatever horror stories I'm sure Gingher told you."

"She said it was really great," said Becca unconvincingly. "That you were great!" Viv only smirked. "I just really want to thank you," she went on, in earnest. "I have *so* much respect for you. I've watched your show from the *beginning*. I always wanted to model myself on you."

"You're not going to *All About Eve* me, are you?"

"No!" said Becca, not knowing what the actress meant.

"Anyway," said Viv, impishly. "You're not Eve Harrington, you're Drew Junior. Which one's worse?"

Becca was too nervous to respond directly. "I just wanted to say that I'm going to do a *great* job for you. I am *so motivated*."

"Good," said Viv, tartly. She lit a cigarette. "But I want to warn you: if you have a *conflict*—an *audition* or a *whatever*—and you can't do what I ask you to do in that particular moment, that is *so* not going to work. OK? If I need you to go to Rexall for Tampax or pick up a tape or a script—messengers do that most of the time—and you happen to have a *fourth callback* for *Steven Soderbergh's amazing new film* at the same time, uh, guess which one you're going to do if you want to keep your job."

"I *totally* understand."

"So were you and Gingher big buddies?"

"Not really. We met through a friend."

"You like her?"

"She's nice."

"I think she stole from me."

"Money?"

"*Oh* yeah. Lots of it. But that's not your problem. I'm not even sure *whose* problem it is because I haven't decided what I'm going to *do* about it. And I'd appreciate your not passing on that bit of information. What we say here, stays here."

Viv stood up as the Pilates teacher came from the back of the house in readiness.

"Do you have my business manager's address?"

"Yes."

"Then see you Monday, Becca," said Viv, shaking her hand.

"Thank you *so* much."

"Call me V. Don't call me Viv."

Home Away from Home

SADGE WAS BACK. He i-mailed someone in Europe while Becca flipped through a magazine. They were smoking weed.

Drew was number 61 on *Premiere* magazine's Power List, but Sadge didn't seem to give a shit. She was wedged between Michael Bay and Sandra Bullock. The tiny paragraph said that Drew "painted the living room of her new bachelorette pad a tawny color called Naturally Calm" and that her boutique production company was called Flower Films. Sandra's paragraph informed that *her* company was Fortis Films. Becca said that she was going to have her own boutique one day too. Sadge kept taking hits off the joint and i-mailing. Becca thought, *Probably someone he was fucking. A backpacking Serbian skeev.* Blue Ridge Films, she said out loud. That's a pretty name. But maybe she needed an *F,* like Drew and Sandra. "Fast Forward" popped into her head. Fast Forward Films was cute! Or Pass/Fail. That was *really* good. She asked Sadge what he thought but he wouldn't talk.

Sadge had diarrhea, something he'd picked up in the Canary Islands and couldn't shake. *A little bonus from the skeev-hump.* Plus, he had some kind of worm in his foot. The doctor said the way you killed the worm was by freezing. You didn't even try to extract it. It gave Sadge the willies to just leave it in there, and Becca thought that was why he seemed underwhelmed when she told him she got the Viv Wembley gig. Maybe he was just jealous.

She slowly chewed an overdone cheese melt. It was too soon to talk about his moving out; she didn't want to kick him while he was down. She read aloud another item, clipped from the *L.A. Times* for her "Drew archives," about the former actor John Barrymore III getting beat up inside his "upscale Mountain View" home by a bunch of crazed teenagers who were after his pot stash. She wondered how

Drew and John III were related—a half brother? Then she told Sadge about how she met this adorable young actress at the Coffee Bean who had actually grown up in the house where Drew and Tom Green lived before it went up in flames. The girl said her dad used to be Marlon Brando's agent, and back then the property had four or five different houses on it. One of them was underground, with windows peeking through the hill—very *Alice in Wonderland*. Without looking up from his i-mail, Sadge said, "Would you please shut up?" Becca blithely ignored him. The girl said they had a screening room, and the mom, who was a painter, had fashioned a studio from inside a famous hamburger stand on La Brea that the dad bought lock, stock, and barrel and had trucked onto the grounds. The girl said she cried when the house burned down but then Ben Affleck had apparently bought the parcel and the girl and her dad drove by and all kinds of construction was already being done. Sadge literally threw his sandwich at her, and Becca burst into tears. She told him he could go fuck himself and that he wasn't even supposed to be here, that he was supposed to find someplace else to live, and Sadge stopped typing, then sulked in that simmering way a man has of signaling a woman he is not a little boy but a coiled snake who by rights could rape and kill her if it weren't for the fact that he was a good person, a good man, who conscientiously exercised extraordinary sobriety, discipline, and restraint. And that one day she would see with what wisdom he had held himself back and would recognize her shrewish ways but by then it would be too late.

She tossed some things into an overnight bag and cried all the way to the car. She was on her way to Annie's, but Annie didn't answer any of her phones so Becca took Fairfax to Washington and then turned and headed for the beach.

The World of Mu

LISANNE MOVED TO Rustic Canyon. The house was empty except for the few rooms Philip inhabited, just as he described. She had her own wing. Mattie took Lisanne on a Beverly-Melrose furniture outing and spent a small fortune. She liked the idea of finally having an excuse to decorate her eccentric brother's house. She couldn't have been kinder if Siddhama had been her blood nephew.

Philip put thirty thousand dollars into an account for her to draw on for living expenses and whatever Sidd might need. They had sex twice a week. He liked taking her pants off and licking her there while she nursed. She remained passive, simply widening her legs. Anything he ever did made him come within a few minutes. He told her it had always been like that, he couldn't hold it, and Lisanne said she didn't mind, which she really didn't. She was actually grateful. Philip became active only when the baby was nursing. As long as he did his business without involving Siddhama, she was OK with it. He drew comfort from her easeful indifference. That she never judged him made him less ashamed.

· · ·

LISANNE RECEIVED AN e-mail from L.A. Dharma, a Buddhist Web site she corresponded with, announcing that a great teacher, Joshu Sasaki Roshi, would be giving a series of talks at a Zen monastery in the West Adams area. She didn't know those kinds of places even existed, locally. Something about his name looked familiar, so she confirmed on-line that Kit had once spent time at the Mount Baldy center where the roshi lived. He was almost a hundred years old.

The zendo was long and woodsy. When she arrived, male and female monks already sat in meditative posture upon cushions lining the walls. A wide bench bisected the room, and people sat on that too. Everyone took the lotus position, spines ramrod straight, but Lisanne knew she couldn't hold that too long (she hadn't really lost much weight since the birth), so she tucked a leg underneath instead and let the other one dangle. The roshi appeared and slowly made his way to a tall oaken throne on a raised platform. He was tiny and broad, and Lisanne thought he looked just like Yoda as he shuffled past in elaborate, impeccably arranged robes. An interpreter sat on the floor in readiness.

There was once a teacher and his student, he began. Teacher and student were in deep meditation when suddenly, a dog appeared between them. The student asked, "Does the dog have the Buddha nature?" To which the teacher replied, "*Mu.*" The roshi explained that both teacher and student represented Oneness. He said that, in an eternal act of cosmic beneficence, Oneness divides itself to make room for sentient beings—bird, dog, self. It then becomes the duty of sentient beings to return to that Oneness, to rejoin the great Source whence they came. The roshi said Buddhists sometimes call such Oneness "the singular reality" or True Love. The act of division itself was an act of True Love.

She struggled to understand, but her mind kept drifting. Slowly, as she grew more aware of her surroundings, Lisanne became cognizant that she was sitting beside the singer Leonard Cohen. How strange. Her back hurt, and she stirred, to avoid spasm. No one else moved— all were yogic veterans of self-abnegation, insightfulness, and zen combat. Why was she even there? She was a coward, a poseur, a grotesque. A dilettante. Unworthy. She thought of Kit, in the Painful and Unnatural Bardo of Neurological Netherworlds. She could shift a leg if her pose grew unpleasant, but what was *he* experiencing? What could *he* shift? How could she dare even presume? One of the books she got at the Bodhi Tree said that, through the vehicle of dream yoga (whatever that was), a person might be able to realize that dreaming life and waking life were the same—mere projections. Last night Lisanne woke up with a jolt because she dreamed she was riding bareback on a gigantic horse, galloping with such primal velocity that it frightened her. She was born in the Year of the Horse; maybe the dream meant this would be the year her life ran away with her. In her own analysis, the horse didn't seem to represent so much her personal life as the wild, rushing force of life itself. (Most of the time, Lisanne felt as if she were in the midst of a dream that she couldn't control, inescapable even by death.) What kinds of dreams was Kit having? Were they mundane or surreal? Or was there even a distinction? When he awakened, when he floated back from dreaming into the waking life of his disconnected body, each time that he consciously inhabited his newly ruined world afresh, the circumscribed, humiliating, crater-pocked landscape far from arc lights and movie sets, from gilded Buddha and sylphlike fiancée and the simple pleasures of food and drink, where exactly did he find himself? How did he perceive? Did he wear a chain-mail shroud made from the vortex of unfamiliar words and faces, where thought and syntax continuously stuck and unstuck like worn gears, veiling the possibility ever to make his most basic or nuanced needs known? Abject and disoriented, unmoored . . . And if, while in such a state, he could actually glimpse with any lucidity the cataclysm that had befallen him, such a revelation alone might be enough to drive him mad. Another scary Buddhist text spoke of the "*kundalini* crisis" sometimes elicited by drugs or trauma, in which subjective and objective states, waking and symbolic, merged together and broke apart in an endless loop until "consensus reality" died as surely as did the proprioception of those suffering vertigo. (A blow to the head could evoke both such crises, she thought.) A person subject to this energetic chain reaction was said to literally disintegrate but not in a *good* way. Oh, who needs consensus reality anyhow. Lisanne comforted herself by thinking, Just because it's something *I* wouldn't be able to deal with, doesn't mean it's something *Kit* can't. Yet what if, on top of everything, his *literal practice* hadn't been "right"? What if he'd made gross missteps (on the Path) that hadn't been corrected along the way, particularly since his root guru, Gil Weiskopf Roshi, was long since dead—making Kit the equivalent, now, of a pilot in a small plane flying by instruments in a thunderstorm on a moonless night. There was no one to guide him but his derelict father and a bunch of lame RNs.

Lisanne shook off her agitation, retucking first one leg, then the other. She took long, discreetly deep breaths to steady herself. She could smell her perspiration and was glad she wasn't menstruating. Leonard Cohen stared ahead with downcast eyes, oblivious.

A gong sounded, and the old man said he was out of time. "What is time?" he casually inquired. "*Time is an activity of the Buddha.* That is not a definition you are taught in schools!" He ended by saying that it was a shame the student interpreted his master's response to the question, Does the dog have the Buddha nature? as "No" when in fact he had said "*Mu.*" *Mu* meant something entirely different. *Mu* meant nothing, non-existence, non-being. "Yet just because he misunderstood does not mean the student was unworthy."

Chanting immediately began, accompanied by drums, as the translator helped the roshi from the throne. After he disappeared, Mr. Cohen was the first to stand. Lisanne noticed that, as he left, the poet kept one arm tucked to his side while the other jutted forward, parallel to the ground, the hand ritualistically cleaving sacred space like the ice cutter at the prow of a trawler.

The morning air stung her cheeks. She smiled at the world and made mental prostrations to the roshi, the gravel, and the trees—to Oneness itself. Everything was clear now. Just as the old monk had benevolently created a space for her liberating insight, Lisanne knew the destruction of the sand mandala had created a space for her child, for she remembered that as the very moment in which she had decided to keep him. The ejection of Viv Wembley's doomed fetus's consciousness into the great Source (a kind of innocent, unschooled *phowa* after all) had created the space for Siddhama Kitchener McCadden's hastened birth. All were part of the Wheel—just as Lisanne herself had been instantly, fatefully bound to Kit Lightfoot through the cauterizing gift of the auction house Buddha. Tiff Loewenstein had obliviously played spiritual midwife. For this, he was and always would be a very important man in her life.

Again Lisanne felt a great peace, the same that had flooded over her on the day of Siddhama's birth—the singular reality of True Love.

•   •   •

ON THE WAY BACK from West Adams, she stopped at Bristol Farms in Beverly Hills. She laughed to herself as the housewives stepped from their Range Rovers and Lexus SUVs—she was practically one of them. Her life had taken a peculiar turn.

"Hey!" said a big woman with frizzy hair. She planted herself in front of Lisanne like some rank frontier hippie. "I remember *you.*" Lisanne stared, blinking. "From the *lawyer's* office. You were at the *meeting.*" She extended a hand. "Cassandra—Cassie Dunsmore."

"Oh! Hi! How *are* you?"

"Couldn't be better!" She rocked her newborn in the crook of her arm. "That's my Jake. Ain't he dreamy?"

Lisanne said, "Oh, he's *beautiful.*"

"Honey, what's your name again?"

"Lisanne—McCadden."

"You should come up to the house, Lisanne! You and your boss— *Reggie.* Oh, hey! We incorporated. *QuestraWorld Productions.* It feels *good.* Man, Grady and I can't even believe it! Actually, it's Questra- World Film and Television Productions. That's the long *and* the short of it. We were gonna call it QuestraWorks but—Hey, know what we want to do? I mean, we wanna make movies and all but, *man,* I wanna do TV *real* fuckin bad. We're gonna do *The Osbournes*—but hard-core. I mean *hard* fucking core. Cause that other shit is so *tired.* Don't get me wrong, the Osbournes opened the door. But we wanna *seriously show fucking.* The final frontier! America's been headin *straight for it,* right? Gonna take the Dunsmores to keep it real, cause it seems everybody's been busy keepin it *un*-real. I am tellin you, folks want to see other folks gettin it on. Honey, we are the next wave! And you know what we got in our corner? *The pathos of Baby Questra.* Not as exploitation but as righteous *inspiration.* Where's the pathos in Sharon Osbourne's gut cancer? The girl had chemo and looks better than she ever did in her *life,* right? And now she's gonna be out there hostin a *talk show*—where's the tragedy? I mean, what's the lesson? Get cancer and get glamorous? Lose weight now, ask me how? Get cancer and get rich? Or *richer*? OK, that's *bullshit.* Let me tell you somethin. Big C ain't *nothin* compared to watchin your baby die. OK? Right? Eric Clapton like to kill hisself when that little boy flew out the window. People at home want to *see* that shit—*not* babies dying!—they want to see *survivors* who still fuckin *hurt,* that you can *survive,* cause the people at home know some terrible shit like that could happen to *them.* An' they need to be able to *commiser-ate.* Grady and I are gonna do it for HBO. Class it *up.* We ain't had the meeting yet but they be *fools* to pass-ola. Gon' be QuestraWorld's first production, that's right. We are *virgin! We! Are! Fam-i-lee! I got all my sisters and me*—Next week, I'm talkin to the *Six Feet Under* people, to partner up."

A Day of Fun

BECCA AND RUSTY spent the afternoon at Mulholland. She liked playing mommy with Jake.

When Grady heard that she had moved in with Rusty, he bought them an expensive robot dog. The droid kept raising its hind leg to pee, and Rusty couldn't figure out why. "This manual is two hundred fucking pages."

Grady sipped his beer, watching the miscreant dogbot like a proud parent. "Every young couple needs an animal."

They smoked dope while Cassandra prattled on about Questra-World ramping up production for the X-rated skein "Been There, Dunsmore" (working title) as soon as the *Six Feet Under* posse signed on. Their new lawyer supposedly was going to hook them up, but Cassandra argued that Becca already had a "relationship" with the show and should be able to get them "entrée." Cassandra said the next time their little girl did "a guest shot"—"If there *is* a next time," said Becca—she was going to come and watch. That way she could introduce herself to Their Highnesses, the two Alans. "Because in *this* town, that's the only way things ever get done." By *extreme measure* (if smuggling in during Becca's corpse gig could be considered extreme). She cited Spielberg as an example of someone who "did what he had to do." Broke into the Universal Studios backlot when he was first starting out—that's how he got hired as a director. Pretended to work there and even scammed an office, just like that movie he did, *Catch Me If You Can.* Rusty interrupted, saying if they *really* wanted the "unreality show" (the catchy phrase Grady had come up with to promote it) to be a success, they should maybe think about adopting a few kids. Especially a few *older* kids. Because that was the secret to a show like that: teenagers. Rusty said that was the main thing the Osbournes got right. You had to have kids, for demographics, drama, and relatability. Ozzy and Sharon had ruthlessly cut the older daughter out of the series, the p.r. cover being that she had declined because she was "private." Rusty said that was pure horseshit. It was "all about demos"—getting rid of their eldest was a smart business move, clean and simple. Cassandra loved the adoption strategy and got a brainstorm that the whole process should become part of the show. *Definitely.* "That is *fantastic.* Why can't *you* come up with a million-dollar idea idea like that, Grady? I'm gonna have to make Rusty here a fucking exec producer." Grady belched and said, "Right on. You go, girl. I don't need me a million-dollar idea cause I already *got* a million. Got *more* than a million. So do what you have to do." Rusty said Web sites existed where prospective parents could go shopping for kids who were currently wards of the state. Cassandra got superexcited. She said the cameras could follow them to the orphanage and they'd pick the kids out right then and there. The audience could even phone in preferences, to make it interactive. "Naw," said Grady. "That interactive shit don't never work. That's a nineties thing." "Yes, Mr. Gates," said Cassandra. Rusty said he read in the newspaper that some of those places had special picnic days where people came to look the kids over like at a slave auction. Becca thought that Rusty knew way too much about it, as if it were all close to home, so to speak. But that was the kind of thing she would never ask him about.

. . .

LATER ON, RUSTY talked about a script he was working on. "You oughta pay me for it," he said. He was stoned. He randomly murmured, "You oughta pay me for it," over and over, a sly, wacko catechism.

"We're gonna pay you for it," said Grady reassuringly.

"First we need to *see* it," said Cassandra, with a smirk.

Everybody was stoned.

"You'll see it," said Rusty.

"Promises, promises," said Cassandra.

"It's gonna be good," said Grady, in his friend's defense. "I know it's gonna be good."

"Got QuestraWorld written all over it," said Rusty.

"Hope it does," said Cassandra. "Hope we *do* make it."

"How much you wanna spend, Rusty?" asked Grady. "On the budge. On el budjo."

"Ten," said Rusty. "But we could do it for seven or eight."

"Hell," said Grady. "Do it for *three* and you can make the cock-sucker *immediamente*. Ipso facto. We'll get Fucko the robot wonderdog to direct."

"*I'm* gonna direct," said Rusty, reminding. "And we can't do it for three."

"Three ain't chump change," said Cassandra. "Lotta movies been made for three."

"What world are *you* living in?" said Rusty, cockily.

"Shit, what'd they make *Reservoir Dogs* for?"

"It wasn't three," said Rusty. "Not in 2004 *dinero*. No way, José."

"You could be right," said Cassandra. "Maybe it was two."

"It's gonna be *good*," said Grady. "Hell, Cassie, if the man's *starrin* in it and the man's *writin* it, you *know* it's gonna be good. We got in on the ground floor—the man's the lead in a Spike Jonze! Gonna be a worse triple threat than Billy Bob. Shit, we're *lucky*, Cass. Motherfuck-ers be givin Van Diesel or whatever the fuck his name is *twenty mil-lion*—I can't even remember the name of that chrome-dome bitch and they're givin him twenty mill. Fucker has about as much charisma as the head of my dick. Fucker *looks* like the head of my dick too!"

"How's that Spike thing goin, anyhow?" asked Cassandra.

"Goin good. Goin real good."

"Gonna start shooting soon?"

They alternated pulling with lazy industry on the pipe.

"Bout six weeks," said Rusty, playing it movie star cool.

"You're in it too, huh," said Cassandra.

"I'm just doing a cameo," said Becca.

"Bullshit," said Rusty, feeling all generous.

"Rusty's *starring*," said Becca, proudly.

"She's got a sweet little part," said Rusty, noblesse oblige. "She sticks her tongue down Drew Barrymore's mouth."

"Duelin Drews," said Grady.

"Bet you're looking forward to rehearsals," said Cassandra, lascivi-ously. "I'd floss my tonsils if I was you."

"I'm actually not!" said Becca.

"Better not blow your lines," said Grady to Rusty.

"Blow this," said Rusty, as he took a hit.

"You might get tongue-tied," said Grady to Becca. He laughed while grabbing the pipe from his friend. "My man Rusty can *write* too!" he giddily exclaimed, to no one in particular. He sucked and nearly gagged. An effete, wincing smile imploded above his chin while smoke poured from his nostrils, four-alarm. "*Help*," he said, wheezing comically through whitened lips. "*I'm having a fuckin heart attack.*"

"Ever seen anything Rusty wrote, honey?" asked Cassandra, ignor-ing her husband's pulmonary spaz.

"I seen how he writes his *name*," said Grady with a joker's grin, as he messily recovered. "It look *real pretty.*"

"Yeah," said Rusty. "*Your* name's gonna look pretty too, when it's on that QuestraWorld check."

It went on like that for a while. Then Grady started tripping that one of the homies at Valle Verde said Kit Lightfoot was there, and was totally twapped out. The homie said the superstar had a wing all to himself, and whenever they let him walk the grounds, the *madre* pulled his pud and had to be hustled inside before some paparazzi in a helicopter squeezed off a shot. Cassandra said they should all pile in the G-wagen and go on down. No one was unstoned enough to drive so Avery, a live-in part-time student and all-around gofer, was enlisted as chauffeur.

•   •   •

GRADY KNEW THE gate guard, who waved them in. They were a few blocks away when de Becker's men turned them back. As they left, Grady asked the guard about Kit.

"Ain't seen him," he responded, with a wink.

Grady was jonesing for a Krispy Kreme. Cassandra pinched his love handle and said, "Why don't you just have one of these? Feels like about a dozen right here." Grady told Avery to find them a Krispy Kreme, *pronto*. Avery called 411 and located a franchise near Knott's

Berry Farm. They went and gorged. Then Cassandra got the urge to visit Knott's and pan for gold, something she hadn't done since she was a kid. They spent a few hours there, and Becca had the best time. As they left, the couple argued because Grady wanted to make a "pit stop" at Hustler's. "I just wanna place one bet." He wouldn't say for how much, and that pissed her off. Rusty and Becca leaned against each other in the backseat, eyes shut, wasted. Cassandra fumed while Grady went inside the casino.

He came out five minutes later with a loopy grin.

"One bet," he said. "See? A man of his word."

"Asshole. How much did you lose?"

"Five large."

"Asshole. Feel better?"

"Fuckin *a* I do. Fuckin *a*, *b*, and *c* too!" Then: "I'm a disciplined motherfucker. I say what I mean and I mean what I say. But it's fuckin *weird*, man. I cannot *tell* you how many times I've gone into a casino and placed *one* bet. I mean for bupkes! For ten, twenty, a hundred. I cannot *tell* you how many times I have done that in my fuckin life. And you know what? Man, tell me the odds, but I have *never fucking won*, not even *once*."

Rusty roused himself from a stupor to laugh, without opening his eyes. Cassandra laughed, then Grady too. Becca was blasted and smiled only because the others were merry and mellow. "And *half* the time, the dealers get blackjack!"

"What does that tell you, niggah?" said Rusty.

Becca stirred, clinging to him.

"*Tell* you what it tells me, dog," said Grady. "*The house always wins.*"

Synchronicity

HIS SON LAUGHS *wildly at something on TV. Burke makes sure the only fare is DVDs like* Shrek *or* Sound of Music *or* Chariots of Fire. *Nothing violent or sexual. And no channel surfing: he guards against Kit mistakenly stumbling across one of his own films, or news reports about his injuries. Doesn't want him watching Viv Wembley cavort on that idiotic series either.*

Lately, Kit erupts into hysterical outbursts in the middle of the night. (The sanghanistas *like to say he's finally getting in touch with the cosmic joke of it all.) Sometimes he sings himself to sleep like a child, but that's the only time he comprehensibly strings more than a few words together, albeit slurred. He possesses an amazing surplus of energy—the* sanghanistas *call it* ch'i—*and Burke makes certain that energy is properly channeled, that his son is occupied by some form of therapy each waking hour.*

His father wants him out of there.

His father wants him home in Riverside, where he belongs.

He speaks in monosyllabic plosives. He says fuck *a lot, eerily reminiscent of the patient with whom Kit and Darren Aronofsky visited months ago. One day, an inspired Tyrone brings Roy Rogers to the private wing for a summit. Seeing the two together—trepanned superstar and blastomaed McDonald's franchiser—watching the Blown-Mind Twins sniff each other like tentative street dogs was a rocky horror show for sure—more like one Special Olympiad passing the torch to another, because it just so happened that Roy was at the stuttering tail end burnout of "I fuck fuck fuck" just as Kit was coming into his full-throated, full-chorus own. Like that summer Tyrone went to New York and John Stamos replaced Matthew Broderick in "How to Succeed" . . . but try as he might, Ty couldn't get a dysfunctional duet goin. Connie Chung enjoyed the impromptu reunion, though Ty didn't think she fully dug the interaction. She wasn't twisted enough; it was a cultural thing. But he thought the way Nurse Connie kept wrangling the veggies so they'd* be face-to-face like sexy toy soldiers was beyond dope. Tyrone shook his head and smiled. It was so messed up.

.   .   .

HE ASSIDUOUSLY LIFTS himself a few inches on the parallel bars. He grins madly, wily and rabid, flashing the erotically mischievous Kit Lightfoot of old. (A bad haircut ruins the effect. Fearful of "anecdotal" leaks to the press, his father shot down Kit's stylist's request to come give a trim.) His body glistens, the layer of posttraumatic fat belying its good bones; Portrait of a Bruce Weber almost-ran, with bad breath.

.   .   .

WITH MOUTH CLOSED, unspeaking, only the wobbly, jerky gait betrays him. After all, he was in perfect shape at the time of the assault; not so many months have passed. He never stopped moving—Burke forbade that— not even in coma. Therapists and sanghanistas threw his limbs around more than Christopher Reeve. Tyrone said, We the A-Team. Put Mr. Reeve to motherfuckin shame.

.   .   .

"HELLO, PIRATE!" said Tyrone.

Kit wore an eye patch because the left lid drooped. He no longer tried to tear it off. Burke arranged for surgery; the docs said it was a simple fix.

"Find any sunken treasure today, Captain Cook?"

.   .   .

VIV LEFT A MESSAGE on Becca's pager that she needed her to pick up the Ambien refill at Horton & Converse.

When she got to the house, Becca punched in the ROCK* code at the gate. As she wound up the drive, the FooFighters blasted. The front door gaped open.

She set the pharmacy bag on the table and called out, "Viv?" She corrected herself: "V?" She thought she heard a response, muffled by music from upstairs. "V?"

Barely audible: "Come up!"

She went to the master bedroom. Viv was on her back, fucking. "Did you get the Ambien?" Becca had already shyly turned around.

She said she brought it, and Viv said, "Where?" "Downstairs." "What about the Norco?" Becca asked what was Norco and Viv said testily that they should have filled that along with the Ambien. Becca said she didn't look inside the bag. Viv told her to go bring it. This time when Becca came back, Viv was on her stomach and the man fucking her faced the door instead of the headboard.

It was Alf Lanier.

Becca *loved* Alf Lanier.

(It looked exactly like Alf Lanier.)

Viv said to put the pills on the dresser and leave. Setting the Ambien down, she couldn't help glancing over to see them sweat-coiled, and Alf caught her eye, either laughing or wincing, she wasn't sure what. She thought that maybe the actors were making fun of her, "having sport" as Dixie used to say whenever Dad was being mean.

. . .

KIT WAS STONED—that was Burke's idea. Pot helped with the pain and the muscle spasms. The staff looked the other way. Half of them were hemp-heads, anyway.

There was so much fear that he couldn't verbalize, which terrified him even more. So much shame and embarrassment. What had happened to him, really? Got his head hit. What hospital was this and what was the one before? Sometimes he went monkey nuts, throwing food and masturbating in front of staff and guests. He was hungry all the time. Ate and ate and started to get doughy. Sometimes he got confused that he couldn't dress himself. He had blinding headaches and threw up, and they gave him shots that made him dreamy all the next day. The Shaved-Head people visited, some in robes but different from the flimsy hospital gowns that he didn't even wear anymore. (Burke liked his boy to be in real-world civvies.) They made him laugh. Things were funny, especially when he smoked the reefer. Things on TV, and things his caregivers would say or do. It was funny when they read from books or said their prayers. They taught him mantras, those were funny too, repeating words he couldn't understand, strings of words, one after the other, going to the end then beginning again. The sounds were strange, and sometimes he panicked he should know what they meant. He would grimace and nervously try to ask if he should know their meaning, and wonder if he ever would or if that was beyond him now, but in his crowned and crowning

agitation, in his disorder, could not get inquiring words to form, and the
benevolent patience and solicitousness of the sangha only made his fear and
panic grow.

•   •   •

STOPPED LOOKING in mirrors.

Not wishing to see his own visage or the purplish white fissures of his
broken, thousand-petaled lotus.

•   •   •

HE FOUND OCCASIONAL respite in remedial Buddhist practice. The edi-
fice had crumbled yet the foundation was there, rooted and unassailable.
By his stalwart guests' incessant cues, he slowly resurrected the meditative
state, starry spangled night on mind-screen—disciplined sits over the
course of a decade had stored in the body and served him well. The sang-
hanistas verbally guided him through: on days he couldn't tie his shoes, he
still crudely focused on the Shaved-Heads drum of Christ consciousness,
seemingly lucid enough to laugh at his hallucinatory predicament. Words
began to rearrange themselves like magnetized particles. A flurry of inter-
change, like a vast hangar filled with square-dancing phantoms, crepuscu-
lar and insolent, dysphotic, drowsy and spooked, orphans and changelings
come to vellicated, marvelous life as the orchestra struck up its synaptic
symphonics.

Sometimes being adrift was his only mooring.

•   •   •

ONE DAY RAM DASS came to see him. That was a great boon. Kit recog-
nized him but couldn't recall their meeting at the Gubers'. (Memory with-
held its muddy welcome mat for the six months immediately prior to his
insult.) Ram Dass floated over in his wheelchair and looked deep into his
eyes. He laid hands on Kit's shoulders and smiled, an electric clown.

Ram Dass said, "Surf the silence."

He told Kit to think of his guru, Gil Weiskopf Roshi (whom Ram Dass
reiterated he had known). "The guru will set you free." He shared some
rambunctious observations about his own recovery that were exorbitantly
pertinent to Kit. He even got him laughing about the Hollywood game—
Burke had steered everyone away from mentioning the Business, but Ram

Dass cut through. "God," said Ram Dass, "will always make more than you per picture!" He began to chant—Om Ram Ramaya Namaha—and Kit tried his best to follow (he'd been play-chanting with the sangha for the last month), swept up in its emphathenogenic energies. The others joined in while Ram Dass held Kit's hand and wept ecstatically. They were all weeping now, even Kit, though water filled his smiling befuddled eyes as it would those of a sensitive child who had been moved not so much by others than by the joy-jangling vibrations of a great and noisy organ during mass.

.   .   .

SHE ASKED HIM to put it in her bottom, the way Kit did. Alf had never done that. Was that sodomy? He thought sodomy was the legal term for assfucking but wasn't sure because every time he read about a sex crime in the paper they called it sodomy—there couldn't be *that* much assfucking going around. (Could there?) Maybe the rapists and molesters knew a thing or two. He had tried before but had never been able to consummate. After amazing heroics, he would manage only to get the head in and the girl would say it hurt and to take it out. He didn't really care all that much but felt it was his duty as a man at least to have the thing on his résumé. Other times, when the girl was seemingly OK with it, he lost his hard-on. Alf reasoned that he probably just didn't get off enough on the deed. Wasn't his kink. Or whatever. He thought maybe he was just lazy. By nature, he had a conservative streak—certain things had always creeped him out, like if a girl went down on him too wildly or tried to suck his nipple. Besides, assfucking was a control trip, and Alf prided himself on not having those kinds of issues with the ladies. Jailhouse issues, he thought. But now the tip of his cock was nudging its way inside the butt of his semiretarded best friend's ex-fiancée. Viv worked it like a pro—kept urging him on, using her fingers to oil him with her juices while begging him to make it hurt, make it bleed—then suddenly he was in. It was a different pressure than pussy pressure for sure. 20,000 leagues under the sea. There was something metallic about it, mechanical, submariney. *Das Boot.* Das bootie. She slowly pushed against him, swallowing him up, and took the whole thing. Like watching a garter snake swallow a fuckin gopher. He asked if she was

OK and Viv said uh huh and her shithole got wet, that's how turned on she was. I didn't even know a girl *got* wet that way. Once, he was with a stripper who shot a warm geyser from her puss when she came, but this was a first. He thought maybe he'd blundered onto the Secret of the Fags. *Dark Tomb Raiders . . . Raiders of the Golden Sphinct*—or maybe the hole was slick with shit. *That* would be fucked. He peered down in the half-light, and his cock looked clean on each outthrust. Wasn't any stink. She probably prepared. Like when his mom went in for a colonoscopy and had to fast for twelve hours before. Sure knew what she was doing. . . . He began to ram her, devil-may-care, and she went crazy. The harder he rammed, the more she groaned and twisted and talked dirty. Maybe she was a pain freak—Fine with me. I mean, I don't want to be inflicting it deliberately, but if I'm feelin good and whatever I'm doin happens to hurt as a sidebar but she gets off on it, then cool. Cool. Although he didn't relish the idea of being back at Cedars signing autographs for the cops while Viv had her poop chute stitched by the same folks who'd tended Kit's wounds. Then she told him to fuck her "up the ass the way your best friend liked to fuck me" and it wigged him but only for a second. All's fair in loving and whoring. (That's what Kit used to say.) *Fuck me up the ass at the hospital, so he can watch.*

It took everything he had to concentrate on not coming.

* * *

EARLIER, HE GAVE Kit some pills, and now Tyrone sat with his charge while he nodded off. Ram Dass and his coterie were long gone.

Ty snorted some crystal and massaged the star's shoulders, oiling the skin. Smooth and unmarred. He rubbed oil into the FOREVER VIV, lovingly polishing the varied tattooed heart, Pacific Northwest Indian, and Sanskrit motifs. He reached around and rubbed the flat-muscled, soft-haired belly; the one-time orderly began to perspire and yawningly hyperventilate. He moved a hand up to the flat tits, tenderly tracing a finger around the nipple. He tongued one, nervously looking around, even though he knew nobody was there and no one would enter. Kit gaped with sleepified incognizance. Ty rubbed the tense muscle-braids of the actor's neck for just a moment, then gently turned him on his back, softly whispering, as if audi-

tioning the words aloud to see if the void would answer: I love you, Kit. He tripped on how the phrase sounded when uttered in the presence of the devotional object itself, tripped on the astonished hyperreality of it. Whoa. Whoa. Moved his hand to the radiant bush of soap-scrubbed pubic hair. Said, louder this time, "Kit Lightfoot is my lover." His heart almost popped from his chest when he touched the shaft. Whoa—nearly fainting as he stood, he needlessly ran to recheck the door, already locked. Light-headed and light of foot . . . Lightfoot is my man. Lightfoot is my man—worked off the pants, fastened onto cock with his mouth, his own already leaking, clear as spinocerebellar fluid. Looked up, still sucking, at the idol of his prostrations and good fortune, to see perchance to dream if Kit was reacting. Any old reaction would do. Perchance to ream. The supernova only stirred, mouth open, and that was more than enough. He imagined the actor to be in some faraway place—a summer place . . . sucked and sucked, gentle, gentle, sucking, kneading, poundingheart, vertiginous stabs of paranoia whenever hearing nonsounds, willing now to lose his job and do hard time for this fleshy succor, this godhead paradise. I deserve this. Whoa. A K-Y'd finger in the ass to get Kit hard elicited a fart. Worked two more fingers in. Still got the touch. In and out till it was easygoing, leisurely cupping and weighing the balls between reentries. Big-time fun. Slid his pants down. Fingers in Kit then same fingers inside his own anus. The superstar groaned, eyes still shut. Heart slammed against steel cage of Ty's torso, graveyard shift foundry, thin black pink-spotted snake cock in hand. Too excited!—oh no. No no no—Kit was half-hard from Ty's expert manipulations. Jacked him fiercely, it was almost over, better luck next time, wanted Kit to come, mouth on it now as he worked his fingers like a safecracker's, turgid ticking cock, lock to catch and spring, whoas! out loud, no no no shit no as he pushed further and sucked on Kit while jacking himself and Alf can hold it no more and is thankful Viv senses that and urges him on—maybe, he thinks, she's in pain or I'm doing it wrong, can't work it like Kit, can't do the real deal dillio, I'm an assfuck loser— but he's grateful she's urging cause the thing he hates most is when a girl says, "Don't come," that means she's totally frigid and wants to drag it out forever, he's slept with so many of them, but Viv can come, can she ever, one of the lucky ones, doesn't have a problem in the vaginal departmento, this he already knew from Kit's innuendoes and Alf says "Now? Now?"—he doesn't want her to think that he has to or needs to or wants to even though all of the above are true—and she says *"Yes,"* so he instantly comes in that tight slick chute and it feels better to come in a pussy but the *cool* thing, the kink of it is, that he comes in her bowel, in a place whose chemical wretchedness kills babies, vilifies and degrades his sperm, and somehow *that's* exciting, that she hereby consents to infernal degradation, such apostasy, adulterous and unadulterated, that is what makes him come so deeply while she arches beneath like an animal being killed *until yes, Kit arches too, sharp coughy intake of breath, Ty's four-fingered hand inside him while the other pulls Kit's cock as he sucks and the star suddenly comes as Ty nudges the G-spot, the Motion Picture and Television Entertainment Liaison quickly bowing to suck the come, coming more himself without even needing to be touched or nudged, climaxing like a woman, immaculately, licking Kit's shaft as it spunks Ty's dark-backed palm-white hand, which has drifted to the tip, not wishing to miss a precious drop* Viv is coming like she hadn't with Kit in so long, Alf doesn't know they used to talk about it more than the actual doing, mostly embedding fingers instead, and now she cries out and is crying too because she thinks of Kit and is getting off on the betrayal, a helpless whore who'd sell anyone or anything out, she would not even make the call to stop the WTC hijackers, she should have put the engagement ring on for this, further frisson, and though she knows that later she'll feel badly, all those useless feelings of guilt, right now all she wants is to be evil, evil, supercallifragalistic axis of evil—*please don't let the coming stop*—and she comes some more because she knows her new assistant is listening to the wolflike screams, in the entry hall or in gleaming $300,000 kitchen, sipping a diet Coke through a straw while taking it all in, the whole house reverbing with screams, CD juke shuffling to lame-ass Bright Eyes-Blur-Sheryl Crow, and she feels the warm narcotic glow of the Norco and the Klonopin, everything so perfect, she, still coming *before plunging the white dick back into his mouth and it goes on, him doing cleanup with his tongue, it takes a few minutes like that to settle accounts and close the books, Tyrone like a runner slowly calms, he's crossed the finish line now, walking aimlessly from the crowd until lungs and worldly locomotion are returned, remembering old History Channel kinescopes of Jessie Owens.* . . .

What a surprise.
I *deserve* this. *(Viv.)* I do, I do. *I motherfuckin Queer Eye do. (Ty.)*
Everyone came together.
  Baby still got the touch

                        That was cool *(Alf)*

The Three Mysteries

. . .

THE NEW YEAR

Four Affirmations

SIDD KITCHENER McCadden was now eight months old, and a regular at Peet's Coffee on Montana. There were a lot of regulars at Peet's, and Lisanne often wondered what those people did for a living aside from drinking tea and lattes. They probably wondered the same thing of her.

In the early morning, she left the baby in the care of a nanny and went jogging along the bluff. The regulars tended to congregate outside, even if it was freezing, and she would see them as she drove to Ocean Avenue. The ones who preferred to stay indoors had special places to sit that they guarded with their lives. When she came at about ten, after collecting her son, the clique was still remarkably intact. They oohed and aahed over "little Sidd" (they assumed he was a Sidney), but she didn't make small talk. Lisanne held them in benign contempt, wondering which was the actor, model, stylist, which was the kept person or whatnot. Sometimes they appeared in absurd spandex cycling outfits; sometimes they celebrated each other's birthdays with slices of cake which they tried to foist on whatever innocents had the misfortune to sit close by. They didn't seem wealthy and no one was famous, although the rich and famous *did* pass through, like Meg Ryan and her son or Kate Capshaw in jodhpurs or Madeleine Stowe and her sweet husband, who looked like a short, stocky dentist. Everyone from local yoga came to Peet's, and Lisanne held out hope she would see Marisa or Renée so she could strike up a conversation about the terrible thing that had happened to Kit. She didn't think that would be inappropriate, but they never showed.

After Viv's miscarriage and her epiphany that Siddhama was the child of Kit Lightfoot (a revelation she guarded from Philip and everyone else), Lisanne had begun to study vipassana in earnest, meeting regularly with a Westside group. They did their sitting at a Zen center tucked behind a post office in Santa Monica and at members' houses too. Sometimes there were all-night *yazas*, but mostly they met on weekday afternoons. She liked vipassana because it was the oldest form of meditation, a technique the Buddha himself was said to have practiced. Philip was supportive even though he no longer evinced much interest in things Buddhist. (She wasn't sure that he ever really had.) Still, he built Lisanne an airy cabin on the grounds where she could do her ashtanga and even let himself be dragged to a loving-kindness workshop just up the road, in Temescal.

• • •

THE SATURDAY RETREAT was led by teachers from a place up north called Spirit Rock. Lisanne and Philip joined about twenty others in sitting and walking meditations. No one was allowed to speak except to repeat four affirmations:

. . . May I/you be safe and protected from harm.
. . . May I/you be happy and live with joy.
. . . May I/you be healthy and strong, or if that's not possible, may
        I/you accept my/your limitations with grace.
. . . In my/your outer life, may I/you live with the ease of well-being.

The affirmations were recited while visualizing first oneself; then a "benefactor" (someone who had bestowed kindnesses or generosity); then a friend; then a "neutral person"; a "difficult person"; and finally, beings one did not personally know.

The idea was to learn to transmit *metta* (a Pali word often translated into English as loving-kindness) to all creatures, human and animal, seen and unseen, newly born and newly dying. The teacher said it was a "practice of the heart." He said that the source of all joy arose from wishing happiness to others and that the source of all sorrow arose from wishing happiness only to oneself.

Lisanne visualized Kit for each permutation. Kit Lightfoot was her Self, her benefactor, her friend, her neutral person, her difficult person, and someone she did not really know. Before the final walking meditation, they were told to send *metta* to all beings encountered on their way—the hikers, the birds, and even the trees. ("Though in classic Buddhism," said the teacher, somewhat reluctantly, "trees lack true consciousness.") The group dispersed, and Lisanne meandered before climbing the hillside trail. As she cleared the ridge, she could see five meditators standing in a small depression, staring down at their feet. She got closer and instinctively slowed, wondering if something lay dead in the dirt. Then she saw it: a snake, sunning itself in the path. Its rattle was translucent and dirty yellow, like a wicked pacifier. The *metta*-heads bombed it with love and then it started to move. All eyes followed as the reptile slithered through the grass, visible for about seventy-five yards before vanishing. She wished that Philip had been there, but he had gone off in a different direction. For Lisanne, it was the highlight of the workshop, but she never told him about the encounter. That would have been smug, and the teachings were against it.

. . .

THROUGH THE *SANGHA* of old and new connections, she became acquainted with a group of practitioners who knew Kit before the mishap. And that was how one day she casually, yet with great portent, came to be invited to do service in a modest home at the end of a suburban cul-de-sac.

The Banks of Riverside

THE OLD HOUSE sat comfortably in its skin.

Spiffed and restuccoed, spit-polished, refurbished, a wall around it now, nothing too tall or ostentatious but nicely done. Thick enough to be serious.

Some new additions graced driveway and curbside—Kit's jet black G-wagen, for one. (A neighborhood boy hand-washed it each week.) His fab old forties pickup, for another. On the lawn, the storied

Indian, teardrop Triumph, and Harley with the handlebar fringe luxuriously hibernated beneath a locked-down tarp. A silver Range Rover with little shark gill vents was there too, blocking the drive—for Burke's use only. The stately, beloved, die-hard DeVille—the junk car gone up on blocks a month or so before Kit came to scan Rita Julienne's love letters—was gone. Scrapped. Tula, the Fijian bodyguard, spent most of his time sleeping out front in a maroon Crown Victoria, a detective's car acquired at auction.

A veritable auto show, but the neighbors don't mind.

The actor, under his father's imposing, vigilant care, could have been stashed anywhere: Arizona, Jackson Hole, Northern California. Canada, Cabo, the Dominican. Hell, anyplace at all could be transformed into a one-man state-of-the-art rehab. The decision might even have been made, with full cooperation of the trust, to fortify the (already secure) Benedict Canyon compound, bunking nurses, M.D.s, therapists, and cooks in guest rooms and guesthouse, stowing *sanghanistas* in the zendo. But Mr. Lightfoot knew such a maneuver would have, at least in the public's eye, made him house nigger; easier for the powers that be to extricate him too, once his boy got better. No, it was all about perception—always was, always would be. He didn't like the view from the back of the bus much. Never did. He would need a modicum of control from the get-go if he was to have a fighting chance against those legal Goliaths.

He lobbied for Riverside and won. Won big.

. . .

ALL THESE YEARS, the old room has been kept pristine, with its desktop aquarium and blackened-pocket catcher's mitt straight off the cover of *Saturday Evening Post*. The shelves in the den were unapologetically lined with clippings from magazines (Cela found the beautiful frames at the Rose Bowl swap): Kit on the receiving end of the People's Choice, the Golden Globe, the MTV-this, the *Show West*-that—Kit with Nicole and Bob Dylan, Meryl, Prince Charles, some crippled kids, the Dalai Lama, Rosie, Oprah, Giuliani and the Singing Fireman, Clinton, Sinatra, Mick, Hockney, Mandela and Sting, Kofi and Gwyneth, George W. and Condoleezza.

Shots of Viv had been weeded out.

• • •

(THE BACKYARD DIDN'T have a pool, but Burke installed an above-ground one with a therapeutic wave machine for Wonderboy to kick against. He bought a humongous steel sectional barbecue too. Cost four grand. Kit loved Cela's burgers more than In-N-Out's.)

• • •

ALL THE WHITE carpets Rita Julienne Lightfoot ghost-walked for years before the divorce, those bitching, toxic, whiny years before she got the crop of cooz tumors . . . All the white carpets, once compulsively scrubbed by that fucking harridan, now torn up and replaced with thick pile.

• • •

NO ONE COULD DENY there was a profound folkloric purity, a demoniac simplicity—the stuff of modern pop myth—in Burke's arranging for the prodigal son's rehab to be in Riverside. *Keep it simple.* (He told Cela that it was a case of "the swallowed returning to Capis-trano.") The homely, homespun formula was a major hit with the media too, featured by every conceivable outlet of the entire wired, warring planet. Lightfoot Senior became his own spin doctor, kibosh-ing rumors that he was trash, a mercenary, deadbeat dad: debonair Burke now vibed caretaker extraordinaire. The lawyers could be counted on to draw out the travails of executorship in order to con-tinue collecting their hourly rape fee. Months went by with nothing resolved. Funds flowed minorly, purse strings tightly cinched; the bat-tle was far from over, and enemies abounded. The estate paid a low-end stipend for a private security detail—Tula, force of one—and an allowance to Kit, which technically, his father could dip into. (The stipend did *not* pay for Tula's meals or overtime, and Burke liked to say he was going broke with all the lunch and dinner runs to KFC.) The lawyers were trying to humiliate him, break him down—get him to settle, then book. To Vegas, or wherever. Out of their face. Classic war of attrition. Make him throw in the towel so they could exact their nefarious tolls, play out their godforsaken sociopathic entitlement motives. Rob him of what was his, by blood. Well, fuck them. Y'all can go fuck y'all. As they say in the South.

. . .

RIVERSIDE LOVED IT.

Because the ancestral home sat on NOT A THROUGH STREET beside a moatlike culvert, access was relatively easy to control. With the enthusiastic urging of residents, the city council quickly approved a gated checkpoint. Unless permitted, only locals were allowed entry to the five-square-block area in question. Per special ordinance of the mayor, those trustees of the stalkerazzi—helicopters, small planes, and hot-air balloons—were naturally disallowed in the airspace above. The neighborhood rallied round its fallen hero amidst a tide of global ink, for it really *did* take a village: Riverside thrilled at its own retooling of image, torqued from homicidal methamphetamine shithole to nurturing municipality. Burke Lightfoot reveled too in his once vaguely hostile hometown's embrace, rejoicing in their newfound antimedia puritanism. He renewed his bonds of affection with this brave new world, county of movers and shakers, of speedy utilitarians, of fast learners that he'd never after all abandoned, kingdom of civic morality and pragmatism, this adroit, far-seeing, unexpectedly *with-it* protectorate whose vivacious, obstreperous, out-of-left-field support had been counterintuitive, and left him with nothing but praise and exultation.

Always, a flotilla of media vans and trucks on the neighborhood's outskirts and the small industry of shiny catering campers that sprung up to feed them (with proper permits, further enriching city coffers). Newshounds made the requisite, random inquiries but were shined by the locals re: purported condition of and/or formal or casual neighborly encounters with the tragic superstar who (allegedly) shuffled, shambled, lurched, and recovered among them. It was unprecedented, but neither grainy image nor insipid anecdote had yet been leaked or sold to tabloids. No bark and no byte. The united front was impossibly, utterly, wholesomely Capraesque, almost as much of a story as its subject. Had a touch of the Branch Davidian too.

Lawns were tidier. This godly little acre took on a lush utopian tinge, a peculiarly Middle-American Shangri-la ruled over by Lord Lightfoot, natty ringmaster and gemütlich Wizard of Kit. If one looked with a very keen eye (the streetlamps did not cast a wide or bright light), one might see them strolling at eventide—wounded wild-child and martyred keeper. By sunny Riverside day (and by night too), troops of saffron-robed monks came and went, polite, amiable, unobtrusive, discreetly stitching themselves into the community quilt. Burke used them for running errands and cleaning house. They engaged Kit in physical therapy, for the father did not trust those sent from the hospital; after their visits, memorabilia seemed to go missing.

Only a few of the old cronies ever called or even asked to stop by. Kiki came just once (it's true she checked in a lot, but Mr. Lightfoot discouraged actual visits), as did Robin Williams and Edward Norton—but not his so-called soul mate ex-fiancée or Alf, putative running partner and self-proclaimed best friend, now rumored to be dining on Viv's snatch, or any of the studio parasites, business managers, or legal eagles who had coolly leeched so many hundreds of millions off his handsome hardworking boy. Fine, then. Better he be ministered to by selfless monks.

Larry King and Barbara Walters called, to cajole. Barbara wanted an interview in the worst way. "I'm very, very, patient," she said slyly. Tough Jew. Ton of moxie. They flirted over time, Burke putting her through his time-tested charmathon workout. Whenever Barbara hung up—after saying she'd call again next week, which she did, like clockwork—he thought: Captivating lady. A real pro, and a hottie in her day, too.

Becca in Venice

BECAUSE OF RUSSELL CROWE'S conflicting film schedules, *Look-Alikes* was shot over the holidays and into the new year. Becca finished the gig just before Thanksgiving. She never stayed on to do camera-double work because Drew asked that her regular double take over. (Drew was loyal that way.) She was kept abreast of any juicy set scuttlebutt by a second A.D. whom she'd furtively kissed on a day Rusty had been mean to her. Lately, there were a lot of those kinds of days.

The big gossip was that the true Russell (his wife, who was expecting, had only been in L.A. for part of the shoot) had some sort of dalliance-dustup with the true Drew and that the Billy Bob look-alike was hitting bull's-eyes with all the female look-alikes (and one of the males), even though he had hopelessly lost his heart to the true and *very* young Scarlett Johansson. Which was funny because, as the second A.D. pointed out, the true Scarlett and the true Billy Bob already *had* a dalliance (on-screen) in that movie where Billy Bob played a barber. The second A.D. said that the true Scarlett, who may or may not have had a dalliance with the true Benicio, *definitely* "had it going on" with the true John Cusack. The second A.D. said that he thought the true JC was maybe having something with either the true Meryl (who had a small, very hip cameo) or the Meryl look-alike, or both. Becca doubted the very married Mrs. Streep would be having an affair with *anyone*, and suddenly all the second A.D.'s whispered intelligences were put into question.

She was pleased that Rusty had spoken of his counterpart with such genuine respect and affection. They'd already shot a few scenes, and Rusty apparently had held his own. He told Becca that "the Gladiator" (though he never called him that to his face) was nothing short of a gent. They'd even had a drink together.

                                    •   •   •

LIVING IN VENICE was fun. Becca loved going for jazzy little walks on Abbot Kinney and having drinks at Primitivo. She loved popping into retro furniture boutiques and making mental lists of what to buy for her future hillside home. (She was thinking Los Feliz. That's where Spike and Sofia lived, and the chief of police too.) Rusty's apartment was cramped and moldy, and even though she enjoyed hearing the sound of the ocean, she was embarrassed to find herself pining for the absurdly decorated nouveau riche Dunsmore aerie.

The desire for a house tugged at her in the way she imagined the desire for a child one day would—craving nest before eggs—and coincided, as usual, with wanting her mom to come from Waynesboro for a visit. She didn't like the idea of Dixie staying at some Surfside or Ocean View–type motel but couldn't afford to put her up at Shutters or the Viceroy, either. (Her mom would insist on paying her own way, anyhow.) But it wasn't like she felt she needed to shoot for the moon either. Aside from being a "Hot Property" junkie, she was always scanning the classifieds in the *Times;* there were lots of great places for half a million or just a little bit more. Becca had a feeling in her bones that she and Rusty had set a course toward that price range, but her practical, thrifty nature prevailed—she resolved that if it wasn't soon to happen, she would bide her time. She could see living communally, if she had to. She read in a magazine that, since her divorce, Drew had been staying with a passel of roommates (like in that old sitcom on TV Land that Becca and Annie liked to watch when they got stoned) and her dogs, Templeton (half Lab, half chow), Vivian, and Flossie (the Lab who saved her life on the night of the fire) in a bright orange—*orange!*—three-bedroom house. Though maybe that was journalistic wishful thinking, as none of it seemed to sync with what Becca had read vis-à-vis the nine-thousand-square-foot gated grounds and servant's quarters, though it *did* seem possible that the orange dwelling was on some *other* part of the property and the publicists were just downplaying how huge and amazing Casa Barrymore really was. (Sometimes they worked like that, in collusion with staff writers, adding or subtracting details in order to make the celeb lifestyle optimally palatable to readership, in terms of the up- or downscaleness of each specific publication.) Becca loved the instant family idea. She'd move Annie and Larry in, *forthwith.*

Waiting for the gynecologist, she found a really good article in *Bazaar.* The cover story said that while Drew wholeheartedly embraced her role as godmother to Courtney Love's daughter, Frances Bean, she wasn't yet ready to have kids herself. And when she did, she would *never* adopt—the implication being that the adoption trend was the result of vain actresses dealing with their sick notions of body image. Becca had never even thought of it like that (instead believing that famous young stars adopted because they were infertile), but the statement rang true. Drew had really opened her eyes.

The article ended with Drew saying marriage was not a goal for her at this juncture. She just wanted to have fun and be alive. "I am so in love with love," she said.

Becca could relate.

THEY HADN'T SEEN each other since the kissing scene, which happened to be the very day Becca wrapped. Making out was fun and got
pretty gnarly, and they bonded but not in a weird way. Becca put so
many of those dissolvable Listerine thingies under her tongue that
she thought she'd get a burn.

There was so much she wanted to ask that day, but as it turned
out, Drew did most of the talking. She, of course, knew that Becca
was working for Viv as a chore whore (Becca was convinced that Viv
had been shamed into letting her take time off for the *Look-Alikes*
role because, as it happened, Drew did a cameo on *Together*, not
because of a friendship with Viv but because she was the casual ex of
one of the costars, and during the taping Drew had raved to Viv in
front of Becca about what a terrific gal Becca was and how funny and
great it was that Viv had hired her "soul sister," and Becca knew that
if Viv forbade her to work on Spike Jonze's movie then Viv would
have been exposed to the scorn of Drew and her movie friends, a
scorn she definitely did not want to inspire) and Drew wanted to
know if what she had heard was true: that Viv was sleeping with Alf.
Becca said yes—she knew that Drew and Alf were once an item—but
that it was a big secret. Drew just laughed and said what a slut Alf
was and how hard it must have been for Viv with everything that had
happened to Kit but that still there was something cheesy and
unheroic about the way Viv kind of dumped him for his best friend.
Especially under the circumstances. But far be it from her to judge,
said Drew. Then she talked about how sweet Kit was and how they
used to hang together when she lived in Carbon Canyon and how he
turned her on to meditating and about the time they all—Drew and
Kit and Tom and Kathy Freston (Tom was the head of MTV, she
said)—went to Westwood to see a vipassana master called Goenka,
who was touring the United States in a mobile home and what a
horrible thing it was that some asshole did that to him and ruined
his life and how she felt kind of guilty for never having tried to go
see him when he was at Cedars. For a moment, it looked like she was
going to cry, but a crew dog rushed over to lick her, almost knocking
her down. She laughed out loud, rubbing its fur and baby-talking

through suspended tears. That's the way Drew was—a big, open heart. A wise old child.

•   •   •

LATER WHEN THEY fucked, Rusty made her talk about the Drew-kiss like it was some big thing that had turned Becca on. She hated when he wanted to hear stuff during sex. He wanted her to talk about their nipples getting stiff and them secretly getting all wet and excited while the camera rolled, but that was so far from the way it actually was. But as long as Rusty got off, what did she care? The more she talked, the more she got into it, and she hated that he could so easily manipulate her. Seeing *him* turned on turned *her* on—sex was power-ful. She would say anything he wanted to hear, do anything he asked, except maybe a four-way again, but when he got her going like that she knew she could never say never. When he came, she came too, and that was all that mattered.

On the Street Where He Lives

THE REUNION TOOK place on a cold, gray January afternoon. Most houses in the cordoned Riverside neighborhood had yet to throw out their Xmas trees.

She felt like she'd been to the cul-de-sac before—not just that months-ago time as a reluctant tourist but in another life. Lisanne dug deep and conjured his mother's beautiful, angular skull, hair gone pre-maturely white from the vile tawdriness of errant cells covertly ripen-ing under the glass of a fractured marital hothouse. The violence of all of it. According to Web sites and unofficial paperback bios, Burke had finally left Rita Julienne—whose very name signaled delicacy and countryside vulnerability!—alone with her son until the sick woman could no longer stand to remain in that godforsaken city and found sanctuary in a $435-a-month studio apartment in the gang-ridden projects of Panorama City. (Burke loitered in Vegas before reclaiming the family seat on the very evening of the day they fled. He got back so

fast, he joked to his running partners, "the toilet seat was still warm.")
Those last months were tough on R.J. Kaiser Permanente was about to
trash her womb and feed her to the chemo dogs.

Lisanne closed her eyes and submerged. She called on Tara to
help with healing divinations, martyred herself to cries and whispers
of unpaid alimony and veiny lymphomas, grapefruit-size divorce
tumors sprouting in the domestic loam of cervical pain. Sitting in
the car just two houses down, a backward-seeing clairvoyant, she
heard all the old sounds and smelled the old smells—witchily raising the zoological mist of Burke Lightfoot's animal funk, tinctured
brew of athlete's foot, jock rot, and unwashed crack, ne'er-do-well
cologne and thirty-dollar parvenu deodorant, Lavoris mouth and
pimpy charisma—invoked even the dark, mystic feelings of wet-
leafed trees and their vermin, damp streets and window frames, sod-
den ungathered newspapers, oil-stained driveways and insular
neighborhood smells, leavened by the crisp spice and blue smoke of
things exaltedly autumnal. The airspace itself spoke in rapturous
tongues of suburban decay.

Miracle: she was now inside that sorrowful house, moving as a
docent within its storied walls, an official cog in the beloved *sangha*.
Her humble reunion with the actor went appropriately unnoticed by
all parties but herself. Lisanne and a gal from the Santa Monica sit
group had been enlisted to accompany a sweet, sallow-faced monk;
they were to do service, whatever father and son required. (Anyone
who came to Riverside underwent Mr. Lightfoot's scrutiny and wasn't
invited back without his approval. Most returnees were female.) The
women housecleaned while the men, say, an ordained monk or senior meditator, sat with Kit in the yard or living room in quietude, or
engaged the actor in gentle conversation. Lisanne tried to be close to
him. During lunch, she rearranged foodstuffs in the pantry or washed
out the fridge's veggie bin a second time, if need be.

She especially loved scrubbing his bedroom toilet. A practitioner
said that toilet cleaning was an old and venerated Buddhist practice—
a particularly honorable way to achieve merit. At first, she didn't
believe it. Then one of the monks told her that cleaning toilets was a
surefire way to quiet the ego. There were even special travel groups
(they advertised in the dharma magazines) that promoted the tan-

dem merit-generating activities of toilet cleaning and the touring of sacred Buddhist sites. Lisanne understood. She knew that her humble efforts were a poem, a kneeling meditation equivalent to the thousandfold prostrations pilgrims endure while circumambulating holy mountains in Tibet. She never used gloves. She reached in to polish the bowl with a little sea sponge as if it was the rarest of alabaster. Sometimes she gave herself a paper cut before cleaning so that her blood could absorb the microbial effluence that remained. Sometimes she wished he left more of himself.

Now and then a woman named Cela came. Lisanne liked her rosy smile. She and Kit had supposedly been schoolmates. Lisanne was reorganizing a closet when Cela and Kit's dad blundered into the room and kissed before noticing her. They giggled and rushed out. A *sanghanista* said that Cela and Kit used to be together, "back in the day." Lisanne thought: Hearsay is the worst kind of poison, and the self-inflicted karmic wounds unwittingly suffered by gossipmongers are more deleterious than any sort of wound those who were gossiped about might sustain, no matter what their misdeeds. Sometimes Lisanne detected Mr. Lightfoot watching her in a curious, vaguely predatory way, but she always deflected his gaze with a beneficent, neutered smile—her Mona Lisa vipassana. There was a line to tread, because she wanted to please him, to ensure he allowed her back.

In a few visits, she had caught Kit's eye only once. He grinned, betraying no recognition of Tiff Loewenstein's honored messenger, the bringer of the Sotheby's Buddha. Better yet, she thought. Better a tabula rasa. Then she had a wonderful idea—she would restore him the idol. How fitting that it come full circle! She recalled Tiff objecting to her impulse to bring the sacred object to the hospital, but now things were different. Now, it would be her privilege and her duty. She was absolutely convinced, *devotionally* convinced, that it was paramount Kit have the bejeweled, copper Buddha and its vibrations at hand. The statue was probably at the Benedict house. She resolved to find the right moment to ask Mr. Lightfoot for his help in tracking it down.

A Special Visit

BURKE WAS SITTING on the can reading the tabloids when the doorbell rang. He looked up, distracted. "Oh shit," he muttered, remembering.

"Just a minute!"

He sucked it in and made a dash to the linen closet.

Kit sat in the pool, wave machine off, smoking one of those herbal cigarettes Tula rolled for him. (Burke let Tula mix in grass when Kit was in spasm.) He held a silver reflector at his neck, a vintage model that Cela had picked up at the Roadium.

Burke rushed into the yard with a stack of towels and a terry-cloth robe, like some freaked-out bellhop.

"Come on! There's some people I want you to meet."

"I'm tanning!" barked Kit, good-naturedly.

He spoke with the long-drawl accent of neurological damage, easily recognized yet easily understood. The manner in which he doggedly scooped words from the ether was cozily endearing and made Kit all the more watchable—the trademark grin shone through, crowned by glinting, CinemaScope eyes.

"Too bad," said Burke. "Come on!" He helped his laughing son step from the pool, buck naked. The homemade haircut was looking worse by the day, and Burke got a whiff of his breath. "Jesus! Try and use a toothbrush once in a while, will you, please?"

Kit cracked The Smile.

"Folks came a long way to see you," said Burke, toweling him down. "Came all the way from fucking Hiroshima."

"Fuck 'em," said Kit, bantering.

"Yeah right, I know. But we already did. We dropped the A-bomb."

"Fuck fuck fuck!"

"I know, I know. Your favorite."

They melodically fuck-fuck-fucked their way to the house, a gleeful trade-off for getting Kit to cooperate. The herky-jerky gait had vastly improved since Valle Verde days.

"And none of that in front of the Takahashis, OK? They didn't fly 12,000 miles on Air Nip to hear you dirty-talk."

The industrialist and his family were gathered in the breakfast room. They began their incessant bows and polite susurrations the moment Kit and his dad came in. The teenage daughters tittered, eyes rolling in their heads like crazed little fillies. The paterfamilias squinted in frozen delight, a tiny DV camera poised in readiness.

"Can't let you use it, Mr. Takahashi," said Burke, cordial but stern. "Sorry. *So solly.* Not part of the agreement."

He acceded without protest, tucking the camera into its case.

"Pretty girls!" shouted Kit. "Made in Japan!"

The dismayed, kowtowing sisters looked as if they might spontaneously combust. Their bold, still furtive glances at the superstar crescendoed to stroboscopic, inhuman speed.

"I have a tan!" Kit shouted amiably. The sisters retreated then all at once advanced, hands over mouths. "You're too pale! Too pale! 'Made in Japan' is too pale!"

"Come on, girls," said Burke. He literally shoved them closer while singing, "*Don't* be shy, *meet* a guy, *pull* up a *chair!*" At first they resisted, but when they actually collided into Kit, the ice seemed finally to have broken. Burke said, in an aside to the patriarch, "My son's a busy man."

Kit bussed their cheeks, which instantly reddened as if bruised. One girl was now crying while the other tenuously kept psychosis at bay. The industrialist slapped his knees with delight, caroming toward some kind of hysteria himself.

"Well, whaddaya think, Mr. Takahashi?" asked Burke, rhetorically. He began to doubt strongly if his guests could understand a word. "Was it worth it? Was it worth it?" He turned to his son. "Mr. Takahashi owns steel factories."

"I fuck!" said Kit and Burke rolled his eyes.

"Oh, here we go. Now don't you *start* . . ."

(The one word they might understand.)

"I fuck! I fuck! I fuck! I fuck! I fuck!"

"Come on now, boy," he chastised.

But no one seemed to care.

Burke laughed along with the Ornamentals, which was what he called them to their faces once he confirmed to his own satisfaction that they were clueless.

• • •

THE CHIEF ORNAMENTAL left twenty-five thousand in cash wrapped carefully in rice paper. The visit had been surreptitiously arranged through a butler at the Bellagio; the industrialist was a whale. Feeling very *Ocean's Eleven*, Burke called to say the deal was done. The butler said he was already taken care of, so enjoy.

They watched an *Osbournes* rerun while Burke discreetly did hits of coke. (He didn't necessarily want his son to see that.) Kit laughed at something on the show, and Burke said, "What's so funny? Ozzy talks just like you. Can't understand a thing he says." "You can *so*," said Cela defensively. Burke leaned over to kiss the nape of her neck but she pulled away—she didn't like him doing stuff like that in front of Kit. Burke got up and walked toward the bedroom, turning back to give her a comical come-hither. She smiled and shook her head, then waited a few minutes before kissing Kit's cheek good night. There were pimples there. The next time Burke wasn't around she'd squeeze a few and cut Kit's hair. Cela made a stagy move to the bathroom before joining Burke so as not to be obvious, but Kit was engrossed in the sitcom high jinks and didn't pay attention to comings and goings.

"Leave the door open," he said from the bed, with shiny, lecherous eyes. *So the kid can have a peek if he wants.*

She shut it.

He pulled her to him.

"All that Ornamental money gave me a hard-on."

Vogue

BECCA WAS EXCITED when the second A.D. called about the *Look-Alikes* wrap party. Rusty already knew about it. He said Grady and Cassandra were coming along.

There was no reason to mention the party to Viv. When it came to her capricious employer, Annie was always reminding Becca to "curb your enthusiasm" (Annie's favorite show). Becca knew that Annie was right. Anything having to do with her being a professional look-alike, i.e., a loser, was fine—Viv seemed to revel in it. Anything else, particularly something that pulled her closer into the fraternity of the Business, was dicey. Whenever she auditioned for something—and auditions were few and far between—or even when she got called to be a *Six Feet Under* corpse, she was forced to lie to escape Viv's punishing ways. Becca secretly crossed herself that first time when she blurted out that her mother was sick with breast cancer and sometimes needed to be driven to doctor's appointments. Each time an "appointment" arose, Viv was so kind and sympathetic, going overboard to ask if there was any way she could help. Becca wanted to crawl into a hole and die when she learned that Viv's mom had passed away from that very thing. She wished she could take it back. She knew that if the truth was ever found out, she would be fired and publicly vilified. Blackballed. Still, Becca didn't feel as if she had any alternative—she'd come to Hollywood to be an actress, not an actress's personal assistant. And Viv had made her feelings clear from the beginning. Becca could always quit. But even though the money was bad, working for Viv Wembley was invaluable in terms of experience and connections. Lots of what she did on a daily basis was boring, though other parts of the job, such as interacting with people she was in awe of and had only read about or seen in movies and on television, more than made up for the downside. (It sure beat going out on jobs for Elaine Jordache.) Viv was rough, but Gingher had exaggerated her bad traits. Gingher had an attitude problem herself. No one, not even Larry Levine, had heard from her since she supposedly left for New York. Maybe Viv got her thrown in jail. Becca was still half-worried that she would return from wherever and try to get her job back.

. . .

VIV ASKED BECCA to bring her a cigarette and brew a pot of decaf green tea. She had just begun Day One of the *Vogue* cover interview.

She hadn't done any real press since the attack. Her publicist said *Vogue* would "only be lightly touching on Kit" and mostly focus on other things, "forward-moving things," such as the usual rumor that *Together* was in its final season. The writer also told the publicist she was anxious to learn more about Viv's just-signed costarring role in the new Nicole Holofcencer with the heartthrob Alf Lanier.

"I would like—and I know this is difficult—to briefly talk about the terrible, and very *public* events surrounding your fiancé."

Viv felt blindsided, even though she knew it was coming. The journalist had merely wanted to get it out of the way, thinking that would be better all around.

"You know, that's not something I'm really prepared to talk about," she said reflexively, with an impenetrable smile.

Becca listened from around the corner. (I wonder if she's prepared to talk about Alf fucking her in the ass while I watch.)

"I completely respect and appreciate that," said the interviewer, realizing she'd made a misstep by blundering in. Now there was no turning back.

"And I know you're trying to do your job," Viv added, salving the sting. Showing class.

"Are you still engaged?"

She smiled again and took a yoga breath. "All I can say is . . . we're *both* recovering from this—and I don't want that to sound any way other than it sounds—"

"I *totally* understand," said the writer, almost chummily. They'd entered the land of Soft Lob.

"—and that we've agreed for now to take things *very slow*. And that it's hard to go forward in the way that we were, not only in a world where people can do the kind of . . . *horrible* thing they did to Kit—but in a world that's incredibly . . ." She trailed off. A tear welled up, elegantly dispersed by a bent, Bulgari-sapphired knuckle. "But he's *very strong.* He's a Buddhist and was, I think, actually, *much* better prepared for something like this—if anyone *could* be—than the average person. He's amazing that way. So he really has this amazing faith, and amazing path, something that I definitely sometimes lack. I have so much faith in him. So much faith that he will come through this."

·   ·   ·

THAT NIGHT, BECCA, Annie, and Larry Levine went to a party with a Kiss cover band whose members were all midgets. It was funny for about a minute.

Afterward, they cruised the Chateau. Annie recognized Paul Schrader sitting on one of the epic couches of the cavernous living room–style lobby. Larry was excited, but Becca didn't know who Paul Schrader was. They were a little drunk by then and went over to introduce themselves. Larry went on about *Raging Bull* and Annie said how much she loved *Auto Focus.* Mr. Schrader was cordial and told Becca that she looked like Drew Barrymore. Annie of course spewed that Becca was a professional look-alike, and Mr. Schrader seemed all interested in that. Mr. Schrader keenly referenced the Spike Jonze movie, in which Becca said she had a small part. Then Larry spewed that Becca's boyfriend was in it too and that he was a Russell Crowe "body snatcher." Mr. Schrader, himself a bit tipsy, really got off on that. Becca gave Larry a little frown while telling Mr. Schrader that she didn't do look-alike work anymore and that she also worked for Viv Wembley as her personal assistant. Mr. Schrader said he knew Viv and that he was supposed to have done a movie with her and Kit Lightfoot that was a kind of sequel to *American Gigolo.* Larry said that he'd auditioned for the Aronofsky movie that Kit was about to star in before he got brained. Mr. Schrader knew all about the Aronofsky movie too and said that, as far as he was aware, the project had been completely scrapped. (They weren't going to recast.) Annie said that Larry was written up in the *L.A. Times* a few months ago because he got a job at the Coffee Bean & Tea Leaf posing as a retarded person as research for his role in that very film. Mr. Schrader, who really *did* seem to know about everything that was happening in the world and especially in Hollywood, burst out laughing and said he actually remembered reading something about that on-line. He couldn't stop chortling about Larry's *I Am Sam* bit. Then Mr. Schrader's friend returned from the rest room, and Becca instantly recognized him from the set of *Six Feet Under*—the "other Alan," Alan Poul. (Alan Ball was the creator, and Alan Poul was, according to Mr. Ball, "the engine.") On inebriated impulse, Becca spoke of her not entirely satisfying, semirecurring role as a cadaver, and Mr. Schrader, deeper in his cups, tried to cajole Alan into giving Becca a short monologue to deliver on the next show. "You're wasting her talents," he said. "Have the writers give the stiff a few lines—that's a no-brainer. Doesn't Alan Ball go for all that pretentious, surrealistic shit?" "No," said Mr. Poul, gamely, "that would be you." "You could have a dream sequence of nude, talking corpses," suggested Mr. Schrader indomitably. "Only if we can insert Bob Crane," said Mr. Poul.

Buddhism for Dummies

WHAT HAD HAPPENED to him?

An untold time, staggered by pain and fear. Drowning: cyclonic; then, a battering of seawalls in his head. The nurses said that for a while he kept asking if he'd been struck by a big blue bus.

There was the period he thought he'd been shot. That someone had abducted him, and stuffed him in a car trunk.

Then he thought he had a bad flu that migrated to his head.

. . .

CEDARS TIME: aside from medical staff, the Quiet People came to sit in chairs by the bed. It seemed like they came just to close their eyes. Nothing ever disturbed them. Others visited, familiar imprints—Agent, Friend, Fiancée—now he could summon their genealogies, but in Cedars Time, he could not. Impossible to trace ancestries. The only faces he knew were those of his parents. For a week, R.J. hovered before him, changing sheets and soiled bedclothes. She comforted him in the night when he cried out. So beautiful. R.J. told him she had learned to live with the cancer and that it was a stern but thoughtful companion who would never leave her like his father did. She said not to be angry with Burke for he was doing the best that he could. It was true: he had been so tender. Sometimes when he sauntered in with that Dad-aftershave and a horny word for the nurses (they loved it), Kit was so happy to see him that he burst into tears—Burke daubed his cheeks with a custom handkerchief reeking of piquant fatherhood regained. He left the handkerchief behind, and Kit held it through the night, burying his nose in the softness like a glue sniffer when he woke up terrified. His father grew fiercely protective; hospital security did a fine job, but it wasn't enough. He hired a gentle giant, a bodyguard from Fiji whose life Burke had saved in South Vegas, to sit at the door and make sure no one trespassed because there were wily, fucked-up people who'd become distraught and obsessive since the incident, who meant well but were determined to lay hands on Kit for a healing. The nurses told Kit he was a famous star, and he took their word at face value even if it couldn't be processed. A large plasma screen was installed in the Cedars suite, and Tula and Kit and the Quiet People (later to become the Shaved-Heads) watched DVDs. Burke fired an R.N. when he found out she'd brought in a stack of Kit's movies. He watched one but didn't recognize himself. Why was his father so mad.

. . .

HE COULDN'T REMEMBER anything that had happened in the months before the assault. (Albeit he never made much effort.) It took everything he had to be present and fight the panic of being entombed, synaptically stuck in a berserk new reality. Not until he was transferred to Valle Verde did Kit try to recall what life had once been like. In rehab, there was much more space and time. Ram Dass came, angel-faced and self-deprecating (Ram was an initialism for run at the mouth, he said). He told Kit to remember his Buddhist teacher, Gil Weiskopf Roshi—and Kit realized he'd been thinking of the guru all along, visualizing his face before him, whenever, as in Ram Dass's phrase, he "surfed the silence."

Ram Dass jovially, gently, literally guided him back to vipassana, got him focused on the breath beneath his nose, on body and sensation, dispersement of pain and dread. The pain and dread would arise and fall away, he said, the fear would come and go, though nothing ever came and nothing ever went, there was only the luminous fullness of the now. Vipassana, he said, was the gift that dissolved all makeshift borders. Ram Dass brought him a light and sound machine so Kit could watch the universe switch on, dancing beneath the goggles. He became a particle in the rainbow's spectrum, a divine, lowly microbe. Now he remembered his first retreat, awakening at four in the morning, sixteen hours of vipassana a day for two weeks, remembered the silence and segregation of sexes, the prostrations, walking meditations, and mealtime prayers, cosmos in a teacup, all barriers transient, dissolved, impermanent. At Valle Verde his practice slowly returned, long preceding the recalled details, the linear landscape, of his life. Wasn't that as it should be? Wasn't the practice the only thing that was real?

He couldn't remember meeting Ram Dass at Yoga House, yet his mind lit on the Getty boy: beneath goggles' pyrotechnics, Kit saw himself in an elevator, rising . . . stepping from the gunmetal door that opened with a whoosh to the invalid's master bedroom, then, as in 2001's finale, standing at the foot of the bed where the ruined scion lay—himself now prone, Coptic prince dead on a sepulchre, though made not of stone: wizened and unborn, timeless and untimed.

Nakedly clothed in the great Self.

.   .   .

THE MONTHS PASSED, and he was not so imprisoned.

His body was stodgily effective and hadn't lost much tone. He had gained weight because the cocktail of drugs made him ravenous. He could finally look in the mirror and court the being who stared back. He knew him a little more each day. He would know him intimately and be filled with compassion and resolve. Such was the power of his will.

.   .   .

(THE WILL THAT, to his celluloid image, had married and mesmerized billions of eyes.)

.   .   .

THE QUIET PEOPLE patiently tutored. They reasserted that the name of the Buddha meant "one who is awake," and again and again offered up the Three Jewels—the Buddha, the Dharma, the Sangha. They said "Buddhism" did not exist. That Siddhartha Gautama was simply a man who saw things as they were: that to live was to suffer, that suffering was caused by attachment, that there was a cure for suffering and that cure was the Eight-fold Path. They said bodily sensations gave rise to aversion and craving and that one could train oneself not to react to what inevitably arose then passed away. Over and over they told him that the difference between buddhas and sentient beings was that a buddha realized all phenomena were totally devoid of arising, dwelling, and ceasing, and had no true existence, whereas sentient beings believed all phenomena to be real and solid; a buddha understood that things and the world were nonexistent, whereas sentient beings believed that things and the world existed. None of this was new to him, but of course everything was new and infectiously, primally urgent. Kit had no choice but to passionately embrace the diamond-pointed construct, to dissolve in it, and in time he became grateful that his own temple had col-lapsed, it had after all been shoddily built, its upkeep wanting, its materials poor, already in shambles when it came down, he was grateful to near ecstasy that the foundation had remained and proved sound, grateful he'd long ago taken refuge in the Buddha, the Dharma, and the Sangha, and that for all his warped and lurid rendezvous, his sleazy affairs of self, the vows still held. At Valle Verde he took refuge again, a sacramental honey-mooner with no choice but to rewed infinity, and all the mysterious rigors and ceremonies that honed consciousness, he could either do that or give himself to madness because his life had at last become nothing but what it always had been—a dream.

          . . . Beginner's Mind. Again and again, over and over they spoke of the irrefutable peace as prescribed by the Great Scientist, guiding Kit through the Four Sublime States and Four Vows, the Three Suf-ferings and Three Stains, the Three Poisons, Three Dharma Seals, Three Aspects, and Three Lesser Pains:

Not getting what one wants.

Meeting with what one does not want.

Being separated from loved ones and encountering enemies.

Mediation

A GRAY DAY at Department 11 of the Superior Court of Los Angeles, California, the Honorable Lewis P. Leacock presiding.

The flag had been dutifully faced; principles for which it stood, recognized; pledges and oaths, sworn. A phalanx of attorneys lined up before the judge, who busied himself with paperwork, ignoring them. An unhappy Burke Lightfoot sat eight rows back.

"I see there was a motion for sanctions and that motion was denied," said the judge.

"Your Honor," said an attorney, "as a matter of housekeeping, the court has bifurcated those original issues."

"What happened to the one-oh-one?"

"The one-oh-one," said another attorney, "has been compromised through the public administrator."

"You're saying the eleven-seven hundred is frivolous?"

"Your Honor, the petition was never consented to."

"Then doesn't it make sense to get all these things before one person?"

"Counsel is asking the court to put the remaining matters over to March," said a third attorney.

"You're not answering the question," the judge said testily. He looked over his eyeglasses. "I repeat: doesn't it make sense to get all of these things before one person?"

"Yes, Your Honor," said one of them.

"We are simply asking that 070441 be consolidated into 070584," said another.

The judge said to a fourth, "Do you have a problem with that?"

"No, Your Honor."

He returned to his paper sifting. "Then 070441 will be consolidated into 070584. This looks like it's ready for mediation. Let's clear the notes. When would you like your hearing date, with the understanding it will not be continued again?"

"We'd like ninety days, Your Honor," said the first.

"All right. How about the week of April the twenty-eighth?"

"Your Honor, I have a three-day trial on the thirtieth," said another.

"How about the second week of May—May seventeenth?"

A third said, "Your Honor, I have a five-day trial on that date."

"June the fifteenth."

A fourth said, "Your Honor, I have a three-day trial on the sixteenth."

There was some laughter from the spectators though not from Mr. Lightfoot.

Or the judge. "Whichever trial comes first takes precedence! There's a *lot* of money involved in this case—I should think that would act as an incentive. See you on the fifteenth!"

.   .   .

AFTERWARD, THE CORRIDOR was choked with lawyers, marshals, pregnant women, and tattooed men.

Team Lightfoot stiffened slightly as Burke approached. "I thought you were petitioning to unfreeze the assets."

"Court won't do it, Burke. We've been through that."

"They don't seem to have a problem disbursing *legal* funds, Lou," said Burke, sardonically. "For *y'all*. And what's this shit about mediation?"

"We're gonna give it a shot, Burke. Frankly, I think we're better off settling than taking this to trial."

"Jerry's right," said a cohort. "We'll have a much better shot."

"I don't know how much longer I can hold out, boys!"

"We can't advance you more monies, Burke."

"What are we talkin' about, guys?" said Burke, livid. "We're sittin on *sixty million dollars*, kids, *ten* of that more or less *liquid*. And you're tellin me the court won't toss me a SAG *royalties* bone? Lou, I got *expenses*. I got a full-time freakin *bodyguard*."

"He's paid out of the estate, Burke."

"Not the *food* he eats, gentlemen! Fill *that* loophole, will ya? I should have stock in fuckin Koo Koo Roo."

"Nothing compels you to buy him dinner, Burke."

"*Right.* Nothin but doin the right thing. Remember that? What a concept. Listen, Tula is the thin blue line between my boy and a *very hostile* fuckin world. I should have *five* Tulas but I *cain't* afford it." He took his foot off the pedal. "I should say *fat* blue line, cause he sure knows how to eat! Eats more than Dick Cheney."

"Keep your receipts," said the counsel. "And submit."

"Keep a log of every expense."

"Have you arranged for the tutor?" asked a cocounsel.

"I'm settin it up."

"Don't drag your feet on that," said the other. "If we do wind up going to trial, it has to look good in terms of provision of care."

"If anyone thinks they can do a better job then I have, they're welcome to try. I can't believe this is even up for grabs! I'm his *daddy.* It's a slam fucking dunk! Listen, kids: it's a *hardship.*" He could see how his personality grated on them, but what could he do? He would rim their greedy assholes if that'd help loosen up some funds. "And I *know* that you know that. And you guys are doin a *helluva* job. So don't think I'm not grateful. I know it's all going to work out in the end. At least I sure fucking hope so. Cause I am sure as hell not going to stand by and watch my son's money handed over to the state. Or Mr. William Morris or *whomever.* But you gotta know that once we're past the established five-block radius, we are *fair fucking media game.* The police do a pretty good job and the neighbors have been great—though who knows how long *that's* gonna last—but I'm tellin ya, it's like living in a serious cocksucking fishbowl over there! Hell, I can't even conduct a romantic life! Fellas! C'mon! What good does Viagra do if you don't have the opportunity for usage? The paparazzi, by the way—in case you didn't know—are now flying choppers over my motherloving airspace! And that's illegal. So put yourself in my Nikes and see how long you'd last. Kit's barely been out of *house*—as his guardian, I can't risk having a telephoto of him not looking his *GQ* best ending up in some tabloid." He paused, inhaling martyrdom. "I'm *tellin* you, kids, I am *really* in the trenches here. Is the court aware of that?"

"Gotta tough it out, Burke," said the attorney, beginning a slow retreat down the hall. "There's light at the end of the tunnel."

"At the end of my asshole maybe."

Counsel fled, en masse.

"But not at the end of *yours*," said Burke to himself. "Fuck it. We'll make do until the ship comes in." He called after them: "My son's in *great* shape—he's fit and he's feisty and he's got a daddy who *loves* him. Tell *that* to the fucking mediator!"

Transference

THERE WEREN'T ANY guards at the Benedict Canyon estate. The gate was flung open to a cadre of indifferent gardeners, who came and went, wrestling with hoses and foliage. Lisanne strode in, businesslike. No one paid attention.

She shivered again with the same feeling she'd had at the Riverside house—that somehow she belonged—except this time, she felt the chill of his absence. The place seemed frozen in time, like an obscure, well-funded theosophical foundation or museum of atrocities committed in past or even future centuries—or the temple where a mythic hero, wounded in battle, had returned to die. Even now, within sight of the flat obsidian column of infinity pool and dark wood cope of the famous zendo in its grove of eucalyptuses, there was blood, there was blood, bone, and death, it hung in the air like gas, oppressively colorless and odorless, and if one could properly read the signs, one might have translated all the terrible things that had manifested: miscarriages and mayhem, and the messy, fragrant anarchy of impermanence.

She stared through the windows, hoping to see the Sotheby's Buddha, imagining Kit home again, in a beautiful robe of Thai silk, having bargained her life away for such an impossibility, brokering a deal with Tara (born of tears shed over the sufferings of sentient beings) for his health and sanctity to be returned—the provisions of the contract being that he would never know of Lisanne's sacrifice, would never even have a thought of her again (which she anyway assumed he hadn't, not a proper thought anyway, since the day they met in the trailer), because she had argued nobly, selflessly for the monstrous event to be forever expunged from history and memory, and her wish had been granted, the assault had never occurred, this was the agreement that Tara, daughter of Avalokiteshvara, had consented to and so decreed. All that Lisanne had asked was that she be allowed to see him one last time in his habitat, vital and free from worry, restored to grace before Tara—whose face gathers one hundred autumn full moons, who blazes with the sparkling light of a thousand stars, who dwells amid garlands and completely delights her entourage—carried Lisanne off to the Realm of Hungry Ghosts.

Of a sudden, it came: she knew what she would do. The omen was that she hadn't glimpsed the Sotheby's Buddha—if it was Lisanne's to give, the fates would have arranged for it to have been prominently displayed for her eyes to see. No. She would pass on to Burke Lightfoot what was *already* hers—the Supreme Bliss-Wheel Integration Buddha that Philip gave her. She felt her impulse instantly sanctified by the Source. The giving of the Supreme Bliss-Wheel Integration Buddha would create a space of True Love, and in that space, Kit's healing could finally begin. Just as the death of Viv's unborn child had created a space for Siddhama, so would the offering of the Bliss-Wheel Buddha create a space for *metta*, the loving-kindness that would heal all things. And after the healing, everyone—Kit, Lisanne, Siddhama—would return to Source. She was determined not to make the same error as the student monk. She would not mistake *Mu* for "no."

As she walked out the gate, a gardener caught her eye and smiled with beautiful knowingness. She took that as another sign that her instincts were sanctified. Still, she would need to prepare the father; simply bringing the Buddha unannounced on her next day of Riverside service would be presumptuous. Best to be humble. Her pulse and step quickened. She would ring Mr. Lightfoot up and tell him she had a gift that was certain to bring the house—and his son—great peace and prosperity.

Turbulence

TIFF PROMISED DANIELLE Steel he would come to San Francisco for the Star Ball, a benefit for the Nick Traina Foundation, a trust named after her late son. When Philip heard about it, he suggested they fly up on his jet. (Lisanne was shocked to learn Philip even had a jet.) A high-end bunch tagged along: Clive Davis and Quincy Jones, Sharon Stone and a friend, Robin Williams, Steve Bing, and Mattie's friends Rita Wilson and Tracey Ullman. When Mattie had to cancel over some kind of dental problem, Lisanne became convinced it was a harbinger that the plane was going to crash.

Until takeoff, she hadn't dwelled on her fear. But just as they began the steep ascent, she said to herself, What have I done? Tucking her head into Roslynn's shoulder, she gripped the poor woman's arm in viselike panic. Lisanne thought of those Quecreek coal miners and how much better off they were because even though the water was rising to their chins they could still be rescued, whereas no one in *this* cave would have the faintest glimmer of a chance. Then she thought of that skydiving woman she read about in *People* whose parachute had failed. The woman plunked straight down onto a hill of red ants and somehow survived. (At least she was already falling *outside* the plane, a detail that now seemed positively merciful.) Her descent had probably been slowed by the unopened chute, whereas Lisanne was locked inside the unforgiving crypt of fuselage and wouldn't be free until an infinitesimal remnant of her charred cells commingled with rocky mountain or gulfstream or wherever it was they'd be blown to. Roslynn kindly stroked her head and said the usual bromide about little jets being safer than big commercial ones, and it sounded like the saddest, most fantastic lie anyone ever told—pure chicanery. The soothing pillow talk of demons when dying children lay their heads down to final rest.

Lisanne set her right hand atop her left, palms up, and closed her eyes. She'd learned a lot from Buddhist classes and workshops, and from her readings too, and thought now might be a good time to put some of it to use. She tried focusing on the breath at her nostrils but only managed to fixate on the rush and precipitation of freezing air outside the paper-thin winged missile—a skittish, sacrificial dance of crazy gusts, currents, and wind shear that teased at flawed engines, themselves nearly spent. The low thunder of turbines reminded her of the diabolically codified sounds described in *The Tibetan Book of the Dead*.

She tensed, bringing herself back with near-violence to the meditation that a friend had guided her through while on lunch break at the Santa Monica Zen Center: she struggled to visualize a tiny rainbow in her heart-center. Lisanne made the rainbow expand while envisioning the dissolution of all fear in her body, all disease, all obstacles. As in the Temescal Canyon *metta* workshop, she tried to imagine herself becoming abstract, losing human form until she was a lamp whose light emanated to all beings, transmuting gross, unmindful, mulish nature into pure awareness, the Pure Land. Why should she cling to this life? The Buddha advised to rid oneself of the defilement of clinging and attachment, but losing Kit and Siddhama would be insurmountable, far worse than losing the Buddha himself. Maybe everything—mind, heart, void—would have to be murdered. True sages were always saying "Kill the Buddha!" but she didn't think that meant literally. Besides, she didn't enjoy a phrase like that; it was antithetical to her true nature. Maybe, thought Lisanne, it was antithetical to her true nature to be liberated. If that were so, than nothing mattered anyway.

A bump of turbulence made her drop the thread. She was panting now, and Roslynn pried loose her grip. Lisanne focused on the others. Sharon and her friend were having a quiet moment, like they were at some romantic beach restaurant. He held her hand and stared out the window. A stewardess served drinks to the Clive-Tiff-Bing-Quincy clique. Q and Bing were laughing at something Clive had said. Q and Bing seemed to laugh an awful lot at just about anything.

Philip, Rita, and Tracey shrieked over some bit of business that Robin was up to. The comedian was spritzing about his good friend

Lance Armstrong and the love-hate relationship riders had with their bicycle seats. He was in the middle of a limp-wristed riff on pinched gonads and ass cancer when Tracey, apropos of nothing, began singing dirty lyrics from the Jerry Springer opera her husband produced. She stopped in mid-aria to say that she woke up that morning with crop circles carved in her bush. She said the same thing happened to Meg Ryan, then did an eerie impersonation of Meg calling her up on the phone to tell her about the "situation." Q overheard the last bit and totally lost it. Then Bing lost it again, then Rita and Sharon and Philip, in that hee-haw way Philip had of laughing that drove Lisanne up the wall—in the grip of her terror, she still had the energy to hate him for not having come over to check up on her, for pretending not to notice something was wrong. Philip was of that emotional school that taught, Ignore loved ones in distress.

There was a jolt and the plane dipped. Sharon woofed and Robin Three Stooges woo-woo-wooed and Tracey mimed an Edvard Munch while Rita, Bing, and Philip split a gut. Clive and Q suddenly began to shoptalk, drinking their drinks, cool as can be. Lisanne was convinced that if the plane had somersaulted, no one would have cared in the slightest. Everyone was rich and celebrated and impervious; everyone had logged God knew how many millions of miles on all manner of rickety aircraft without the faintest whiff of anxiety; everyone was blessed and they knew it. Lisanne tried her rainbow vipassana again, but as the jet chop-surfed jagged currents, she felt something collapse like scaffolding within. That Tibetan Book blackness rolled toward her like a carpet of smoldering asphalt, and try as she might she couldn't remember anything of the teachings except the parts about the Wrathful Bloodthirsty Visions and the homeless souls gathering during intercourse at the genitals of a couple like flies on a piece of meat—

"How's our girl doin?" asked Philip. Finally.

"She's going to be fine," said Roslynn, herself shaken by the force of Lisanne's naked agonies.

Philip took a closer look. "Wow. We should have given her a Xanax."

"I have Ambien," said Roslynn. "But by the time it kicks in, we'll be on the ground."

"I think you should give it to her." Philip stroked Lisanne's head and said, "She'll be fine."

"Oh Jesus," said Roslynn.

She'd been smelling something, and as she got up for the pills, she saw that Lisanne's seat was soaked in urine. There were other smells too, and she quickly went into nurse mode, telling Philip to grab some blankets. A steward came with a pile, and after he returned with towels, Rosylnn dismissed him with a curt nod. Philip lifted his girlfriend, and Roslynn shoved a towel then a blanket under her to sop it up. She put a blanket on the floor beneath Lisanne's stocking feet, covering her up with a third. Sharon, Rita, and Tracey came over and, once they understood what was happening, tried to comfort. Sharon stroked Lisanne's head, and Rita said, "Poor thing, poor baby," while Tracey said her daughter Mabel hated flying too, and that the turbulence they'd just been through was really nothing, nothing at all, they all said they'd been in a hundred times worse. Tiff broke away from Bing, Q, and Sharon's friend, joining Philip and the ladies. He started talking about a bad flight he once had into Aspen, but Roslynn twitched her eyebrows at him to stop. Philip made Lisanne swallow a pill, and then the choppiness got bad enough that the pilot told everyone to strap themselves in.

Swathed in blankets, sitting on a cushion of terry cloth, Lisanne made a game of the speed in which she told the shit to leave her body. She nudged the feces back and forth before expelling it with slow, determined gallantry, envisioning the putrescence first as dark clouds of turbulence, then as disease and fear, finally transforming to rainbow light. In the relative silence that ensued (born not of the rough ride, but of the stymied group's concern for Lisanne), she recalled the noble practice of cleaning Kit's toilets and the peace it had bestowed and made the entreaty and promise that she would take formal refuge in the vows if only the Source and Oneness would now spare her, if only the Source and Oneness would let her return to Riverside for her sacred chores again, if only the Source and Oneness would allow her to live long enough to give her man the conciliatory gift of the Supreme Bliss-Wheel Integration Replacement Buddha.

Special Needs

BURKE WORE A chef's hat and apron. Tula stood at the grill, in uniform: gargantuan three-piece C & R Clothiers relic and equally outsize grin. With fierce concentration, Kit Lightfoot, human pendulum, stood barefoot on the leather swing and propulsed a hair-raising arc. He was the biggest swing daredevil that Ulysses S. Grant or any other school had ever seen. No butterflies; no fear. Cela remembered watching when she was a girl, afraid he would fly off into space and shatter himself on the blacktop. Her heart used to pound, and there was something sexy about the pounding, even though at the time, she wasn't sure what those kinds of feelings meant.

. . .

BURKE WAS LOADED. He went off on Cela about some shit or other while she did the dishes. Cela said she didn't even know why she was doing the dishes because they mostly used plastic plates. She was loaded too and shouted back. Tula went to the car and read Robert Ludlum, which seemed to be the only thing he ever did read, same thick paperback, week in, week out. (When he finished, he'd just start over again.) Burke went out to the yard and stripped and sat naked in the pool with a bottle of Jack. Kit curled up on the grungy sofa and watched himself on an E! bio.

. . .

TULA STRETCHED HIS legs and smoked. Squatted down to sponge-soak the bumper sticker that someone had inexplicably gonzoed him with: MY KIDS THINK I'M AN ATM.
Razored it off.

. . .

KIT SAT IN PJ'S at the end of the bed.
Walked to the window and stared at the moon; heard a moan.

Padded through the dark hall toward his father's room. Stood there at the open door. Burke's bedside lamp was on. He was fucking Cela. She was on her stomach. He sensed Kit's presence, swiveling his neck to stare at his son. They looked at each other awhile before Burke went back to his business. Kit fished out his cock and started to rub. He rubbed until he came, then ran to the living room and turned on the TV, ashamed. Cried and rocked and ate an entire bag of chips before getting engrossed in an old CSI.

The Standard Wrap

RUSTY AND BECCA waited in the vaulted living room. There was a shindig going on, and Rusty thought they'd forgotten about the wrap party. Then Grady popped his head in and said a limo was coming and that Rusty and Becca should just smoke a doobie and chill.

There was always some kind of happening on Mulholland. Cassandra usually had one or two QuestraWorld interns wandering around with a DV cam recording the nefarious goings-on for a work-in-progress prototype of "Been There, Dunsmore." You had to watch your behavior.

"Hope they don't do anything too weird," said Becca, once they were more or less alone again. "Especially in front of Spike."

"Like what?" said Rusty.

"Like *embarrassing.* Sometimes Grady and Cass can just be . . . *really weird.* Haven't you noticed?"

Rusty laughed, coughing out weedsmoke.

They wandered outside, where Dr. Thom Janowicz held court by the pool. He'd met the Dunsmores through Grady's lawyer, Ludmilla Vesper-Weintraub. Ludmilla sent a lot of clients Thom's way, including those who had reaped windfalls from the city by settling wrongful arrest or racial profiling suits. It was Ms. Vesper-Weintraub's feeling that having a ton of money dumped on you could be a hardship in itself; the golden downtrodden needed all the help they could get. Thom was an old college friend and someone she prized for easily relating to people of all colors and income strata. Aside from his workshops on SWS (sudden wealth syndrome), Dr. J was a novice screenwriter, and Ludmilla thought that he and the Dunsmores would make a nice fit. She was right. With his flair for storytelling and winning disposition, the amiable raconteur in horn-rims and tweed was already a regular in various "Been There, Dunsmore" episodes that Cassandra cobbled together on Final Cut Pro. Dr. J was also engaged to write a movie for QuestraWorld, for which, not being a member of the WGA, he'd been generously paid guild minimum.

Rusty wasn't thrilled to hear that a wanna-be like Dr. J was already on the Dunsmore payroll. He was nearly finished with his own screenplay—they knew as much—and no one had offered *him* a god-damn thing. Grady countered that was because Rusty's script predated the incorporation of QuestraWorld; he admitted having worked on it, at least in his head anyway, for years. Grady said that he *still* thought of Rusty's "spec" as a QuestraWorld project, regardless. Well that's good, said Rusty, peevishly. Keep thinkin. Think away. Have big ol' happy thoughts. Because Rusty said that maybe he'd just take his script elsewhere. Fine, said Grady. Rock on. Prob'ly plenty of folks out there who *love* unfinished scripts. Shit, said Grady, you don't even have a *title*. The *fuck* I don't, said Rusty. Then I'd like to hear it, said Grady. Rusty got a far-off, suavely proprietary look in his eye and said, Gonna call it "To Kill a Unicorn." Grady sat there nodding his head, quiet. I like it, said Grady. I *like* that. Shit, I *really* like that. Out from nowhere, in the kitchen somewhere, Cassandra shouted, Somebody already *used* that title. She said she saw a biography about Dorothy Stratten on the E! channel and that somebody already used that title in a book. About Dorothy and her murder. Grady said, So the fuck what, I *like* it. Hell, it's good enough to use again. You can't do that, said Cassandra. Bullshit, said Grady. You can't copyright a title. Ask our lawyer. Anybody knows that. Oh yeah? said Cassandra. Then let's you and me write a script and call it *Star Wars,* she said. That's what we'll call *Rusty's* script, she said, laughing. Rusty said sagely, That book about Dorothy Stratten was called *The Killing of the Unicorn.* Mine's called "To Kill a Unicorn." See? said Grady. Know-it-all. See? Man knows his shit. Man done *researched.* Man knows *all* the titles out there. Knowledge is fucking *power*! Cassandra said, Whatever. But I still think it sounds like *To Kill a Mockingbird.* Yeah, snapped Grady, only it's "To Kill a Fucking Unicorn," which is not a fucking *mocking-bird*, unless a mockingbird has a fucking horn in its head, which it *doesn't*, last time *I* looked. You ain't never even looked at a mocking-bird, said Cassandra. Ain't never even seen one. Yeah, well *you're* gonna see one in a minute goin tweet tweet *tweet* with my fucking fist like a horn in your head if you don't shut the fuck up. Fuckin hag. He turned to Rusty and said, I *like* it, man, I do. It rocks. You got the gift, man. You got it. Always knew you did. Then Grady said that Questra-World should have "first option," and Rusty parried that people usu-ally had to *pay* for first option. Just like you're paying Dr. Phil. Oops, I mean Dr. J. Dr. J's the man, said Grady. Gonna win hisself an Acad-emy Award. They went on like that, having a friendly go at each other, jousting their unicorn horns.

Becca had been telling Rusty for months that she wanted to read the script, but he always said he wasn't ready. She never really saw him working on it. He kept saying she could see it soon, and she thought maybe he was planning to show it to Spike. Whenever Grady or anyone asked what the script was about all Rusty would say was it was a murder mystery that took place among horse train-ers. Rusty used to work a lot around stables, at least he said he did anyway. On the sly, Grady told Becca, "You cain't trust to believe half the shit come out that boy's pretty mouth." But Grady liked the whole racetrack thing. Ever since Cassandra told him about the *Spider-Man* kid starring in *Seabiscuit*, Grady thought that horse and jockey stories, or anything having to do with the track, were a sure bet. (Rusty said his movie wasn't gonna be "no sobby, suckass *Seabiscuit* turd.") He became more and more convinced that *Look-Alikes* was going to make Rusty Goodson a star and incessantly spoke to Cassandra about drawing up a contract to lock their home-boy into a QuestraWorld film at a bargain basement price. Grady read in *The Hollywood Reporter* about how even Kirsten Dunst's hot-shot agents got stuck honoring some craphouse deal she'd made with a studio way back when, before *Spider-Man* spun its billion-dollar web worldwide—if Rusty got hot off of *Look-Alikes*, Questra-World should already have him in the bag. Cassandra wouldn't bite. She was more focused on the new baby than on Rusty's screenplay anyhow. Focused on the reality show and managing their money.

She loved getting loaded and sucking Rusty's dick in a group thing, but she'd be damned if she was going to shell out cash for something that wasn't even real. She pissed Grady off, but he kind of loved her for that.

.   .   .

THE WRAP PARTY was on the roof of the Standard. There were so many stars, it seemed more like a premiere. Being downtown and high up like that was such a different perspective, skyscape-wise. Becca and Cassandra were stoned and kept pretending they were in Toronto or Vancouver, places they'd never even been. When her mom came, Becca for sure wanted to bring her there for cocktails.

The costume ladies and makeup girls and all the funky women that Becca saw hauling equipment during the shoot were dressed to the nines, showing lots of skin. Wrap parties were like that—they were all about sex, and majorly blowing out the pipes. Celebrities were wraparound because Spike and Sofia knew everyone and everyone wanted to know them too.

The look-alikes showed up in full force: her friend the Barbra, the Cameron and a Cher, the Billy Bob, the Pope and a James Gandolfini, a Mike Myers, a Reese, the Benicio and the Cusack, and of course Becca and Rusty. Whenever an official shutterbug flashed a photo of him Rusty knew (even though he was hands-down the best "specialty" actor, and had the biggest role) that attention was being paid because of his look-alike status, and not his own merit. She saw that he was ashamed. He said to her that being a look-alike was like being a porn star. You could never escape your caste: Untouchable.

Becca disagreed, though not to his face. She didn't mind having her picture taken at all. After a few drinks, she got the courage to say hello to Spike and Sofia. They were always so courtly, especially Sofia—just folks. Mrs. Coppola-Jonze immediately said, in her sweet, disingenuous way, "Oh, Drew's in Turkey," as if Becca and Drew were officially linked. Sofia asked how things were going with her boss. Becca said fine, and Sofia asked if Viv was coming to the party. Becca got a shiver because that was something she hadn't thought of—that Viv had been invited and would probably show. (Suddenly, it seemed superlikely.) Becca didn't want to run into her, fearing that a whole petty cycle of hassles would be set in motion. Even if Viv acted nice, she knew there'd be hell to pay during the workweek.

Sofia introduced her to Charlie Kaufman. (They had already met, once at the Chateau, and a few times on the set.) The writer was with a woman he said had done the novelization of the Ethan Hawke–Gwyneth Paltrow movie *Great Expectations*. Charlie kept saying how great it was that his friend had "novelized Dickens," but Becca felt kind of bad because she didn't get it. Sofia kept smiling in that mysterious way; you could never figure out what she was thinking, or, for that matter, Spike either, and Becca was always on guard because as far as she was concerned being around either one of them was like an audition for one of their future films.

She ran into the second A.D., and they made out in one of the crazily decorated hotel guest rooms (in addition to the roof, a whole floor had been consigned). The second said that Drew was vacationing in Turkey before returning to work on *A Confederacy of Dunces*. Becca said Sofia already told her that, then went back to the roof to find Rusty. That was when she saw Cassandra in midconversation, wildly gesticulating before Viv Wembley and Alf Lanier. Becca's heart went straight to her throat. That was *another* thing she stupidly hadn't considered—that the Dunsmores, knowing she worked for Viv, would of course approach the television star and act like the shameless freaks that they were.

I am fucked, she said to herself with a carefree shrug.

Reentry

ROSLYNN BABY-SAT her at the Fairmont while the others went to the Star Ball. There had been urgings among the group that she be hospital-assessed—her behavior after landing continued to be worrisome—but Lisanne always emerged from cloaked silences to resist deftly and cogently, against their better judgment. Mattie and Phil were from San Mateo, so a doctor they knew dropped by the suite to give Lisanne something to settle her. He told Philip and the Loewensteins that he wasn't sure what was going on but that some sort of "abreaction" should probably be ruled out. Not really his area.

On Monday, they sent her home in a Town Car. She asked the driver to take the coastal route. She loved Carmel and Big Sur. They stopped at coffee shops, and ate club sandwiches and fries.

From her backseat nest, Lisanne caught up on newspapers and magazines. One of the ads featured a gorgeous, buff young black girl.

> Shanté puts all kinds of heat on the world's torturers. And then she hits the gym. Shanté is a member of Amnesty International. Every month, Shanté sends e-mails to world leaders, urging them to stop torturing and killing the prisoners in their jails.
>
> Torturers worldwide wish they never heard of Shanté Smalls.

She read an article in *The New York Times* about people who have recurrent infections acquired in hospitals, mostly from health-care workers who neglected to wash their hands. The infections were of the type that could no longer be cured by antibiotics. One of the sick persons was an older woman whose sternum had been eaten away by bacteria, and now whenever she went for a drive she had to wear a bulletproof vest because if she got in an accident her chest would be crushed by the air bag. Another article was about a little Jewish girl who was snatched from her crib and killed by a black bear in the Catskills. On the next page was a financial ad with the head of a big black bear staring out. "Are you managing the bear?" read the copy. "Or is the bear managing you?"

· · ·

LISANNE VISITED THE Bel-Air home office of Dr. Calliope Krohn-Markowitz, Holocaust survivor and legendary shrink to the stars. Roslynn Loewenstein, a client for years, had arranged it.

"Did you ever lose control like that before?"

"You mean," said Lisanne, embarrassed, "on the plane?"

"Yes."

She shook her head.

"Were you a bed wetter, Lisanne?"

Again, a modest shake of the head.

"You know, all kinds of things happen—to our bodies—when we fear for our lives. When that fear is genuine. Right now, there's a disconnect. Have you heard of a 'false positive'? When a test comes back positive but it's actually negative? Well, right now I think you're dealing with *lots* of false positives. You've got to replace the faulty wiring, so to speak. I can certainly help you with that."

"How?" She hadn't understood a word of what the woman had said.

"There are a number of ways," said Calliope, assuredly.

"Drugs?"

"Medication is one avenue. In that regard, I'd like you to see a friend of mine, a very talented psychopharmacologist."

"Can't you give me something?"

"I don't prescribe." She paused. "We can also try hypnosis. I've had phenomenal results. I like a multidirectional approach. We can do things on a practical plane, no pun intended! There's a wonderful class—I think they have one right here at LAX, we'll check the Internet—to overcome flying phobias. I've known many, many people who've taken that course and now fly like *banshees*."

"I know *one* way to get over my fear."

"What's that?"

"Not fly," said Lisanne, smiling.

"That *is* a solution," said Calliope, pleased that her patient had lightened up. "I won't even say it's not valid. We all make choices; that is our prerogative. We do what is best for us. To survive. But I think, Lisanne, that with you there are some other issues. What we call a constellation. Your crisis on the plane might be an indicator that it's time you *faced* some of those issues, head-on. I want you to visit my friend—and think about what we spoke of today. If you decide you'd like to come back, then we can do some exploring."

Cadillac Escapade

TULA PULLED THE Escalade out of the drive. To the casual observer, he was alone.

"OK, keep hide now!" he said.

"This is too goddamn weird!" said Kit excitedly from the back.

They were under a Mexican blanket; he smelled Cela's warm, giggly exhalations. It brought him all the way back to their preteen make-out sessions.

"Kit, it was *your idea!*" she said.

"Yeah," he said, cockily. "*You're fuckin right.* Time to go to the fuckin mall! Get E! channel more shit for their documental!"

"You are such a wack job," she said, tweaking his rib cage. "You are *such a wacky goofball.*"

He squirmed and spasmed at the tickle, then put a thumb in her side, sending her into contortions. Tula gravely *shushed* as they approached the guard at the barricade. Then Cela shushed Kit, clenching his fingers to neutralize him. It was all so sexy. As the car slowed they grew seriously still and hot-breathed, like children during the critical part of a game.

The rent-a-cop waved Tula through. They rolled past the crowd of fans, photogs, and media trucks.

Once they were in the clear, Kit started singing, "Tommy, can you hear me?" He replaced *Tommy* with *Tula*, and Cela had a fresh conniption.

A rogue paparazzo grew suspicious. He ducked under the ever-present WE LOVE YOU GET WELL SOON banner and broke away, discreetly slipping into a Corolla. He accelerated and drew closer. When Kit lifted his head to take a peek at the world, the freelancer saw him and gave spirited chase. Tula muttered Fijian expletives then upshifted into *Bad Boys* movie maneuvers. The bodyguard, extracautious because his charges were unsecured, reveled in finally being able to do what he was paid for.

Rubber was peeled; corners sharply taken; horns honked; accidents barely averted. Kit and Cela went gleefully bonkers, cheering Tula on. The driver was proficient, hyperconcentrated and adrenalized, his sweaty, scarily resolute, block-headed, thick-necked countenance thrilling them to no end. Then it was over as unexpectedly as it had begun—the paparazzo's car flipping onto its back like a bug.

"*Oh my God,*" said Cela, aghast, looking back. "Do you think he's hurt?"

Tula slowed, and peered in the rearview. The Corolla had toppled again in slo-mo, absurdly righting itself. Its owner stared ahead in a daze.

"No," he assessed. "Just shook up."

"Good job!" said Kit. "Good job, Odd Job!"

"Should we go back?" asked Cela.

"No!" said Tula. "No go back! Not our fault!"

"Girl," said Kit, jokily somber. "You can't go home again."

"He just shook up," said Tula, with a parting glance before motoring on. A pedestrian helped the pursuer from his car; he was already walking under his own power.

Kit put on an Elvis-sneer, singing, "All shook up! Ooh hoo hoo. Ooh hoo. Ay yeah!"

Everyone—even Tula—cracked up.

                    •   •   •

THROUGH THE COLD bright Riverside Galleria, wide-eyed.

Holding hands—delirious fugitives.

Kit, unchained. Mall, uncrowded.

The occasional look of stunned recognition from passersby cum well-wishers.

"Wow wow wow!" yelps Kit.

The freedom of it. The old *feelings* of it.

The spatial newness. Nowness. Wowness.

"Oh my God, that *chase,*" says Cela. "That was *so amazing.*"

"Like Steve McQueen!" says Kit. "What that movie? *Bullitt.*"

"Burke is gonna have a flying *shit*fit," she says, slightly paranoid. "He's gonna kick our *ass.*"

"I will motherfucking kick *his* fucking ass!" shouts Kit.

Cela shushes his too public swagger. "Can you please, like, lower the volume?"

"Oh shit, man! I am fucking *hungry.*"

"OK, Bullitt, what do you want to eat?"

Pause. Then: "Everybody!"

They laugh. A gawking schoolgirl approaches.

"Excuse me, but are you Kit Lightfoot?"

"Steve McQueen!" says Kit.

She turns to Cela while her friends hover nearby.

Awkwardly: "Is he Kit Lightfoot?"

"Yeah," offers Kit as Cela nods. "The one and only."

"Oh my God!" says the girl, taking a few steps back. "It *is* him, it's *him* . . ."

The clique rushes over in pleated parochial school uniforms, waists turned faddishly down to show hipbone. Tula puffs up, bodyguardlike. Needless but endearing—still in hero mode.

"Can we get an autograph?"

"Do you have a pen?" asks Cela.

They dip into North Face–Powerpuff backpacks.

"He can sign my arm," says the girl, proffering a Sharpie.

"He can sign my leg!" says another.

"Is he retarded?" asks one of Cela.

"Girls," Cela cautions. "Be *nice.*"

Kit signs an arm while saying, "Not retarded. Just a little . . . fucked up."

"He *sounds* retarded," says a girl, not quite sotto.

Her friend examines the signature like it's a rash and says, "Oh my *God*, what does it *say*?"

The other takes a look and says: "It's like a *scrawl*—"

"I said, *Be fuckin nice,*" says Cela. "You're being *rude.*"

The girls say reprimanded thank-yous, then dash off. When they're far enough away, they break into laughter.

"Little cunts," says Cela.

"It's OK," says Kit thoughtfully. Then, with a nasty-assed grin: "They make me horny."

.   .   .

INSIDE BLOCKBUSTER NOW.

Rushing down aisles, exhilarated, nature boy in the video forest. (A very strange enchanted boy.) Touching the hard, hollow, garish boxes, wide-eyed, tactile, inhaling collective memory of film. The store is huge and empty, except for clerks, discursively restocking.

"I was a movie star!" he shouts, thumping his chest like Tarzan.

"You still *are*," says Cela. "You're still the biggest star on the planet, OK?"

He ponders then says, matter-of-fact, "OK." The effect is unintendedly droll. "We should get popcorn." They walk past the new releases wall. (Like a 99 cent store display.) He asks, "What movies was I in?"

Before she can answer, a Norman Rockwell geek with chin acne enters their frame.

"Excuse me—are you Kit Lightfoot?"

(Cela braces herself. Tula puffs up.)

"Yes, I am!"

"I *knew* it! I put on *World*"—there, suddenly, it is, on all hanging monitors, *World Without End*, the famous scene at Children's Hospital where Kit and Cameron Diaz erupt in dance, the crippled kids following suit, to Supertramp's "Logical Song"—"and I just wanted to tell you what a great—how amazing I think you are as an actor and as a person."

(Cela sighs with audible relief.)

"Thank you."

"And what an honor it is to have you in our store."

"Thank you." A daub of Elvis again: "*Thankyouverymuch.*"

A little daub'll do ya—

"I just want you to know that everyone in Riverside, everyone in the *world* is pulling for you."

(Cela, nearly in tears. On her period. Quick to cry.)

"Thankyouverymuch."

"May I show you the Kit Lightfoot section?" he asks, as if coaxing a girl at cotillion to dance. (Includes the others in what he says next.)

"We have a whole Kit Lightfoot section—I organized it myself."

"I would like some popcorn."

"You can have all the popcorn you like, sir!"

By now, a few other employees curiously make their way toward the little group.

The clerk turns to Cela.

"Think he'd mind signing a a few posters?"

"Ask him," says Cela, proudly. Feeling like the missus.

True Confessions

MOTHER AND CHILD dropped in unannounced to the Sunset Boulevard penthouse suite.

Lisanne felt bad because she never thanked her old boss for his kindnesses in those first few months she and Siddhama were home alone. (He had continued to pay her salary.) In fact, she'd never thanked him at all—through the years, he'd been stand-up and generous to a fault. It was true she had made herself indispensable, but it was Reggie, with his sunny, contagious confidence, who, long ago, had so generously opened the door, helping Lisanne to overcome her initial insecurities. He was startled by the hidden pregnancy but, like a true gentleman, withheld judgment. She would have been lost without his emotional support after her baby came into the world.

They hadn't spoken since she moved to Rustic Canyon, and the fact that the life-saving arrangement with Philip came about under the auspices of Tiff, Reggie's client, made it even worse. She felt so ungrateful, but nothing could have been further from the truth—now was the time to face him, to reveal all. Reggie Marck, if anyone, should be privy to the certain details of the child's parentage.

He held the baby in his arms.

She said: "I wanted to tell you that this is the son of Kit Lightfoot."

"OK," he said, smiling. Waiting for the punch line.

"And I wanted to give you the supramundane Secret Thatness offerings." She knelt upon the ground and opened her blouse. He stood there holding the child, looking down at her. "Here is my mustard seed, my scoops of barley and clarified buttered bread, here are my nipples large as the purplebruised toes of homeless children. I, Vajrayogini, generate the celestial mansion with this wide and brazen cunt. Look! at the cervical fire of my stink-necklace, looped through 700 dew-fresh skulls. O, I am asking you to disarm! For these are the weapons of mass instruction. I am the blue dakini, door of membranes and remembrance, the green PHAṬ HAM. Let us kneel on the carpet of the cathedral like pilgrims humbled by disaster—O Reggie, join me now! Offer and observe the materials to be burned in bodhiwood! OM OM OM SARVA PHAṬ PHAṬ PHAṬ SWAHA—Reggie, please—OM NAMO BHAGAWATI VAJRAVARAHI—Reggie!—BAM HUM HUM—why oh why Reggie is everything so wrong?—PHAṬ OM NAMO ARYA APARAJITE HUM HUM PHAṬ—"

A Disturbing Call

WHEN BECCA ARRIVED at her *Six Feet Under* gig, they said there was some kind of fuckup. Her services weren't needed until later that week.

She'd already given Viv the trusted alibi—caretaking moribund Mom—this time even going slightly overboard in the drama department because of what she felt to be the necessity of washing the taste of a certain recent rooftop encounter out of her employer's mouth. (Becca said the Dunsmores were crazy and she'd only met them once or maybe twice and didn't want anything to do with them. Fortunately, Viv dismissed the whole incident with a kind of blithe, disgusted wave of the hand.) Instead of going back to Venice, she went shopping on Third. She phoned Dixie on the cell to say hi, in a cheap attempt to mitigate her guilt over the creepy cancer cover story.

She hooked up with Annie. They ate lunch at the Grove with Larry Levine then went to a movie.

Afterward, Larry split and the girls smoked weed and baked cookies at the apartment on Genesee, gossiping about their exes. At suppertime, they decided to go to Forty Deuce, but Becca was reluctant because she couldn't reach Rusty to tell him.

"What is he, your fucking keeper?" said Annie.

The TV report caught Becca's eye. "Oh my God! Turn it up!"

[STUDIO ANCHOR] *Lots of excitement in Riverside today when a member of the paparazzi "flipped" for Kit Lightfoot. More now, from Macey Dolenz.*

[OUTSIDE THE RIVERSIDE GALLERIA] *That's right, Raquel. The actor, who is still recovering from an assault last year in a West Hollywood liquor store that left him with extensive neurological damage, evidently went on an unscheduled outing this morning* [FOOTAGE OF FLIPPED CAR] *and was chased by Jimmy Newcombe, a freelance photographer. Newcombe was in hot pursuit of the reclusive superstar when he lost control of his car as Kit Lightfoot's driver continued on. The photographer was briefly hospitalized before being released. Photos of the recovering actor, at a premium, are said to be worth hundreds of thousands of dollars on both domestic and world tabloid markets.* [OLD FOOTAGE OF RIVERSIDE HOUSE] *Lightfoot, who has not given any interviews since the tragic incident, has been sequestered at his boyhood home since his release last Christmas from Valle Verde Rehab Center in Valencia, where he spent a closely guarded six months.* [BACK TO MALL; SCHOOLGIRLS/-BOYS IN B.G., JOCKEYING TO BE SEEN] *But, today, it seems like he went on a field trip to the Riverside Galleria, where he cheerfully signed autographs for supportive fans. Macey Dolenz, for KTTL, in Riverside.*

[BACK TO STUDIO] *A much needed, and hopefully, much enjoyed field trip at that. A tragic, fascinating story—and one we haven't heard the end of yet.*

[OTHER STUDIO ANCHOR] *Little bit of an old-fashioned movie car chase there, huh?*

—*Keystone kops.*

Coming up: a wild Wednesday for the Patriots, when they found their offense "up for grabs."

BECCA'S CELL PHONE lit up: CALLER UNKNOWN. She didn't think it was Rusty because when he phoned it usually said PRIVATE.

"Hello? Rusty? Hello?"

The club was too noisy for her to hear anything. She said "Hello? Hello?" through the crowd until she was outside.

"Hello, who is it?"

"Becca? Is it you?"

"Yes, this is Becca. Who is it?"

"It's Elaine!"

"Elaine?"

"Elaine *Jordache*. Did you hear about Kit Lightfoot?"

"The chase?"

"They caught the person who did that to him."

"They what?"

"The one who hit him on the head!" she said, adding testily: "He worked for *me*." Then: "Have you talked to Rusty?"

"No—"

"Then you don't *know* any of this?"

"Know any of *what*, Elaine?" said Becca, getting peeved.

"The police are supposedly looking for him because of something that person said . . ."

"That person—"

"The idiot who cracked Kit Lightfoot's skull! They were *friends*, they *knew* each other."

"Friends? *Who*—?"

"There supposedly was a *murder*, in *Virginia*—"

"Elaine, I don't understand this! I don't understand what you're saying."

"If you talk to Rusty, *do not tell him that we spoke*. All right? Will you promise me, Becca? Because we could be in *danger*, and I am *scared shitless*. I am in fear for my life!"

A Decent Proposal

BURKE CALLED FROM Vegas to tell Cela that a suspect in his son's assault had been arrested.

He said the police were sitting on it for the weekend but to expect a burst of media activity on Monday, when the announcement would officially be made. He didn't want Kit to know anything and was only mentioning it in case something leaked before he got back. Try to keep him away from the television. Just in case.

That night Cela invited Kit to her house for dinner. She lived outside the media-free zone; there was an element of delinquency, but more so because Burke was away and wouldn't have approved. It was just like the old days, when they snuck around their parents after dark.

Steaks sizzled on the Foreman. Kit leaned over to inspect the water bowls with floating votive candles that dotted the yard.

"So who died?" he said with a smile.

"Very funny," said Cela.

His limp was no longer pronounced. He wore a white button-down Gap shirt and new Levi's, and was three days into the haircut she'd given him.

"You look nice," she said.

She'd chosen a short little black dress, but Kit didn't comment.

"Dad in Vegas," he said, declaratively.

"That's right."

"When coming back?"

" 'When is *he* coming back?' "

"When is *he* coming back?"

"You can really speak beautifully when you *want* to."

"When is *he* coming back, when is *he* coming back," he said, gently mocking.

"Depends on how fast he loses," she said. "He *loves* giving them his money."

"Loves giving them *my* money."

Cela laughed. His sense of humor was intact—everything was pretty much intact. He just moved a bit more slowly, in mind and in body, a bit less elegantly than before. He sporadically discarded words and consonants, his inflection unpredictably emphatic or slurred, but Cela was convinced that was because there was no one riding herd.

"Ever go with him?" he asked.

"To Vegas? Couple of times."

"Where did you stay?"

"The Bellagio. He knows some people there. Or the Mirage."

"You fuck him a long time?"

She turned from the grill, narrowing her eyes. "There is *nothing* between me and your father."

"I saw you," he said. She went back to grimly futzing with the blackened steaks. Kit's smile became bittersweet. "I don't . . . judgment. No energy to judge. Have got . . . energy for eating and shitting and . . . *maybe* signing autograph. Autographs," he corrected.

"Your father," she said awkwardly, "was good to me. Burke has his flaws—does he ever. OK? And I know that. I'm well aware. The bottom line is he took care of me when I got out of rehab. *More* than once. And I know he did some *really shitty* things to you, Kit—to you and your mom. And I respect whatever feelings you have toward him about that. OK? That's not really my business. All I can deal with is how he—what he did for *me*. And that he's a human being. He was *right there*, Kit. He was there for me. My father wasn't, and neither were *you*—and that's so not your fault! I'm sorry. That's bullshit, and I shouldn't have even said it. I'm sorry. It just—it had nothing to do with you. I'm not a perfect person, Kit—never said I was. OK? But I love you and I just don't even really want to talk about any of this anymore. Or right now, OK?" She choked back tears and said, "*I just want us to have a nice dinner and be sweet to each other—*"

"I'm sorry, Cela."

"About what?"

"I'm sorry I had a . . . *big movie star life.*"

She hadn't seen him angry since the injury—anger was probably a good thing. Still, it hurt to be the target.

"That's not what I meant—"

"But I don't anymore! So don't worry!"

His face contorted with rage, then he broke into raucous laughter. Always with the practical jokes. She wanted to hug him, but he turned the tables again. "You're using," he said.

Cela poignantly winced. "Once in a while."

She went back to her business at the grill. (Actor's prop for a difficult scene.)

"You shouldn't do it."

"How about a urine test?" she said, stung. "But can we do it *after* dessert? Look: *I'm well aware* that I'm fucking up, OK? Does that make you *feel* better, Kit? I'm gonna start going to meetings again, I already decided that." She shoveled the meat onto plates and sighed. "*Shit.*"

He grew quiet. The table was beautifully set with white cloth, white flowers, white candles.

They didn't talk as they ate, but she watched him. The world had been upended though some things would never change. She was reminded of when they first went out and how she was nervous and always trying to please him.

After supper, they sat on a porch rocker, staring at the moon.

"Tula's probably freaking out you're here, huh."

"I told him to . . . get a life. I told him—go guard some chicken tonight. At Koo Koo Roo."

"Now that he's a famous stunt driver, you better look out. Some headhunter's gonna poach him." She lit a cigarette. "So, what's up with those Buddhists? They're kind of a trip. I mean, they're like full service, huh. They *cook*, they *clean*, they *meditate* . . ."

"Yeah."

"I mean, I think they're great. You've been into that a long time, huh."

"Yeah right. Buddhism has been berry, berry good to me."

Cela laughed, not really catching the reference. "Kit," she said, earnestly. "Do you remember anything about what happened? I mean, the night that guy hit you?"

"No."

"Nothing about the hospital?" He shook his head. "What about when you visited with Burke a few weeks before? You came and looked at some things that belonged to your mom." He shook his head again. "We went over to Grant, on your hog."

"I don't remember anything that happen. *Happened*. For about maybe a year or maybe three month—*s* before I hit my head."

"Do you . . . do you remember Viv?"

"I do!" he said, stalwartly. "I *do* remember . . . Viv Wembley! But I am not assure . . . that Viv Wembley remembers *me*!"

Without warning, he groped her. He wetly kissed her mouth and squeezed a tit. She kissed him back, then said, "I don't think this is such a great idea."

"Dad won't mind," he said.

"That has *nothing* to do with it," she said. She quickly decided it was absurd to be offended by his remark—everything was so ridiculous and heartbreaking.

"Could you at least . . . *think* about it?" he said.

She shook her head wryly and pulled out a joint. "I think," she said, "I'm gonna become a Buddhist."

A Tangled Web

"MOTHERFUCKER SNITCHED off my *boy*. Leaves Kit Lightfoot droolin in his soup, then goes and ruins a *major* QuestraWorld property! For sport! For fuckin sport!"

"He was up at the house, wasn't he?" said Cassandra.

"That's right—the look-alike *wanna-be* was swimmin in our motherfuckin *pool*. Man, how low can you go to be a look-alike *wanna-be*? No offense, Becca. Cause you and Rusty the real thing."

"He was here," said Cassandra as she fiddled with a two-carat diamond created from the ashes of their beloved little girl. "Sniffin round Rusty like a puppy dog. Talkin shit about how he was big in Tokyo doin Kit Lightfoot look-alike gigs. I don't even think Elaine *Jordache* would hire him."

"She wouldn't get fuckin *near* his raggedy *un*look-alike ass. And you got to be pretty low for Elaine not to try to squeeze some fuckin money out of you. That lady knows her shit."

"He sure didn't *look* like Kit Lightfoot."

"He looked like Kit Lightfoot as much as I do."

"Not unless he did his hair up a certain way."

"He was a fuckin *housepainter*, Cass! Shit mother*fucker*." He stomped around in front of the picture window. "And he snitched off my boy! We was about to lock Rusty *up*, wasn't we, Cass?" He turned to Becca, who was struggling to remember whether or not the Kit look-alike was at the Chateau table-read. "We was about to give your old man *major dollars* and stamp 'Property of QuestraWorld' on his hairy butt. Wasn't we, Cass?"

He made the sizzling sound of a cattle brand while his wife took a hit of pot.

"Maybe," she said. "Maybe we was."

"That's *right*, you better *believe* it. That was *my call*. Cause you might be CEO and COO but *I'm* the president and secretary-in-motherfucking-arms. So motherfuck that 'maybe' shit." He maddogged Cassandra though both knew who'd win in a fight. Grady did a line, then handed the rolled bill to Becca. She shook her head but he wouldn't have it. He watched like a scientist while she snorted up. "Man," he said. "You gotta write something *down* about your *killer boyfriend*." He got a neon brainstorm. "I know! We'll get Dr. J to do a *script*. Cause Rusty's gonna be hotter than *shit*—*Access Hollywood*, *Dateline*, *Sixty Minutes*—ev'rybody gonna line *up*. Old Larry King too. Rusty gonna be hotter than the dude who killed Versace."

"Andrew Carnegie," said Cass.

"Whatever." He looked like he just goosed himself. "Oh shit. *Oh shit*. What's *Spike Jonze* gonna do? Shit, man, this is good! The plot gets fuckin thickerer! I'll *tell* you what Spike's gonna do, he gonna *love* it, *that's* what—"

"There ain't no such thing as bad publicity."

"—*especially* with the motherfucker who whacked Kit Lightfoot on the *head* bein a Kit Lightfoot look-alike *hisself*!"

"It's tawdry, baby," said Cassandra. "It's real tawdry!"

Grady began to squeal. "Spike and his peeps gonna be happier than motherfuckers! All hot and bothered, cause now they got Russell *and* they got Rusty in the *can*—I don't mean the *penitentiary,* neither. That's somethin to *Crowe* about! Got the two of 'em on *film,* man . . . it's a motherfucking wrap!"

He sucked and squealed and clapped his hands together while doing a little dance. Then he fell to his knees before the table like a spent soul singer and sucked up two pencil-thick lines.

Cassandra held the diamond ring up to Becca's eyes. "Ain't it pretty? That's my little girl. Didn't they do her beautiful?"

"Got your boy on Murder One!" said Grady, gleefully. "Whacked some fucker in the horsey set, in Virginia. Ain't that your hometown? Didn't he never say nothin to you about that?"

"Why *would* he, Grady?" said Cassandra, drowsily. "He and some . . . fancy lady—" She nodded out, then came to. "Gettin it on at some ritzy equestrian center . . . now why would he want to—"

"Ritzy *whuh?*" he said, furrowing his brow. "Some ritzy bar-mitzy *whuh?*"

"—killed the husband? Or whatever? Now why would he mention that to our sweet little *Becca?* Why would he want her to even know anything *about* that? Huh, Grady?"

"Shit," he said, shrugging his shoulders. "How the fuck would *I* know? Could be nightie-night talk. You and me used to nightie-night talk shit, didn't we? Never know what goes on behind closed doors."

Cassandra drunkenly warbled, "When you get behind closed doors, and you let your hair hang low . . ."

"Who *knows* what these two look-alikes here shared?" said Grady the horn-dog. "I'll *tell* you who—the shadow do!"

"And you make me feel like ah'm a man! No one knows what goes on behind closed doors—"Cassandra shrieked, collapsing in rheumy laughter.

"Man," said Grady, regarding her with disdain. "You like that fat crazy bitch on *The Sopranos.* You jus' like Tony Soprano's sister." Jake cried from his crib. Grady cast a lecherous eye on Becca. "*Lotta* shit goes on behind closed doors . . . if you know what I mean."

He touched her thigh and she pulled away. She was sad and stoned and had no energy to leave. Outside the window, a ghostly pool man drew a long pole through the water.

"Tell you one thing," said Grady, lighting up. "Tell you one thing, for *sure*—that boy gonna need to get *lawyered up*. Mr. Russell Crowe Junior's gonna need hisself some *legal* funds."

"And we ain't gonna give him shit."

"Oh yes we are."

"Oh no we ain't."

"Oh yes we are. And I'll tell you why."

"OK, baby. You tell me why."

"I'll tell you why and you're gonna *like* it."

"Right—I'm gonna love it. I'm gonna love it like I love your crusty ol' butthole."

"You gonna love that too when I'm through. Gonna love it when I'm prairie doggin. Gonna wanna pitch a *tent* in there. You gonna wanna up my salary too."

"I'll up it. Love to. Up it till it hurts."

"We gonna buy that screenplay he wrote."

"We ain't gonna buy shit."

"I got five words for you: *To Kill a Unicorn.*"

"That's four, dickwad."

"Now what'd Rusty say when I axe him what that screenplay was about? What'd he say, Cass?" She thought about it as she went on the nod. "*What'd he say?* Yeah, that's *right—now* she finally cain't say nothin—now she *won't*—cause she *knows* what he said. The man said it was a *murder mystery.* Right? OK? And where did he say it took place? *At the track!* Or some kinda horsey farm. 'Member, Cass?"

"That's right," said the wife, eyes sealed. The cigarette was about to burn the tip of her finger. "That's right." He knew that she knew where he was going. "I'll give you that."

"Yeah well, you gonna give me more than *that*, Mamasita. While my guitar gently fuckin weeps. I wouldn't be surprised if Russell Crowe Junior laid the *whole motherfuckin crime* out in that *scriptuh* his. OK?"

"OK," said Cassandra. When you're right, you're right. "OK, Columbo?"

"I ain't *shittin*, Sherlock. And I mean *everything* that fucking happened, all right? OK? All right? QuestraWorld gonna *own* that shit—the *whole fuckin deal.* All right?"

"I see what you're saying," she said.

"I knew that you would. Took *me* to think of it, though, didn't it?"

"You just might get that raise, babylove."

"Better believe I'm gonna get that raise, Mommy!" he said, then whooped. "You gonna suckle my grody anus too. Taste like tutti-frutti. Gon' give in to *all* my hostage demands! Fifty thousand in change, for a night at Hustler's! In beautiful downtown Gardena!"

"We ain't closed no deal with Rusty *yet*."

"*When we close*. That's fair. That's fair—I'm a fair man. Though I *do* think you should give me ten up front, for a finder's fee. For puttin the fuckin pieces together. But I'm fair and I got a mind like a mother-fucking iron trap and don't you or anybody forget it! That's why I got all my millions. Trick is, to get the screenplay off him before it becomes evidentiary."

"Fore somebody else buys it."

"That's right. That's right. Now you got it. I don't think he gonna be in a hurry to tell the police about it. But when HBO find out, HBO gonna want it."

"Naw," said Cassandra, shaking her head. Her lids were heavy, like a groggy seer's. "We wan' somebody else. HBO is for the TV show. Don't want to dip in that well too many times. We want this for a DreamWorks."

"That's why you're QuestraWorld CEO," said Grady respectfully.

"Could be for a Soderbergh," said Cassandra.

"Maybe. Hell, George Clooney love to get his hands on this!"

"Too old to play Rusty."

"Then he could just direct or exec produce. They gonna be linin *up* for this motherfucker! So get your checkbook ready, girl! Get your yayas out!" He clapped his hands, rubbing them together as if to make a fire. "Whoo-eee! We got ourselves a *major project acquisition*." He did a war dance, then turned to Becca. "You gonna help, ain't you? Help persuade him? Make *you* an E.P. for that. Wanna exec? We can swing that, cain't we, Mama Cass? Cain't we swing exec prod for our girl here?"

"Associate," said Cassandra.

"She gonna be an invaluable part of the package—she was the girl-friend *and* she's hot *and* she's a look-alike! Look-alikes 'bout to be hot as *mother*fuckers! And *shit*—bitch works for Viv Wembley! I didn't even *think* of that shit! It all ties in!" He coughed a dewy fogbank of smoke. "Our little girl works for the wicked witch former fiancée! The bi-atch who dumped Lightfoot—in sickness and in health my *left nut*. Bi-atch left his twappy rear end standing at the altar!"

"Waitin around for that slut with a buncha bald old Buddhists with hard-ons," said Cassandra, stirring from a nod.

"It's a Shakespearean fucking tragedy, man! I love it! I love it!"

"Associate producer," said Cassandra, from the viraginous depths.

"That's what I said."

"You said *exec.*"

"Well associate's what I meant."

Negotiations

LISANNE CALLED TO SAY that she was from the *sangha* and had a gift for the house. Burke said that, since the arrest, things had been kind of crazy and he wasn't having anyone over until next week. She didn't want to intrude and suggested they meet somewhere nearby. Burke was half-intrigued and wanted to check her out. Maybe she was fuckable.

The voice on the phone had been familiar but he couldn't quite place it. When he saw her, he laughed: the chubby one with the angel's face who loved cleaning toities. That was all right. He liked 'em with a little extra padding.

She had that blissed-out look, scarier in a nascent fattie—bit of a red flag but so what? He'd seen crazier. Anyhow, what could she do, suffocate him with her tits? She was a Buddhist, and they didn't act out. He got right to it and asked about the gift. She said she was good friends with the studio executive Tiff Loewenstein (Burke, of course, knew who he was, even though the connection to his son didn't at first compute; maybe Loewenstein was a *sanghanista*) and how Tiff had entrusted her to bring an ancient Buddha statue to Kit's trailer during his last shoot. As a present. Out of curiosity, she asked Burke if he'd had a chance to see that Buddha and he said no, everything in the Benedict house of any value had been inventoried, packed, and stored by the insurance folks. That's when Lisanne told him she had an "energetic replacement." She called it by its unwieldy name and Burke couldn't help but laugh out loud. He was starting to think she was a certified wack job, but what the fuck, she cleaned a mean toilet. He was in an expansive mood. Lisanne remained unperturbed. She said she'd been given the Supreme Bliss-Wheel Integration Buddha as a gift herself—not from Tiff—and that it was now her desire to pass it on as a sacred offering to the Lightfoot household. When she told him it was extraordinarily expensive, that got his attention. The piece, she said, celebrated Paramasukha-Chakrasamvara, a tantric deity that Kit seemed destined to possess. Lisanne recounted how she saw his son at UCLA on the night the monks ululated over that very god in the midst of their solemn public ritual. "Tantric" got his attention too, and he asked Lisanne if she knew anything about tantric sex. Burke said he read somewhere that Sting was into it and that it was all about holding back orgasm. Lisanne said she didn't know much about that but was sure that all things tantric could only be taught by an authentic guru. Burke said he had a special guru when it came to sexual matters and she asked who and he said Master Bates. He said his friends called him Stormin' Norman and he ran the Master Bates Motel. She smiled but didn't get it—any of it. His blood was up and he got horny for her. Burke asked if she knew anything about *kundalini*. Lisanne said that it was "serpent energy" and began talking about chakras from the little she'd learned in books. Burke started calling it *cunt*alini—what the hell, she'd either leave the table or not, she was a wack fattie and he wanted to ball her, he didn't give a shit what her reaction was—and said Master Bates told him that after *cunt*alini it was always important to smoke a cigarette and eat Rice-A-Roni. He couldn't get a rise out of her and that made him hornier. He asked when she wanted to bring over the Super Tampon Piss-Wheel Segregation Buddha and without batting an eye Lisanne said the best time would be when no one from the *sangha* was there because she didn't want others to think she was currying favor. He thought: Well well well. Maybe this fat cuntalini's a dirty bastard. Maybe ol' loosey-goosey's in what we call a righteous orangutan heat. Lisanne said the

Buddhist community was a bit incestuous and even enlightened people gossiped and misinterpreted. Incestuous—you got that right,
fatso. Daddy's going to do some major rectal probe enlightening.
Show you nirvana six ways from Sunday. She said the Supreme Bliss-
Wheel Integration Buddha would do wonders for the house and was
even partially responsible for the arrest of the person who did his
son—and all beings—such a terrible wrong. Get on that Piss-Wheel
of Fortune. Integrate that Buddha-bootie. Super-ream that lard-ass
bumper butt. She said the Buddha would help Kit to heal his crown
chakra. Burke said *his* crown needed healing too. Said he had a purple crown with a big ol' hole that needed healing, big-time. Master
Bates called the geyser-hole Old Unfaithful.

Lisanne smiled vacantly, unhearing. She looked through him but
saw only Kit, who was her breath and her benefactor, her friend and
neutral person, her enemy, and the being she didn't even know. She
looked through him and saw all things human and animal, seen and
unseen, waiting to be born and waiting to die.

They made a plan when she should bring it.

After the Fall

THE DETAILS OF the arrest of Kit Lightfoot's assailant, himself a
Lightfoot manqué, predictably became a nightly news staple, as did a
legion of seamy *Hollywood Babylon*-redux celebrity crime scandal
minidocs in general—and the shadowy fringe world of look-alikes in
particular. (Becca and Annie noticed how they always used clips of
Kim Basinger from *L.A. Confidential*.) The creep turned out to be one
of Elaine Jordache's third-string loser-hires; when he wasn't working
low-end convention sideshows or Mar Vista bachelorette parties at
the Look-Alike Shoppe's behest, he made his living as a housepainter
and petty grifter. When they pinched him, the Kit got nervous, and
hastened to cop a plea. Herke Goodson immediately came to mind.

The down-and-out look-alikes hooked up around a year ago on
the rent-a-star circuit. They became friendly but hadn't spoken in a

while—the Kit still being miffed at a beating Goodson gave him out-side a club in Playa del Rey. For months before, "Rusty" had been showing off pages of a script he'd written, a murder mystery entitled "The Trainer." Because of certain coy remarks and a plethora of plot minutiae that struck him as a little too authentic, the Kit always had a hunch the story was based on something real. After he shared his potential Get Out of Jail Free card with the LAPD, Virginia detectives were quick to ID Herke Lamar Goodson as the subject of numerous outstanding warrants for home-invasion burglary and aggravated assault, and as the suspect in a high-profile local homicide.

·   ·   ·

BECCA MOVED IN with the Dunsmores on the same day she was interviewed by the police. Investigators went through every square inch of the Venice love nest. The idea of pervy old detectives handling her underthings made her skin crawl. Rusty's arrest hadn't yet been announced, and Becca was glad—she wasn't in the proper frame of mind to be stalked by the tabloids. Annie said she'd probably be in the national papers too. Becca dreaded that. When the time was right, she would have to call her mom to preempt any freakouts.

The cops were like cordial pit bulls. They brought her in every day, for a week. They talked to the Dunsmores, and Grady started getting paranoid. He was afraid that even though he never had a clue about Rusty's bad boy status, they'd bust him for "consorting." Cassandra reminded him that one of the outcomes of the Rampart suit was that his record had been expunged—he was no longer classified as a parolee. Grady said it didn't matter: they were gonna nail anybody who won a settlement. "Payback's a motherfucker." He threw out their dope. They cleaned up their act for a while.

Living at the Dunsmores' was handy. Becca signed a contract mak-ing her coassociate producer with profit participation on any project or projects that QuestraWorld produced re: the compelling saga of Herke Lamar Goodson, a.k.a. "Rusty" Crowe. (Annie and Larry told Becca that she could be "like Rosanna Arquette in *The Executioner's Song*.") The contract also stipulated that Becca's rights as a real-life personage in said project(s) would be waived, that a writer or writers could deem to make her life or her person "more interesting" (Cassandra's words) without fear of legal reprisal and that Becca would make herself available for attendant press and publicity chores, lending name and/or image to the promotion of said QuestraWorld product(s), electronic press kits, print ads, et cetera. The contract came with a five-thousand-dollar check and Cassandra's word that there would be more—which really helped because Viv had fired her and she was completely broke.

. . .

ON THE WAY TO Elaine's, Becca pondered Rusty's innocence—the one thing no one seemed to have considered. Her attempts to visit him in jail had been rebuffed. A sign of guilt? Not necessarily. Becca knew her man; he was prideful. He probably just didn't want her to see him that way, encaged like an animal.

The door to the Look-Alike Shoppe was ajar. Everything was in boxes. Only some banged-up furniture remained.

"This has been the day from *hell*," said Elaine, as if she and Becca were in midconversation. "The *LA Weekly*'s doing an 'investigatory' piece—I don't even want to be in the fucking *country* when that comes out. I heard they might put me on the cover. Can you believe it? Why! Why! I called them up and said *no*—but they don't need my fucking permission. *I am not Heidi Fleiss.* Read all about it! Elaine Jordache, the Low-Life Look-Alike Queen!"

"But isn't that good? I mean, for business?"

"You must be kidding."

She went back to her packing.

"What about that guy?" asked Becca. "The Kit look-alike?"

"What about him?"

"Well, you hired him for stuff. Do you know what happened?"

"What's there to know? Kit Lightfoot dissed him in front of his girlfriend so he went *off*. When they split up, she turned him in for the award—end of story." She spoke with the *noir* affect of a court stenographer, indifferently reading back notes. "Haven't you talked to the police?"

"All week long," said Becca.

"Didn't they tell you what Rusty's accused of?"

"That he killed some rich lady's husband?"

"In Albemarle County," she said, again with hard-boiled noncha-lance. "Didn't they tell you *who* he killed? Daddy. That's right: his fucking father. And guess who the rich lady was—they didn't say, huh. Well, I'll give you a clue. Little Rusty slid out of her pussy. Need more than three guesses?"

Contact

THE ARREST AND pending extradition of Herke Lamar Goodson a.k.a. "Rusty" Crowe took media center stage, ratcheting up the hulla-baloo over all things look-alike. The frenzy escalated, if that were pos-sible, upon the revelation that the defendant had a "starring role" in the celebrated director Spike Jonze's latest offering. The auteur's reps smartly underplayed their hand. A press release stated that Mr. Good-son had indeed participated in the film, "along with a dozen other look-alike actors," but his screen time had been substantially reduced, for reasons which—so they claimed—had nothing to do with current controversies.

· · ·

WHEREAS KIT RESPONDED to the capture of his double with a cryptic half smile, Burke Lightfoot, who at least publicly, had limned the part of selfless caregiver to such perfection, vehemently demanded assurance from the lawyers that all measures would be taken to guar-antee that his son be spared a circus-like courtroom confrontation with the man who had so grievously injured him. He even said as much on Fox News—after cannily alerting Barbara Walters before-hand so as not to subvert the chance of father and son making a future appearance on one of her specials.

The Buddhists were allowed back in. Burke hadn't heard from what's-her-name and found himself ruminating on her fat ass. Ought to hang a sign on it: WIDE LOAD. He smiled to himself—he sure did like 'em crazy. Maybe he'd put her off with the cuntalini shtick. Who knew? Still, all that talk about how no one should be there when she brought over the Super Tampon Tit-Wheel . . . hmmm. Made ya wonder. Might just make a late-night bootie call yet. Buddha call. Whatever. Ask me if I care.

* * *

RAM DASS WANTED Burke's permission to bring someone special to the house, a holy man that Kit had met shortly before his injury. He said that H.H. Penor Rinpoche was a reincarnated lama; it was from him that Kit's root guru, Gil Weiskopf Roshi, had received "the transmissions and secret sealed protector empowerments." Burke didn't know what the hell Ram Dass was talking about. He thought Mr. Dass was just fine so long as the conversation didn't get too out there—aside from the Moses beard and the electric Kool-Aid bug eyes, he was kind of a regular guy. But the idea of a quasi-royal visit from a Tibetan big enchilada tickled Burke's fancy.

A few days later, Ram Dass, a fellow called Robert Thurman, and the yellow-robed guest of honor arrived with an entourage of orange-swathed monks and khenpos, the sight of which impressed even the neighbors, who by now were more or less inured to the unusual if not the outlandish. Thurman was a bearish, convivial man around Burke's age, the first Westerner to be ordained as a Tibetan Buddhist monk by none other than the Dalai Lama himself. He was a professor at Columbia and a prolific author who had translated scores of sacred texts. More important for Burke, he was Uma Thurman's dad (father-in-law of Ethan Hawke), making them comrades-in-arms of the rarefied Movie Star Parents Club.

While his son communed in the backyard with the holy man, Bob—the others called him Tenzin—put Burke at ease. He said that he could relate to what had happened to Kit because he had sustained a life-altering injury when still in college. Bob had lost his left eye in an accident; forced to confront his mortality "head-on," he dropped out of school and embarked on a journey whose road inexorably led to Tibet.

"That was more than forty years ago."

"That's a good thing," said Burke, humbly nodding. "A heroic thing. Wish something like that had happened to *me*—minus the pain, of course," he said, winking. He was genuinely impressed and thought the doctors had done a helluva job with that glass eye. "Though it'll probably'll take dick cancer to get Burke Lightfoot to straighten up and fly spiritually right."

Bob laughed. He was unpretentious that way—a heavyweight who wasn't about to proselytize. A mensch, and Burke appreciated that.

"Who exactly *is* His Holiness?" he asked.

"Extraordinary man. Left Tibet in 'fifty-six, a *huge* group. Only thirty or so made it. Built a monastery, practically with his own hands—Namdroling, in Mysore. I'm pretty sure your son was there, maybe ten, twelve years ago."

"Did you know Kit?"

"We did meet but unfortunately never got the chance to spend much time together. I think we were introduced at a benefit in New York, at Tibet House. He was very sober, very centered. Not at all interested in the 'movie star thing.'"

"Guess he and Uma must have hung out."

"You know, I spoke with her and said I was coming out to see you. They never worked on a film but she said they spent some social time."

"Did she get teased a lot? About her name?"

"Oh, I think when she was younger! But not too much anymore."

"It's a beautiful name."

"She was heartbroken when she heard what happened."

"Well, the next time everyone's in town, we'll have us a dinner. Ethan too."

"That'd be terrific. She would love that."

"We'll go right over to the Mission Inn—that's just a few miles from here. Diane Keaton is rumored to drop by now and then to partake of the prime rib. But you're probably some kind of vegan. Isn't that what they call that?"

"I *have* been known to be carnivorous."

His mind returned to the rinpoche. "So, our friend—is he a 'lama' like the Dalai Lama?"

"Well, yes, but not of that lineage. He's also called a *tulku*, or reincarnated being. His Holiness is actually recognized as the incarnation of the Second Padma Norbu, a great Buddhist saint and meditation master."

"He's a saint?" said Burke, eyebrow arched in playful skepticism.
Bob smiled and said, "In Buddhism, *saint* means 'realized being.' "
"You know, I've been doing a little meditation myself."
"Ya have? Great!"
"M & M—meditation and *medication*."
Bob laughed.
"We have a *lot* of Buddhists moving through here—it's like Grand Central, can't help but rub off on you. They seem to calm Kit down pretty well, that's for sure. He still gets frustrated. You know, with everything that's happened."

"I can't stress enough the importance of Kit getting back to his practice. *Feeling* it again. And that *you're* meditating is great—this can't have been easy for you, either, Burke. It's a *wonderful* gift you've given your son, bringing the *sangha* into your home. That's great, great merit. And I hear Kit's doing phenomenally well—I don't have to *hear* it, I can *see* it. He's just flowering."

"He's a tough kid, Tenzin. Tough like his old man."

Red Essence Rising

LISANNE BROUGHT over the Supreme Bliss-Wheel Integration Buddha at the agreed upon time. She noticed a general stillness; even the neighborhood seemed more deserted that usual. She could feel the Source all around her.

Mr. Lightfoot said that Kit was in the shower. He asked if she wanted anything to drink, and when she said no, he sat on the couch, eyes focused on the box. The copper-leafed mandala was in its original velvet-lined mahogany container. He enthusiastically bade her remove it. Lisanne smiled and looked toward the bathroom. She could hear the water running and tried to indicate that she wanted Kit to be present for the unveiling, but he said they should go on ahead. That way, it would be "in full regalia" when Kit came in.

She carefully took it out, and the father inhaled appreciatively. *That's really something.* When he asked somewhat boyishly if he could touch it, she said the Buddha was his, that it belonged to the house now and he could do with it as he wished. He held the antiquity high in the air, as if already appraising its fair market value.

He asked her to come sit beside him. He put his hand at the nape of her clammy white neck, resting it there while he complimented the sculpture. He said that such a thing was "probably priceless" and wanted her to be certain she wished to make a gift of it. And would she mind signing a paper to that effect. He began rubbing her neck to see if she would balk at his attentions. When she didn't, he let the hand drift to her collarbone, then out to the shoulder, telling her what a generous gesture it was she had made, all the while making tight semicircles with his fingertip. The pudgy skin was soft and unblemished and turned him on. Kit emerged from the steamy bath in one of Burke's silk robes. He smiled, and she smiled back. When Burke's hand deliberately brushed a big tit, Lisanne stood and asked if she could use "the ladies' room." She wasn't sure if Kit was finished in there, but the impulse was too strong. She excused herself and entered the space Kit had been only moments before. She closed the door. She got the can of Comet and a brush from below the sink and began to scrub the basin of the stall. The mirror was fogged. It was humid and there was no fan. She was on her knees, sweating as she leaned into the crud. When she didn't come out, Burke boldly opened the door without knocking. He laughed in a friendly way. You really like to clean, don't you? he said. When she started in on the toilet with that spacey smile, he knew what he always knew—she was the Grand Imperial Super Tampon Wack Job. He fished out his cock, just to see if she'd notice. "You know," he said, "we had a holy man here the other day. And evidently he said—this is what *Ram the Ass* told me but maybe I got it wrong because *Ram the Ass* sometimes talks out of the side of his fucking head, goo goo guh-joo, but Ram the Ass *supposedly* said that this *holy* man said that my Kit was showing signs of being a reincarnation of some kinda holy man him*self*. H.H. Kit Lightfoot. Now what d'ya think of *that*?" He pulled on his pud and moved closer, brushing the cock against her face as she scrubbed. He kept talking, trancelike. "You like to clean shitters, huh. You're pretty good, huh. Gotta pretty big throne on you yourself. I'd like to sit on that fucking throne. Hey, what do you get when you cross a king with a toilet? A royal flush. Come on. This king's crown has some dust on it. Do a little cleaning." He bent his knees and put the tip of his softish penis in Lisanne's mouth. He moved it in and out with his hand. She was a slack-jawed corpse, and he joked, "You're a real party animal, aren't you?" He took her by the elbow and helped her up. Come on, Big Bertha. Time to get a load off. He led her to the bedroom and sat her on the coverlet. Are you a holy woman? Are you a holy girl? Cause I think you're a *hole* woman. That's right. You a whole lotta hole. He laid her down. He stripped his clothes off while asking if she wanted to be with his son. "Oh c'mon now, that's some kind of great honor. And you know what? Time he get himself some! Cause he's had less pussy than a Muslim cleric, and I don't want him on Cela either. He may have been on her already—I don't put *nothin* past that girl—but I don't play that shit, not in my house. He had his time. This is *my* time. I own that cunt. Hell, own the *both* of 'em. And I think you should be with the holy man. In Xanadu, I so decree: you are hereby the Chosen One. Or maybe you're fat enough I should call you the Chosen Few." He laughed at his joke, shouting, "Son! Get *in* here!" Kit entered smiling, not knowing at first what was going on—so bizarre and unthinkable. Burke was in the middle of pulling Lisanne's shirt up over her head. Wow, those are big. Jesus H.—real Louisville Sluggers. Stinky too. Y'oughta wash 'em now and then. That's a Howard Hughes special. Haven't seen a brassiere like that since the freakin forties. Fuckin zeppelin catchers. Her head got trapped in the blouse then emerged and Kit recognized her, not just from minutes ago but from all the weeks she'd come and tidied, so polite and helpful. When he saw his father's stiff dick, he backed up. He asked what he was doing and Burke said, "Lookin after you, *tulku*-breath. Your Analness. Your Holy Dipshit." Then, as Bogart: Here's lookin' after *you*, kid. Kit said, It's wrong. Burke said, Wrong never felt so right— or so tight, neither. You gonna see. You gonna see. He pulled off her jeans and panties and said, Now *that's* a fuckin bush! Jesus! Know who had a bush like that? Your mother. R.J. had a bush like that. Kit said, Shut up, and Burke said, When I saw that bush on your mother, I said: Gonna marry that girl. *Got* to. That's right. 'He gotta have it.' Oops, what have we here? It was a Tampax string. Houston, we have a problem. Gonna need a towel. Ground control to major towel. He started for the linen closet before saying, Oh fuck it. He looped the end of the string around a forefinger and slowly pulled. Woo, that stinks. That's *muggy*. That's a New York subway, summertime. When it came out he said, Plop plop fizz fizz oh what a relief it is. Woo woo woo. Sunday bloody Sunday. Burke got tired of his son's lame, chivalrous reticences and ordered him to take off his pants. Kit got hard right away, in spite of himself. Thar she blows! That's right. Made him an offer he couldn't refuse. Lisanne opened her eyes long enough to see the tattoos: the FOREVER VIV and the Sanskrit she didn't understand the first time she saw it on him in the trailer but had since learned to recognize as Om. She was on her back, beached. Burke led him down, grabbed Kit's pecker, and put it in. There now. Fits like a glove. Fire in the hole! Kit said, Shut up, then Lisanne put her hands on his ass and worked it. Burke got a kick out of that. She ain't dead yet, he said. He ain't heavy, he's my lama. Burke jacked, watching the bloody cock. In and out. That's what a hamburger's all about. Now that's a beautiful thing. That's a *very* beautiful thing. But I'm gonna have to burn these sheets when you lovebirds are done. And those are Ralph Lauren, they ain't cheap. Gonna have to do a serious burn. Cause Fatty Arbuckle is hemorrhaging. Gonna need to find ourselves a tourniquet for that clit. Lookie that thing. Gonna have to tie it off. He got down and peered under his son's flat, pistoning stomach. Yee-haw. Looks like someone stuck a buncha Bazooka gum on a goddamn Brillo pad. Lookit that belly. That's a Goodyear blimp belly. When I was seventeen, he sang, it was a very Goodyear . . . As Kit fucked her, Lisanne thought, I am in the in-between. In the bardo of their lovemaking she saw his white essence sink in the sky like the moon and her red essence rise from the earth of her navel like a sun through karmic winds. Father and Mother merged—she couldn't feel her own body but saw them copulating as if staring down from the ceiling. She waited for the wrathful deities, but they didn't come. Lisanne stroked his skull, caressing the double surgical scars where the rainbow light would one day emanate. He was oblivious to her touch. He pounded her, dry-mouthed and ecstatic. His eyes were closed, but they opened as he came, shuddering, that was when she saw the energy leave the scar, she was rehears-

ing him for *phowa,* she'd read all about it and listened to the audiotapes but had never spoken of the esoteric maneuver with her teachers or anyone in the *sangha* but now here she was, performing like a
natural. Coaching, guiding, evoking. She'd sent away for the tapes
from Boulder and vigilantly done the meditation, and in the second
week, she even got a nosebleed—the tapes said that wasn't uncom-
mon, external signs were indicators of the power of the practice. (You
were supposed to repeat the *phowa* meditations twenty-one times a
day but no more, because if overdone, they could have a deleterious
effect.) The tapes said to imagine the white male drop falling from
the crown chakra and the red female drop rising from the lower
loins, both drops merging to form a pearl in the heart chakra. (The
Dalai Lama said that when a body died, the heart was the last organ
to lose its warmth.) After the merging, you said a prayer, asking for
purification and forgiveness for all negative thoughts and actions
experienced in this life, then you expelled the pearl through the
fontanel or soft spot at the top of the head with an audible *Hic!* or a
Pung!—straight into the heart of a Buddha or deity that you visualized to be floating somewhere above, though it didn't necessarily
have to be a Buddha, it could be your grandma or your best friend or
anything really that was beloved. For Lisanne, of course, it was Kit—
friend and benefactor, lover and enemy, human and animal, seen
and unseen, newly born–newly dying—Kit, who was in her breath
and the breath of her son, now inhabiting the lungspace of her very
womb—the pearl was delivered, the merging, complete. She was certain that invisible wanderers sensed his godliness and already
swarmed like flies onto meat: *Imagine the multitudes of lost souls cir-
cling this bardo!*—all this she thought while ejecting their mutual
awareness into the heart of the ethereal Buddha-Kit floating above
their heads through the corridors of dharmakaya. The tapes said one
had to be certain that the person having his consciousness ejected by
proxy was dead but Lisanne's intentions were to elicit a gentle run-
through, unlike classic *phowa,* which is always done *after* final respirations . . . a temporary, anomalous, honored *healing* instead, a kind
of ventriloquistic bloodletting (wasn't Kit letting *her* blood? She felt
it streaming down her legs like a martyr in some religious painting
but shook herself, careful to climb out of any unhelpful or confusing

theistic mind-set and return to the Source, Oneness, the manifestation of True Love) or medieval trepanning. She had mingled their minds, energy, and ejaculate, catapulting them to Infinitude; they clambered into the lap of the Great Mother like unruly children, holy beggars, snow lions. *Train right now in the path luminosity,* the guidebook said, *so that at the moment of dying you can dissolve confusion in the ground luminosity—*

Suddenly their bodies were overturned.

A woman shrieked.

Mr. Lightfoot yelped, guffawing.

The lady called Cela was in the room.

Kit grabbed his robe and ran. Cela swatted Lisanne, shouting, "What are you doing! What the *fuck* are you *doing!*" Lisanne jiggled and trembled, modestly covering her sex with a smeary hand while Burke, still laughing, put himself between them, urging Goodyear to get dressed.

Cela struck him. "You motherfucker! She bled all over the bed! The bed where we *fuck.* How could you do that? And how could you do that to *him?* He's your *son,* he's your fucking *son!* You're *sick!* You're sick sick sick sick *sick!* You sick *fuck,* how could you bring a fat fucking whore in here like that! Oh God, look at the blood! She's like a pig! You put your dick in that—she could have fucking *AIDS!* How could you *do* that? How could you *do* that to me! And your son, your son, your son!"

·   ·   ·

HE SAW HER STANDING in the driveway, disheveled. He brought her to the house—his wing, where she'd spent so little time. She was docile. He asked if she was hungry, but she shook her head. He gave her water from the kitchen tap, the Bulthaup/Poggenpohl kitchen that she called the mothership because it was capacious and made of steel, and the housekeeper made sure there were always steel bowls of fruit and redolent flowers there. Then he brought her to the bedroom and laid her down as she'd been brought to the Riverside bedroom and laid down hours before. He saw that she wasn't wearing panties. Her thighs were smeared brown with blood. She's been fucking, he thought. But who? Someone on the street. Maybe someone on the bluff, there was that section from the pier on up to Wilshire where he told her never to walk, where the woebegone held court, lying in wait under newspapers and ratty quilts, pretending to be sleepy and harmless so the liberals would continue to condone and indulge their predatory verminlike presence. She was vulnerable. She was prey. Her heart was kind and large and damaged—it grew larger each day and pumped less blood to its own system, an aneurysmal craving to burst and reabsorb into the generalized heart of needy humanity—and if it weren't for his patronage he knew she would become one of them, dissolved into that scabrous communal wound. He hoped that wasn't so and she'd just been out wandering because he worried about her catching a disease. Not that she would give him anything; their relationship wasn't that way. His concern was unselfish. Also, he saw the end, and his seeing of that perhaps was the one selfish thing. He did not delight in the end, even though he had seen it coming for so long and had recognized Lisanne as its instrument. He soaked a rag in hot water and sponged her down with soap. (Maybe, he hoped, she'd been roughly, crazily masturbating and hadn't been raped.) She was numb and bereft and he understood those things with tough and poignant insularity as might the translator of an astonishingly moving text who cannot then pass on what he knows. Yet who better to know those unknowable things and silently commune with her than he, the benefactor? Philip did this very thing with his mother when he was twelve, after she went out wandering. But my mother, he thought, was not a whore. My mother went out wandering to forget herself, to forget her wealth, to forget her husband—who himself had fled because he knew a wandering was coming and could not bear it—to forget how she had been crushed, her dreams eliminated. (Neither she nor the father nor the son nor his sister knew or would ever know what those dreams had been. It is a tragedy to forget what it was that was vanquished and merely be left with emotional detritus, the dried up tears of phantom loss.) Mattie would be with his father in La Jolla and Philip with his mother when she came back with her scrapes and contusions born of brambles, various small stones and the brushings-by of domesticated bark and branches— nothing more, nothing less—such damage could be done without leaving the property, which was vast. As he damp-toweled his mother, he would linger at her fine white wrist scars, thicker by a hair than a hair's width, wispy keloids whose origin it had been ingrained within him never to ask, the way some Jewish families never discuss the murky prehistory of modified noses. No, this was not his mother before him but rather it was as if he had swallowed

her and regurgitated Lisanne's soft white form and that he was now respon-
sible for that form's maintenance and comfort and for all of the forms it
would beget. This was a tender lozenge before him, living and corpuscular, a
sentient being whom he must protect, its cocoon rent, blown away like a
bruised gown in the gusty albeit warm, sacral winds of the Santa Anas and
it was up to him to father her—though he saw his own energy at an ebb, and
that frightened him, he could see the recession of his earthly powers at hand.
All that kept him here, and all that ultimately would send him away, lay in
the animal eroticism of mother and son communion. All that kept him
attached to the world was the sheer abandon inspired in the gaudy firelight
of that act, by its holy, meretricious witness.

Bygones

TWO WEEKS LATER, his father in Vegas, Kit made an appointment
to see Alf.

(While Burke is away, the mice will play.)

He tucked into the backseat of Cela's Volvo while Tula spirited
him away. They knew the drill—same old same old. Not too much
action on the barricade, anyhow.

They drove past old haunts.

(He'd gathered up the addresses and given them to Tula, who
spent the night before hunched with the Thomas Bros.)

The Chateau and the Strip . . .

(Though not a glance to or thought of the liquor store.)

His old house, in Benedict . . .

(Had the impulse to go in but forgot to ask the lawyers for a key.
Was of a mind to sell the whole caboodle, but legally, nothing could
be done until issues of conservatorship had been settled. At least
that's what Burke said. He sat and stared, trying to imagine living
there again or having lived there.)

Viv's house.

(Imagining himself and Viv inside; then being replaced by Alf.)

Last stop before Alf's aerie—the grave. *Old haunts . . .*

•   •   •

THEY DROVE THROUGH the gates, high above Sunset Plaza—mini-malist, hipster digs, as if Lenny Bruce still lived and had commissioned a Richard Meier redo. There stood barefooted Alf, grinning from the porch. Both men nervously self-conscious. Kit wore the gray Prada suit that Cela had selected on a rare after-hours expedition. (Maxfields had stayed open late, so he could shop without hassle.)

Big hugs. Awkward stuff. Alf offered Tula entrée, but the bodyguard declined. More hugs inside. Water and foodstuffs dispensed by a nondescript helper who then vanished for good. Kit was laconic, weighing and measuring words far more than he would in Riverside. They settled into couches. Alf took a brief phone call. Apologized. Said it was business.

"Think you're going to sell the house?" said Alf. (To have something to say.)

"Maybe," said Kit. "Not sure."

"Now, don't do that," said Alf, with a pleading, country-western star smile. "Shit, that place should be on the historic registry. We had some *crazy* times there, huh."

"Very crazy!"

Alf laughed with tension release, and Kit laughed too, spittle boisterous; still finding his way. It got a bit easier—the court and spark exchange of trademark grins. "If those walls could talk! *Speaking* of which, what ever happened to our old friend Mr. Raffles? What's he doing now, workin escort?"

Kit had to be reminded of the canine casanova, more on account of nerves than anything else.

"He died," said Kit.

"Oh shit," said Alf, genuinely sorrowful. Any sort of loss now had a larger context. "That's fucked up." Then, joshing again: "Thought he might have met a nice Beverly Hills socialite and settled down."

"Great Danes don't live too long."

"Sure you don't want a martini?"

"Can't. Take all the medicines. For seizure."

"Oh, right. Right." Awkward. "You know, you look really great. And you *talk* well too—I mean, you're well-spoken. Much better than the last time I saw you."

Wished he hadn't said it. Sounded patronizing. And it had been too long since they've seen each other—his fault.

Everything his fault . . .

"Yeah," said Kit.

"I been workin," said Alf, by way of explanation and apology.

"Me too," said Kit.

"Oh yeah?" he said, intrigued.

"Physical therapy!" said Kit, grinning at the joke.

"Right!" The attempt at humor shot past. "They're workin my *ass*, Dog. But you ain't missin much—ain't shit out there. Scripts are all shit. Showbiz is a *shambles*, dude. I mean, there's always one or two people out there keepin it real. But hey! You've really managed to stay fuckin *hidden*, man, I'm *impressed*. Guess your dad's done a pretty good job. After Osama, you're the world's most wanted man!"

Awkward again—coming in waves.

"But it's good over there? I mean, with Burke?"

"Pretty good. Pretty good." He shifted on the couch. Reached for the water, drank, set the glass back down. Cleared his throat. "Hey, Alf, I want to ask you something." Cleared his throat again. Reached again but pulled back his hand before it got to the glass. Shifted. "OK. I want to see Viv. I know she feel bad—feels bad. Maybe afraid. Maybe she's afraid. Not of me! I want to tell her it is—that it's OK. I want to tell her that, Alf. That I am OK. That it—it's cool."

"She knows that!" Alf said, too congenially. "She *knows* that, Kit. She's smart, she's really smart. *You* know how smart she is. But, you know, she's away." Lit a cig (skittish actor's prop). "Yeah, she, uh, was doin a film, you know, the David Gordon Green, while they were on hiatus? That's why she couldn't come see you. Pretty much. Cause you know she *wanted* to . . . but she got really run-down and shit. Then her grannie died. Her *mom* got real sick too, no lie. Got all jaundiced, but I think she's cool now. The mom's cool. Out of the woods and all. But it was *fucked up*. Been kind of a fucked-up year for her. Not to take away from *your* fucked-up year." Levity, then amended gravity.

"I feel bad for her!" said Kit, earnestly. Winced and shifted some more—stabby nerve-ending pain out of nowhere, per usual. Pressure in the temples. He could deal but hoped his eye didn't start to twitch; hated that. He could feel Viv's sorrow and only wanted to comfort her. "I really want to see her!"

"Here's the thing, man." Actors Studio–size drags off cig. "And look—I didn't think this was a good time to tell you but I guess it's that old cliché. Ain't no good time to give bad news."

Kit panicked, envisioning the worst. His lips went bloodless and he began to tremble. To Alf, it looked kind of pathetic.

"She OK? What is happening to her?"

He shifted into Samuel French/Dramalogue mode—Alf Pacino. "She's fine," he said, to allay him. "She's got a pretty good support system. I guess that—Well, I guess *I'm* the support system. Now. I'm kind of the one she turns to for comfort. Know what I'm saying? I know it sounds like a bad movie or some . . . *fucked-up* Mexican soap opera or *whatever*, but it's—it's *life*, man, it's what *happened*. And it wasn't right away, it didn't happen right away, you gotta know that. No lie. It was a gradual thing, something that happened out of a *grief* thing. I mean, that girl was *seriously hurting*, Dog! Like, crazy out of her mind. Takin pills to sleep. Doin whatever— I don't mean it that way. But we both were. We spent a lot of time together. Most of that time was all about *you*. And it just fucking happened. And we knew it was fucked up but we couldn't do anything to change it. I'm sorry, Kit. I'm sorry about fucking *every*thing, man! I'm sorry we went to that *club*—I'm sorry you went to that *liquor store*—and you know what? I'm gonna hire someone to full-on fucking *kill* that punkass motherfucker in prison— that'll be my gift to you, bro. And I'm sorry about Viv . . . and I'm—I'm all sorried out. And you know what? I'm glad I can finally be telling you all this—that you're at my house, and you're happy and healthy and look fuckin hunky-dory—cause it's been eatin me up. Been killin Viv, too."

"OK." Laughed. Pains in body. Shifted. Quick water drink—smiled and winced like it was ninety proof. "Bad movie . . . bad Mexican movie!"

"Are you OK?"

"Yeah! It's like, cool. I'm all cool. I'm all, like, yeah. Yeah!"

"Looks like we're gonna be doin this Nicole Holofcener thing together. The 'Lovely and Amazing' chick?"

"Lovely and—"

"We're doing a movie. It shoots in Maine . . ."

Softly, Kit said, "*Fuck fuck fuck fuck fuck.*"

"Sorry, man." Alf sheepish and mewling now, redundant with self-contempt. "Too much information. I'm an asshole. *Shit.*"

"Shit."

"It's crazy," said Alf, lamely.

Spastic laughter from Kit: "Crazy fucked up!"

Alf managed an agonized grin. His grins were getting old.

"Hey, know what . . . dawg?" said Kit, slapping his thighs as he stood. "I'm gonna go home. I—I real tired."

Alf nodded like a jack-in-the-box while staring at the ground.

"Thank you for having me as your guest."

"You're family, man."

A clumsy O.G. soulshake, segueing to standoffish, gentlemanly hug.

"Tell Viv *I* am happy because *she* is happy. And I am happy for *you.* Because I love you both and I am . . . happy for everybody!"

Sincere relief. Worst part over. He can smell Viv again. Wants her terribly now—will rush to her as soon as Kit's gone, rock-hard the whole way. She paces at Beachwood as they speak, a woman awaiting her man's return from battle, salty and bloodied. This morning, after it was agreed that he would tell Kit everything, she said that she'd shave her pussy. For when Alf came home. He flashed on it, banishing the image.

"You don't know what that means—to me. *And* to Viv. I *know* she wants to see you, Kit. She just needs a little more time."

"Bye, Alf."

Walked out. The air was good. The house oppressed like a cage. Tula jumped, opening the passenger door.

As Kit got in, Alf said, "Hey, Cameron sends her love, Dog!" They pulled away. Alf shouted, "I talked to her last night. She's in Africa, doing a thing with Bertolucci."

Apologies

A COUPLE OF GAYS shouted from their car while rolling out of Fred Segal.

"Oh my God! An Undergirl!"

When the same thing happened a few hours later as she was leaving Elixir (a less flamboyant shout-out from a passing dyke), Becca thought she was being mistaken for someone in a band. Then it happened again, near Agnès B.—but this time, the person scarily invoked her name. She grumpily assumed it had something to do with recent notoriety. The article in the *Weekly* had come out (an LAPD mugshot of Rusty on the cover, not Elaine) with a photo of Becca inside captioned DOUBLE TROUBLE. One of the tabloids—RUSTY NAILED!—ran a grainy picture of the two walking hand in hand, just like Penélope and Tom. That was actually kind of cool.

When Becca got home, she went on a crying jag. She was about to call her mom (who had actually been really great about everything) when Annie and Larry phoned. Larry, being the Internet troller that he was, had discovered that Becca was part of an unofficial *Six Feet Under* Web site paying tribute to the show's legion of mortuary extras (Undergirls and Underboys) via a rogues' gallery (the Not Ready for Lifetime Players) of "toe-tag bio" pop-ups called "The Not So Vitals." The dead, subclassified as "Dying to Be Taft-Hartleyed," were sorted by personality type, according to popular vote. There were Undertakers and there were Undergivers; a competing Web site for *CSI* cadavers had since sprung up.

Larry was giddily on-line as they spoke and assured Becca that she was the most beloved Undergirl by far. Her "gurney-cam" shots (*"Dead! From Los Angeles! It's Becca Mondrain!"*) had already registered many thousands of hits—Mr. Levine's theory being that it was distinctly possible her popularity was based upon the fact that in one or two downloaded stills (each snapped directly from the TV screen as the show aired), part of a tit was visible as she lay on the slab. Becca remembered being forewarned by the casting people that the director of that particular episode wanted her breasts exposed because it tied in with the comic dialogue of the scene. She had agreed, because you really couldn't see her face. She probably would have agreed anyway.

In another inset blowup, the Web site lovingly called attention to a production glitch: a strap of Becca's thong was showing. The whole spectacle made her feel kind of violated, but Larry said she should get over herself. He said it was a hoot—with all the negative attention she'd gotten lately she should feel good about it and just do what everyone else did in this town, which was to find a way to exploit whatever press came their way. It had been Larry's opinion all along that, instead of running from it, she should be actively milking the look-alike cause célèbre. She totally felt like Monica Lewinsky.

.   .   .

BECCA WAS A little uncomfortable lodging at the Dunsmores—she didn't like being beholden. (Annie said she could stay with her awhile, but Annie was the kind of girlfriend who would get too dependent, and resent Becca when she finally found her own place.) She could have used the money Cass gave her to pay first and last on an apartment, but then what? In a few months, she'd have been scrambling again. At least this way, she could feel what it was like to have a nest egg. Besides, if she split, the Dunsmores might get grudgey, and that was one more problem she didn't need. They might try to fuck with her. Since Rusty's arrest and Grady's attack of nerves, they'd actually been behaving pretty well. Their attempts to enlist her in ménage à whatevers were half-assed, and she'd made her feelings about that *exceptionally* clear.

She thought about going home. She couldn't even *believe* Rusty was from Virginia and had lied all that time. He'd lied about a lot of things. (Though she felt ambivalent about him these days, Becca still nursed the hope he hadn't lied about his feelings for her.) But she kind of needed to stay put awhile because with Rusty about to be extradited, if she flew to Waynesboro it would almost be like they were going back as a couple. Becca didn't want to be psychically, or tabloidally, linked. She was still kind of in shock about it all.

One thing she *did* know was she wanted her mommy. Needed her—called and said she better come to Hollywood, *right now*. Sang into the phone while Dixie laughed: "Right here, right now, there is no other place I want you to be. Right here, right now, watching the world wake up from history." They'd share the bed and spoon like when she was little and everything would be all right. Grady had better not perv on her, but Dixie could handle herself—hell, if she handled Daddy, she could sure handle Grady. Besides, the Dunsmores had more bark than bite. Dixie would have *fun* and be so impressed because the whole Mulholland Drive *experience* was kind of a magical mystery tour. And poor Dix never got a chance to go anywhere. She actually did visit New York three years ago as a job performance bonus and loved it so much she'd been planning another trip. Who needs loser New York? Everything's so expensive the only thing a person can afford to do is go stare at that open grave. The dirty Bath Tub, or whatever the fuck they call it. Oh, Becca, you are terrible. C'mon, Mama, don't you want to come see your baby? Don't you love your baby? Now course I do, you know I do. Course I'm gonna come. Then c'mon, and she started singing "Right Here Right Now" again. She said the Dunsmores would rent limos and take them to all the fancy clubs and restaurants, the ones Dixie read about in *Us Weekly* and *InStyle*.

Dixie said Sadge had called, looking for her. He'd been trying to reach her ever since Rusty's arrest. (Annie said he'd been calling her too.) Becca was avoiding him because she knew that whatever sympathy he put on, all Sadge really wanted was to gloat. He was still in love with her and that was his way.

·   ·   ·

VIV WEMBLEY WAS mortified that the waif whom she took into her home and her trust had been exposed as the lover of a suspected murderer and his associate—the latter being the very man who, for all intents and purposes, had killed her fiancé (and, uh, had creepily made his living *impersonating*). It was like one of those old Vincent Price movies that Kit used to love. When she thought of this Trojan horse, this Manson girl, roving through her Beachwood Canyon home unsupervised, her blood ran cold. (She wondered if Becca had been in cahoots with Gingher, that other thief and criminal, from the very beginning.) When at their last meeting, as part of an ill-timed, messy catharsis, a hysterical Becca had tearfully begged Viv to believe that she knew nothing about her boyfriend's *or* his psycho friend's "alleged" crimes while at the same time misguidedly confessing to myriad deceits regarding her noncancerous mom, Viv had literally pushed her from the house, run to the front bathroom, and thrown up.

•   •   •

RUSTY FINALLY consented to a visit.

(She could never bring herself to call him Herke.)

Grady had already been to see him and supposedly closed the deal on "To Kill a Unicorn," privileged information that the Dunsmores shared with Becca only after becoming amazingly shitfaced on a hellacious combo plate of she knew not what. Even though the LAPD were aware of its role in ensnaring their suspect, they still didn't have, as Grady liked to say, a "habeas scriptus." To date, the prisoner's creation was hearsay (though its whereabouts were a recurring theme of Becca's station house interrogations). But Grady had a feeling the detectives were beginning to write "Unicorn" off; from everything he had heard, the Virginia D.A. was building a case just fine without it. After all, they had their corpus. Rusty talked about that missing screenplay like it was the Holy Grail, and Grady could understand why. Shit, he'd done the same type of thing when he was incarcerated—a man in prison had to hold on to something—but for the QuestraWorld president and secretary-in-motherfucking-arms, "To Kill a Unicorn" wasn't so much the grail as it was his ace in the hole, a heat-generating ticket to ride in the Hollywood Derby. Rusty said it was buried in the desert somewhere, to be revealed at a future date. Mama Cass said her husband was a fool for believing him, but Grady fronted seventy-five hundred into his jailhouse account on good faith before declaring the whole topic *verboten*—it being the pardoned parolee's superstitious opinion that even mentioning "the property" would not only endanger his own actual freedom but quite possibly jeopardize the Dunsmores' most valuable holding, ergo threatening the very existence of QuestraWorld itself. He was certain the Mulholland digs were bugged.

Becca told Annie she couldn't understand how anyone survived even a minute behind bars. It was funny—now he looked more like Russell Crowe than ever, all tousle-haired and gorgeous, sulky and dreamily wronged. Even his sweat smelled sweet. He told her he was sorry he'd "withheld" certain things and that he never meant to hurt her. When she asked if he loved her, he lowered his head like the genius in *A Beautiful Mind,* mumbling, "Pretty much, yeah. I pretty much did. And do." She was glad he tacked on "and do."

She asked about his crimes, but he simply shook his head. "Has your mother been to see you?" The tender question came unexpectedly from her depths. Again he shook his head, with forlorn indifference. He hadn't really known the woman—his mother—all that long, he said. Their first meeting had occurred just three years ago. Becca presumed that Cassandra's hypothesis was correct and that Rusty had been raised as an orphan. (Perhaps the tragedy had been set in motion when he decided to seek his ancestry.) Now was not the time to probe; it was a story she might never know. He wondered if she knew anything about the release date of the Spike Jonze film. Becca said she'd heard it was sometime in the fall. "Ah," he said, with a scampish wink. "Did a little A.D. tell you?" He said that Grady told him there was something in the paper about his role being chopped down to nothing. Becca had heard the same thing on *Access Hollywood* but said she didn't really know anything about it.

When she finally asked about Herke, he said it was short for Hercules. That had never occurred to her, and she thought it touching because at that moment he really did seem to bear the weight of the world on his shoulders. He told her he was happy that she was living with the Dunsmores. "Don't do anything I wouldn't do," he said. Becca said, "You don't have to worry." She was going to ask if he'd been sleeping with Elaine Jordache all the time they'd been seeing each other and if it was true he really did kill a man and if it was true what she heard that he was related to that man by blood and why was it only three years ago that he'd first seen his mom and she wanted to tell him that she still loved him and that maybe they would make a

QuestraWorld movie of his whole life and saga and write to each other every day until he got out as long as it was true that he still loved her—but in the end, none of it seemed to matter. She recounted the very last part to her mom, trying to sound hardened and nonchalant and mature, but when Dixie replied, "Honey, *everything* matters," Becca burst into tears.

And that was the last time she saw him, in the flesh anyway.

Blackout

MATTIE WAS CONCERNED about Lisanne, as were Reggie Marck and the Loewensteins. Since the episode on the jet, she'd been going downhill.

When she stopped by his office to deliver that deranged soliloquy, Reggie got seriously spooked. She left before he could take any action—not that he knew what that action would have been, though he kicked himself for not having "detained" her. He was worried that Lisanne might potentially harm herself or the baby. He phoned Roslynn, and they tried to sort things out. Reggie asked about the boyfriend, but Roslynn said he was out of his league when it came to her troubles; Philip had grown too dependent on Lisanne to be objective. The sister, she said, was the one with the head on her shoulders.

Reggie and Roslynn initiated a conference call with Calliope Krohn-Markowitz to discuss some sort of intervention. (Lisanne saw the psychiatrist for a few sessions, but had since gone AWOL.) The Muskinghams were also on the line. Calliope asked if there were any new developments. Mattie said that Lisanne had been spending a lot of time in the "yoga cabin" and appeared withdrawn. Also, there was a "growing diminution in personal hygiene." Roslynn spoke of what she felt to be a "continued inappropriate response" to the plight of the actor Kit Lightfoot. Impatient with the pussyfooting, Reggie circled back to the astonishing office visit. "That was a crazy person," he said. "That was a deeply disturbed woman who either needs to be taking medication or should be locked up. Probably both. Period."

There was a pause. "Frankly, I'm *very* concerned for the welfare of that baby. I don't think we can in good conscience sit by while there's a tragedy in the making." Calliope asked Philip about his thoughts—he was, after all, the one closest to Lisanne in a number of ways—but he said she seemed fine. Reggie said, sotto, "He's got to be kidding." In her role as mediator, Calliope reiterated Reggie's concern about the well-being of Siddhama, and Philip said the nannies hadn't noticed anything strange. Not that they'd talk about it if they had, said Mattie sardonically. And why is that? asked the doctor. Because, said Mattie, one of Lisanne's eccentricities was, she was always giving them cash on the side. Roslynn wanted to know how much cash. Philip said there was a daily limit on the ATM. Reggie said, "What is it? Three hundred? Four hundred? That's a lot of money to be giving a nanny." "Is that 'hush money'?" wondered Roslynn. "I mean, what's she doing? Money for what?" "It's just misplaced largesse," said Mattie. "She has a big heart," said Philip. "That's all very well and good," said Reggie, in hard-nosed attorney mode. "But I think we really need to be in *reality* regarding this woman. This is a *damaged lady.* Look, I've known her a lot of years now, and I am telling you this is someone who needs to be hospitalized. And I think we should take that step. Because we don't want a tragedy on our hands. Hey, maybe it's something that only needs a few days—or a week—or whatever. Great. Maybe it's strictly a medication thing. I don't know, Doctor, could having a child have brought this on? I mean, the whole concealing of the pregnancy . . . is this a postpartum psychosis thing?" "It may be," said Calliope, with caution. "Of course that needs to be ruled out. But I can't rule out anything if I'm not able to meet with the patient." "Maybe Phil can help with that," said Roslynn, knowing that his sister would chime in. "Yes," agreed Mattie. "Phil and I can definitely talk to her about coming in for another session. Don't you think, Philip?" "Uh huh," said her brother. "And if not," said Mattie, "we can talk about something more definitive. We're actually all going out tonight for an event." "Great," said Roslynn. "Maybe that would be a good time for discussion," said Calliope. "But I think it's important you use your own judgment. If that's a conversation you think would be better suited to have at home, then wait until you get home." It was agreed all around that Lisanne wouldn't be left alone with Siddhama. Reggie said, "Won't that be difficult?" Philip said Lisanne was rarely alone with the baby anyway. Mattie said she would have a talk with the nannies, and Roslynn said that Philip should take her ATM card away. He assented. Calliope told Mattie and Philip to check in with her as soon as they spoke to Lisanne, even if it were late tonight.

After everyone had hung up, Reggie called Roslynn back and said that he couldn't understand why the call hadn't ended with more of a concrete plan. Roslynn contradicted him. She definitely got the feeling things were "coming to a head" and that hospitalization was imminent. "I missed that," said Reggie skeptically. "I guess I zoned."

.   .   .

IT RAINED HARD that night.

Months ago, Philip had got tickets to see the Dalai Lama at UCLA. He engaged a driver, but when his sister arrived at Rustic Canyon, Mattie said, "I refuse to take a chauffeur-driven Mercedes to see the Dalai Lama."

Their seats were up close. As they arrived, tantric monks gargled timeless liturgies from the foot of the stage. Ushers handed out pamphlets that told the story of a little boy who had been recognized by His Holiness as the eleventh Panchen Lama of Tibet. He had been kidnapped by the Chinese government, who then replaced him with a Panchen pretender.

It made Lisanne think of her own Siddhama. Since she'd given away the Supreme Bliss-Wheel Integration Buddha, whenever she looked in her baby's eyes it seemed as if he wasn't there. As a mother, she could no longer recognize his energy; the bond had been swiftly, elegantly severed. She cursed herself for being on her period when Kit came inside her. She'd been too hasty—she should have waited until she was ovulating. Now her fate was sealed. Craving estrus, the flies of all those souls awaiting human rebirth had been repelled by her blood's brackish, viscous, tarry rejection of the "liquid gold" of H.H. the venerable Kit Clearlightfoot's semen. In that very instant, she had slammed the door on the Buddha, his teachings, and the holy community, forever.

Philip discreetly pointed, alerting Lisanne and his sister that Viv Wembley was just a few rows away. How perfect! The succubus was with Alf Lanier. Both had dressed down in a ridiculous attempt at self-effacement, so shabbily casual as to almost backfire, evincing disrespect, shallow, wicked, radiant poseurs come to gawk at His Holiness as high society once did the Elephant Man. Anyone with two eyes could see that Alf had replaced Kit in her life the same way the Panchen pretender had supplanted the true lama, wherein Lisanne saw an even more sinister motive for their attendance at the arena. Because Viv was an actress, Lisanne knew that she needed to be loved above all else, begging exoneration for her abandonment of Kit (and subsequent flagrant transgressions). The miscarriage and all-around fickle public sympathies were not enough to salve an ego of her proportion. Lisanne was certain the *Together* star was of a mind that merely being seen in the Dalai Lama's presence with copper petals humbly spread, ready to receive the nectar of atonement, would by necessity gather great merit, as sure as the wealthy sinner once obtained indulgences by the pressing of exculpatory lucre into the hand of the Pope. Still, she admired Viv's cunning, her élan, her pirate's nature, and with a twinge in the womb, admonished herself: *Viv Wembley* would never have gone over there while menstruating. *Viv Wembley* would have waited until she was in heat. She was so angry because she had bested that rich and famous woman—Viv Wembley's cervical loss had been Lisanne McCadden's magical gain— but the executive assistant had choked at the moment of truth. And now her baby, her Siddhama, was abducted and unknown to her, as unknown as the child Viv had coldly flushed away.

A ripple of applause became a torrential ovation as the exiled head of state was led to the stage, surrounded by monks and bodyguards. His English was difficult to understand. Lisanne spaced out on Viv and Alf until half an hour later, when the Q & A began. Someone asked, "What is the best way to become spiritually pure?" His Holiness said he didn't like the word *best* because it usually meant fastest, quickest, easiest. "That is *wrong*," he said, sternly. "Wrong, wrong, wrong!" The cultivated mob laughed obsequiously. He went on to say that the answer to the man's question was "everything I have been talking about tonight." There was a testy, imperious edge to his words, and Lisanne thought: Good for him. It must be tough to talk to shits and dunces. Then some jerk-off wanted to know if he ever "just relaxed and enjoyed" himself. His Holiness smiled and said, "I am going to enjoy this cool glass of water." With that, he dramatically hoisted the glass and took a long, steep drink while the mental midgets laughed, wept, and clapped. "And now," he said, "I will enjoy going to sleep!"

He left the stage without fanfare. Barely an hour had passed.

As they filed out, Philip said, "What a pro."

Mattie said, "Amazing."

Philip said, "Short but sweet. He's the Man."

Mattie said, "We *have* to go to that Kalachakra thing."

Philip said, "Where do they do that, in India?"

Mattie said, "*Wherever*. Sign me *up*, I'm goin."

. . .

KIT AND CELA danced, drank, and smoked weed. Kissed and groped. He told her about Viv and Alf being a couple. She commiserated. (She'd already read about it in *Entertainment Weekly*.) He literally cried on her shoulder. She knew they were going to fuck tonight—that whole scene with the Super Size Hare Krishna girl had clinched it.

The motherfucker was in Vegas again. She didn't even want to think about what he was doing. Why kid herself anymore? She'd done enough of that through the years. The dad had been a perverse aberration—Kit was her man. And now like some romance novel he'd come back to her. She would take him, any way she could. He wasn't even that fucked up. Hell, everyone was damaged goods. And he was getting better every day. All Burke thought about was the money anyhow. Cela never thought about the money. If she could guarantee that Burke and the whole shitty world would just leave them alone by signing a piece of paper giving away Kit's money, then she would. She sure-ass would.

He asked her to put on the "blockbuster," *World Without End*. He wanted to fast-forward to the dance scene with Cameron Diaz. As they watched, Kit sensually mirrored his on-screen movements while Cela mimicked Cameron's.

—Acceptable, Respectable, Presentable, A Vegetable!
   At night . . .
   when all the world's asleep . . .
   the questions run so deep . . .
   for such a simple man . . .

He turns the volume up as loud as it will go, gyrating toward the sliding glass. Rain sheets crashing. Shirtless now, coiled and muscular, swaying to the beat, hands gliding over each other tracing wet forms, shadows of mutual tattoos, snaking into the downpour through mud-grass puddles, shoes off, wrestle-wriggling jeans over ankles, oblivious to torrents, no longer lip-synching but shouting lyrics full-bellow, eyes closed—

Won't you please
please tell me what we've learned
I know it sounds absurd
please tell me who I am . . .

Something happens.
   Stops singing.
   Eyes open wide now, as if finally in complete awareness—the enormity of what befell him.
   Lifts his head to the star-dead Riverside skies and yowls.
   Cela, who is not finished with him, who cannot, will not leave him, never has and never will, Cela, who is not yet done with her epic love, love of her life, not yet done in this life or childhood life or life any other, sobs and sinks to her knees, holding, ballasting, rooting this tree that tears loose from its mulch, pointing with rent goblin's thicket of caterwauling branches toward freezing (star-dead) Riverside skies: Cela bears him down, afraid he'll loosen and ascend, forever lost, gasping with the horror she may not have what it takes to hold him, that her love will not be enough to make it so.

• • •

SHE SLAUGHTERED the pug—Philip's pug, the one Mattie gave him for his birthday, the one he loathed at first but in three short weeks had learned to love—by hurtling it against the wall, then doing some eviscerating with a pair of antiquey, gilt-edged scissors that she got at Restoration.

The dog was an obstacle between student and teacher, novice and guru, between the Vulnerable Lisanne McCadden and H.H. the Venerable Kit Clearlightfoot. The dog came uninvited to the in-between, where only empty spaces may reside. That was a karmic violation—there was only so much room for official bardos. (The guidebook said there were supposed to be only six, but the dog made for a seventh.) That sort of thing had been studied and decreed for millennia and was certainly not beholden to the whims or policy makings of an errant pug. Lisanne was unconcerned about the implications of the killing. Hadn't Milarepa, poet-warrior and student of the supreme *phowa* master Marpa, committed dozens of murders before his fated enlightenment? Anyway, it was a *mu* or moot point whether dogs possessed the Buddha nature. If this one did, she thought, it sure doesn't now.

She used masking tape to cover her apertures, as the guidebook suggested. "During the practice of *phowa*," she read aloud, "one must first block all the openings in a special way so that only the aperture at the crown of the head remains open. When the mind leaves the body through the crown of the head, one will be reborn in a pure land beyond samsaric existence where the conditions for practice are perfect." She wanted to bypass the disintegration of the five winds and the dissolution of gross and subtle thoughts. When, through the Brahma-hole, her life-winds ceased at last breath and came the merging of red and white, of earth and sky, she wished to remain conscious and not panic. Otherwise she worried that she would have to endure the three and a half days of darkness and the gang of wrathful demons—the 100,000 suns and 100,000 thunderclaps. No: only the fourth *rigpa* would do. According to the guidebook, "The first sign of a result in *phowa* practice is that a strong itch is felt at the top of the head. Later a tiny hole appears into which a straw of grass can actually be inserted." She needed one-pointed concentration in order to eject consciousness, "as a competent archer shoots the arrow from his bow." She taped a sanitary napkin over her bottom holes before sealing navel, ears, and mouth. As she plugged her nostrils, Lisanne imagined blood and lymph leaking there, a classic sign to whatever monks were present (she wished some were here now) that recitations from *The Tibetan Book of the Dead* should begin. Finally, she covered up her eyes.

Some texts said it was best to die standing up. Some said it was best to die sitting, in full lotus. If one couldn't manage either, the guidebook suggested one simply recline, in the posture of a sleeping lion. That was how the Buddha had died. Then it is good enough for me. As she lay on her right side, she punched at her skull with the gold-handled scissors in the complementary area of Kit's surgical incisions. She stabbed to the cadence of measured oracular tones, and shouted out loud: "Listen, Lisanne! Now has come the time for you to seek a Path! As breathing stops, the clear light of the first phase of dying, as shown to you by H.H. the Venerable Kitchener Clearlightfoot, will dawn! This is primordial mind, empty and radiant, without horizon or center! See that for what it is! H.H. the Venerable Kitchener Clearlightfoot will describe it and help you!"

. . .

GUESTS SCREAMED, in revelry.

Becca locked herself in her room. Every now and then some drunk stumbled into her door or tried letting himself in.

She was checking out *Us Weekly*'s Celebrity Look-Alikes page, with its paired photos of famous people who supposedly resembled each other—like Kate Spade and Kate Beckinsale, or Tina Turner and Beyoncé Knowles. It was sort of a goof. There was also a famous/nonfamous section, and there she was: a picture of Becca beside one of Drew. Without her knowing, Larry and Annie had sent in one of Becca's eight-by-tens—along with a link to the Six Feet Undergirls Web site.

If you're like Drew double Becca Mondrain, a twenty-two-year-old actress, Internet goddess, and "Six Feet Undergirl" in Los Angeles, and people are always saying to you, "You know, you look just like . . . ," send your photo along with your name and daytime phone number to Letters, *Us*, 1290 Avenue of the Americas, New York, NY, 10104-0298, or e-mail it to letters@usmagazine.com. If we run your picture, you'll win a prize!

A body slammed dumbly against one of her walls, and she startled. She flung herself to the bed and cried.

"I will not leave this town a loser look-alike!" she exclaimed, then thought: I sound like a bad actress. (Out of some fifties film.) She giggled, then picked up the phone to call Annie. They talked excitedly about the *Us Weekly* piece, and Becca said she wondered what the prize would be. She told Annie she should get her horny ass up to Mulholland *right here, right now,* then hung up and went to the bathroom and did a line of coke as she peed. She washed the tears from her face, put on a thong, and looked at herself in the mirror. Flat stomach, belly ring, high ass. Tried on a short black Barneys skirt. Thought of Rusty, then pushed the thought away.

Ready to party.

Ground Luminosity

. . .

HOLLYWOOD, ONE YEAR LATER

The Eternal Return

COLD L.A. SPRING.

A luxe, hidden warehouse space just off Fountain.

An audience of twelve, each sitting apart.

Handsome pair onstage—young woman, young man.

The unkempt harridan in a mohair cape forbiddingly occupies an aisle seat. Pinches nostrils between thumb and forefinger as she focuses. Famous old habit. Reading glasses hang low on a long garish chain.

"Don't you feel how good it smells?" asks the actress of her partner.

(Strindberg chamber play.)

Doesn't "own" the scene—hasn't cracked it. Running on fumes. Actor fumes . . .

"That's from the palms that are burning," she says. "And Father's laurel wreath. Now the linen closet's on fire—it smells of lavender—and now the roses. Little Brother, don't be afraid! Hold me tighter!—" Lurches into him.

Without moving a muscle, Jorgia Wilding screams from her perch, in full-tilt boogie nostril pinch. "You're making *emotional choices* without *physical commitment*. Gerda ain't just *fidgety*—watch your body, Toya. Choreograph the inner landscape, distill the gestures! Otherwise, it's Strindberg Lite. It's Nick at Nite."

An intern approaches, votive before an altar. Bends and whispers into Ms. Wilding's ear—the old woman flinches at his announcement—before receding into darkness.

She stands, commanding the troops: "All right—from 'Don't say anything bad about Father.' "

She exits. The actors softly rappel to the foot of the scene.

In the lobby, she cannot suppress her emotions upon seeing him.

(A large Fijian stands in the doorway blocking the sunlight.)

"Kitchener, my God! What a wonderful surprise!"

They embrace. She presses him close—he feels right as rain.

"How *are* you?" he asks.

She pulls back to take him in.

Right as rain!

"I'm well, I'm well!" Jorgia says, discombobulated. "But more to the point—how are *you*?"

"Gettin there. It's a . . . long and winding road!"

Notes the smallest slurred impediment, and emphatic tone that she shrewdly ascribes to nervousness. The Henry Higgins in her thinks: Easily modulated.

What an effort his journey must have been!

"I *cannot imagine*," she says, with mother's tender grace. "But I'm right in the middle—Would you like to come watch class?"

He knows the sacred teaching comes first.

"No—not now. Thank you. But I have a question."

She cocks her head expectantly.

"Jorgia, I would like to know . . . if you—would have the time . . . to help—me."

•   •   •

TULA DRIVES HIM back to the bungalow at the Bel-Air.

He steps from the car with a slight lope but overall gliding gait.

Media hunters and gatherers have tread heavily since Turkey Day, when Kit and Cela made their move—since the Götterdämmerung ugliness of the Riverside decampment. Kit makes an effort not to be mobile before dark (Jorgia was an exception), so as to cramp the stalkerazzi's style. While still lucrative, bounty for stolen images has suffered devaluation, the trouble being that Mr. Lightfoot looks much like he always did: a rough prince. There has not been captured, nor could be now, that pesky drooling onto stubble; no shambling *Rain Man* heart tuggers; no scary Chris Reeve telephoto rehab cum-shot. Glam, dignified, and amazing looking, he is nothing short of the hunky poster boy for neurological recovery. There's a gold mine in the girlfriend, though, God willing: fourteen weeks pregnant. Shoot both in one frame—though the couple make sure they're never together, outdoors—and the gross is around $400 K, worldwide. Tabloid-fueled rumors of incestuous *scandale* (was she Dad's galfriend too?) goosed the price even further.

Cela's swollen belly floats toward him as he walks through the door. Everything smiles at them now. He rests a hand on the ripeness; then her hand on his, warming the womb. Her once and future kings.

On Her Own

ALREADY MARCH, and the tree isn't down. The maid carefully dusts the ornaments. She told her mom she was just going to leave it, and her manager loved that because it was great, quirky shtick for interviews, which she'd been doing a lot of since the Spike Jonze movie came out.

Becca went to Waynesboro for Thanksgiving, then Dixie brought two favorite cousins out for Christmas. She came back again for her daughter's birthday—the Ides of March—when Becca threw herself a party at Boardner's. The entire talent team was there plus Annie and Larry, Becca's new acting coach, fellow dramatis personae from Metropolis, and last but not least Sharon Belzmerz, the angel in her corner from the very beginning, who not only introduced her to Spike Jonze (more or less) but got her a part on *Without a Trace* and hooked her up with a former associate who placed her in national Ford and Cingular spots. (Whenever they were in public and she'd had a few Flirtinis, the casting director liked to refer mischievously to Becca's Six Feet Undergirl "moment" like it was some kind of softcore skeleton in her closet.) More important, Sharon had been instrumental in getting Becca the A & E pilot she'd just finished shooting, *1200 North*, in which she played Rhiannon, wild-child Paris Hiltonesque daughter of a rich Bay Area matriarch (think Danielle Steel). After the overdose of a boyfriend, Rhiannon decides to take a nun's vows. Testing her faith and resolve, Marlee Matlin (family friend and wise mother superior of an East L.A. Carmelite monastery) bids Rhiannon first do a year of volunteer work at the nearby USC-County trauma center.

Dana Delany plays the chief surgeon. Seeing aspects of herself in the young girl, Dana takes Rhiannon under her wing.

Becca was shocked when Dana swept into the Boardner's patio with her sometime beau David Gough, a TV star in his own right. (She hadn't expected her to come.) Dana was so elegant, chummy, and unaffected, and a slightly tipsy Mrs. Mondrain kept saying to her face how she was "television royalty." But when Marlee made her entrance, Becca's mom really lost it—she'd been such a huge fan since *Children of a Lesser God* and even done volunteer work with deaf kids in Charlottesville. Larry Levine took some portraity digital shots of Dixie with Marlee, Dana, and David (which she downloaded to the family Web site as soon as she got back to Becca's) before calling in the Cameron, the Jim Carrey, and the Barbra, for a campy group pose. Becca had invited them at the last minute because she'd panicked that none of her invitees would show; most look-alikes were so needy, they'd go anywhere they were asked. They were sweet and harmless, and now she felt sad for them—a million miles away.

.   .   .

THE DUNSMORES didn't know about *1200 North*, and Becca wanted to keep it that way for as long as she could. She had escaped the Mulholland guesthouse last year (on the anniversary of 9/11, which felt appropriate), the very day that Grady was arrested for assaulting a UTA agent during one of their out-of-control theme parties. Last summer Cassandra took a lover, a gaunt woman with hep C that she'd met through Dr. Janowicz's sudden wealth syndrome support group. (She had recently won an eight-figure settlement on behalf of her obese husband, whose death had been attributed to a ride on the Magnum XL-200 roller coaster at Cedar Point.) It seemed that almost immediately after they'd been introduced, Cassandra had insisted her new friend become an equity holder in QuestraWorld, sharing CEO, CFO, and COO duties. This became a bone of contention with Grady, whose OxyContin intake rapidly escalated around the time the threesomes became Sapphic, behind-closed-doors twosomes, which egged him on to calamitous Hard Rock Casino sorties; Cassandra, conferring with their Encino lawyers, took a flurry of steps to limit his monthly draw, concerned that he was "blowing the legacy." Though

Mama Cass had given up on the family (such as it was) reality skein, as far as Becca knew, the "entity"—at least Grady anyway—was still actively hyping "To Kill a Unicorn," the buried, Saran-Wrapped pages of which he had finally uncovered at a site one hundred yards from a Lands' End outlet in Primm, Nevada. (Once retrieved, he kept right on, to the Hard Rock.) But even with the low buzz in the press about Herke Lamar Goodson's upcoming trial, "Unicorn" was going nowhere fast. The Dunsmores tried for months to get her to call Viv Wembley to see if she would be interested in starring or maybe just producing (as a full QuestraWorld partner), and Becca thought that was a measure of how crazy the couple was because they already knew that Viv had threatened Becca with a restraining order and was terrified of her at best. Months ago, the young actress made the mistake of telling Cassandra that Viv's business managers had fucked up and she'd never signed a confidentiality clause like Gingher and the rest. Cassandra said that if Viv didn't help with "Unicorn," Becca should just tell her she was going to sell a memoir "to the highest bidder." Becca said that was blackmail and she was going to pretend she didn't even *hear* it. The Dunsmores continued to be psychotically oblivious to the fact that "To Kill a Unicorn" happened to be written and conceived by the homicidal friend of the man who'd assaulted Viv's former fiancé—hel-*lo*! Apparently, they didn't see that as an obstacle. Annie said they should definitely be committed.

Meanwhile, Grady got "Unicorn" to Eric Roberts with $300,000 attached even though Cassandra and the gaunt woman, as co-CEOs, -CFOs, and -COOs, hadn't approved the offer. Fortunately or unfortunately, Eric passed. (Grady suspected he was lied to when told that Mr. Roberts had been given the script for perusal—else why would the actor have Pasadena'd? Becca presumed the party-pummeled talent agent was somewhere in the mix.) The gaunt woman thought they should approach Adrien Brody, ASAP. Cassandra couldn't believe it when Grady emerged from a narcotic haze just long enough to inform them that the property was now "out" to Mickey Rourke. The gaunt woman said Mickey Rourke had his face beat in a Florida prize-fight, and looked like "a ghoul in a Lara Croft." "Mickey just might say yes," Grady said gallingly. "Mickey likes money. He's doin his comeback thing. Mickey wants to be a star."

Becca's only wish was to get these people and their bad karma *off* her. She knew they'd turn into heat-seeking missiles the minute they got wind of success—if *1200 North* was picked up for September, Grady and Cass would be all over her. By then, she hoped to be able to hire a bodyguard, or even have a big agency like ICM or CAA looking out for her: if she was going to be making potential millions, they'd be highly motivated. But until that day came, the Dunsmores had to be considered loose cannons. She'd keep a distance but play the coddling game too.

Becca used her Cingular checks to rent a place in Silverlake. She hung Chinese lanterns around the patio that overlooked the sloping house from the hill's high end. That's where she finally moved the yuletide tree, as a kind of performance piece installation. But the flocking was gray, and nothing smelled like Christmas anymore.

Under the Medication Tree

AFTER LISANNE'S hospitalization, Reggie Marck spoke with a certain party in upstate New York who was dismayed to learn that her niece had given birth. Lisanne had talked freely of the old flame (the boy's alleged father), and while she had kept the details to herself, the lawyer didn't feel he was in violation of a confidence when revealing as much to the aunt. She immediately put him in touch with Robbie Sarsgaard.

While Reggie knew that Lisanne was where she should be, at least in the short term, he didn't feel the same about little Siddhama. He had a gut aversion toward Philip Muskingham and, for all his money, felt him to be of questionable parenting skills. Moreover, he didn't think it practical or even appropriate to lean on the sister or the Loewensteins to fill that role. As an attorney and longtime friend of Lisanne, he was mandated to protect the welfare of Siddhama at all costs and, though it was unlikely, to block any potential efforts of the DCFS to gain custody of the child. (Philip had shown no inclination to petition for an even temporary guardianship.) That was why he decided to take a flier and, through the aunt, contact the blood father, for whom, during a rare conversation about the gentleman, Lisanne had evinced a historical, more than glancing affection. His initial idea was to suggest that he come to Los Angeles—if amenable—and stay awhile on Reggie's dime. Mr. Sarsgaard listened and immediately acceded, but said he would pay his own way.

He was joined by his elderly spouse. Reggie and the Muskinghams took the couple for dinner at the Grill, the sanguine result being that Philip had them relocated from the Embassy Suites to a spacious Fairfax District duplex where they might live with the baby (an arrangement happily promoted by the Sarsgaards that would, perforce, be perfunctorily reassessed upon what turned out to be the first of Lisanne's many releases and readmits). Robbie said neither he nor his wife had anything to tie them to Albany and were free to stay "for the duration." The Rustic Canyon nannies were retained. Philip felt unburdened, and gratified in doing right by Siddhama and those concerned. Further, his good deed assuaged the of late morbid fear that, in her madness, Lisanne might confess their sexual secrets—more to the point, his own aberrations—to the hospital staff. (Though he sneakily comforted himself with the notion that her claims would most likely be dismissed.) At any rate, this particular chapter's end had been considered a fortuitous one, not least because there was great relief that it was the pug and not the precious child who'd been harmed. That Lisanne had somehow stopped herself from committing such an unthinkably atrocious act allowed a measure of optimism about her future and the future in general to creep in.

· · ·

SHE SPENT SO MUCH time in the hospital, first at Cedars, then in private facilities that Roslynn and Mattie found by research and word of mouth.

H.H. the Vulnerable Lisanne McCadden—that's how she always signed in, on admission.

Between stints, she would be released to Rustic Canyon, then, after only a short while home, returned to lockdown. For months and months she vanished to the world and to herself. She felt like the ghost of a burnt-out barge floating on a wide, dark river.

On bright construction paper, a bardo-diorama of dementia, she pasted a mandala montage of the Materialized Realm of the Paradise of the Med-

icine Buddha. For who was the Buddha if not the Great Physician, Great Healer, the Lord and Scientist who held the vaseless vase of ambrosia in his hands? He would cleanse her of toxins and set her free. Look what he kept in his beggar's bowl: the Three Nectars that cured disease, reversed aging, and propagated Ultimate Awareness. Honey that broke the chains shackling all sentient beings to the Wheel of Deluded Existence . . .

OM AH HAM

She knew she needed

to say it over and over while spinning Kalachakra—the great Wheel of Time. Everything was Great. Great OM,

seed sound for the two-petaled

sixth chakra, was fixed at the brow, the area of Kit's injuries, its vibration heard whenever male and female energies merged. HAM

emanated from the throat chakra while preparing the

gullet channel for devotional receipt of nectar.

   Yet only

OM AH HAM

could rally the Three

Ambrosias to vanquish the Three Poisons—aggression, greed, ignorance— the very same fires that stoked the conflagration called samsara.

Snake! Rooster! Pig!

Lisanne had long since memorized the Wheel of Becoming—the laminated poster she'd picked up that day at the Bodhi when she ran into Phil not yet Philip, pervert and—no, that wasn't fair—sweet-souled benefactor and god-father to her son not of him, and she rotated its twelve radiating rungs in her mind each moment of every hour of the nuthouse day until they became swift second nature. For what was a mandala but a visual mantra, so said the guidebook of guidebooks, her mantra through its turning was "Kitlight-foot/Clearlightfoot/Kitlightfoot/Clearlightfoot," and like the blur of spokes in a carriage wheel, they soon became one. As she hummed, she began (as was proper), with the miniature painting that depicted Ignorance—rendering of a blind man with a cane. "That's me," said Lisanne. "For I am but a cripple surrounded by fields of brilliant jewels, a cripple who has chosen not to see." She wanted to help him, but he just went on, tap-tap-tapping, alone. Who

*was she to think she could help? She could smell his stubborn breath, stag-
nant and ketotic, like her own. Right beside the crooked man, moving clockwise, came Actions, bearded thrower of clay pots, busily making karma. (The
Wheel said that even thoughts and intentions bore the burden of consequence. Every time one had a bad thought it was like putting another pot in
the kiln, a pot that would need to be shattered if one was ever to be free.)
The hairy, red-faced golem was born of mud, and now here she was in this
wreck room bardo because she had worshiped gods with clay feet. How could
the humble workshop of a wise old pot thrower be a place of such misery? So:
there was no solace, not even in the touch of wet earth. Then came the restless monkey of Consciousness, swinging compulsively from tree to tree, harbinger of the talking ape—it had taken all this, Lisanne thought with a
smile, doped up, locked in bedlam, to at last understand what the* sangha
*meant by "monkey mind." The fourth spoke, a scene of passengers in a boat,
reminded Lisanne of the time her parents brought her to Disneyland and she
sat in a theme-ride canoe (like the passenger section of an airplane with its
wings detached), methodically ratcheted by track and chain through still
then rushing waters . . . This part of the Wheel was called Name and Form,
and she watched as the boat of her pale, heavy body drifted down the great
polluted river of* samsara. *Kitclearlightfoot Clearlightfoot Kitclearlightfoot
Clearlightfoot Kitclear—others in the dugout being simply Forms and
Aspects, luminescent phantoms of her own personality and nonphysical self.
Leaving the river behind, Lisanne shook herself dry and approached an
empty house with six windows that always reminded her of the cover of a
Nancy Drew mystery. The bodhisattvas said the windows were the Six
Senses through which we perceived the world.*

She continued her clockwise march.

There: a couple, tangled in erotic embrace.

*Whenever she saw them, they rekindled emotions of that historic day in
Riverside. If only she knew then what she now knew to be so simple—that by
copulating, the star-crossed pair hadn't merged but instead created a duality,
a space between them, as Joshu Sasaki Roshi presciently foretold in his story
of Monk, Novice, and Dog. Unwittingly, monk and student had carved a
divide in which something could arise then fall away, be it thought, mood,
or sentient being. (Lisanne felt she must instinctively have known that. For
the pug, though pure, was an obstacle to their merging.)*

She came to a man with an arrow in his eye. She thought it the most haunting of her encounters, because he offered both eternal chastisement and eternal hope. Neither sadistic nor morbid, the message was so clear— she was saddened the whole world couldn't instantaneously understand— ALL SENSATION IN SAMSARA IS PAIN BECAUSE ALL SENSATION REINFORCES THE DELUDED SELF. If only we could awaken, we would see: even cancerlike pain could be turned to bliss!

She dreaded the adjacent image-form: a woman drinking wine. This was Craving. Remorsefully, Lisanne hovered o'er. She knew she had thirsted too much—for Kit's love and his child, his approval and energy, his amazing, oversized world. Standing next to the wino was a slut reaching out to a tree that burgeoned with fruit—she was the one they called Grasping—then came a third termagant, flat-footed and smoky-haired, heavy with child. (The bodhisattvas had given her the name of Existence.) The trio taunted, and Lisanne's womb panged for the Panchen boy she no longer knew.

Resurfacing in the hospital's rec room, the last few thangkas came in a blur. Exhausted by her centrifugal self-reflection, she tearfully blotted out Siddhama's face, closing ears to his cries, nose to his smells, letting herself be jostled by the watery turbulence of Birth, Aging, and Death. In the last scene-spoke, a man was carrying a corpse on his back: the corpse was that of Lisanne. The carrier was Lisanne too, trudging to sky burial grounds, where her white, cotton-clad load would be unraveled by itinerant monks, its flesh- and-bone cargo feasted upon by turkey buzzards. Perforce, Lisanne would move on—was this not the legacy of all sentient beings? As a unit nurse called out her name, she felt her vision clouding over; the tip of the blind man's cane hardened in her hand. Reborn on the Wheel, she feebly made her way forward, blind, crippled. Soon she would come to the pottery shed of the bearded thrower of Karma . . .

I must escape the Wheel or I'll be crushed. On the ward, the only thing she could do was accelerated phowa *practice, not 21 but 2,100 times a day, for Lisanne knew that was the only way to overtake karma accrued from past lives. She prayed to outrun the Wheel held by Yama in his tall white teeth. Yama, Lord of Death.*

"For I have no choice and cannot endure the pain any longer."

. . .

HE WOULD GO *and sit with her. Mattie never did. Reggie and Tiff came, during that first month at Thalians. Roslynn too. Mrs. Loewenstein usually* visited once or twice for each admission, as long as the hospital was in California. But Philip sat three times during the week and every Sunday, no matter where.

They did not learn the circumstances of their mother's birth until after her suicide. (The death of their father by heart disease had come a year later.) Their mother's mother had been abducted by a middle-class, overweight white girl who was unable to bear her black boyfriend a child. Later in court she said she was afraid the boyfriend would leave her. The white girl went to trade school to study vocational nursing. This was in Chicago. She was especially rapt by the class in which cesarean technique was discussed. She feigned pregnancy (with the same enthusiasm as Lisanne concealing her own), disappearing in her alleged fifth month owing to the alleged infant's premature entry into the world. She lay in wait. She struck Philip's grandmother on the head, shoving her into the open trunk in a dark suburban parking lot. (She'd been following her for a week.) She drove to her parents', who were in Milwaukee, and with whom she had been living since things got rocky between her and the boyfriend, whom they had actually met and urged her not to see. In the basement—her father was a woodworker—she cut the baby from his grandmother's womb with a car key and her father's cooper's adze. It was nearly to term. By some miracle—the lord smiles at drunk, dogs, and eviscerated fetuses—Phil and Mattie's mom survived. The coroner said (it came out at trial) that their grandmother was most likely alive during the procedure and may even have lived to see the girl holding the baby in her arms, trying to make it suckle.

Philip sat with Lisanne's pale, troubled form. They sat outdoors, and at partially-roofed-over picnic tables and in sundry rec rooms. She didn't say much. Sometimes they held hands. His mother, after many bramble-scratched wanderings, had killed herself with barbiturates and a plastic bag, just the way the "Final Exit" book said you should. The old newspaper articles Philip's father had left in the bank box with his will told the story of how the overweight white girl hanged herself with a bedsheet during the trial and how it took her ten days to die. Now here he was with Lisanne, and sometimes it felt like sitting with the Chicago girl, the sick marooned white whale who delivered his mom, sitting beside her mournful ICU deadweight, and an indomitable pity overtook him, for all God's lacerated children. Here he was with Lisanne, who he thought had (comparatively) been

shown great mercy, and who he tenderly prayed would one day see that and
come back to the world, not for his sake but for her own and for that of
their beautiful Siddhama.

An Actor Prepares II

HE MET WITH Jorgia three days a week, hours at a time. She imposed diction, rhythm, and presence, forcing him to project until hoarse and lung-numb. All the nonsense sounds, guttural, chirpy, and ludicrous, the Sid Caesared ornithological speaking tongues, brought him back to Viola Spolin and Del Close and the exhilaration of his improv glory days. She forced characters, broken accents, unbroken focus. They sang false soprano, belched and drummed, hiccuped and fizzed, coughed, vaudeville-sneezed, then howled at the rafters—Jorgia was one wily coyote. Cackled, wheezed, farted, and masticated, rolled on the floor like bellowing spastics, ejaculating hot breath, arses upright on sore kneecaps, shitting vowels into space. Set about to *righteously* erase the Self. He plunged and soared, banking on thin hot air—wailed, hooted and yippeeed, dowsed for water and delved—into all realms of senses: common-, horse-, -memory.

Did sits together too. (Jorgia, the old yogini.)

• • •

AFTER A FEW months, he had the notion to put up a Sam Shepard play. The timing would have to be right. So much had been wrong; he was changing all that.

• • •

THEY MOVED to a house on Stone Canyon Road.

The private cops were gladdened—hotels were harder to secure than houses, and the Bel-Air was a bitch.

A restraining order against the dad, but so far, no problems. Hadn't proved inflammatory, as sometimes happens.

"I DON'T WANT you driving my car," said Kit.

"What?"

"My G-wagen. I—don't want anyone driving it."

"This a joke?"

"This is no joke!"

Cela, conciliatory: *"Then we won't drive it, Kit."*

Burke biliously mocked. *"Then we won't drive it, Kit."* Mad-dogged her. *"Who the fuck died and made* you *CEO?"* To Kit: *"I know what this is about. This is about your little meeting with the attorneys last week, ain' it?"*

Kit vociferously shook his head.

"I knew you were having that meeting. You didn't think I knew you were having that meeting? News flash! *That meeting would* not *have* happened *if I didn't approve it. Cause* I *approve your shit."*

"I don't want anyone drive my car," Kit said, nervously holding his ground. Self-corrected: *"To drive my car."*

"Oh, you don't?" said Burke, smugly. *"Really?" Lolling the tongue in his mouth like a big ol' bored lion. "Well how bout if those Century City attorneys drive it? Would you make an exception, Kitchener? For your precious G-wagen? I mean, you're the head of the* fleet—*you can* make an exception. You're the man. I know I sure as shit would—cause they're such good people! Oh, the attorneys (each time he said* attorneys *he had a gigglefit) really have your best interests at heart! The attorneys wake up each morning and say, 'Now what the fuck can I do to help Kit Lightfoot today!' So howze about you make a little exception, Kitchener, and let the fucking compassionate altruistical attorneys* who *love* you *so much drive your fucking car—"*

"Burke, stop," said Cela.

"You! Shut the fuck up!" Swiveled back to Kit. "In fact, the attorneys *can fucking move right in! The* attorneys *can fucking change the sheets on your bed in the morning after you've soaked 'em with your superstar piss, just like I do. Oh, they would* love *that so much. The wonderful* attorneys *can watch you stand in the kitchen and choke the chakra whenever Pam Anderson or Viv Wembley or whomever comes on TV—"*

"I don't do that!" shouted Kit.

"The fuck you don't. You're a horny fuck, just like your old man." The

sly smile again. "You liked porking Buddha-puss, didn't you? Buddha-puss was a bleeder, huh. You like porking bleeders."

"Burke, stop it! Leave him alone!"

He brutally backhanded her. She flew onto the couch. Kit grabbed at his father.

"Don't—you—touch—her!"

Burke pranced and sang, "Macho macho man! I wanna be a ma-cho man!" Shoved his son, bam blam bam: "Don't you think I'm tired of your shit? Now I got to hear you telling me not to drive your faggoty G-wagen? Fuck you! Where'd you think you'd be without me, Dr. Demento? Think all those people with your best interests at heart would be taking care of you?" He pretended to pound hard on a door. " 'Hey! Open up! Let us in, we want to take care of Kit! For nothing! We're the compassionate attorneys, open up!' They don't give a flying shit about you, got it? OK? If anyone really gave a shit—except for yours truly—you'd be living with your fuckin agent. Or your fuckin fiancée, who as we all know loves you so fucking—"

"You sonofabitch!" shouted Cela.

"—so fucking much she can't tear her ass away from you! Loves you so fucking much she hasn't been to visit, not-a-wunst. Loves you so much she's gobblin your homey's dick like it was Jimmy Dean pure pork saus—"

Cela climbed onto his back as Burke pinned his son to the unvacuumed shag. Held him there while turning to Cela with full force. "That's right, go where the money is, babe, you're good at that. That's where Cela goes— whoever's got the fuckin money. Open wide for Chunky! Stuff that money in the junkie cunt—" (Back in his son's face while the weeping Cela ineffectively clawed.) "Well, let me tell you something. I'm your father. And I should be fucking compensated. What are you gonna do with fifty million dollars, buy yourself a new brain? 'When a man's an empty kettle, he should be on his mettle in company or'—I'm the one doing the heavy lifting! Me, OK? Not your mama, may she rest in peace—not your precious beloved attorneys—not anyone! Capiche?"

Kit wrestled free and ran to the yard.

Burke chased him out.

Cela raced after, shrieking.

Burke tackled him. Pinned him. Kit squirmed, struggling to breathe.

"We're in this together, or I'll put you out on the street! I potty-trained you when you were a baby! When you were at Valle Verde, I fuckin potty-

trained you again—that's the kind of commitment I made! Because that's the kind of father I am!"

Kit *frothed and spat.* "Fuck you! Fuck you! Fuck you!"

"Oh yeah?" Burke *creepily reprised:*

> Oh I could tell you why
> the ocean's near the shore
> I could tink-uh tings
> I never tunk before

Then drubbed and walloped, breaking two ribs and Cela's jaw too before Tula rushed to put him down.

·   ·   ·

THAT WAS THEN. This is now.

Trials and Tribulations

RUSTY'S TRIAL HAD begun on Court TV, engendering a fresh wave of press about the bottom-feeding world of look-alikes. Someone was full-on blabbing to the *Post* about Becca's relationship with Herke Lamar Goodson *and* her deposed gig as Viv Wembley's chore whore. She suspected it was Gingher, though it may have been Larry Levine, because the two of them, Becca and Larry, had stopped talking after he got drunk at a party and made some insinuations that she didn't care for about the nature of her even then defunct relationship with the Dunsmores. Annie said Larry was really hurt when he found out that Becca thought it was him. Annie was certain it was Gingher.

The idea of being forced to testify terrified her. She'd already told the detectives everything she knew, none of which seemed particularly special. Months ago, a Dunsmore attorney had assured her of the unlikelihood of a subpoena, but now Becca felt more vulnerable than ever. Her career was just taking off, and she was convinced that kind of exposure would finish her. She had trouble sleeping. The only thing that calmed her was when Dixie brushed her hair, which she did at all hours, at least when she was in town. Her mom was a rock.

How strange it was watching Rusty on television! He wore a tie and was clean-shaven, more *Insider* than *Gladiator*. She glued herself to the set and sometimes (especially after smoking weed) actually strained to make eye contact. It was totally surreal. Whenever the trial recessed or got bogged down in sidebars, they played Rusty's "reel," an anthology of forgettable ads that Elaine Jordache had pro-cured, mostly from foreign countries—and, of course, the surviving microscene from Spike Jonze's *Look-Alike*, courtesy of 20th Century-Fox. (The network was unsuccessful in getting hold of any outtakes.) The commentary provided by resident Court TV glamgirl wonks was filled with repetitious effulgence of the case "having all the elements of a Hollywood thriller," the Greekly tragic (or Shakespearean, depending on the pundit) kicker being that the patricide's victim, Rader Lee Goodson, was a reformed grifter and short con who had risen to be a kingpin in the world of identity theft. *Identity theft:* the "look-alike" son inheriting the sins of the father, then knifing him up in a fit of Oedipal rage! It was almost too "written," too good to be true.

Still, after careful consideration of QuestraWorld's submission, the studios deemed "To Kill a Unicorn" strikingly inept, contrived, and off-point—which under normal circumstances would have been enough to put it on a fast track to production. (The project remained a novelty item whose only generated heat emanated from the oddball producers' curious, heavy-handed innuendo that its creator was none other than the murderer-protagonist himself.) An article in *Vanity Fair* wound up being optioned by a pair of former Fox executives with close ties to Tiff Loewenstein. Eventually, CBS and Showtime got into the action, but ultimately the bizarre story of the look-alike killer and his Tinsel Town sojourn slouched toward Babylon, never to be born.

· · ·

"THANK YOU *SO* much for having me read. I loved the script *so* much."

"No, it was my pleasure."

"I *so* didn't think I'd be reading for *you*."

"I'm known to sit in on auditions," he said, sardonically. "You were terrific. Sharon raved about you."

"She is *so* great—she's gotten me, like, every part I've *ever had*. And I know you're sick of hearing it, but I loved *When Harry Met Sally* so much!"

"I never get sick of hearing nice things."

They had bumped into each other in the hall, after the read, when Becca was leaving the powder room. He looked like he was angling to get away. But maybe not.

"Thanks again, Mr. Reiner!" she said, pouring it on.

As he walked off, he added, "And by the way, you were *very* funny in Spike's movie."

She thought: A "very funny" from Rob Reiner is pretty fucking great. He'd lost about fifty pounds and told Jay Leno that it was because he wanted to be around for his kids. Becca thought that was so sweet. The audience had even applauded.

He ogled her from afar, with a kind of quizzical charm. "You know, you look much more like Drew in the *movie* than you do in real life. If we can call this real life."

She laughed. "So much of the Drew thing is how I wear my hair?" she said, with an old-style Valley Girl (Southern belle) upturn. "And it's partially *attitude*. I mean, I gotta be in that *Drew mood*—know what I'm sayin?"

She felt feisty and carefree, talented and desired.

She felt like Ashley Judd.

"Thanks for coming in," he said. "We'll be in touch."

She almost *never* read with directors—the casting person put her on tape and that was the end of it. Usually, you had to get called back maybe three times before something like that would happen. She told Annie that when she came in the room and saw Rob Reiner sitting there she almost lost it. He was so down-home and had her do the scene a bunch of different ways. It wasn't a huge role, but there were two scenes with Ed Norton and one with Dustin Hoffman, who played Ed's dad. Dixie was gonna *die* when she told her. Dustin Hoffman was her mother's all-time hall of fame fave, and Becca thought that was funny because Dixie always seemed to go for the Jews. In the movies, anyway.

Labor Day

LISANNE AND PHILIP were in Rustic Canyon, watching the remains of the Jerry Lewis telethon.

Philip was sniffling. He said that around four in the morning he'd called the on-screen number during a five-minute pledge rush to gather funds to send kids to a special MDA camp. It cost $540 a kid, he said. Lisanne thought he'd been moved by the poignancy of it, but then he confessed. Philip said he got connected to a young volunteer and told her he wanted to buy twenty pledges. That was almost ten grand, and the girl got excited. He said he would give her his credit card. He unhurriedly doled out the numbers, while saying he was also doing a certain something to himself and she told him she didn't know what he meant (she really didn't) and then he said that he thought she did know what he meant and he warned her not to hang up because if she did that would mean *twenty disabled children* wouldn't be going to camp. The girl whimpered but stayed on the line—she was so young that she didn't know any better. What excited him most was that he could actually see the girl crying in the back phone-bank row as she took down the bogus info. He said that, to the home viewer, nothing appeared out of line because half of the people on the telethon were always crying anyway.

. . .

"THAT'S THE THING about Jerry that always bugged me," said Robbie.

(Lisanne left the house in Rustic as soon as Philip finished his little story; the telethon was on at the Sarsgaard's, too.)

"He's *mean*," said Robbie. "I mean, I love 'im and everything—and he's the world's biggest softie. But Mr. Lewis can be meaner than hell! Right, Max?"

"That is correct," said the old woman from her La-Z-Boy.

Lisanne recalled the first time she saw her, in Albany, standing in the dusky kitchen. At the motel, Robbie had lied, and said he was sharing his home with his paternal grandmother. She remembered thinking, Something fishy there. Maxine Rebak was in her late sixties, and the alliance was comical to Lisanne at first but then poignant—everybody loves somebody sometime. Looking back, she wondered why he drove them over to see Max in the first place. Maybe it was some kind of ambivalent last gasp defiance toward his wife-to-be. But whatever ambivalence he might have had was now gone. They had the soft, comfy edges of any long-married couple.

Robbie met Maxine on a singles Web site. A Christian Scientist, she had registered her age as ten years younger. He advertised himself as a retired ambulance driver who became further disabled during WTC cleanup efforts, the truth being that on 9/13 he actually did start into Manhattan but was sidelined when a piston blew. That kind of bravado was pure Robbie. He was more a dreamer than a deceiver, and Lisanne loved him because he didn't have a malevolent bone in his body. (Doesn't have a bone at all, her dad would have wryly said.) He was a passive, sweet-hearted man. Maxine was a widow with a little bit of money. Shortly after they introduced themselves at a coffee shop rendezvous in Syracuse, she sold her house and moved in. She'd grown ill over the last few months; the road trip to L.A. took it out of her. They were married in Vegas, on the day they visited the Hoover Dam, "a thing of profound beauty" that Maxine had always dreamed of and wished to see before her death. But Siddhama superseded any morbid notions—she loved the idea of her husband being a sudden father, and seeing him with the boy gave her renewed life.

Lisanne had been in the hospital only a few days when Reggie tracked Robbie down. Reggie and the Muskinghams met Robbie and Maxine for dinner, and that was when Philip offered to lease them a duplex in the Fairfax area. The nannies' living quarters were on the second story (that way, Max wouldn't have to negotiate stairs), and they worked in revolving shifts so that the Sarsgaards were never without help. Between hospitalizations, Lisanne visited Siddhama whenever she wished, and while no one broached the topic of the baby returning to Rustic Canyon to live, she knew she wasn't ready. But she was no longer afraid of her child. The aberrant ideation of his Panchen-like abduction receded, as flotsam upon floodwaters, and she reveled in their communion, staring deeply into his eyes with unneurotic affection. It was in this fashion that she willed Siddhama into being, assembled him with her love, and that he grew more real with each passing moment. She could not fathom this luscious, magical creature not being in her life.

Meanwhile, Lisanne did everything she could to reclaim her health and spirits. She went to an obesity clinic at UCLA and drank protein powder packets each day. She chugged down potassium pills with sugarless Metamucil, morning and night. She lost thirty pounds in the first month. She did yoga, Pilates, and Gyrotonics, returning to her five-mile walks along the bluff. She lifted weights and submitted herself to the energetic meridian needlings of Dr. Yue-jin Feng. (The only thing she didn't do was meditate.) She saw Calliope Krohn-Markowitz for talk therapy five hours a week in conjunction with cutting-edge palliative care provided by Chaunce Hespers, M.D., the renowned Camden Drive psychopharmacologist. All was relatively well with the world.

She emphatically knew who this baby was—a beauteous boy child, born of the union of Lisanne Emily McCadden and Robert Linden Sarsgaard.

"Did you hear what Jerry said just before Julius La Rosa came out?" said Robbie, poised before the campfire of the TV. "Lisanne, you didn't hear? Maxine! Max, come on, you guys have to *watch*! Ed McMahon was announcing Julius La Rosa—Maxine, *you* know Julius La Rosa"— she nodded from her chair and said, "He's of the where-are-they-now ilk"—"what they call a singer's singer. Tony Bennett *worships* him. And if *Bennett's* considered a 'singer's singer,' I guess that means La Rosa's a singer's singer's *singer*. Whew! That's a tongue twister. Sinatra loved him too—Lisanne, you're too young. But I happen to know my saloon singers, and La Rosa coulda been big as Frank. Right, Max? Hands down. But he was *cantankerous*. This guy pissed *everybody* off . . . Arthur *Godfrey*, Ed *Sullivan*, the *mob* guys. Everybody. So McMahon introduces him—this was just twenty minutes ago!—and Jerry says, 'Is he still alive?' And you know that had to hurt. Jerry, with that pumpkin face full of cortisone, like he should talk! The guy comes on and sings—*beautifully*— What'd he sing, Max? 'Cat's in the Cradle'? Beautiful. And I was never wild about that song—that's Harry Chapin, a Brooklyn boy—but it was like we were hearing it for the first time, huh, Max. La Rosa was in a tux, that's their thing, all those saloon guys, but *handsome*, like he was born in it"—Maxine said, "*Very*"— "and probably older than Jerry, if that's possible! So, after he sings,

Jerry looks in the camera with those crocodile tears and says, 'It don't get any better than that, folks'—and how if there's a pantheon, the top guys would have to be Frank and Tony and Julius (he throws in Jack Jones only cause Jack's coming on later), and you kind of get the feeling he means it but it's too late! OK? He's already made the Is he still alive? remark, and *that's* the thing that makes me uncomfortable about Jerry"—"So why do you watch?" interjects Maxine, without expecting an answer, then says to Lisanne, "You can't tear him away"—"A *mean* motherfucker, pardon my German. And that's why if *I* was famous, I would *never* do that show"—"Fortunately, you will never have that problem," said Maxine—"I don't care *how* many sick kids you supposedly cure. And I don't think they've cured one *yet*. But they will, and I'm not taking that away from him. But if you *do* go on that show, and I don't give a hoot if you're the Pope, Uncle Jerry is gonna take a crap on you *sooner* or *later*. He'll take a giant shit on your head—pardon my French—that's from *Full Metal Jacket*—great movie—Uncle Jerry will crap on your head and you'll never know until it hits you."

True West

THE PLAY OPENED in a ninety-nine-seat house for a run of twelve performances. *Access Hollywood* reported that scalped tickets were going for nineteen thousand dollars on eBay.

As the curtain fell on opening night, the crowd thundered, screamed, and wept. No one had ever seen anything like it or ever would. At the star's insistence, the uncharacteristically tearful Jorgia Wilding emerged from the wings to join the cast in deep bows. That bittersweet mix of first and last hurrahs.

Though critics had been barred, many in the audience (culture vulture luminaries) posted Internet opinions—word of Web being that while Kit Lightfoot's transcendent performance was at times halting, it was more haunting than anything else. Toward the end, representatives from a few national publications smuggled themselves past the box office, yet by the time their reviews ran (breathlessly)—the *New York Observer* headlined "Long Day's Journey Into Lightfoot"— they sounded dated and glowingly apocryphal, for production had already triumphantly shuttered, having spiritedly entered the death- less annals of mythic theater lore.

Viv Wembley sent flowers.

The Leno Show

THE BAND PLAYS the Supertramp theme from *World Without End* as he comes out. The longest ovation in Leno's history.

For the next five minutes, hoots, catcalls, coughs, and whatnot as the mob cathects then settles upon its collective seat.

"Wow," says Jay. "I cannot tell you how happy I am—how happy the *world* is—that you're back."

Tsunamis, then tidewaters of applause. Kit humbly smiles and begins to respond—forced to give up, as the audience dam breaks. Awash again.

Second longest ovation in Leno's history.

Kit's jaw is clenched, his eyes wet. Bodysurfing the no-silence.

Jay, too, wipes away a tear. "I'm getting very emotional," he says, sweetly shaking that ridiculous-sized chin. Slightly embarrassed, or playing at such. Now and then it's OK to be unmanly.

Kit smiles and says nothing. Stop-starts, charmingly stymied. Audience, charmed too—way, *way* on his side. Still, though, he hasn't said a word, and they're kinda nervous about that. . . .

How will he sound? All retardy?

Time now overdue for that *first sentence moment*—utterance to be reported the next day, the quip heard 'round the world.

(That one-giant-leap-for-mankind moment.)

Finally, after a great sigh it comes:

"What a long, strange trip it's been."

Laughter, tears, ovation! The sentiment funny and true! *And* he sounds normal!

Just like they knew he would.

. . . more than anyone could have dreamed or hoped for.

Kiki had six writers spend two weeks brainstorming. Then Cela heard the Grateful Dead song on the radio—her suggestion. Kiki agreed. The writers' picks were too jokey. This, the most *real*.

The crowd deftly replays his words in their heads, picking them clean for slurs, impediments, *I Am Sam*–type aftershocks.

Nothing!

(The collective Eye had already searched for skull craters beneath the chic, barely grown out buzz cut—none visible.)

"I just have one thing to ask," says Kit.

They hang on his words. You could hear a pin drop.

"Because people worry about my mental faculties."

All anxiously hold their breath. He's going to say something . . . serious—

"You *are* David Letterman—aren't you?"

Hilarity! Foot-stomping ovation! The kid stays in the picture!

Now Jay and Kit ease into the familiar, comforting shuck-and-jive *What was it like?/How does it feel to be back?* shtick.

Ice-breaky stuff to give guest and host (audience too) their sea legs.

Jay says, "Now, one thing the people out there may or may not know is that there was an *irony* connected to this whole 'event.' "

"Event? You mean, when I got hit on the head?"

Laughter. A man of the people, regular guy. Deserving, courageous.

"Yes!" says Jay. "Mind if we talk about it?"

"That's why I'm here. But *you* talk—I'll listen." Laughter. "Because, man, I am *tired*."

Applause. Whoop-whoops.

Jay says, "OK. That's fair. Fair deal."

"I just flew in from rehab," says Kit, on a roll. "And boy, is my mind tired." Laughter: tidewater ripple: tsunami applause.

"Carrie Fisher wrote that for me."

Jay cracks up.

Kit adds, "And I'm [bleeped] *nervous*."

With the unexpected obscenity, Leno joyfully loses it. The crackling *realness* of the moment. Rapture from the crowd, then—

A (lady's) voice, from audience: "We love you, Kit!"

Jay, sternly: "Have that woman escorted from the studio . . . and immediately taken to Mr. Lightfoot's hotel room."

Laughter. Whistles, catcalls. Applause.

A (man's) voice, from audience: "I love you, Kit!"

Jay and his chin lose it again.

Giddiness, contagion. Punch-drunk love. Admiration for the conquering hero's return.

Jay gently admonishes the audience like the old friends they are. "All right, *calm down* now." Back to his guest. "And I want to talk about the play, *True West*—what a triumph— [applause begins; Jay deftly thwarts another prolonged salvo by continuing] but . . . and *this* fascinates me. You were preparing to do a film when you got [awkward] hit on the head . . ."

Kit nods matter-of-factly. "Darren Aronofsky. Wonderful director."

" . . . now the irony is that you were actually going to play—to *portray*—a character who was very much like you. A famous movie actor who was normal—at least, relatively!—until he was involved in an automobile accident that rendered him with [awkward for Jay now], well, not 'diminished capacity,' but I guess what you'd call a kind of neurological disa—"

"Brain damage," says Kit tersely.

The audience laughs, though slightly discomfited.

"Oops," says Kit. "Sorry to be political incorrect." (In a nanosecond, sharks to blood, the mob registers possible retard-omit of -*ly* from *politically*.) "Politically incorrect," says Kit, self-correcting without fanfare—and all is well again. Just a case of nerves.

"Come on!" Kit says boisterously, throwing down a challenge to the crowd. "You can say it—*brain damage!*"

Raises his arms like a conductor while Jay bashfully shakes his head at the mischief making. The audience reverberates: "Brain damage!"

Not once, not twice, but three times.

Applause—ovation.

They are his.

Together Again

"HOW LONG HAVE you lived here?"

"About a year. It used to be Woody's—Woody Harrelson's."

"Very cool."

The Taosified beach house sat on two lots, north of the Colony.

She invited him over after seeing him on Leno. Why not? She apologized for not coming to the play. She said, with a laugh, that she was worried he'd have seen her in the audience and freaked out.

"Does Alf stay with you?"

"No."

A vexing beat as the waves crashed.

"Did you know that Woody's father is in jail for shooting a federal judge? He's a professional hit man! People even think he might have been the guy on the grassy knoll." Kit nodded indifferently. "You look . . . *so great*. You were *so funny* on Leno."

"I missed you," he said.

Past tense. The air went out of her. "I missed you too! It's just . . . I—I . . . Kit, it was so *hard* for me. It's been really hard! And . . . I know that sounds *so self-obsessed* and it's *true*. I *so* fucked this up . . . and it's been so *weird* just to try and stay *present*, to *see* that—to see that that's the kind of person I am, or wound up being, because I don't even think I'm— Sometimes it's like, I look back and say, 'Who *was* that?' "

He smiled sardonically. Then, with the smallest hint of a stammer: "This—this is the part where the girlfriend hasn't seen him for a long time." She wasn't sure if he was being cruel. "This is the scene where they feel bad together."

"Kit," said Viv, starting to cry. "I am *so sorry* for what happened. I am *so sorry* that I—that I couldn't *deal* with it."

"Not your fault," he said stalwartly, determined not to get emotional. Not to give her that.

"The whole thing with Alf—"

"Not your fault, Viv."

"—has been pretty much over for three months." She felt like she was on the witness stand of her own court-martial. "Not that that means anything. Or should. But he— Alf was my connection to *you*. And I know that sounds weird and like a cop-out . . ."

"It's OK." He wouldn't look at her.

"It's *not* OK. And I just need you to—I just walk around this planet feeling so fucking *miserable*. Kit, I still love you so much! And when— when you got hurt . . . I know it sounds like some stupid cliché—I was talking to Steve Soderbergh (not about this), and he said, 'Clichés are true, that's why they're clichés'—but I think I just *loved* you too much to go to the hospital and *see* you that way—"

He looked toward the ocean. "I thought I saw a seal out there."

"Probably just paparazzi," she said, vaguely relieved to be taken out of her moment. "Their Malibu disguises are really resourceful."

She changed tack and gossiped about the business. Who was sleeping with whom, who'd been fired, who was at Promises. That she'd signed with Gerry Harrington, and Angela wanted to throw Kit a dinner—Angela was working for Dolce now. They walked on the sand and smoked weed. The conversation got looser. Viv asked if he still liked to fuck. He said that he did and managed pretty well. She took a flier and said maybe they should, "as a healing thing." Kit laughed, then she said all actresslike that no one ever fucked her like he did.

"I have a girlfriend," he said. Square business.

"Oh. Who?"

"You don't know her."

"Is she an actress?" He shook his head. "Is she a *Buddhist*?"

He smiled. "Civilian. High school sweetheart."

"Oh right—the old flame. I think I read that in the *Post*. What's her name?"

"Cela."

"So if she's the old flame, what does that make me?"

A beat, then: "Candle in the wind."

Crash Course

THE AWFUL THING was that Rob Reiner wanted her to come back and read with Ed Norton but she had to say no because of a scheduling conflict with *1200 North*. Becca said, "When it rains, it pours." Dixie said, "You mean, it's either feast or famine."

A & E ordered twelve, and while Becca wasn't in every show, her contract guaranteed she'd be paid for at least six. As yet, only the pilot had been written, but according to the show's "bible," Rhiannon's arc called for at least five more episodes. The agent said that if the stars (and writers) were in alignment, Becca could wind up doing eight or even ten.

It was great news. Still, she was bummed at not having a Rob Reiner film on her résumé and almost felt worse that she wasn't going to read with Ed Norton. (She talked herself into thinking she'd have absolutely nailed it.) She sent Mr. Reiner handwritten regrets, as Sharon Belzmerz so classily suggested. Sharon was sweet and said Rob Reiner was an old hitless fogy anyway and that she'd already gotten Becca "a meet" with Brett Ratner and was working on the Coen brothers. Her near miss was still a good story—one of those gripping Hollywood yarns she could share with everyone in Waynesboro next Thanksgiving, a shining example of what her agent liked to call a "high-class problem." It was also the kind of surefire anecdote to maybe bring up one day during a Conan or Letterman preinterview, as long as it didn't sound stuck-up.

Hollywood Palace

PHILIP HANGED HIMSELF on Halloween night while Lisanne was at the hospice.

For the last few months, she'd been helping out at Lavendar House, a Victorian-style building over by the VA. A friend from the *sangha* said it would do her great good. Though Lisanne had abandoned any formal or even informal Buddhist practice, the friend had been right—working at the hospice took her out of herself and put her in touch with what was real. The mundanely majestic drama of life and death.

She was sitting with a comatose woman when the cell phone vibrated in her purse. It was Mattie, with the news. She went home to Rustic Canyon and sat another vigil. There were bodies all around her now. She felt like that kid in *The Sixth Sense*.

•   •   •

THE NEXT FEW days were filled with snakes.

Lisanne heard a paramedic on the radio, talking about the hair-raising adventures of his trade. He spoke of a Korean man who skinned snakes and ate them raw, for health purposes; he swallowed the heads too, but this time a fang sunk into his tongue. The man stumbled into the fire station saying that he had "a problem." They were able to save him.

At night, she conjured the Temescal Canyon *metta* rattler, the one she never told Philip about. In her dream, they stood over it, together. The serpent spoke to them, but when she awakened, Lisanne could never remember what it had said.

On the morning of his funeral, she read an article in the *Times* about Amber, an eight-year-old girl killed by the family's pet Burmese.

Robert Mountain testified that he was kept awake by the python the night before his daughter was attacked as the snake tried to escape from its makeshift cage.

Mountain said he applied about four layers of duct tape to hold a screen on the lid in place and checked on the snake before leaving for work the next morning.

Both he and his wife said they knew Moe had outgrown its cage, a particleboard bin bought from a fabric store, with a hinged clear-plastic lid that Robert Mountain had attached.

They found Amber on the kitchen floor, the snake coiled around her neck and chest. Lisanne wondered how it would feel to die like that. And what would it be like for the rescuers, to get the snake off her, seeing what they would see?

. . .

THEY BURIED HIM in a pricey Westwood mausoleum beside the Bel-Air waste management king, Louis Aherne Trotter, kitty-corner from the drawer Hefner had reserved for himself above Marilyn Monroe. Mattie was gaunt and wobbly, flanked by the stoic Loewensteins, and she pinched a handkerchief to her sopping face as if the fabric itself was her sole source of oxygen. Even Dr. Calliope attended.

Lisanne was glad to see Robbie and Maxine. He brought their son because Mattie had requested it. Lisanne was holding Siddhama in her arms as she came over. Taking the handkerchief away from her face at last, Aunt Mattie said, "My brother loved that baby so much."

After all was said and done, Lisanne knew that he did.

. . .

THAT NIGHT, Lisanne stayed with her at the beach house. They watched *Mildred Pierce* against an appropriately wild-dark backdrop of ocean, and ate pumpkin pie à la mode while thumbing through old family albums. Mattie said that her brother was a "lost soul." He'd tried to kill himself in college, then again right after Dad died. Lisanne couldn't believe Philip never told her that.

She had left her psychosis behind. As she drifted off, pulled closer now by the amniotic rhythm of cold swells that arose and fell like mantras never-ending, shattering so near the Joan Crawford picture window, her body relaxing beside Mattie's nameless, nearly formless form, Lisanne remembered the loving-kindness workshop teacher's definition of a meditation practice: it is nothing but the abiding calm a man learns as he carries a bowl of scalding oil upon his head while walking through the rooms of an enormous palace.

Christmas Eve Day

AT THREE IN the afternoon, in the patio under freezing refulgent crystal blue heavens, Cela told her man she was going to Rexall Square for a bagful of nonpareils. That was her alibi.

She blasted an old Bowie CD in the BMX, south on Beverly Glen all the way to Pico, a right to Overland, down to the 10 east.

She'd done all the major shopping—*loved* Christmas—and had just about finished this crazy collage thing (corny paper cutout tributes to their love), thinking she was so clever until suddenly realizing what a *fool* she was for having completely spaced on the mother lode of oldies—a treasure trove of Ulysses S. Grant stuff, photos of Kit with R.J., and God knew what else—that was sitting in storage, gathering dust. Imagining the bounty that awaited her, Cela began to think in terms of actually doing an oversize triptych. That was OK by her. Kit would *love* it. She'd stay up late like she did when she was little, cutting and pasting, giggling to herself while he chilled in front of the $20,000 slimscreen. She'd have to chase him off if he snuck up to see what she was doing.

The 10 to Azusa, then north to Badillo toward the Covina U-Stor—down the road from Uncle Jimmy, who'd helped move all her Riverside belongings. She hadn't seen any of the packed things since (or Uncle Jimmy either), but now and again they spoke on the phone. Cela wanted him to visit the new house, but they hadn't been there all that long and she thought it better to hold off. (They were phasing out some of the security guys, and it felt nice to have the place to themselves.) Uncle Jimmy wasn't sensitive—all he ever wanted to know was when was she gonna invite him to a big premiere. He had a thing for Nicole Kidman and kept saying, wickedly, "When you gonna hook me up with Nicole? Time she had a *man's* man." Uncle Jimmy had a heart of gold. He was diabetic, and had had a few scares. She gave him Christmas money so he could spend the holiday up at Russian River.

She went by his house, knowing he wasn't there. Wouldn't it be funny if he was? Then she realized her true impulse, and made the detour, heart beating faster.

There were tenants in her old place, but it looked woebegone. Cela changed her mind about driving past Burke's; too radioactive. She grew faintly nauseated. Everything was saturated with sunlit anomie. Neighborhood kids were staring at the BMX. She gunned it.

. . .

SHE RUMMAGED among the stacks and laughed: she was Pack Rat Supreme, always had been. (That was always Burke's joke, whenever they went to Vegas. There was Frank Sinatra and the Rat Pack, and Cela Byrd and the Pack Rat.) What a sad bunch of shit—broken lamps, fucked-up chairs, dusty file boxes marked COURT, REHAB/JOURNALS, MAMA, LEGAL, TAXES, MISC., SWAP MEET . . .

—there it was: PIX/YEARBOOKS.

She pried the carton out from under and took the lid off. *Whoa.* Better make that *two* triptychs. Mebbe three. The first thing she laid eyes on was a half-ruined Polaroid of them smoking a doobie in front of a bonfire, age thirteen. Couldn't remember a thing about it. Blurry, smudged, time-sealed—might be fun to blow up and wallpaper the den with. Or hang on the side of the pool house, ten by ten, with a special outdoor coating.

She had planned to throw everything in the car but couldn't help getting engrossed. Accordingly, she didn't see the silver Range Rover, the one Kit allowed his father to keep, the good riddance "bone" as Burke called it, quietly berth a few doors down. There was a small crack in the windshield; a few holes had been punched in the passenger door, to fix a dent.

Cela startled as he sauntered over, framed in the metal roll-up door against the cloudless Covina sky.

"Hey, babe."

"What are you doing here?" She stayed down, kneeling and semi-sorting, trying to be cool.

"I rent a unit," he said, smiling. "For my unit." Always the salacious double-entendre. "Dr. Phil, is that not OK?"

"Did you follow me?"

"Saw you in the hood a little while ago," he said. "Gettin nostalgic?" She sighed and went back about her business. "A preggers gets *mucho hornito*. Thought you might be havin an 'afternoon delight' moment."

"You are *disgusting*," she said, coldly.

"Might just wanna DNA the kid, you know," he said, lasciviously apprising her belly. "Could be mine. But in order to do so, I may have to serve you with a su-penis."

"Can you just leave me alone?" She decided she would motor in about thirty seconds. "We've already done this dance, Burke."

"*Done this dance?*" he said, ascerbically. "That's some shitty dialogue, babe. Right out of a Kit Lightfoot movie."

She stood up. "I think you better get in your car."

He stepped back, as if in mortal terror. "Mommy! Mommy, you're scaring me!" A lurid quick change to fawning admiration: "Oh *boy*, you've gotten tough. Wow! You are *one tough macha*. Wouldn't want to tangle with *you*, chola, *huh* uh. No *way*."

"Burke, I don't want to do this."

"You don't have a restraining order against *me too*, do you, Cela? Cause far as I know, my *ungrateful shit-heel son* is the one who filed. Though I do believe it'll come out in the wash it was counsel's idea."

"I wonder why someone would have had the *audacity* to get a restraining order." Now that she was on her feet, she felt bolder. "Isn't that outrageous? Could it *possibly* have something to do with the fact that you beat the *shit* out of your own kid and broke my fucking face?"

"You know," said Burke, "experts *will* tell you that restraining orders aren't always a good thing."

She got adrenalized. Her brain told her to run, but she walked resolutely past. He spun her around and forced her back.

"Get your fucking hands off me!"

"Hey, hey, *hey.*"

"I'll call the police—"

"Here's my phone," he said, jamming it to her cheek. "Call Chief Bratton and tell him you're being diddled by an armadillo. Who *gives* a flying fuckito? *Listen,*" he whispered. "You went with the money and I cain't blame you. Hell, I *admire* you. You fucked the money with my come still runnin down your leg. *Mo better power to ya.* You testified against me at trial. Dragged my name through the mud and left me with *squat.* I put a lot of bread into that piece of shit rental you were living in, Cela. Put a lotta money into *you.* Hey: my prerogative and my pleasure. Where you livin now? A fifteen-million-dollar house? Is Catherine Zeta-Jones knocking on your door to borrow sugar, all neighborlike? Bra-*vo,* baby. You were sucking his dick right under my nose."

"I didn't do *anything* under your nose."

"Cept let me eat your pussy. *That* was under your nose." He laughed. "No—that was under *my* nose. And you let him watch, remember? Cause that's your thing. Your freak thing. That's what you're into."

"*Stop* it."

"You cunt."

He pulled a gun. She shook—gone bloodless.

"Take your pants off."

"Please don't—"

He punched her face and ordered her again. She hunched, dizzy and bloodsprayed, struggling to stay upright. She took them off. He kept the gun on her and flicked the roll-up switch. The iron drape descended with a sickening, inexorable grind. He pushed her face to the cement, unzipping his fly and greasing the cock with a gob of spit.

        She is only worried about the baby. She is determined not to bring it up for sympathy, for she knows he will not respond. It may only enrage him. She is beyond pain, protest, and tears. She is beyond.

"You coulda stayed with me," he said, panting as he forced himself in. "He coulda cut us a check. We had a good thing. Why'd you have to go get greedy on me?"

Absurdly, he riffed on the good times: the barbecues, Bellagio, Sunday Rose Bowl swap petty larcenies. What a team. Riffed on this and that, then popped one off in the tummy. *Whoops,* he said, with a grin. She looked at him, astonished. Writhed beneath as he dug in deeper. Squealed, gasped, and bled. "Not such a bad way to go, huh?" She made other sounds now. Dire. Rattling. "Though you may have some trouble coming. I know *I* won't." Shot twice more as he came. Who needs Viagra. Her eyes widened. She wheezed and made sounds again. He said, *Shake, rattle, and roll.* Climbed off pretty quick, clucking and tetchy, recoiling at the mess. *Lock and load.* Wiped himself with her Levi's before zipping up, then used the jeans to dam the blood so it wouldn't run into the thoroughfare just yet. Flicked the clappety roll up. Ducked under it macho-style, then ambled to the Range Rover, sucked in snot, and spat it out while looking first left then right like a badass B-movie bandito—peering down empty conjunctions of deserted asphalt alleys, in unwitting parody of the careful killer.

He stood catching his breath in the cool air. Had second thoughts. Walked back and triggered the door, ducking out again. It descended, shutting Cela's body into darkness.

Clear Light

. . .

Like the death of a child in a dream,
through holding the erroneous appearance
of the varieties of suffering to be true
one makes oneself so tired.
Therefore, it is a practice of Bodhisattvas when meeting
with unfavorable conditions to view them as erroneous.

—FROM *THE THIRTY-SEVEN PRACTICES,*
BY THE BODHISATTVA TOK-MAY-SANG-BO

The Healing

HE ENDURED the loss of his beloved, but could not endure being alone.

As always, the *sangha* mercifully engulfed him. Monks read aloud to Cela's wandering soul from long wood tablets of painted Sanskrit. Friends who'd feared to visit during Kit's own ordeal now overwhelmed with their generosity of heart. Even Viv came to cook for him.

All around the new zendo (deliberately humbler in construction than its Benedict Canyon forebear), pristine and by nature impervious to the farrago of tabloidal gore, a balm of practitioners did contemplations. Row upon row they lay in *Shavasana*—the corpse pose.

They breathed in death.

In just a week's time, he was ready to visit the jail.

. . .

THE PRISONER was led in, unshackled—that had been Kit's request. It was agreed that he posed no threat. Besides, there were enough guards in the room.

The look-alike assailant (who'd consented to the meeting) seemed suddenly intimidated by circumstances.

Kit measured his own breaths, collecting himself.

"Thank you for seeing me. I—I have thought about you every day." His diction was stilted. The slur came back from nervousness. He breathed through it, moving on. "I could not live with your hate— or . . . hate inside. It was kill me. Killing . . . always want—I always wanted to see you. To come to forgive. Forgive and to *thank*—you. I don't know why! It is the godly thing. It is karma. My karma and *yours*. We are the *same*. You look like me. They pay you to be me! How could I not forgive? So: I forgive you as you forgive me! We do the same. *We do the same thing.* OK?" The look-alike appeared to nod subtly, dipping his head. "My father is in jail now," said Kit. "I want to forgive him. I would like to forgive and would like to thank him too! If you see my father, please tell him that I am—that I forgive him. But don't tell him thank you—not that I said 'thank you.' . . . I will do that myself. One day. I hope I will love him enough to thank him. And forgive." Eyes loose with tears, the trademark superstar smile eked out, in spite of himself. "But not today."

Vanity Fair

FOR A MINUTE, it looked like David Gough and Dana Delany were breaking up.

Becca was floored when the actor phoned out of the blue, hinting they attend the *Vanity Fair* gala at Morton's together. He never really *asked*—he just seemed to want solace on the rocky Dana front, nervously betraying there was a chance he'd be "solo" on Oscar night. It was the kind of confusing call a girl might get from her older sister's drunken heartthrob boyfriend. A terrible idea anyway—Annie told her the last thing she needed was to foster bad vibes on the *1200 North* set. Set yourself some boundaries, girl. David said he would call back to let her know what was happening but never did. The whole thing seemed like a setup, and she kicked herself for not having had the moral fiber either to express outrage or at least tell him he was a numbskull not to patch things up with Dana because she was amazing and he knew he'd never find another gal like her. Though it was juvenile, Becca realized that her heart had become set on going out with David on Academy Awards night.

At the last minute, instead of crashing an Oscar viewing party at the Mondrian, she decided to take Annie to the Dunsmores'. She no longer worried about them sabotaging her career and even felt a little sentimental toward the old days. Anyhow, she'd heard that the Cass and Grady Show had been "discovered." Everyone who used to like to go to Robert Evans's—Wes Anderson, Nick Nolte, Aaron Sorkin,

Robert Downey Jr., Gina Gershon—now had a hard-on for the notorious biweekly bashes on Mulholland Drive.

. . .

CASSANDRA GREETED them like long-lost daughters. After standard issue nods to her newfound *1200 North* fame, she was chastised for "being such a stranger." Cass blathered on about how they'd supported and discovered her "when you were still *Drew,*" and then Grady stumbled in, bestowing hugs and sloppy kisses. He acted like Becca had never left the guesthouse. When he asked if she'd spoken to "Mr. Herky-Jerky," she said, bemused, "Why would I?" Grady feigned being dumbstruck, before answering back, "Well, you, uh, used to *fuck* him, didn't you? I mean, correct me if I'm *wrong*. You *loved* him, right?" He laughed, wheezing like a discount devil. "*1200 North* got you *uppity*." He said he needed to go find "Miss Maryjane," and excused himself.

Becca wanted everything to be copacetic. She asked where the bar was, but Cassandra said she first had to introduce them to Dr. J. Becca reminded their host that she and the doctor had already met.

"He's doin scripts for us. We just sold a pilot to USA."

"UPN," chimed her gaunt ladylove (and QuestraWorld coprincipal).

"Whatever. He likes Dr. J, but *I* call him Dr. *Doctor*. Anyhoo, it was Dr. *Doctor* who had the bright idea we start filming our Tuesday and Friday fiestas. Now why haven't *you* shown up for any of those?"

Thom Janowicz turned toward them as they hove into view. "Well, if it isn't the all-seeing, all-knowing Dr. *Doctor*!" said Cassandra.

"Hey, I know who you are!" said Dr. J—Becca was in his coked-up sights and he grabbed her. Annie followed as he led Becca to the window overlooking the pool. Cassandra & Co. dropped back, waylaid by Alan Cumming and Dana Giacchetto.

"Now I know you had a boyfriend who got into trouble. I've talked with Grady and Cass about it, that's one helluva story and you're one helluva lady to have been on that ride. And I'd like you to share your experience at a future date, now is not the time. But I think that is something we could definitely turn into a beautiful, beautiful screenplay and I want to talk with you about that but now is of course *not* the time. I'm sensitive to time and place. You had a bad egg experience and soon it'll be time to make an omelet. There *are* bad eggs, as you well know. Like that beanpole there—see him, over by the Lava lamp?—I'm working on a script about him. I'm five weeks in. He lied to a lady, corresponded with a widow for two years saying he was John Lithgow's brother. There's a slight resemblance, but mostly, he's tall. She was starstruck and he stole her money. End of case. Wound up giving that cad right over there about $96,000. He's awaiting conviction. Not a bad guy. Smart kid. Knows he did a bad thing. He's turned to Jesus and that's his prerogative. Who am I to judge? You get in trouble when you start to judge. Big time. But you know that. And there's a woman down by the pool. You can see her talking to—who is that, David Spade?"—he gestured through the window—"Hey, who's that way over there? Andy Dick? Anyhow, see that lady? Well, that lady was a dear friend of the late great Dorothy McGuire. Now you're too young to know about Dorothy McGuire. Go on IMDb and you'll learn all her movie credits. Go on Google or the AMC Web site. Well, Dorothy McGuire died a few years back and the Academy Awards failed to mention her passing during their much-touted annual memorial montage. And now this dear woman—the one by the pool—is waging a letter campaign to right a wrong because the Academy *failed to acknowledge*. Can you blame her? There's a whole group of people here tonight with similar beefs: there's Peggy Lee's people and Troy Donahue's too. The Academy didn't acknowledge either one! And it's a travesty. A few years ago, Peggy Lee got bumped for some little girl named Aaliyah. Now I never even *heard* of this little girl Aaliyah. She was black and she was in a plane wreck and maybe all that had something to do with why they put her on. You know, the tragedy of it, a life cut short. And she was a hottie—a hottentottie! But what about a life long lived, and lived well? I never *heard* of Aaliyah but I can tell you I sure heard of Peggy Lee! Gave lots of people lots of pleasure. Hell, even the young kids worship her now. And the Dunsmores freely give of their time and their counsel because they're for the underdog—the Dunsmores feel a wrong should be righted and they are currently engaged I believe in putting up a Web site—they're giving the money to put up a Web site for anyone of note who died but was not subsequently honored or acknowledged throughout the many many years of televised Academy Award memorial segment history. Cass and Grady are lobbying to have a special segment air with all those who were never acknowledged. These are *not* bad people—the Friends of Dorothy McGuire, the Friends of Troy Donahue, the Friends of Peggy Lee (my folks always called her *Miss* Peggy Lee)—and I don't believe the folks at the Academy are bad guys either. I've spoken to them. Oh yes. I've spoken to *all* parties as a mediator. That is sometimes my role. Role and raison d'être. I spoke to that woman—the McGuire friend or relative or whatever. Spoke to her *many* times. I've had counsel with her the way I would with anyone. And she's a wounded person but not a bad person—hell, we're all *wounded*. Jesus Christ our *savior* was *wounded*. We wouldn't be human beings if we weren't wounded. Would we? Would we? What are your names?" The girls offered them. "What's my point, Becca and Annie? My point is that we're all *people* and the Dunsmores just go right to the heart of that, they are fearless, they take everyone in, they are for the underdog, they do not pass judgment, they do not have lofty opinions, they do not—"

Trans World

SHE SAT AT Lavendar House with perspicacious George, who lay dying. It was George who actually wanted to watch the Barbara Walters interview with Kit Lightfoot after the Academy Awards. Lisanne thought how funny the world was because she hadn't even been aware of it. She'd tuned all that Hollywood stuff out.

She turned on the set—there he was before her, so handsome! Still the rumpled élan, rapscallion glint in the eye. But the Kit Lightfoot who had ruled her life and her energies was dead to the hospice-worker of the present moment. *This* Kit was a movie star and just that, a fallen idol risen again in the popular imagination. He was a human being who'd been through a great ordeal, just as she had, but the commonality ended there. He was not her lover nor was he the father of her child. He was not the Buddha; light and nectar did not pour from his crown. He was a man, plain and simple.

The segment began with Barbara showing clips from his films followed by a medley of breaking-news edits, both local and international, related to the assault. They strolled through Kit's new house and garden (how lovely the zendo was, thought Lisanne) and spoke about what he had been able to mentally reconstruct—with gentle, yet somehow obscene inelegance, Barbara probed the arduous process of rehabilitation and what returning to Riverside was like, especially to stay in the room he'd occupied as a boy ("So you *can* go home again," she said, eliciting oddly genteel laughter from the interviewee). She wanted to know just how it felt to live with a man he'd been estranged from since the death of his beloved mother, a man of questionable character and motive who was abusive to him even when he was a child. She did not refer to the father's incarceration nor to his crime; Lisanne couldn't decipher if that would come later or if it was simply off-limits.

"Kit," said Barbara, all hard-nosed *metta*. "Can you talk about Viv—Viv Wembley? Can you share with us why you're not together?"

He smiled, and Lisanne saw him take deep, yoga breaths—she knew he was doing *ujjayi*, yet the knowing was of itself free from obsession. She felt sane and at ease. A magisterial compassion for his being washed over her.

"Barbara . . . I wouldn't wish that on anyone—not just what happened to me but . . . I wouldn't wish it on the *partner*, of whoever becomes ill or debilitated. It's a terrible, terrible burden."

"And a great test, isn't it?" she said, sowing seeds of doubt and betrayal with that copyrighted wince of scurrilous sympathy. (Viv Wembley had failed out.) Kit smiled ambiguously. "And yet," she went on, "couples *do* survive a catastrophic occurrence. Christopher and Dana Reeve are one example that comes to mind."

"I think every situation is different," he said generously. "People move on—or through—what happens to them, in different ways. Everyone has a path, Barbara."

"*You* certainly do. And that path is called Buddhism. And I'd very much like to talk about that in a moment. But have you spoken? Have you spoken to Viv?"

"Oh yes—"

"You have?"

324 | Bruce Wagner

"We're good friends."

"Really?" she asked. Copyright honeyed skepticism.

"Yes, really!" He laughed. "I was at her beach house. You know, Barbara, we've been through a lot together and we respect that. We honor that. Have to! But Viv's moved on with her life—as I have with mine. We both know that we're there for each other when we need to be."

It was time to go for the jugular. Barbara segued with kill-shot celerity to Cela. Lisanne wasn't sure if she wanted to see this part. She looked over at George, who was asleep. She shut it off. Kit would be all right. She didn't need to protect him anymore. She never had, never could. All she wanted was to wish him well.

.   .   .

HE WAS A SWEET old man without much time left. Anyone could tell by looking at him how handsome he must once have been. He lost his wife in 1970. Their only son died five years ago in a car crash. George had never remarried.

She'd spent the last month or so sitting with him. He was often chatty, but lately his strength had waned. Lisanne sat through the blank spots, night sweats, and myriad terrors. Some afternoons, she gave him sponge baths which he stoically endured, too polite to tell her the pain of being touched was excruciating. As the end approached, she closed her eyes and drifted with him to this moment, to unconsciousness and beyond. Sometimes she rubbed baby oil over the corroded tattoos of his jaundiced skin or blotted water onto colorless lips. He stank, but it wasn't hard to transform death smells into balm. She thought of her dad a lot and how narcissistic fear had banished her from the very moment of his death. Now she understood that sitting with George was a gift from God, any god, pick a god. She had come serenely, she had not rushed to this room at Lavendar House as she had rushed to her father's deathbed from the platform of that train, like a fool. She was already here—one of his hands pressed between hers. Already here, to comfort to the end. She was present, and accounted for.

As she sat with him, she meditated on her father's library. She remembered waking up in the middle of the night and restlessly communing with the forest of volumes, some with their backs turned as if to snub her late arrival. Lisanne's finger had strummed against the spine of Milarepa's *The Hundred Thousand Songs.* What was it doing there? She'd since had time to puzzle over that. Dad was a learned man, but how had the book been acquired? Was he simpatico to Buddhism, or was he indifferent? Was he a cognoscente? And what, after all, did he actually know about the great saint Milarepa? Maybe not a damn thing. Maybe the book had been absorbed rather than acquired, had belonged to a hippie lover, one of his students, say, from back in the day—someone he took a fancy to while her mother was shut in the guest room with migraines. There was so much she'd never know about Dad—or Milarepa or her mother or Philip, and George too. She was OK with that.

As she emptied the bedpan, she thought about cleaning the Riverside toilets and how crazy she'd gotten. It was hard to believe—she would have laughed if it wasn't so gut-wrenching. Lisanne thought about the claustrophobic Amtrak water closet too, then shuddered at her shaming and violation by that horrible man, now behind bars, reaping the karmic whirlwind. Burke Lightfoot had orchestrated and overseen the rape, not just of her, but of his own son, and Lisanne wondered if Kit would ever try to contact her to make amends. She hoped he wouldn't, but if he did, she'd tell him that there was no one really to blame, that she had allowed it to happen, that she had been in a bad place but now was well. The pills that Dr. Calliope's colleague prescribed had stabilized her, but mysterious forces were at work, forces that conspired to provide a healing, an occult glissade of grace and nonresistance, and love unperverted. Now her life was filled with the light of Siddhama and nonsectarian prayer, a humble dyad between Lisanne and her faith. Each day, she and God created a simple space, wherein hope and regret, splendor and sorrow—and love— could be born.

When Lisanne came from the bathroom, she lit a scented candle. She was drawn to a photo of George and his wife and son that hung upon a wall. He wore a gleaming smile and captain's hat: suspended in time, like one of those fallen astronauts. He'd been a pilot for TWA in the fifties and sixties. She took the photo in hand.

It was time for her to shed the last of her fears, and fly.

With Rob Reiner in the Patio
of the Ivy on Robertson

"HOW DO YOU memorize?"

"Jorgia taught me some tricks."

"Jorgia Wilding."

"Yeah. And I do some—neurolinguistic stuff. With therapists. I'm just a dog who jumps through hoops."

"Well I think you're being a little modest. I really did want to tell you that your performance in *True West* was . . . pretty damn seamless."

"Thank you. I try to go with—the feelings. Behind the words."

"There were so many levels there. Will you do more theater?"

"I want to do Beckett."

"That's funny."

"Hopefully," he said, smiling.

The director laughed. "Beckett *can* be very funny, it's true. But it's also funny because I've been talking to the Geffen about putting up *Krapp's Last Tape.*"

"Whoa! That's a trip. I love that play."

A youngish man in a suit approached the table. "Gentlemen," he said respectfully, "forgive me for interrupting." He turned to Kit. "Sir, I just wanted to say that I am honored to even be sitting in the same restaurant."

"Thank you," said Kit.

"No—thank *you*," he said, and left.

"Lou Petroff. Do you know him?"

"I don't."

"Sweet man," said the director. "And a good agent."

"Mr. Reiner—my managers said you had a script."

The director leaned in, his hand cupping a bread roll like it was a healing stone. A peculiar but effectively intimate gesture.

"It's all very weird. You know, originally—and I'm sure they told you this—Ed was going to be doing it. Ed Norton."

"Ed's great."

"But there was a conflict."

"Ah!" said Kit. "I love 'conflict'! *Creative differences.*"

"Exactly. We had *lots* of those. And what *happened* was—your agents probably already told you this—what *happened* was, I literally woke up in the middle of the night—because I'd seen your play a few weeks before so you were already bouncing around my subconscious—and I'll never forget. I sat bolt upright in bed and thought, BAM! *Kit Lightfoot.*"

"Eureka. I found it."

"My Eureka moment. And I called Ellen—Ellen Chenoweth . . ."

"I know Ellen. You called her in the middle of the night?"

"I had the sense to wait until morning. And I said: Ellie, does he wanna do movies? Is everybody asking him? Or is *nobody* asking him?"

"That's closer!"

"And I said that out of total respect. Because right now you're like the pretty girl who everyone's afraid to ask out—that's what I was hoping, anyway. The bottom line is, this project is something I've been wanting to do for about five years." He pivoted the bread roll, wheeling it this way and that. "It's about a man who suffered an injury not dissimilar to yours. He was a law student when the accident happened—"

"True story?"

"Yes. A true story. In fact, I had lunch with him two weeks ago, in Boston."

"What's his name?"

"Stan Jiminy."

"Jiminy Cricket!"

"Jiminy Cricket was his nickname," intoned the director, as if all—especially Kit's involvement—had been predestined. "A brilliant guy. The injuries he sustained left him damaged but with 'a beautiful mind,' if you will. And after years, many years of incredible discipline and hard work—something you're certainly not unfamiliar with—Stan became an attorney. Now of course I'm making a very long story short, which is the challenge we'll have with the film."

328 | Bruce Wagner

"He became an attorney—"

"Right. And along the way, this *amazing* woman was his mentor and kind of guardian angel, who hired him to assist with pro bono work. She was a criminal lawyer. Rhoda—that was her name, Rhoda Horowitz—had a sister who the family kind of shunted off to a state home. The sister was retarded, and Rhoda always felt that was kind of the skeleton in the family closet. Which it was."

"Like Michelle in *I Am Sam*."

"I wouldn't say Rhoda Horowitz was quite in the Michelle Pfeiffer mold," he said, wryly.

"Who plays the mentor?"

"Susan Sarandon's going to do that for us. And Dusty's the dad—Stan's father."

"Ah—"

"Do you know Susan and Tim?"

"Yeah! I like them!"

"And of course, you've worked with Dusty."

"She's a real angel?"

(He had spaced on that part of the pitch. Nerves.)

"No, no. Not a real one—a guardian. Not that I'm above using the device of an angel, if I need to!" The wry smile again. "Anyway, one day in the middle of a very important trial, she dies."

"Susan?"

The director nodded.

"How?"

"Embolism."

"True?"

"All true."

"Did you know Susan?"

"You mean, Rhoda?"

"Rhoda! Yes."

"I didn't have the pleasure."

Kit sipped at his water. "Mr. Reiner, does it seem— I don't want to knock your project! But—"

"No, please . . ."

"With me in the role, does it seem, maybe, a gimmick? You know—stunt casting?"

"No. No, I don't think so, Kit, not if we do it right. I completely understand the question—and it's a *good* question—but I don't think so. By the way, I read the Aronofsky script. Very intriguing—as Darren always is. And I think Darren is absolutely brilliant, a visionary. But it was a bit 'postmodern' for me. I guess it's all about sensibilities but I found it hard to get under the characters' skin, emotionally. And there was another thing. I really strongly feel that for these kinds of movies—if one can say we're doing a 'kind' of movie without instantly losing integrity!—that you really need to be in the courtroom."

"I loved *A Few Good Men.*"

"Thank you. Which is what the Aronofsky script lacked. Because that script you were going to do was essentially a courtroom drama—*without a courtroom.* And that's something the audience demands, the kind of classic catharsis a courtroom setting provides. Otherwise, it's *Gladiator* without the Colosseum. Of course, there's a romance too, but we haven't cast your 'lady' yet."

Dark Horse

BECCA GOT THE CALL while she was at Whole Foods.

The Rob Reiner film was back on track—with Kit Lightfoot in the Ed Norton part. Her agent said that casting the recovering actor was a brilliant stroke ("No pun intended") and amazing coup. He told Becca the director was anxious for her to read with his new leading man. Rob liked her original audition so much that he had phoned personally.

She was ecstatic. But the moment she hung up, Becca knew she was doomed. Her agent didn't even get it. She examined the impasse from every angle—the problem being, it was only a matter of time before someone connected to the movie snapped to the fact that Becca Mondrain used to sleep with the daddy-killer whose buddy had whacked Kit Lightfoot in the head. It was an insane predicament, a tragically ridiculous checkmate, and the more she thought about it the more surprised she was that the Reiner camp had been caught unawares. What should she do? The oblivious agent would probably just say she was paranoid, but she knew that wasn't the case. Even Annie agreed.

She was about to call Sharon Belzmerz for advice when it came to her: she would go in and audition for the sheer incredible experience of it—she owed herself that much—and if fate decreed he hire her, she'd bite the bullet, and come clean. *Look, Mr. Reiner, there's something that I think you don't know but that you probably should because it's kind of a big deal. And maybe you know already but I don't think so. See, I used to pretty seriously date Herke Lamar Goodson, the guy who was on trial in Virginia last year? We went out for a few months before he was arrested for a . . . for homicide. He was the one who killed his dad? Everyone— including me!—was* totally *shocked when that happened. I had* no *idea he had anything like that in his past or was even capable of such a thing. Anyway, it turned out—as you probably or might already even know—that he also* happened to be friends with the crazy person who did that awful thing to Kit. The man who hit him in the head with the bottle? When I found all of this out, it became totally one of the worst periods of my life. Because I'm from Waynesboro, Virginia, and we just don't live life in the so-called fast lane there. Mr. Reiner, I cried my eyes out on the phone to my mama every night. And I know I probably should have made my agency "tell all" before I came in to audition—I didn't conceal any of it from him, but to tell the truth I don't even think he—my agent—was thinking straight—but I was just so amazingly honored to even be asked or considered by you for your film and that you remembered me and were gracious enough to totally ask me back was just almost too much! It's almost like I didn't want to let you down or disappoint you. Aside from "Rusty"—that's what Herke Goodson called himself—he lied to me and everyone else about so many things, even his name—aside from the crazy coincidence of me auditioning with Kit, and my ex-boyfriend knowing the man who struck him on top of the head, I just wanted you to know, wanted to be sure that you understood that I so* totally *did not know at the time that Rusty, or Herke, had this terrible double life! It was* beyond *the worst thing that ever happened to me, worse than when my closest friend was hit by a car on prom night! And I am so sorry if I caused you any hassle or wasted your time but you have been* so *nice to me and I wanted to say all this because I thought that if things went any further*

it would potentially be embarrassing for all parties down the line, notwith-
standing the studio. From a public relations standpoint. And I would never
want to embarrass you or Kit. I know that you know that. And I just wanted
to thank you for giving me the opportunity—it is something I will never for-
get. And that I would love *to work with you one day* in any capacity *and*
just feel that my best chance of doing that is to open up to you in the way
that I have today. So thank you, Mr. Reiner, thank you, thank you, thank
you for even listening and hearing me out!

·   ·   ·

THEY SAT face to face.

A camera taped them as they read.

Kit seemed shy, but maybe she was just projecting. It was difficult
for her to be in the moment. She knew Mr. Reiner was looking for
chemistry more than anything else; she was a long shot but didn't
care, because as far as Becca was concerned, she'd already won. If I
have to pack my bags and go home tomorrow, she thought, by God's
grace it would be all right. Here she was, all the way from Waynesboro, Virginia, where she'd slaved in a store just like the one Jennifer
Aniston did in *The Good Girl*. She thought of how hard it had been for
others before her—especially Drew, who, at thirteen, spent a year in
lockdown. Her own mother had put her there yet she still had JAID
tattooed on her back, with angels. Every night from the hospital,
Drew looked up at the moon and cried her heart out to her dead
Grandpa John.

Here she was, after all the hard, hard times. She'd finagled her way
onto a classy cable show and even been some kind of cult figure on
the Web, and now she was in a room with Rob Reiner and Kit Lightfoot, cohorts and fellow artist-travelers . . .

No regrets!

·   ·   ·

OUTSIDE THE Coffee Bean, two teenage girls breezed by. One of
them made a little gasp, then excitedly turned to her friend. A familiar
reflex foretold the actress had again been mistaken for Drew.

But the whispering girl said, *"That's Becca Mondrain."*

Graduation

LISANNE SIGNED UP for a Fearless Fliers clinic at LAX. The woman said there would be around twenty-five in the group. Enrollment in classes for "aviophobics" had diminished in the months following 9/11 but over time had rebounded to previous levels. In fact, the woman said sunnily, because of the war in Iraq people were confronting their fears with newfound confidence.

The three-weekend course began with an informal overview. The counselor, a retired airline pilot, said the most important thing the group would learn was that their phobia emanated not from the fear of death but from the fear of losing control. They couldn't really grasp the distinction, but he reassured them they had come to the right place. Everyone seemed to exhale at once when he quoted a statistical study from MIT that said if you took a commercial flight every day for the next 29,000 years, the odds were you'd be involved in just one crash.

The enrollees formed a circle and introduced themselves. They gave their names and occupations before delivering what Lisanne imagined to be AA-style confessionals of how each had found his or her way to Fearless Fliers. One woman, a pediatrician, said that years ago on a stormy night in Minnesota she'd boarded with a syringe of Demerol and given herself a shot in the ass, only to awaken hours later to find they were still on the runway. (Lisanne thought that was someone who probably *should* be in AA.) Everyone had their own special niche, like the generic panic freaks, for whom fear of flying was a midsize subsidiary of a much larger corporation—or the seasoned claustrophobes, who equated entering a plane with being sealed into a coffin. Lisanne enjoyed the eccentrics the most: the ones who thought that the plane would run out of gas or that God might snatch whichever aircraft happened past Him at whatever arbitrary moment in time. (God was superpremenstrual.) Some in the circle worried about pilots having psychotic breaks or passengers having psychotic breaks or air traffic controllers having psychotic breaks or terrorist passengers simply being themselves. One or two self-proclaimed divas admitted to having been escorted from flights due to pretakeoff "arias"—groans, moans, and high-pitched wails that erupted from seemingly bottomless depths as runways were taxied toward. A man in his sixties was possessed by wind shear and "sudden rollover," a phrase he invoked and muttered, both prayer and imprecation, with near-comic insistency. (The common denominator of horror being turbulence, hands down.) A sardonic librarian said that whenever she booked a flight, she couldn't help imagining an AP wire photo of some Middle American farmer's field strewn with the debris of metal and body parts, being picked over by an FAA crash team. Torsos in tree branches and whatnot. Everyone laughed when the same woman—Lisanne thought she was funny enough to do stand-up— said she'd even attended multiple showings of a theater piece at UCLA that was basically actors re-creating dialogue from black box transcripts of fatal air crashes. Lisanne could relate, though it'd been a while since she'd lulled herself to sleep with the dog-eared paperback. She didn't share that with the group. Still, when it came her turn, Lisanne found herself saying aloud what she'd never told anyone, let alone strangers—that because of her phobia, she took a train to her father's deathbed, and missed his passing. Her story opened a floodgate; astonishingly, she wasn't the only one. The classmates became emboldened. Together, they stared into the face of cowardice and did not like what they saw.

They were encouraged to write essays on worst-case fantasy flying scenarios and were shown how to "stack positive imagery," slowly replacing bad thoughts and images with good ones. The counselors guided the class through breathing meditations—Lisanne was glad to be reminded of something so familiar. She had done a lot of "sits" at the hospice, but it was well over a year since she'd meditated on her own, as she used to.

On the last weekend, everyone trooped into a hangar and boarded a 727. They talked to pilots and stewards, mechanics, air traffic controllers, and engineers. They revolved through the cockpit for comprehensive demonstrations and Q & A. They sat in coach seats (seat belts on) while the counselors played a tape reproducing all the sounds one might hear in the course of a normal flight. The tape was constantly stopped and started, each sound discussed and overexplained.

•   •   •

THE GRADUATION FLIGHT to San Francisco was optional, but nearly everyone signed up. The airline gave them a special rate.

At the suggestion of the counselors, some Fearless Fliers wore rubber bands around their wrists to snap away negative thoughts and feelings. The librarian offered Lisanne herbs and essential oils that she picked up at a health food store. The blue "Fear of Flying" package read, "This box contains enough remedies for one flight."

All of them sat together. Lisanne took her place by the window—hardly anyone wanted a window seat, and besides, she didn't need to be bothered by the bathroom comings and goings of someone in the midst of a preflight freak-out—and quickly got into meditative posture. She focused on her nostrils, following the breath as it filled up her lungs. Sounds of the cabin—the bustle and stowing of bags by unneurotic passengers not in their group, the little suck-rush of air through vents, the buckling and unbuckling, the coughs, sneezes, and throat clearings, the sporadic groaning gallows humor of fellow graduates along with the soothing running commentary of Fearless Fliers counselors—floated in and out of her awareness. (She wondered if anyone had cheated and taken a tranquilizer.) Whenever a bad thought intruded, say, the jackscrewed Alaska Airlines Flight 261 plunging into the Pacific—they would soon be flying over the very place it had gone down—or the documentary she'd watched a few months ago on the Discovery Channel about the famous golfer and his buddies who died on a Lear—the plane broke contact and inexplicably drifted off course, fighter jets were scrambled and got right up close to see the windows frosted over, meaning the cabin had lost pressurization—or the time she had a drink with a temp Reggie hired and the gal said she was supposed to have been on the PSA flight to San Francisco that crashed because a vengeful employee went berserk. The temp said that at that time of her life she was commuting a lot and always took that particular morning flight and this one time she was late: she remembered being at the gate begging them to let her on but they said the flight was already closed. That reminded Lisanne of the English movie she saw when she was a girl, about the supernatural. A woman in a hospital kept dreaming that each night she awakened to ride the elevator down to the morgue, where a man stood and said, "Room for one more." When the woman was finally discharged, she was about to board an airplane, and the attendant at the gate said the same thing—"Room for one more"—and because she'd had the premonition, the woman didn't board and of course the plane crashed. Whenever Lisanne was jolted by a morbid train of thought, she used one of the relaxation techniques the counselors had walked them through. She was able to get back in touch with the core of her *zazen* practice and found that its reawakening served her well.

There came that iffy time when taxiing was over and things got serious because there was now no turning back and the engines roared and the plane and all its guts began a sprint to the void. Lisanne's eyes remained closed, but she noticed her section was quiet—that animal-fear quiet, before slaughter. *Poor things. They'll be all right.* She was doing OK and suddenly felt maternal. She would meditate on their behalf, to help them through. She actually didn't mind this part too much because you could really feel the power of the machine, the aircraft flexing its muscles, strutting its stuff, and it was so mightily definitive that it was a comfort—a hint of the kind of majestic strength the machine could summon if called on. (Besides, it was common knowledge that most crashes occurred during descent.) A jet like this one could take a lot of roughing up. That made Lisanne think of another documentary she'd seen about a research plane that flew into the eyes of hurricanes. (It even had propellers.) She remembered being shocked to watch it pierce the "wall" of a thunderstorm system, amazed that could even aerodynamically be done.

The graduates broke into huzzahs as they leveled off from the ascent. Soon, the drone would become that all-encompassing vibratory OM, filling ears and senses, the collected, collective hum of airspace within and airspace without. They were now over the Pacific. She pushed Alaska Airlines from her mind and tried to think of the water as a good thing, but again, it was common knowledge that crashing in water is actually worse than crashing on land, experts said the impact was somehow more devastating—even putting aside the likelihood of drowning if by some insane miracle one had managed to survive the collision. (It was one thing for Tom Hanks to endure his ocean crash in *Cast Away*, she thought, but would be quite another for Lisanne McCadden.) Still, this wasn't a long flight, they weren't even going all that high, nowhere near the altitude of a plane on its way to New York. Or maybe they were. If something went wrong, they could probably just glide down and land on the 5 or the 101. Regardless, she didn't want to break meditation or pseudomeditation to ask one of the counselors about altitude because somehow she thought that might trigger something bad, some kind of small mechanical failure—when she caught herself having that nonsensical, superstitious notion, she laughed—and breathed—and suddenly felt normal again—then remembered something she hadn't thought of in a long time. When she was nineteen, a friend asked her to fly with another couple in a Beechcraft to Catalina. Even though the trip was relatively smooth, she had been so unexpectedly terrified that she hadn't flown again until the shit-filled jaunt with Philip et alia. Years later the friend who'd invited her to Catalina had crashed in the very same plane, and though he didn't die, he had his jaw clamped shut for six months and everywhere he went carried wire cutters in case he choked on something or got sick and vomited. It was eerie that she had actually ridden in the same machine that had subsequently gone down and been damaged beyond repair. *Room for one more . . .* The soothing 29,000-year MIT statistic floated back to her and then the OM drone came and the FASTEN SEAT BELTS light went off and there was more jubilation from the grads. She thought of Philip, poor Philip and his unseemly death, death by hanging, what would that be like, and what a strange personage he was in her life, what a marvel it was that he'd come along to protect her, taken her in, her and the boy, and his perversions didn't matter because he never touched Sidd or made him bear witness, and Lisanne thought how glad she was that she'd never judged him, Philip had enough pain, and her judgments would have hastened his death. Imagine your mother being cut from her own mother like that. She knew that children of Holocaust survivors were damaged by their parents' mind-sets just the way people's lungs were damaged by secondhand smoke. It is so common for the child of a suicide to commit the same act, she imagined the suicide of a parent like a magnet or dare, an enticement to join the dark fun. He'd written Lisanne a final note that had disturbed her. He said she had given him a book on rebirth that spoke of the Buddhist realm of the gods. In that they died, the gods were actually mortal yet because their lives were of such incomprehensible length and because they had lived them in unfathomable luxury it was particularly agonizing when they realized the end was upon them. He rambled in his letter and said that he had lived like a god and America had lived the same way and now the end had come, for both him and America, and what a fantastic shock it was for him and the Republic but that it was her duty, hers and Siddama's, to carry on—he said he would make sure to think of them at the end because the Buddha said how important was one's final thought, that if one had lived one's life raging then one would rage at the end or if one had lived one's life lusting one would lust at the end and Philip said he wished he could be like Gandhi was at death's door and call out for Krishna or whatever the equivalent but was afraid he would shout something fearful or profane not devotional though he would do his best to think of her and the boy and even if he wasn't sure that he could or would he joked he would die trying. She never showed those last words to anyone, not even Mattie—he was not in his right mind and no one would benefit. Philip bequeathed her the Rustic Canyon house and what he poignantly called a "dowry" so she would never have to work again in her life. To put it mildly. She asked Robbie and Maxine to move in and they did, but they kept the Fairfax duplex, and sometimes she and Robbie even slept in the same bed, without sexing. It was a comfort to have a body to curl up into. And he was a decent man. She didn't understand his relationship with Maxine, but why should she? What business was it of hers, or anyone's? She was a firm believer in "whatever gets you through the night." No one understood anything anyway. All she knew was that Robbie was kind to Max and loving to Siddhama. What more could one ask for than loving-kindness?

Something jolted the plane and she opened her eyes. A counselor smiled vacantly, patting the arm of a frightened Fearless Flier, and then it happened again and the plane rolled over, plunging downward. Oxygen masks popped out, uselessly entangling themselves, and people in the aisles slammed into each other, concussed by flying debris. The jet righted itself with as little warning, and she noted there wasn't even a scream because what happened had been so shocking and dreamlike. The librarian clutched onto Lisanne, who watched the scene in front of her with great stillness as a child would a snow globe he had shaken and stood on its end. A dazed and bloodied steward threaded the aisle. A loud whooping alarm went off with a robotic male voice attached, but she couldn't understand what it was saying. Lights flashed too, then came the rhythmic bloodcurdling screams of a passenger, contrapuntal to the lights and alarm, and a baby choked and bawled, maybe it was more than one baby, and whimpering rose up from somewhere—from mindstream, mindground, or buddha-field, she couldn't tell, and when it seemed as if all was not lost or at least that small deathless moment arrived when things seemed to set-tle, relatively, because nothing had or really could settle at all, just then the plane lurched and thudded and the metal itself shrieked and came a primal chorus of *Ohs!*—more screaming—this time of those who knew whatever impossible hint of a sliver of chance they were absurdly thinking they might have had was now irrevocably gone and Lisanne saw a counselor screaming too and the plane was nose-diving. She watched all this with her strange stillness, wondering why it was so and wondering why she was unruffled, knowing of course that planes rarely pull out of such dives. Bodies and everyday flotsam rained down past, a true rain because there was coffee and water and even blood, and the librarian nearly got her head chopped off by a PowerBook and everything slowed down: anatomies careening or flopping or weirdly edging their way under dictates of velocity and g-force through clouded, ruined aisles, and Lisanne went deaf but her eyes and heart opened and oddly she thought, Should I have known this, did I know this, was this meant to be, everything so still, she even had time to think of the guidebook that said if on the first day of the month the pinpricks of light and color that normally appear when-ever one closes one's eyes, if those pinpricks should on the first of the month appear no more, then soon death is coming. That when one no longer hears a subtle ringing in the ears, that ever-present subtle sound-presence that all of us, even children, are so familiar with, then soon death is coming. *She closed her eyes and saw only blackness, and in her ears heard only blackness.* The guidebook said that if one should have a recurring dream of donning dark robes and descending or if one recurrently dreams of the sun and moon descending in the sky, then soon death is coming. *Amidst everything, she thought about it but could not remember her most recent dreams. She could not remember ever having a recurring dream in her life, except the one about the snake after Philip died.* The librarian was dead, but her hand was still in Lisanne's. Now everything sped up again to faster than real time, if there could be such a thing, because of the brutal velocity and dreamlike movement, and Lisanne tried reaching to the librarian, whose disfigured face kept getting slammed torn pummeled rivened by debris, tried grabbing the head with her free hand to cradle it from harm's way, and during those epic librarian labors fittingly all she could think of were books, the black box book whose nearly biblical concordance they once both laughingly shared, and that Lisanne had carried with her on the train to Albany: a chapter that now came to mind with eerie, still, cool remembering was of the plane that crashed because the maintenance crew forgot, after scrubbing down the fuselage, to take a piece of masking tape off a certain hole that in flight always needed to be left uncovered, in order that all kinds of vital gauges and readings could be taken. She recalled puzzling over that account again and again, never understanding how such an essential indicator could be a simple hole and not an actual piece of attached equipment, or why such a hole wouldn't at least have had some kind of protective grate around it the way meters or pipes do, and if the hole didn't, which it didn't seem to, why hadn't this sort of tragic thing happened before, or if it had she'd never heard about it or read about it, not in all the time Lisanne ever spent reading about crashes. And that seemed strange. In the case of the covered hole, the heroic pilots had flown the plane blind, in the darkness of night, without idea of direction or altitude, for well over an hour before it finally came down. She remembered thinking how cruel that was because the transcripts revealed them to be so noble and meticulous under the circumstances, pilot and copilots continuously alternating glimmers of hope, adroitly skillful, drawing on their collective expertise, natural born problem solvers, yet they were never to know what went wrong or how hopeless their situation was, all because of a masked-over hole, and

Lisanne thought with great empathy about the pilots of her own plane just now, what they must be going through, the terrible sorrow of an unflappable captain and his sinking ship, the transcripts sometimes revealed that pilots shouted out the names of wives or girlfriends at the very end or simply said "Mother" or "Mama" (she remembered that the Alaska Airlines pilot had said, "Here we go"), and part of her was grateful everyone was going to die soon, less cruel than flying on and on in delusion, righting the plane then rolling over again then righting it and so forth, postponing the inevitable. She remembered covering her own holes that terrible time she stabbed Philip's pug. She contrived to cover every orifice as did the careless maintenance crew but in Lisanne's case it was mindfulness not negligence because the guidebook said one made such coverings during *phowa*, taping over the apertures of the dead, all but the crown, in order to force ejection of consciousness through the fontanel or top of the head now

a

voice

told her there wasn't much time. A lama wrote somewhere that even the riders of horses may have a moment to rest during a race but not mankind who from birth with each breath gallops toward the arms of the Lord of Death.

Lisanne was twisted by g-force to lay on her right side. Something so strange popped into her head. She once saw a TV show about a woman who trained orangutans to talk. The university lost their funding and the orangutan that she used to have conversations with was now encaged, awaiting transport to a zoo. He hadn't seen her in a long time and became excited when she left her car and walked over. He began to "sign," and the woman translated for the camera crew. Clinging to the bars of the cage, the orangutan said, "Where's the key?" Then, "Where's the car?" and

I want to go home

A great force stole the air from her and Lisanne didn't know if she saw or had merely imagined the moon dip and the sun rise, real and imagined were as

one, *dreamed and nondreamed, expansion and con-
traction, guest and host, and she tried to merge the
white and red mustard seeds in her heart as darkness
came and thunder returned to her ears with utter
determination she prayed for the winds of* prana *to
blow the pearly droplet from the central channel
straight out the top of the librarian's head even
though the audiotapes said only trained masters
should attempt such a thing let alone effect it—but
how could any of that matter because Lisanne's heart
was so pure—pure as her Intent—and she rammed
the librarian's consciousness through the dead
woman's thousand-petaled lotus into the heart of
space then did the same for herself just as she'd practiced, did her very best to send her own awareness like
an arrow into the heart of space, the heart of love, she
conjured no Buddha above, the tapes said imagine
something beloved suspended there but she envisioned
no deity, no Kit, no Philip or dead father with bor-
rowed Milarepa, not even her boy, the love-child
whom she of late had taken to calling Rob Jr., not Siddhama anymore, please forgive,* forgive me that
jejune demotion, *nothing above for that arrow to
pierce except light, the pure light that was everything,
clear light and blissful heart of space, that's where she
sent whatever she had, nectar, nectar everlasting, for
herself and librarian, for all beings alive, dead, and yet
to be born, and that her final thoug——*

CODA

Ordinary Mind

H.H. PENOR RINPOCHE formally recognized Kit Lightfoot as a *tulku*, or reincarnation of a twelfth-century Buddhist master. Both Ram Dass and Robert Thurman were present when Kit was told. The actor was profoundly moved. Later, Tenzin judiciously cautioned him not to "go public" with the announcement; it was the sort of thing, he said, that could easily be misconstrued. Kit, of course, agreed. His ego made no demands in that regard.

His Holiness had noticed auspicious portents on the occasion of their first encounter at Tara Guber's, more than three years before. Further clues to his enlightened status became manifest when Penor Rinpoche visited the Lightfoot home in Riverside, and during subsequent meetings at the Stone Canyon compound. Aside from an abstruse welter of personal characteristics tying Kit to his centuries-old predecessor, His Holiness had perhaps been most impressed by the movie star's equanimity and consistency of desire to help others—the compassionate jailhouse meeting with his assailant being a prime example—despite the experience of great trauma related not only to his injury but to the death of his girlfriend at the hands of his father. After H.H. Penor Rinpoche consulted with the peers of his lineage, Kit was recognized but not enthroned. *Tulku*hood was something to be earned, rather than conferred.

Unfortunately, the revelation was leaked to the press, and skepticism, however briefly, prevailed. It was broadly hinted (even among those claiming to be spiritually evolved) that Kit Lightfoot's *tulku* status had been bestowed by virtue of his many generous donations, both past and relatively recent, to certain clinics and monasteries in Mysore, Burma, the Netherlands, and elsewhere. No one seemed to care or take public note that his root guru, Gil Weiskopf Roshi, had close ties to H.H. Penor Rinpoche and the Nyingma lineage that stretched back many years or that Kit had visited the Namdroling monastery with his teacher.

His Holiness still felt a measured response to the controversy was in order and released a kind of elegant disclaimer, via the Internet, stressing that no relevant persons or entities had received any substantial donations from Mr. Lightfoot. Moreover, the announcement of his being a *tulku,* far from being frivolous or ill-conceived, was measured and sober minded. Such a recognition, he said, was to be celebrated, not rebuked. The statement of his rebirth was a simple fact and not meant to imply that Mr. Lightfoot was a realized being, merely that he possessed special gifts and the potential to aid others. Much training lay ahead. There were no guarantees regarding each *tulku*'s "success." Taking the high lama road, the Rinpoche closed his statement by reiterating that the discovery of a jewel should provoke joyousness, not cynical dissent. He hoped that one day, that would be so.

•   •   •

"DID YOU KNOW we worked that thing out with Charlize?" said Rob.

"Cool," said Kit. "When's she gonna be here?"

"She's in South Africa now. End of next week."

"Now *there's* a long flight," said Kit.

"Tell me about it," said Rob. "I've done it—more than once. You guys know each other, right?" Rob called through the open door to his assistant.

"Maybe we met at some benefit. Toronto? Maybe, yeah. I think it was the film festival."

Megan poked her head in.

"When's Charlize coming, do we know?" asked Rob.

"Saturday," she said.

"Saturday?" said Rob, with a minifrown.

"She had a family thing and had to wait until the weekend."

"OK," said Rob, resigned.

"Excuse me, Kit," said Megan, respectfully. "The camera crew's ready."

"Great!" said Kit, standing.

"What's going on?" said Rob, nonplussed.

"Kit's being honored next Sunday by a group in Washington."

"NIF," said Kit. "The Neurological Injury Foundation."

"How great," said Rob.

"I'm sorry," said Megan to the director, deferentially. "I thought you knew."

"No," said Rob. "But that's fine."

"That's probably my fault," she said. "Anyway, Kit's not able to attend the gala because of our rehearsal schedule."

"Galas are a good thing," said Rob.

"That's why they're going to tape. It shouldn't take very long."

"If I'd have known," said Rob, "we could have worked our rehearsal schedule around it."

"I mentioned that to Kit—"

"It's OK, it's OK—I didn't want to go to Washington," said Kit. "Didn't feel like doing the poster-boy thing this week."

"You can use my office for the taping if you like," said Rob.

"They're pretty much all set up in the courtyard," said Megan.

"Let's do it," said Kit.

(Trademark grin.)

.   .   .

KIT SAT IN the courtyard in a safari chair. The makeup artist zapped a zit while the D.P. tweaked lights and meters.

The director said, "OK, folks, are we set?"

"Ready," said the A.D.

"Mr. Lightfoot," said the director. "Are you good to go?"

"Ready-steady," said Kit.

"Ready Steadicam," said the D.P., nonsensically.

"Do we have a Steadicam?" asked Kit.

"No, but I wish we did," said the D.P.

"Just like a *cinematographer*," said the director. "They want a Steadicam for a stationary shot."

"We could shoot this *Russian Ark*–style," said the D.P.

"Dream on," said the director. "Ready?"

"Ready-teddy," said Kit.

"Let's roll tape."

"Camera is on."

"Kit," said the director, standing just behind the D.P. "Can you tell us why this new role is so important to you?"

"You mean, as spokesman?"

"I'm sorry—no. In the Rob Reiner film."

"Sure, be happy to. I—I guess I've always liked a challenge. And . . . this—this has been the hardest one."

"Hold it," said the D.P.

"I'm sorry, Kit," said the director.

"Not a problem," said Kit.

"OK," said the D.P. "We are good to go."

"Rolling?"

"Rolling tape."

"Kit, can you tell us why the role in your new film has been so important for you? Why it's been important for you to take on?"

He hadn't prepared, but that worked in his favor. He began to talk, heartfelt. "I've always really liked a challenge. And this has been a hard one! There are . . . so many people in my corner—friends and colleagues—so many fans. The fans helped pull me through. And there's my mom, who was so brave. She passed away. I learned a lot from her! I still have that picture in my mind of my mother's courage, and that was something to help me in my dark hours. And my dear friend Cela, who I knew since I was young. Another strong woman, important woman in my life. I am an artist, and just because I was injured . . . I still *think* like an artist—or hope I do! I have to do the things an artist does. So I do what I am doing for all artists and all friends—and all the friends and all the people who are alive who have suffered for . . . neurological injuries and trauma, and even for those who are dead but whose courage and struggles should not be forgotten . . ." His eyes filled with tears. "I— If I have one special wish, it is . . . to do my *best*—if I am *real*—to make people *believe*, with all their hearts, that this journey and this *struggle* can be so beautiful . . ." He looked down then back up, smiling sweetly. "To show the world. That you *can* be anything and *dream* anything . . ."

He trailed off, emotional.

Long silence from crew, punctuated by makeup girl sniffles.

The director softly conferred with the D.P., then said, "Kit, we had some technical difficulties, and for that I am *very sorry*." The actor shifted in his seat and minorly grimaced. "I'm being told the problem has been corrected and *will not happen again*." The last he lobbed toward the repentant D.P., who, avoiding his eyes, nodded militarily. "But that was *fantastic*, and I hate to ask you to do it over . . ."

"That's OK," said Kit, affably. "Shit happens."

"OK, then let's go once more! That was *amazing*, Kit—if you could do pretty much the same thing then I think we are *golden*."

"No problem," said Kit. "*No estoy problema*. No estoy problemita, Señorita Pepita."

"Rolling tape!" said the cameraman.

"All right, Kit—when you're ready."

Give me, O God, what you still have.
Give me what no one asks you for.
I don't ask you for wealth
Nor for success,
Nor even for health.
People ask you for all that so often
That you can't have any left.
Give me, O God, what you still have.
Give me what people
Refuse to accept from you.
I want insecurity and disquietude.
I want hardship
And struggle with no end.
And if you should give them to me, O God,
Give them to me once and for all,
For I will not always find the courage
To ask you for what you still have.

—ANONYMOUS

About the Author

. . .

BRUCE WAGNER is the author of three novels: *Force Majeure, I'm Losing You,* and *I'll Let You Go.* He has written and directed two films, *I'm Losing You* and *Women in Film,* based on his novels. He lives in Los Angeles.

About the Author